William Sharp

The life and letters of Joseph Severn

William Sharp

The life and letters of Joseph Severn

ISBN/EAN: 9783337136505

Printed in Europe, USA, Canada, Australia, Japan

Cover: Foto ©Raphael Reischuk / pixelio.de

More available books at **www.hansebooks.com**

Seymour Kirkup f.
Rome 1822

THE
LIFE AND LETTERS
OF
JOSEPH SEVERN

BY

WILLIAM SHARP

Severn's recollection in old age of Keats

LONDON
SAMPSON LOW, MARSTON & COMPANY
LIMITED
St. Dunstan's House
FETTER LANE, FLEET STREET, E.C.
1892

TO

WALTER SEVERN AND ARTHUR SEVERN

THE DISTINGUISHED SONS OF

A DISTINGUISHED FATHER:

INHERITORS OF A NAME IMMORTALLY ASSOCIATED WITH THAT OF

ONE OF THE GREATEST OF ENGLISH POETS,

THESE MEMOIRS ARE INSCRIBED.

PREFACE.

SEVERAL years have elapsed since the Severn MSS. consisting of a great mass of letters, journals, reminiscences, and fragmentary records, were placed in the hands of the present writer to be edited at his discretion. One or two editorial considerations, as well as other equally potent causes beyond his control, necessitated delay after delay; but it will suffice to say now, that in the main the original procrastination was due to the constantly recurring discovery of much relative matter (chiefly correspondence) which could not be overlooked, and also to the need, on many points, of difficult inquiries and careful investigation. The book was practically finished, in Rome, by the winter of 1890–91, but since then it has been wholly re-written. The original project was that the Memoirs should be issued in two large volumes, the first of which would practically justify the title 'Keats and his Circle,' while the second would for the most part be occupied with Severn's middle period in London (1840 to 1860), his consular life (1861 to 1870) in Rome, and his last years in that city (1871 to 1879). But ultimately it was decided that this biographical scheme should be abandoned in favour of a more concise record. Of course, there is loss of a kind. A mass of correspondence of considerable interest has had to be wholly disregarded, and records and diaries covering many years have had to be condensed into even fewer pages. On the other hand there is the gain involved in the exclusion of much that would, in all probability, interest only a few specialists, and of a still larger quantity of what in a sense may be called historical matter—either irrelative to the story of Severn's life, or which is to be found elsewhere, set forth with wider knowledge and greater skill. There can be little question that the life of Joseph Severn is of interest to the present generation not so much by virtue of his achievements as a painter, his consular services at a vital period when the re-birth of Italy was yearly, daily, almost hourly in process before his eyes, or even by that winsome personality to which such generous testimony has been borne by Mr. Ruskin; but on account of his intimate connection with the great English poet who, howsoever we may differ as to the qualities and reach of his genius, is, of all his kindred, the singer who is nearest to our hearts. Severn himself, declares a friend in Rome who knew him intimately, remarked, not long before his death: "With a truth that was ever inapplicable to Keats, I may say that of all I have done with brush or pen, as artist or man, scarce anything will long outlast me, for writ in water indeed are my best deeds as well as my worst failures; yet through my beloved Keats I shall be remembered—in the hearts of all who revere my beloved Keats there will be a corner of loving memory for me." Truly, Joseph Severn is worthy of remembrance for much beside his perfect friendship for Keats; yet his own foreknowledge is not to be gainsaid in great degree, for, notable as he was, and noteworthy much in his accomplishment and artistic and literary experiences, he would, dissociated from Keats, be, at this late date and in the inevitable pressure of more immediate and more vital interests, only as it were a voice to charm those among whom the personal tradition of the man is still more or less potent.

It seemed to the present writer, therefore—as well as to those who are also immediately concerned—that, from every point of view, the wisest plan was to make the

Memoirs in great part a record, in the first place of Severn's youthful life, and his early intimacy with Keats; in the second, of the whole episode of Keats and Severn in Italy, with, to repeat a useful titular phrase, all interesting new correspondence and often matter concerning 'Keats and his Circle;' and, finally, of the last five-and-fifty years of his long life, a life coloured and even directed from the outset to the close by the abiding influence of the poet. Naturally, again, with this biographical scheme, it was thought best, at the expense of any arbitrary considerations of proportion, to educe from the available new material as much as possible relative to Severn's early years, friendship with, and subsequent correspondence concerning Keats; to deal much more succinctly with the doings, experiences, and correspondence of Severn and his wide circle of distinguished friends, during the middle period of his life (1830 till 1860); and to concentrate, within the extreme practical limits, the record of what he justly viewed as the eventful and interesting period of close upon twenty years posterior to his return to Rome in 1861. Indeed, necessity as well as judgment demanded the condensation of the correspondence, and above all the minutely detailed and uninterrupted diaries from 1860 onward; for the alternative was a record so ample that the fundamental scheme of the Memoirs would be destroyed.

The only rival of Severn, in the minds of those who revere the genius of Keats, is Charles Armitage Brown. As many letters and part-letters by him have been quoted as was found practicable; a volume might easily be written from the Brown-material alone. But, at any rate, even the Keats-student will, in the following pages, gain a fuller knowledge of Charles Armitage Brown's life and personality than hitherto has been possible. The prevalent impression seems to be that Brown was merely a man of independent means and literary tastes; but he was, in truth, and of necessity, much more a professional man of letters than were most of the minor members of the Keats-circle, certainly not less, for instance, than was John Hamilton Reynolds, though Reynolds had a finer native talent and a more distinctive expression. Brown's letters extend from the days of his trip to Scotland with Keats to the year of his death in New Zealand. They contain ample evidence that he was at once a shrewd man of the world and an impulsive enthusiast, loyal and unselfish in his affections, bitter and often unreasonable in his dislikes, at all times ready to resent an affront, real or imaginary, or to smoke the pipe of peace whether as forgiver or as the forgiven. But with all his hot head and warm heart he was an excellent counsellor for others, and no one of his friends benefited more by his good sense, discretion, and intelligent sympathy, than did Joseph Severn. Of his writings nothing has survived, save his share in the tragedy of *Otho*, his ingenious and painstaking volume on Shakespeare's life and genius, and, in another sense, that MS. Memoir of Keats which is re-embodied in Lord Houghton's 'Life' of the poet. His early productions are valueless, and even the humour of his comic opera *Narensky*, is of that broad farcical kind which sounds so flat to our ears. Some of his tales, and more particularly his miscellaneous descriptive and critical papers, are creditable performances, and as a translator he is at once sympathetic and able. It was a strong wish of his at one time to render the whole of Goldoni's comedies into English, and among his posthumous papers were many translations, and a long and exhaustive critical study of the Venetian dramatist. In his latter days in New Zealand he often talked of writing his reminiscences, not only a more detailed record of Keats, but of all the men of letters, artists, and other interesting people whom he had known. As he was a good *raconteur*, and a shepherd of all the vagrant amusing stories of his day, it is a pity that he postponed his work till too late. Every one who knew him delighted in his company. Keats, as we know, rejoiced at a letter from the friend whom, in well-known lines, he once parodied as "a melancholy carle." Bailey, Reynolds, Haslam, had a high opinion of him, and he was esteemed by Byron and Leigh Hunt and Samuel Rogers. There is much in his letters that would no longer be of interest, somewhat that is of too personal or private a nature to be disengaged from the gossip of a bygone day, and occasionally passages in that broader humour which has ceased to please; but in the main they are the letters of a gentleman and a good fellow, of a scholar and of a man of quick sympathies and native insight. His indomitable energy of mind and body (though not as a ' Russia merchant,' retired or otherwise—for Brown's youthful experiences in commerce were of the briefest, and consisted chiefly in winding up the business which his father and elder brother had suffered to decay)—this indomitable energy was, no doubt, part secret of his power to refresh and stimulate those whom he encountered as friends; a faculty he had in no common degree, as Severn, who himself possessed this happy gift, has emphatically and again and again testified.

Certain words of the latter may fitly be quoted here, applicable as they are to the person who uttered them as well as to Charles Brown :—" One of the best fellows who ever lived; a creditable writer [painter]; a natural wit; a man of the world in the best sense; and possessed with a happy genius for friendship."

It has been no easy task to select from the vast mass of Severn's correspondence (and from his earliest days in Rome he was a great letter-writer, though ever an irregular correspondent) those letters and part-letters which seemed to bear most directly on the matter in hand. No doubt much has

been omitted which, were it included, would interest many
readers; on the other hand, it was obviously impossible to
satisfy all in this respect, and the MS. material was sifted
over and over to the end that no useful sidelights should be
lost, no really valuable matter be overlooked. Severn kept
most of the letters which were addressed to him, even when
these were mere notes of no other interest than that of the
moment; and frequently he preserved the first drafts or
later copies of the epistles which he himself sent.

His biographer has, of course, primarily been indebted to
the great quantity of MSS.—letters to and from Severn
during a period of nearly sixty years; reminiscences, fragmentary, and more complete, written at different times in
his life; and many volumes of scrupulously explicit
journals—placed in his hands by Mr. Walter Severn.
Thereafter he has to express his obligations to Mr. Charles
Severn, Joseph's younger brother, for much interesting
information of a personal nature, and again to him and to
Mr. Rayner Storr for their joint courtesy and assistance in
entrusting him with a large quantity of Severn's home-
letters for examination, excerption, or quotation. There
are so many persons to thank for all manner of aid that
it is best to make no attempt to specify each generous
collaborator; but sincere acknowledgments are in particular
due to the friends and strangers, not only in this country
but also in America, and Italy—and above all to those in
Rome—who by loan of letters, communication of interesting
facts and anecdotes, and records and memoranda of various
kinds, have helped to animate what is even now a less
comprehensive and living portrait than the limner would
fain have wrought.

To already published writings he is also, of course,
indebted. The most important single book or article is
Severn's own paper in the *Atlantic Monthly* for 1863 on the
'Vicissitudes of Keats's Fame.' Thereafter should be

mentioned Mr. H. Buxton Forman's monumental edition
of 'Keats' (to which, in particular, acknowledgments are
due in the instance of a few of Severn's letters or part-
letters, copied therefrom instead of from the originals);
Mr. Sidney Colvin's admirable monograph on Keats in the
English Men of Letters series, and to his delightful edition
of the poet's letters, a compilation edited with so much
patience and care, and distinguished by such discreet
sympathy and judgment, that it must be accepted as the
standard 'Letters of Keats;' and, almost needless to say,
to Lord Houghton's original and revised "Memoirs."
Naturally all noteworthy writings bearing upon the personality, circle, or period of Keats have been consulted;
but further specification would be as undesirable as it is
unnecessary. Finally, thanks are due to one or two literary
friends for advice on matters of detail, and for assistance in
research where a more or less arduous quest proved necessary—and notably to Mr. Richard Garnett, LL.D., and to
Mr. G. K. Fortescue.

A word upon the portrait-illustrations in this volume.
The interesting silhouette of Keats is reproduced for the
first time. The original, in the possession of Mr. Walter
Severn, was discovered only within the last few years,
having been accounted lost or destroyed at a period long
anterior. To all Keats-students it will have a particular
value; and specialists will note those indications of strength
which are inconspicuous in certain familiar likenesses of
the poet. The vignette-head of Keats, on the title-page, is
not after the early miniature, but a reproduction of a late
drawing; the latest portrait, indeed, which in his old age
Severn made. Rightly or wrongly, he was wont to declare
that it represented the poet as he commonly was; it is
certainly different in several respects from the well-known
engraving after the earlier miniature, which stands as a
frontispiece to Lord Houghton's 'Life' of Keats. The

pathetic sketch of Keats in the extremity of his last illness
is already known to every lover of the poet's work. The
original is one of the finest things Severn ever did, and
though it has necessarily lost much in process of reproduction, it will still, to those who look upon it—with the
eyelids closed as they are in mortal weakness, and the hair
matted with the dews of coming death—give that touching
sense of nearness to the dying poet which so many have felt.
Another instance of loss in reproduction is the engraving
after the autograph portrait of Severn. Here certain features are too pronounced, and the more youthful look of the
original drawing has evaded the translator. Fortunately,
Seymour Kirkup's beautiful drawing of Severn, made early
in 1822, and depicting him as Keats must have known him,
has been admirably reproduced. It is further interesting as
the handiwork of an eminent man and an artist who has
scarcely had his meed of recognition. When one looks at
this portrait of Severn in the prime of his early manhood,
it is easy to understand how readily he fascinated men as
well as women by his good looks and grace of manner, and
how it was that in his early days in Rome his 'head' was
so often 'taken' by his fellow-artists. It is quite likely
that, in common with all Seymour Kirkup's portrait-work,
this likeness is somewhat idealised; the artist himself,
however, thought it a vivid portrayal of his friend as he was
in the early Twenties. At a first glance, there is not much
in common between this portrait by Kirkup and Severn's
autograph likeness, though they belong to the same period
of his life—even when allowance is made for the different
way in which the long hair is brushed; but even here a
similarity may be traced in the eyes and still more
obviously in the mouth. In the originals the likeness is
more readily recognisable.

It may be added that the illustration in the last chapter,
that depicting the graves of Keats and Severn, is from a

recent photograph, taken at a time when the interwoven clusters of violets grew as thickly as tangled grasses.

On one point, it seems necessary to add a few words. Severn had a capricious memory, and was at no time heedful of the exact verity of his statements. Thus it is that one set of reminiscences will sometimes contradict the other, and that even letters written in the same month (occasionally, on or about the same day), will be at variance in matters of more or less importance. The same picture will be variously sold at £70, or £100, or £150; the same event will occur "this year," or "last autumn," or "a few years ago;" this friendship or that acquaintanceship will date confusedly now from a period anterior to the writer's first encounter with the person concerned; now from a year or month when intimacy had long been established. In advanced age the old painter's memory often played him strange tricks, though in the very last years of his life his remembrance of the days of his youth grew clearer and more intensified, and much, it seemed, that he had forgotten in early manhood or middle-age, came back to him. It was this that underlay his exclamation in his eighty-fifth year, that he was fortunate among men in literally recovering in his old age his lost youth. A good reason, accordingly, is afforded for a certain suspicion of any positive affirmation in Severn's letters, reminiscences, or conversations; without verification, or, at least, consideration, one might easily be led to false conclusions. Possibly some of the Keats-anecdotes he used to narrate in his latter years were either coloured, or actually created, by retrospective imagination; on the other hand, he was so reverent of the genius and dear fame of his beloved friend that, in narration, he would not consciously derogate from the facts. A friend informed the present writer that the first time he heard Severn tell a new story about Keats he would doubt its all-round veracity; that on the second telling he would think it was probably true in all essentials; and that if the story ever reached a third presentment, " it was certain to be an absolutely trustworthy record." So far, the present biographer has, in many like instances, followed this rough-and-ready means of judgment; that is, he has utilised no anecdote or reminiscence which did not seem to bear upon it the impress of actuality, or could in some degree be borne out.

In the same way that he has purposely refrained from dwelling on much of Severn's private life during the fifty years that followed his marriage—convinced that with the sayings and doings of Joseph Severn as a private individual, the public had no concern—he has also neglected many opportunities to diverge into mere gossip, and omitted much of personal family interest, which he need not have done were he a relative of Severn and engaged on a memoir practically intended for private circulation. Yet there is one point of general interest which should not be disregarded : the strong hereditary æsthetic strain in the Severn family—an inheritance exemplified in divers ways, but always notably. As stated in the early pages of the following Memoir, the father of Joseph Severn had a native love of pictorial art, and was, for a prolonged 'period, a teacher of music, a science which he almost passionately admired. His wife, too, loved it as one of the best things in life ; and in her judgment, both of music and painting, showed an exacting refinement which, no doubt, was in some degree due to the French strain which she inherited from her Huguenot grandparents. Of the sons of their marriage, as noted at page 5 hereafter, Joseph became eminent as a painter, and might have won repute as a musician; Thomas was a popular composer ; and Mr. Charles Severn was, for more than fifty years, a musician of high standing, the associate of the most eminent composers, singers, and executants of his time, and in his old age still

delights in his nominal vocation as organist. The lady
whom Joseph Severn married, though not an artist, had a
keen sense of colour and form, and was, moreover, a woman
of culture and refinement, native and inherited. Of their
six children, three were girls: Claudia, Mary, and Eleanor.
Of these only the third (Mrs. Furneaux) survives, and
shares in no slight degree, not only the family love of Art,
but, in particular, that of her twin-brother, Mr. Arthur
Severn, whose name is so familiar as that of a painter of
much originality, power, and poetic insight. Claudia
Fitzroy Severn married Mr. Frederick Gale, so well known
to cricket enthusiasts, and died in 1874; in her, the
æsthetic strain betrayed itself in a delicate love and understanding of music. The second daughter, Mary, showed
exceptional promise as an artist; some of her drawings had
a refinement and grace which proved her possession of a
strong and original talent; but, subsequent to her marriage
with Mr., now Sir Charles, Newton, she died untimely in
1866. Of the three sons of Mr. and Mrs. Joseph Severn,
Mr. Walter Severn, the eldest, has already had a long and
distinguished career as an artist; and in the craft of letters,
also, has proved that he has inherited something of that
literary faculty which his father had in a secondary degree.
It would be altogether inappropriate for the present writer to
dwell upon the life and achievement of Mr. Walter Severn;
while, as an artist, what better word could be said of him
than has already generously been uttered by Mr. Ruskin?*
The same reasons obviously apply in the instance of Joseph
Severn's youngest son, Arthur, to whom allusion has already
been made. Born in London in 1841, Mr. Arthur Severn
is now in the prime of life, and is fortunate in having
sustained and enhanced the high repute which he won at
an early age. This is neither the time nor the place to
dwell upon his devotion to the illustrious friend of whom he

* *Vide* Letter of March 26th, 1875, quoted at p. 219, *post.*

has been the intimate companion for many years, but it is
significant that, with much else, he has inherited that
genius for devoted friendship which was the good fortune
of his father's life.*

The late Henry Augustus Severn was a man of exceptional intellectual energy. Ill health interfered to some
extent with what promised to be a brilliant scientific career,
and in 1884 his constitution yielded to a prolonged strain.
The eldest of Mr. Walter Severn's six children has also shown
a marked scientific bias, and is now a member of the Royal
College of Science. Two other sons perpetuate the family
tradition; Mr. Nigel and Mr. Cecil Severn—the latter at
present a midshipman on board the *Immortalité,* whence
he has sent to the 'Daily Graphic' and elsewhere, clever
sketches of naval life and marine experiences. It is not
often that an artistic strain is at once so dispersed and
so strenuous throughout three generations.

In a sense the writer of this 'Life of Severn' may repeat
what Lord Houghton wrote of his Memoir of Keats: "I
came to the conclusion that it was best to act simply as
Editor of the Life which was, as it were, already written."
He hopes that, at any rate, he has educed from the mass of
material at his disposal enough to give an adequate idea of
the life and achievement of his subject, and to make the
personality of Joseph Severn live again. The story, at least,
of an immortal friendship has for the first time been set forth
in full detail. That friendship, as Severn was ever the first
to recognise, was the golden gate whence issued the success
and happiness of his life; and in the shadow of death, as in
life, he turned his eyes longingly towards it. *Sic itur ad
astra.*

WILLIAM SHARP.

* Mr. Arthur Severn married a lady who is a cousin of Mr. Ruskin,
and for many years the three have been one family, residing together at
Brantwood, Coniston.

CONTENTS.

CHAPTER V.

CHAPTER VI.

CHAPTER VII.

CHAPTER VIII.

CHAPTER IX.

CHAPTER X.

JOSEPH SEVERN'S MISCELLANEOUS WRITINGS.

CHAPTER XI.

CHAPTER XII.

ILLUSTRATIONS.

LIFE AND FRIENDSHIPS

JOSEPH SEVERN.

CHAPTER I.

*Early training—Boyhood vicissitudes—Apprentice to an engraver—
Beginnings in Art—Rivalries—Mrs. Siddons as Queen Katherine—
First steps to success.*

THE name Severn, writes Mr. Freeman in a private letter,
" is a curious bit of philology. The Welsh is *Hafren,* or
some such name, which is said to mean *divider* or frontier
stream. The Lake *Sabrinas* is according to a very old
analogy, by which the initial *h* in Welsh, as in Greek,
answers to initial *s* in Latin. The puzzling thing is that a
law of change of that sort should be applied at so late a
stage of the language. It is possible that the modern
Welsh form may be later than the Roman Conquest, as in
old Greek we find $\sigma \hat{\upsilon} \varsigma$ for $\hat{\upsilon} \varsigma$. But, as I am not a Celtic
scholar, I do not much like guessing at these things."

The Severns were a family of good West-country stock,
for several generations settled by the banks of the Severn
in Gloucestershire. In the latter half of the eighteenth
century trouble came to them and caused the wide
scattering of what had been almost a clan. One member
of the family settled in Bedfordshire, and his eldest son,
James, was the father of Joseph Severn. Mr. James Severn
married a Miss Littel, belonging to an old Huguenot

family, and shortly before his marriage definitely adopted, owing to a collapse in the small remaining family fortunes, the profession of music. Mr. Severn was a man of an excitable and somewhat flighty temperament, with native, though untrained æsthetic tastes. He was fortunate in his wife, a woman whose comeliness was only less remarkable than her sweetness of nature and alert sympathy. Despite her husband's headstrong temper, their life seems to have been a happy one. The Severns are a long-living family, and Miss Littel brought to that strenuous stock her share of the proverbial hardihood of the Huguenots; for, through troublous times, she preserved her notable vigour and serenity, and survived to a great age. Her eldest son lived to his eighty-sixth year; one of her daughters died three or four years ago, well on in her eighth decade; her youngest son, Mr. Charles Severn, after a long and honourable career as a musician, is happily still living, and as active at the age of eighty-six as are most men younger than he by a score of years.

Early in 1793 Mr. and Mrs. Severn settled in Hoxton, then a somewhat remote village to the north of London, and there, on the 7th of December in the same year (not in 1796 as sometimes stated), the eldest of their six children was born, and duly christened Joseph. The boy was precocious, for while still a child of five he drew a portrait of his father. The drawing was in profile, and was sufficiently good to attract more general attention than infantile attempts generally do; indeed, an artist friend of Mr. Severn declared that it was, in everything except firmness, excellent. One of the hobbies of the lad's father was to collect old pictures at local and second-rate Metropolitan sales, and though in one of his MS. confessions his son irreverentially alludes to the "rubbishy old pictures which [his father] was always picking up when other people dropped 'em'," he admits that this paternal fancy, and the tolerable and intolerable pictures themselves, helped to educate his own latent sense of line, mass, and colour. Father and son were companionable while Joseph was but a child; in great part, as the latter admits, because he was never tired of staring up at the canvas treasures (which came and went with almost tidal regularity), and of listening to explanations of their subjects or expositions of their merits.

As soon as Mr. Severn became convinced that his first-born possessed an exceptional faculty, he lost no opportunity of assisting its development. He helped the boy with hints in the elements of drawing and composition, and sometimes took him for a walk into the country, where he would point out a cottage, or a hamlet clustered under tall elms, or a wayside inn nestling like a huge white-and-red-strawberry among a mass of foliage, and explain the value and methods of pictorial selection. Occasionally he would insist on the boy's attempting one of these familiar subjects; once, for instance, at Tottenham, he prevailed on him to sketch an ivy-mantled cottage, for which purpose he borrowed a stool from the old lady who occupied the cottage, who watched the child with an astonishment which culminated in profound admiration followed by profuse offers of cake.

He was, moreover, a good story-teller, and held his children entranced with historical tales : sometimes he would simulate the personages of whom he spoke, as when he so impressed the imagination of his firstborn by his re-presentation of the ' Ghost ' in *Hamlet* that Joseph made, though in fear and trembling, a drawing of the gruesome apparition. Occasionally these peaceful interludes were momentarily broken by swift wrath at some misdeed of the precocious Joseph, when Mr. Severn would inflict unexpected chastisement with bewildering suddenness. Nevertheless, these summary punishments caused no feud between father and son, and in the main the boy seems to have been brought up wisely enough. The long walks in the country were good for body as well as for artistic training, and as the lad grew older his father was wont to take him with him to the various country-houses where he taught music, and show him the pictures and tell him particulars of the painters. Sometimes Joseph showed originality in his drawings, as when he painted "a bright gamboge glory all round the coffin " in his drawing of the Nelson Car. This, however, must have been when he was no longer a child : and it was before he passed into his teens that some of his father's patrons noticed the drawings which Mr. Severn often took an opportunity of displaying, and encouraged the boy to persevere. In later life Severn was wont to attribute to his mother all his heritance of good qualities, and to her, certainly, he owed his joyous serenity of temperament : yet to his father, except in the matter of temper, he bore distinct resemblance. From him he inherited his most characteristic traits—sudden enthusiasms, swift emotions, personal vanity, with extremes of self-depreciation.

Mr. Severn deserves credit for having discerned his son's artistic tendencies, and for having done his best to cultivate them. Even when a mere child, the boy's education in this respect was not neglected, for drawings, engravings, and picture-books were frequently lent to him : and so keen was the lad's pleasure in these that, when given him at night, he used to go to bed early so as to "get up at dawn to devour them." Some of Severn's kindly-worded complaints against his father, therefore, must not be taken too literally ; the " hardness " to which he more than once alludes was no very severe infliction after all—even the casual chastisements already alluded to, seem to have had no ill-results, and, as Mr. Whistler says of an apologetic critic's remarks, were " meant friendly." Moreover, as he fully admits, his father had several excellent qualities. He was thoughtful for his family despite his extravagances ; he was generous, in the fullest sense of the word ; and he invariably set an example of scrupulous honesty. His inability to bear contradiction was a cause of frequent disturbance, particularly as his children grew older ; and no doubt here he had only himself to blame. Devoted to his wife, and not averse from domestic existence, he was something of the household-tyrant, for he would allow no domestic work to be done in his presence, and kept no restraint upon his anger if one of his children made any noise. Withal, he had the virtue of industry, and displayed rare ingenuity in everything concerning the science of music and musical instruments.* It was well for Joseph Severn that he had so good a mother to counteract the somewhat too eccentric influences of his father, particularly as he seems to have been anything but a tractable youngster. Again and again in his "reminiscences," journals, and letters, he refers to his mother as his guardian-angel, as a woman of incomparable tact and rare sweetness of nature. From various accounts, it is clear that her charm of manner was peculiarly winsome. To her son she was something holy almost, and often in after years he wrought into the faces of the Madonnas whom he painted the expression of the mother whom he loved so well and reverenced so deeply. Among those who were almost equally impressed by the beauty of Mrs. Severn's character was Keats, who loved his own mother with passionate affection, and mourned her death, when he was in his fifteenth year, with poignant grief.†

Young Severn went through the usual vicissitudes of boyhood. It is needless to follow him in detail through his diffuse and discursive early reminiscences: it will suffice to refer to one or two incidents. During the celebration of the Victory of Trafalgar, the lad, enthusiastic for Nelson and the glory of a naval career, ran away from home; an act which had an untimely, not to say an ignominious ending, for, overcome with fatigue when but a short distance from home, he sank by the wayside and fell asleep by a post. There his alarmed parents found him, and so practical

---

* Unquestionably his three sons derived their musical faculties from him. Joseph, as he was assured again and again, might have been as successful as a composer as a painter; Mr. Charles Severn has won deserved repute; and their brother, Thomas, was a popular composer as well as a good executant.

† In the MS. of "Early Remembrances," Severn records a statement of Keats, "that his great misfortune had been that from his infancy he had no mother." There is palpable forgetfulness, or confusion of some kind, here. Probably Severn, who did not become acquainted with Keats till after his mother's death, believed that Mrs. Rawlings (for she had married again) had died during his friend's infancy, or perhaps that she was but Keats's step-mother, and remembered or misapprehended some casual remark by the poet.

was his father's argument that he did not again attempt surreptitious flight. Of an emotional and imaginative temperament, he seems to have been permanently impressed by a tragic incident which occurred in his eighth year. He had gone with a schoolmate named Cole to bathe in some water-filled gravel-pits, and in one of them his companion ventured beyond his depth and was drowned. There was no one near at the time, so the child had to watch his comrade perish, and then to make his way home, carrying the drowned boy's clothes, and break the news to Mrs. Cole. No doubt his extreme horror of sudden death was in great part due to this experience.

When Joseph was in his fifteenth year his father began to look about for some suitable vocation for him. If he had been able he would have himself instructed Joseph in the technique of Art, but notwithstanding his mania for collecting and dispersing old pictures, he had little trained taste or knowledge, and could not draw in the least. An artistic education for his son was altogether beyond his means. Entering his house one day, and seeing Joseph engaged in copying with great accuracy some old plate, it occurred to him that he could not do better than apprentice the boy to an engraver. Here again the question of means nearly brought about the abandonment of the project, for in almost every instance a premium was asked, varying from £100 to £300. At last Mr. Severn saw an advertisement which promised more satisfactorily, for no premium was demanded, but only an undertaking as to board and partial lodging. The advertiser was Mr. William Bond, whom Severn describes as "an engraver in the chalk manner," and who was then engaged in reproducing some paintings by Singleton. Young Severn had never drawn from oil pictures, and was delighted; moreover, in comparison with the canvases he was accustomed to see in his father's house those at Mr. Bond's seemed to him works of high art. In a word, he was fascinated by the novel artistic atmosphere, and, inexperienced as he was, imagined that with Mr. William Bond as guide he would soon become an artist.

Mr. Bond, on his part, was satisfied with the drawings which Mr. Severn showed him, particularly with one of the Ghost in *Hamlet*, and agreed to take Joseph as an apprentice for seven years on his father's guarantee as to the fulfilment of the stipulations concerning partial board and accommodation.

It was an important change for the young would-be artist, no doubt, and perhaps may have been more influential for good than he was ever willing to allow. Yet it was the beginning of a long period of fret and unhappiness. In his own words, he "was popped unwittingly into slavery, and doomed to stab copper for seven long years." In the first few months he was well content, for though he had some qualms at being so rigidly bound by the indenture, after he had made such rapid progress that Mr. Bond became anxious lest so promising a pupil should leave his service, he rejoiced in his new surroundings and comparatively congenial work. After some months of exercises in drawing, chiefly in copying in Indian ink prints by Bartolozzi, he was set "to stab the copper." At first this interested him greatly, and he was an apt pupil; but when he wished to devote himself more exclusively to drawing, Mr. Bond held him to the terms of the agreement, and in every way discouraged all original effort. A feeling of resentment towards the engraver grew in young Severn's mind, unjustifiably in some respects, for Mr. Bond had bargained for an assistant in his trade and not for the superintendence of an ambitious and restless young artist; though, on the other hand, neither he nor Mr. Severn seems to have made the youth clearly understand the nature of the indenture.

It was about this time, however, that he began to find some solace in the study of literature. The " epics and histories " which he read eagerly in his few periods of leisure when he could not be working at his drawings further stimulated his inventive faculty. The desire to create became almost a passion, and slowly he began to feel his way towards independent accomplishment, though as he had never been able to work in colour save with Indian ink or at best with indifferent water colours, he was conscious of his painful limitations. Occasionally he rebelled against his circumstances, and it was all his parents could do to persuade him that he would be foolish as well as wrong to desert the honourable trade to which he had been apprenticed. Ultimately Mr. Bond consented to his pupil's having some more time to himself for purposes of recreation as well as of study, for the boy's health was delicate.

Severn's arduous, if intermittent, studies enabled him to learn one invaluable lesson for a young artist, namely that his ignorance was out of all proportion to his aspirations, and more than this, that he had much to unlearn as well as to acquire. Sometimes there were pictures to be engraved which were really works of art, and from these, and his effort to reproduce them in monochrome or water-colours, he perceived wherein he fell short, as well as obtained glimpses of the goal towards which he was fain to strive. Among these pictures he particularly mentions a 'Laughing Girl,' by Sir Joshua Reynolds, and a Portrait of himself by the great artist. He also refers to a fine painting of Lord Stafford by Vandyke, which, he says, was offered to Mr. Severn for 2*l.*, an offer declined by his father, who "cared for nothing in Art except landscape." Untrained as he was, Joseph Severn at once recognised the beauty of the old picture, and for half-a-crown persuaded the dealer to let him take it home to copy. The copy was duly valued at Hoxton, not so much for its artistic merits as because it bore a striking resemblance to the head of the household. Twenty years later, when Severn returned from Rome on a visit to London, he saw at the British Institution this identical picture— "one of the finest specimens of the master, which had been foolishly lost owing to my father's ignorance of Art."

As his small circle of acquaintances extended, and with the renewed hope and artistic energy which were the result of his occasional holidays, Severn's health began to improve. The long walk to and fro between Hoxton and Newman Street, in all weathers; insufficient and monotonous diet;

and the deep discontent which possessed him—one and all
had wrought upon him to such an extent that he feared he
could not endure the strain for long. But when he found
himself free every now and again to do as he willed, his
spirits rose, and all threatenings of a decline passed away.
On these holidays (granted at first on condition that he
would be more assiduous in his apprentice-work at other
times), he frequently painted small portraits in water-
colours, at the rate of half-a-guinea apiece, and the money
thus obtained was spent on the materials of his craft and on
books. He became, indeed, an eager student: for, more
and more conscious of his ignorance, he set himself to self-
instruction, not only in *belles-lettres* and history, but in
mathematics, with rare and uncertain wanderings into the
unknown ways of other sciences. But as time went on, and
he found that he was no longer really gaining ground, and
as, moreover, he realised keenly how fatal for him was his
lack of training in anatomical study and drawing, he determined at all hazards to become a member of the Royal
Academy student classes. A long time elapsed, however,
before he gained his point. A drawing that he made, of
'Joseph interpreting the Butler's and the Baker's dreams,'
seems to have been instrumental in convincing Mr. Bond
that it would be best to let the youth find his level, whatever
that was to be.

From this time forward Severn made rapid progress in
the preliminaries of his art. When at home he lost no
opportunity of useful experience, and he makes particular
mention of one undertaking which helped him in no slight
measure. For a long period, he says, " I was engaged at
home making a little theatre. All the scenes were carefully
drawn and painted, both in architecture and landscape ;
then the figures were equally well studied in cardboard, and
in this way my ingenuity was called forth and many good
opportunities afforded of learning not exactly to draw, but
of knowing how much I wanted to learn, how much I needed
to acquire." But all this enthusiasm and determination was
looked at askance by Mr. Severn, who could not believe

that his son had sufficient talent to enable him to overcome
the apparently insuperable obstacles to success, and thought
his indifference to the engraver's trade as foolish as it was
reprehensible. In vain he pointed out that a master-engraver
was an artist, and that there was artistic scope for the ablest
draughtsman in so worthy a profession. His son replied
that it might be the finest calling on earth, but was not to
his liking, as even the finest engravings the world had
seen were interpretative and not creative, and that he wanted
to create, and to have free scope for his development to that
end. The seven, or rather eight, years that were passed in
more or less close apprenticeship to the art of " stabbing
copper," were undoubtedly hurtful to Severn in other
respects than by occupying the best years of his youth
with labour at once enforced and alien to his tastes,
and by circumscribing his opportunities for drawing
and anatomical study. For the long apprenticeship
meant all manner of adverse influences upon both his
mental and physical development. He had no time for
healthy exercise, little leisure for reading, and that at the
expense of his already tired eyesight, and of his almost
exhausted stock of energy ; and, moreover, such reading as
he could manage was haphazard, and so sometimes calculated
to cause mental confusion rather than aid his intellectual
growth. " The years of youth are as a mirror, fore-
shadowing the years to come," says an Oriental proverb ;
and with some such sentiment Severn closes the first section
of his earliest reminiscences. No after-care, he says in
effect, can absolutely readjust the balance lost through the
expenditure in a wrong direction of those years of youth
which should be bartered to a particular end with a heed at
once scrupulous and far-seeing. " Owing to those limited
beginnings," he admits, " I may perhaps have been induced
since to undertake works that were rather the effect of love
than skill, of enthusiasm than judgment. This may have
been always an evil for me." It undoubtedly was, and credit
is due to him for the self-criticism. Indeed, throughout life
Severn was a strange mixture of childlike vanity, genuine

humility, high aims and ambitious efforts, with accomplishment often far short; profound belief in himself and his artistic calling, combined with swift readiness to see and admit his shortcomings; of a habitual self-criticism ranging from generous apologetics or depreciatory condemnations to a calm survey of facts and judicious estimates.

The evening art-classes, however, though serviceable, were not so pleasant in other respects as the eager young student had anticipated. Rivalries which were often carried to the pitch of bitter jealousies made the course of true art-life run anything but smoothly at times, and the system then in vogue, by which money and influence together made a student's career one of pleasure or, by absence of either, one of hardship, rendered comradeship by no means so easy as it generally is wherever the bond of Art exists. Severn does not seem to have made any friends among his student acquaintances at this time, but rather to have incurred some ill-feeling by his self-confidence, perhaps self-assertiveness, and by his enthusiasm—then, as now, and always, a quality unacceptable to the many.

In the fortunate years of youth even seemingly untoward accidents as often as not induce new and welcome developments. Through having been nearly crushed to death at a theatre Severn, as he declares, gained a new insight into Art. Writing in 1857, he affirms he had been so many times near death and in its actual presence that, though constitutionally not of a courageous nature, he had gained a coolness in the front of danger which would mislead many people into thinking him possessed of no common valour. Strangely enough, he was conscious of less fear, of a self-possessed calm, whenever the peril of death was actually imminent: the more remote the possible mischance the more harassing and almost prostrating the effect forecast by it. To some extent he attributed this idiosyncrasy to the drowning accident alluded to above, but even more to his narrow escape from death at the Haymarket Theatre. He had often heard of the superb acting of Mrs. Siddons, but as she had retired from the stage he could not hope to see her once more enthral a metropolitan audience. On the occasion, however, of her brother, Charles Kemble, requiring aid, she generously came forward with an offer to impersonate Queen Katherine in *Henry the Eighth*. The advertisement appeared in due time, and besides the irresistible attraction of Mrs. Siddons's name, playgoers read that John Kemble would appear in the part of Cardinal Wolsey, Charles in that of Cromwell, Pope in that of King Henry, Miss Foote as Ann Boleyn, and that even the subordinate parts were to be filled by actors of assured repute. The popular Miss Stephens, moreover, was to sing, in Queen Katherine's dream, 'Angels ever bright and fair,' and altogether it was calculated that the little theatre in the Haymarket would be crowded to its utmost limits. When Severn and a friend, William Haslam,* reached the doors an hour before the time of opening, the crowd was already large : ere long it became so great that the Haymarket was almost blocked by it. The entrance to the pit was through a small door and along a narrow passage. In the struggle which ensued upon the opening of the doors Severn was separated from his friend and soon afterwards stumbled and fell, with the result that he was speedily trampled into unconsciousness and, indeed, escaped death by little short of a miracle. At last, as the crowd thinned, some one noticed that an unfortunate was being done to death, if not already dead, and gave the alarm. The unconscious body ("thin as a skeleton almost, to start with, and now flattened out like a pancake") was uplifted and conveyed over the playgoers' heads to the front of the pit, where there was less risk of suffocation. When it was found that the sufferer was not dead, but at the same time that he could not "come to," several doctors and medical students from various parts of the house volunteered their

---

* William Haslam, whose name is so familiar to all students of Keats's life and work, will be referred to frequently further on. He was about a year older than Keats, as he was born some time in 1795. He died in 1852.

assistance, though for three-quarters of an hour the patient remained insensible, and scarcely shewed signs of life. But just before the performance began consciousness returned. Although everything in his pockets was smashed (two oranges, he says, were reduced to a kind of marmalade-like pulp), and his clothes were so torn and soiled as to be thenceforth useless, no bones were broken or any serious damage incurred beyond a "universal bruise from head to foot." Either he could not or would not be removed, and when the curtain rose he was left in peace. He watched the performance in a dazed fashion till Mrs. Siddons appeared, when "her impressive demeanour and magical dignity and pathos" so affected nerves already feverishly excited that he sat as one entranced and conscious of some new and vital influence in his life. Severn believed that "something had been trampled out of him:" that thereafter he was "well in spirit." Probably his excitable nature had been so wrought upon by the shock, by the physical suffering, and by the sudden change from a long-continued apathy to a state of comparative exhilaration, that he became subject to a kind of happy frenzy. He never forgot the performance nor its effect upon him. From that day, when the power and magic of Art was borne in upon him, he determined to live the life of an artist, whatever the sacrifices involved, the cost to be paid. In his eightieth year, even, he would recall with vivid speech and gestures his emotions of that far-back night. In all his life, though a frequenter of the theatre and at one time passionately fond of it, he declared that he never saw such acting: no man could expect to see twice, he says, such a combination of the highest dramatic genius and personal beauty, with such altogether admirable helpmates.*

* It may be worth while to give part of Severn's recollections of the great actress: for there must be few now living who once were moved to deep emotion by the genius of Sarah Siddons. Her " farewell appearance " was as Lady Macbeth, at Covent Garden, in June, 1812. But between the summer of 1813 and that of 1819 she acted publicly again some six or seven times, from motives of friendship or generosity. The performance at

Weak and in suffering though he was, and enthralled too by the pageant upon which he looked, Severn was yet able to make several drawings of Mrs. Siddons in her most striking and characteristic attitudes. From these

which Severn was present took place on May 31st, 1816. " Her large and imposing figure," he writes, " was well suited to the character and situation of Queen Katherine in *Henry the VIIIth*. Her noble countenance not only impressed all, but, despite her years, was winsome by those additional marks of beauty such as only a good and dignified length of life can give. Her brow was Juno-like, and when she uttered the words, ' Lord Cardinal, to you I speak—'tis you hath blown this coal betwixt my lord and me,' her large black lustrous eyes flashed fire, and it was such an inspired glance as I have never but that once seen. Then, after maintaining this majestic front till she is about to leave the Court, when the crier calls out ' Katherine, Queen of England, come into Court,' and her maid reminds her that she is called back, when suddenly she descended from the Queen to the woman, and showed her private anger in saying *sotto voce* to her maid, ' Fool, why need you notice it '—the change was wonderful. Afterwards, in the dying scene, she was not less impressive, calm and resigned, still beautiful though so different, altogether changed from what she had been, save for that deep touching voice whose tones, whether loud and impassioned or soft and pathetic, were like the finest music, for they thrilled the air with melodious tones, and at the same time touched the heart with such deep pathos that the audience seemed to think it a merit to shed tears and thus appropriately accompany such sublime acting. One seemed, indeed, to be an onlooker on the actual pageant of life rather than auditor to an acted tale of history. The Cardinal was impersonated by John Kemble, in all the pride of intellect, and beauty of person and countenance, that so raised him above his fellows. The profound show of humility he assumed at first in the trial scene, and thereafter his haughty pride to the nobles when he suspects imminent danger, were masterly; but nothing could be more superb in acting than his discovery of the wrong paper given him by the King, when he trembled from head to foot, with convulsed underlip, which quivered like a leaf as the paper dropped from his nerveless grasp. The part of Cromwell was in its way not less perfectly rendered by Charles Kemble, whose handsome face and youthful figure made a good foil to the worn and o'er-ambitious Cardinal. And how am I to describe the lovely Miss Foote as Ann Boleyn?—for she was a paragon of beauty, which was set off rather than detracted from by the unassuming nature of her acting. She was fair, and might well have been the real Venus of the antique world, as Mrs. Siddons would then have as certainly been the Juno. To complete the greatness and individual splendour of this unique performance, Miss Stephens (whose voice and simple style surpassed anything I have ever heard since, even in Italy) sang ' Angels ever bright and fair ' as though an angel had silently and invisibly (for she was not seen) descended to console the dying Queen. The pure voice and unaffected style made the illusion perfect—and the dream itself, as represented so wonderfully by Charles Kean in 1855, with the groups of angels bearing palms, and with rays of heavenly light, even this, with all its magic, was not comparable in effect with the solitary voice of Miss Stephens singing her sweet vibrating song. I have been studies he made other drawings, for which he found a ready sale at the small sum he asked for each, and so at last he found himself able to purchase an easel, oil-paints, and other paraphernalia which till then he had lacked.

thus particular in recording this unique dramatic representation, as, apart from its influence on me, perhaps none so perfect may ever be seen again; moreover, the record will tend to prove how strong my mind and feeling must have been for such triumphs of the imagination and the moving spirit of history that, almost in the grasp of death (for nearer death I suppose I at no time ever was), my spirit was not only unquenched but rarely exalted."

CHAPTER II.

SEVERN was still an engraver's apprentice and casual student at the Academy schools when he formed an acquaintanceship which rapidly developed into friendship, and became ultimately the chief factor from without in his life. Every incident of his friendly relationship with Keats is of interest, for surely there is nothing in the history of art and letters more deeply affecting than the story of the untimely death of one of the greatest of English poets, and the self-sacrificing loyalty and love of the young painter whose name is for ever indissociable from that of his illustrious friend.

There is some uncertainty as to the date when Keats and Severn first met. The latter wrote once that the event occurred so early as 1813, but as he added that Keats was then "walking Guy's Hospital," it is clear that he was mistaken, for the poet had not then begun his hospital experiences. On the other hand, there is some likelihood that he met Keats either when the latter was staying at 8, Dean Street, in the Borough, or in St. Thomas's Street; and there seems no doubt that his introduction by William Haslam certainly was not later than the spring of 1816, just before Keats went to reside with his brothers in lodgings in the Poultry. It has been commonly asserted that the meeting occurred in 1817, and that the introducer was either Haslam, Holmes, or Haydon; but it is unquestionable that Keats and Severn had met by the autumn of 1816 at latest, though probably in the spring of that year, if not, as I am inclined to believe, earlier.[*] Keats, despite his genial manner, was apt to be reticent with new acquaintances, and it is possible that when he first met Joseph Severn he was not sufficiently impressed to seek familiarity of intercourse; while Severn, on his part, though he has stated several times how immediate and irresistible was the spell cast over him by the poet, may not have felt entitled to demand the privileges of friendship, particularly as he had then so little leisure, and, moreover, no lodgings to which he cared to invite a friend.

In the MS. sketch entitled 'My Tedious Life,' Severn does explicitly state that the event happened in 1817, adding, "we soon became the greatest friends;" but the genial artist's dates are at all times untrustworthy, and with one who used words so loosely, "soon" might indicate a few months as well as a few weeks, or even a year or so. From various vague statements in the MSS. it would appear that lengthy intervals occurred between the meetings of the friends during the first part of their acquaintanceship, and even when there was no longer any reserve betwixt them, but genuine affection and sympathy. Keats had many friends, Severn few, and, moreover, little leisure. Yet Severn seems to have resented any lengthy interval in seeing John, or for that matter George Keats, with whom he had also formed a firm friendship. There must, in all likelihood, have been an intimacy of some standing before George Keats would write as follows :—

Hampstead,
" Wednesday Evening.

" MY DEAR FELLOW,

" What a most unconscionable fellow you must be for fearing my brother has forgotten you without knowing the ' how '—and the ' why.' Take

---

[*] In a letter to Charles Cowden Clarke, of 17th December, 1816, Keats alludes to Reynolds having promised to be with him that evening, and adds : " Yesterday I had the same promise from Severn. . . . "

my assurance that he has not; that he has heard where your Picture is situate, and notwithstanding that disadvantage looks so well and attracts so much attention, pleases Haydon, and moreover, that a very clerkly written review of it has appeared in an esteemed magazine, and what the praise thus bestowed amounts to—all this he has heard within this week. Can he, then, have forgotten the complaining Severn? Be like that River

> 'That makes sweet music with enamell'd stones,
> Giving a gentle kiss to every sedge
> He overtaketh in his pilgrimáge;
> And so by many winding nooks he strays,
> With willing sport, to the wild ocean.'

"He shall know your feelings about the treatment of your picture, but I think he'll agree with me in thinking that all those who are likely to have tastes to boast of, will be pretty well acquainted with the delightful passage the directors of the exhibition have thought proper to omit. Who does not know one of the best jewels, set in the midst of the richest gems, that ever proceeded from the Brain of Man? The *Midsummer Night's Dream* is the masterpiece of fanciful Poetry—no exceptions—oh, yes, *The Tempest*, one! I have read them both since I have been here, all in green Fields, under green Hedges, and upon green Mounts, surrounded by nature in her prettiest dress, decked in the flowers of Spring. One may say with truth that Shakespeare carries you where he pleases, but the quicker the senses the more he is enjoyed—and how the free air of the hills quickens the Brain, I can witness. I did not know our grand, awful Bard till now, but now he comes upon me with all his light, darkening the name of every other votary in proportion (—— might be "The" with an omitted word, or perhaps "Jno") is not just—I am taken by surprise—'tis true! I could go on a great deal more of this sort—but 'methinks I prattle something too wildly'—what profanation to place such a line here; I deserve to be pilloried for it. Whatever may be the merits of this case about your picture, you may depend on victory, since Shakespeare will be sure to side with one who so well illustrates the pictures of his imagination. 'Twas my intention to have made you a visit on Monday when I was in town, but the villainous rain (I cannot say refreshing rain) kept me away; as it was, I was soaked, and obliged to walk to Hampstead through it. Since then I have passed my threshold only once. To-morrow I shall be in town, but business of importance calls me another way than your house. If you should be inclined to spend a day in the Country, and have a look at the beautiful scenery of this place, please send a note mentioning the day, and I will be careful to be in the way. I would offer you a bed, were that possible; that it is not is a cause of regret to

"Your friend,
"GEORGE KEATS.

" *Observe.*—Let me know at least two days before you come, unless you choose to run the risque of my being from home, which I would not have.—G. K. John and Tom are at Canterbury—(no time for more)."

Intimacy, at any rate, did not begin till 1816, or possibly early in 1817. There is, at least, no question as to the profound impression made upon Severn by Keats. It was his good fortune to encounter in his youth, he says, one of those incidents which change or make the whole course of a man's life.

"This was the congenial meeting with a young poet near my own age,* and so gifted with a bright imagination and with such charming manners, and with great communicativeness,† that I felt raised to the third heaven. Fortunately for me we soon became the greatest friends, for there was much in common between us in addition to a mutual love of nature." [This common love was in itself sufficient to form the basis of friendship, and later, if not at first, the two young men often went long walks together beyond Highgate Woods or across the Hampstead Weald. Their friendship was further based on an unequal reciprocity, he adds in effect:] "on my part, in the reception of such intellectual largesse with a warm feeling of gratitude, and on his part, the freedom of generous bestowal of his mental richness, and the free imparting of his poetical gifts, as well as his taste in the arts, his knowledge of history, and his most fascinating power in the communication of these. Thus a new world was opened to me, and I was raised from the mechanical drudgery of my art to the hope of brighter and more elevated courses."

What most impressed Severn was his new friend's singular compactness; "just as his mind was atune with the divine harmony," he wrote to a friend, "so he was in his bodily self a melody of humanity." Though small of stature, "not more than three-quarters of an inch over five feet," he seemed taller, partly from the perfect symmetry of his frame, partly from his erect attitude and a characteristic backward poise (sometimes a toss) of the head, and, perhaps more than anything else, from a

* Severn was the elder by two years. Keats was born in 1795.

† This seems contradictory to what is said above, but Keats was often frankly communicative with new acquaintances, though in intimacy subject to moods of almost austere reticence. The circumstance of Severn's allusion to his "communicativeness" as one of his immediately obvious traits goes to decide the question as to the date of their first meeting.

peculiarly dauntless expression, such as may be seen on the
face of some seamen. Severn noticed too, even then, the
almost flamelike intensity of Keats's eager glances when he
was keenly excited or interested; "they were like the
hazel eyes of a wild gipsy-maid in colour," he said once,
"set in the face of a young god." The only time Keats
appeared to him as small of stature was when he was
reading, or when he was walking rapt in some deep reverie;
when the chest fell in, the head bent forward as though
weightily overburdened, and the eyes seemed almost to
throw a light before his face. In some of the walks they
took together Severn was astonished by his companion's
faculty of observation. Nothing seemed to escape him, the
song of a bird and the undernote of response from covert or
hedge, the rustle of some animal, the changing of the
green and brown lights and furtive shadows, the motions of
the wind—just how it took certain tall flowers and plants
—and the wayfaring of the clouds : even the features and
gestures of passing tramps, the colour of one woman's hair,
the smile on one child's face, the furtive animalism below
the deceptive humanity in many of the vagrants, even
the hats, clothes, shoes, wherever these conveyed the
remotest hint as to the real self of the wearer. Withal,
even when in a mood of joyous observance, with flow
of happy spirits, he would suddenly become taciturn, not
because he was tired, not even because his mind was
suddenly wrought to some bewitching vision, but from
a profound disquiet which he could not or would not
explain. Certain things affected him extremely, particularly when "a wave was billowing through a tree,"
as he described the uplifting surge of air among
swaying masses of chestnut or oak foliage, or when,
afar off, he heard the wind coming across woodlands.
"The tide! the tide!" he would cry delightedly, and
spring on to some stile, or upon the low bough of a wayside
tree, and watch the passage of the wind upon the meadow-
grasses or young corn, not stirring till the flow of air was all
around him, while an expression of rapture made his eyes

gleam and his face glow till he "would look sometimes like
a wild fawn waiting for some cry from the forest-depths," or
like "a young eagle staring with proud joy" before taking
flight. This "eagle" appearance of Keats at certain times
much impressed Severn. "He was a nightingale only
when he sang," he remarked to a friend once; "at other
times he was a wild hawk." "I can never forget the wine-
like lustre of Keats's eyes," he said, on another occasion,
"just like those of certain birds which habitually front the
sun." "Those falcon-eyes," as he wrote in his account of
the poet's last desperate days.

The only thing that would bring Keats out of one of his
fits of seeming gloomful reverie—when he would answer
with cold, almost harsh brevity, or not at all, although his
eyes would have no hardness, but appeared larger than
usual and as though veiled in profound shadows: so darkly
pathetic, as Severn thought long afterward, though he did
not specially note this at the time, that the poet might
have been a woman consumed by some secret and fatal
anguish, rather than the bright, joyous, and genial, even
jovial, Keats—the only thing, during those country-rambles,
that would bring the poet "to himself again" was the
motion "of the inland sea" he loved so well, particularly
the violent passage of wind across a great field of barley.
From fields of oats or barley, Severn declared once, it was
almost impossible to allure him; he would stand, leaning
forward, listening intently, watching with a bright serene
look in his eyes and sometimes with a slight smile, the
tumultuous passage of the wind above the grain. The sea,
or thought-compelling images of the sea, always seemed to
restore him to a happy calm. Naturally these were
memorable walks for the impressionable young painter,
who from the first was conscious that he was enjoying the
companionship of a master-spirit.

But ere the acquaintanceship had grown into intimacy,
and while Severn saw rather more of George Keats than
of his elder brother, he was preparing for an ambitious
encounter with fate. The picture alluded to in George

Keats's letter, 'Hermia and Helena,' brought neither profit, direct or indirect, nor praise from those quarters where the artist most eagerly wished it to come : and for a time Severn was almost in despair. But gradually he discovered that he was making way in the "Antique" class at the Academy, and that not only his fellow students but one or two artists of high standing, including Fuseli (then Keeper), were attracted by his rapid progress. He grudged neither time nor labour in the effort to approach mastery in draughtsmanship. Thus, in his determination to succeed in a perfect drawing of the Laocoon group he strove (after his day's employment under Mr. Bond, his couple of hours' careful drawing at the "Antique" class, and his long walk out to his father's house in Hoxton) for two hours each evening throughout a whole winter. During the evenings of the ensuing summer he worked away at a drawing of two Gladiators fighting, and felt no small encouragement when Fuseli complimented him upon his success and began to take a genuine interest in him. One day Severn read an announcement about the Grand Prize in Historical Painting. His· heart beat with excitement as the idea flashed across his mind to try to win, or at least make a creditable struggle for it, notwithstanding his inexperience in painting in oils ; though his courage sank almost to vanishing-point when he read further that the prize had not been awarded for twelve years, as no competitor had proved himself sufficiently worthy to carry it off. He had need to remember all the encouragement he had received at the "School" of late, even in the life-class ; where, he records, he was first set to draw the feet of Hercules, from a model, and found himself companioned by a young artist afterwards to become famous as Sir Edwin Landseer. Yet even then he hardly dared to regard himself as worthy to be a candidate for a prize, the winning of which would mean more than customary repute. The subject, however, allured him. Keats had spoken to him enthusiastically about Spenser, and had read and recited passages of *The Fairie Queene* till Severn had been fired to an ardour which would not rest content without possession of the precious volume. He had come to love the poem almost as much as did the young poet, though naturally enough it did not give him the same ecstatic pleasure in its subtle under-music and quaint, picturesque, vivid, happy epithets. Thus it was that, when he read in the announcement that the motive for the prize-picture was to be found in Spenser's lines descriptive of the seizure by Una of the dagger from the despairful Red Cross knight, he felt as though the scene were in a sense familiar to him. When, later, he told Keats the subject of his picture, the poet smiled with pleasure, and at once repeated the lines of the fifty-second stanza.

> " Which whenas Una saw, through every vaine
> The crudled cold ran to her well of life,
> As in a swowne ; but, soone reliv'd againe,
> Out of his hand she snacht the cursed knife,
> And threw it to the ground, enraged rife,
> And to him said; ' Fie, fie, faint-hearted Knight !
> What meanest thou by this reproachful strife ?
> Is this the battaile which thou vaunt'st to fight
> With that fire-mouthed Dragon horrible and bright ?"
> —(*The Fairie Queene*, Bk. I., Canto x.)

So much for the subject. As to the size of the canvas, Severn saw to his relief that it was to be an ordinary half-length, that is 4 ft. 2 in. by 3 ft. 4 in. There was a year's time before him in which to work at it, and he began forthwith to think over the subject, make studies for the four figures, and accustom himself to painting in oils. It was to this end that he also ambitiously began another picture, that alluded to in George Keats's already quoted letter. It was this Shaksperian picture which was his first attempt in oils, and not, as sometimes stated, the prize-painting of ' The Cave of Despair.' The subject was a figure-study of Hermia and Helena in *A Midsummer Night's Dream*, which Severn had been reading at the instigation of Keats.

Having quite, or nearly, completed ' Hermia and Helena,' Severn set himself in earnest to attempt ' The Cave of

Despair'—a title, he says, which was only too painfully significant of his state of mind. The picture was in part painted in the winter, in a cold room without a fire and with insufficient light. The progress made was slight, partly because the artist persevered in secrecy concerning his undertaking, and mainly from the circumstance of his inability to devote to it more than the brief leisure when he was not occupied with the painting of his miniatures. With these small portraits he had gained some success. Miniatures were frequently commissioned, and though his prices ranged only from half-a-guinea to three guineas—more often the smaller sum—yet he was fortunate in having found even this demand for his artistic work. So well, indeed, was he progressing that if he had not resolved to do something in oil-painting he would probably have become a professional painter of miniatures in water-colours. Notwithstanding his industry in this direction, however, he found it difficult to obtain what he most needed. When the cold weather set in he had to paint, as already stated, without a fire—except, he adds, that supplied by his own enthusiasm. In two of his 'Reminiscences' he alludes to the fact of his having painted the limbs of the figure of Despair from his own naked shivering legs, as seen in a looking-glass in the chill morning or afternoon light. Often he thought of giving up the task as one beyond his means; but as time advanced he became more and more determined to go on with his attempt. Ere long the painting of the picture had become a kind of passion with him. With ever fresh hope and determination he devoted all his spare time to it, and finally sold his few treasured possessions, including his watch and his books, so that he might not lack the materials he required.*

* That there were bright episodes as well is evident from a passage in a letter of Keats to his brothers, dated from Featherstone Buildings, on the 5th of January, 1818. At that time Charles Wells, author of 'Joseph and his Brethren,' &c., lived in Featherstone Buildings, and Keats saw much of him. "Wells and Severn dined with me yesterday. We had a very pleasant day . . . . we enjoyed ourselves very much; were all very witty and full of Rhymes. We played a concert from four

In course of time the canvas was duly despatched to the
Royal Academy, and Severn's mind relaxed to "a certain
despairful case." About the end of October he received
the following letter from Keats :—

" Wentworth Place,
" Wednesday [October 27th ? 1819.]

" DEAR SEVERN,

" Either your joke about staying at home is a very old one or I
really call'd. I don't remember doing so. I am glad to hear you have
finish'd the Picture, and am more anxious to see it than I have time to
spare; for I have been so very lax, unemployed, unmeridian'd, and object-
less these two months that I even grudge indulging (and that is no great
indulgence considering the Lecture is not over till 9, and the lecture
room seven miles from Wentworth Place) myself by going to Hazlitt's
Lecture. If you have hours to the amount of a brace of dozens to throw
away you may sleep nine of them here in your little crib and chat the rest.
When your Picture is up and in a good light I shall make a point of
meeting you at the Academy if you will let me know when. If you
should be at the Lecture to-morrow evening I shall see you—and congratulate you heartily—Haslam I know is very Beadle to an amorous
sigh.

" Your sincere friend,
" JOHN KEATS."

Severn was glad that he had worked so hard, and, though
conscious of the fact that he had gained some valuable
artistic knowledge during its composition, yet his ambitious
deed now seemed to him little short of preposterous. Yet
he knew that his hazard was to prove the turning-point in
his Art life, whatever its result.

The early winter-weeks passed without any news, though
Severn attended the students' class at the Academy every
evening; but about the beginning of December a rumour
spread that the Council had decided to award a Gold
Medal, though none had been given for twelve years, notwithstanding the fact that among the competitors had been
several sons of Academicians.

---

o'clock till ten . . . . Severn tells me he has an order for some drawings
for the Emperor of Russia." There is no other record of his serious illness
in the autumn of 1818 than the allusion in a letter of Keats to his
brother George and his sister-in-law, written in mid-October. "Severn
has had a narrow escape of his life from a Typhus fever: he is now
gaining strength."

The name of each competing student was in turn bruited about as that of the favoured individual, and Severn had the doubtful pleasure of hearing his picture alluded to as "the dark horse that might win"—doubtful, because he had always the mortification of hearing the suggestion scouted, and, indeed, of believing that it was a mere play of guess-work and that he had no chance. Still, the praise he obtained from one or two friends gave him encouragement, and though he could not persuade his angry and sorrowing father, or surly Mr. Bond, to go and see the picture where it hung, he had the pleasure of inducing Keats, among others, to inspect it.

In answer to Severn's letter of the 4th December, Keats replied two days later as follows :—

> " *Wentworth Place* [*Hampstead*],
> " Monday Morn.
>
> " My dear Severn,
>
> "I am very sorry that on Tuesday I have an appointment in the City of an undeferrable nature; and Brown * on the same day has some business at Guildhall. I have not been able to figure your manner of executing the Cave of Despair, therefore it will be at any rate a novelty and surprise to me—I trust on the right side. I shall call upon you some morning shortly early enough to catch you before you can get out—when we will proceed to the Academy. I think you must be suited with a good painting light in your bay window. I wish you to return the compliment by going with me to see a Poem I have hung up for the Prize in the Lecture Room of the Surrey Institution. I have many rivals; the most threatening are 'An Ode to Lord Castlereagh,' and a new series of Hymns for the New, New Jerusalem Chapel. You had best put me into your Cave of Despair.
>
> " Ever yours sincerely,
> " John Keats."

Keats was delighted with his friend's picture, though he had himself conceived a very different setting for the episode ; and he even ventured to prophesy that if the work did not gain the medal it would be the most honourable of the failures. Personally, he liked it the best of the several competitive canvases. Though, as he protested, he

---

* Charles Armitage Brown, afterwards (and till his death in 1842) the most intimate friend of Severn as well as of Keats.

was no judge in the technical merits of painting, Keats had so quick a sympathy with, and so sure an insight into Art, that Severn felt greatly encouraged.

The 10th of December was the date when the name of the successful competitor was to be published. Already there had been jealous whisperings to the effect that Joseph Severn, the miniature-painter, was, for all his inexperience, to be the fortunate man; but even when he overheard the rumour he could not realise the chance as anything more than a vague possibility. The ceremony was to be held in the Council Room, which had been specially prepared for the occasion, and all the students were invited. "The solemnity was increased," adds Severn, "by the ceremony taking place in the evening after eight o'clock."

Prizes were to be given to three students, it was announced, and the Gold Medal for painting, so long unawarded, was to be bestowed upon a young candidate whose efforts were all the more praiseworthy in that he was entirely self-taught. After this preliminary announcement there ensued a few moments' strained silence. Then, to the bewilderment of the successful student, and perhaps to the surprise of most present, the President mentioned Joseph Severn as the Gold Medallist.

As soon as the Gold Medal was placed in the successful competitor's hands, and he could get away, Severn made haste to carry home the news. He writes that when he reached home his father had gone to bed in despair at his son's inveterate folly. He ran up to his room, and with a few eager words told his good fortune. His father looked incredulous, and inclined to be angry at what he resented as worse than levity; but "the sight of the large Gold Medal weighing some half a pound instantly enabled him to believe, and see the truth that I could be an artist without 'apprenticeship to the business.'"

Severn was delighted with his success, but, some fifteen years later, in a fragmentary chapter of autobiography, he wrote: "For the first time there seemed a chance for me, but only seemed; for the solid pudding never showed, and all I got was such an amount of ugly envy that I was obliged to forsake the Royal Academy."

So there was nothing for it but miniature-painting once more, and the familiar difficulties and worries. It was at this time that Keats's friendship meant much to him. The two young men saw each other frequently, Keats often journeying to London expressly to see Severn and to go with him to the National Gallery, the Sculpture galleries of the British Museum, and elsewhere. Severn, also, often made his way to Hampstead, generally for an afternoon walk, though occasionally he stayed overnight with a friend who lived in the neighbourhood. On these occasions he met Leigh Hunt, Haydon, Reynolds, Haslam, Charles Brown, and several others, though he seems to have formed intimate friendship with Brown and George Keats only. Haslam, as we have seen, he already knew and greatly liked.

Early in 1819, after he had been " driven away from the Academy," he gave up his lodging in Goswell Street, and went to reside again at his father's house in Hoxton. Thence it was easy for him to reach Hampstead, and, as a matter of fact, he declares that he had almost daily inter-course with Keats. So interested was the latter in every-thing concerning Art that he was always glad to learn anything he could about the technique of painting ; and his friend tells how their frequent communion was really mutual instruction. The poet learned much about certain mysteries of line and colour, and it was through those lessons that he came to see how greatly his much-admired friend Haydon had over-estimated his powers. One great debt, on the other hand, the older owed to the younger. He was almost wholly ignorant of the charm and beauty of the old Greek myths, of ancient classic literature and art; yet from no scholar, in the common sense of the term, could he have learned so much.

Keats, therefore, was to Severn as a young Moses, dis-closing a golden land of promise. The world had a new meaning for him; no doubt he often saw the familiar Hampstead Heath through the same glamour as it was viewed by his friend. He was proud of having taken Keats to see the Elgin marbles and of having pointed out their beauty, but he had not really understood them aright till his novice had enabled him to see with a new and happier vision. It was not till after the poet's death, however, and when Severn was alone in Rome and with the sense that it was to be his home, that he realised how deep was his indebtedness. "Rome," he says, "the *real* Rome would never have become a joy to me—not, at any rate, for a very long time, and even then with difficulty and at best obscurely—had it not been for Keats's talks with me about the Greek spirit,—the Religion of the Beautiful, the Religion of Joy, as he used to call it. All that was finest in sculpture—and, as I came to see directly or indirectly, all that was finest too in painting, in *everything*—was due to that supreme influence. ' I never cease to wonder at all that incarnate Delight,' Keats remarked to me once : nor do I either, now that in inferior measure I too see something of what he saw."

"Keats," he remarked once to a friend, "made me in love with the real living Spirit of the past. He was the first to point out to me how essentially modern that Spirit is : 'It's an immortal youth,' he would say, 'just as there is no *Now* or *Then* for the Holy Ghost.'"

It was a time of earnest effort and keen living for both young men, and Severn was ever wont to recall with lingering memory the days when he and Keats were "in almost daily intercourse."

From the moment of their first meeting, the elder had been deeply impressed by the genius of the younger. Writing of this some five-and-fifty years later he alludes to his newly-won friend's "poetical gifts, his taste in the Arts, his knowledge of history, his most fascinating power of communicating all these. Thus a new world was opened to me, and I was raised from the mechanical drudgery of my Art to the hope of brighter and more elevated courses." "The first example for me of his magic power," he adds, "was the 'Sonnet on First Reading Chapman's *Homer*.'"

"I confess that at the moment he recited it to me I also felt like Cortez when he stared at the Pacific with a wild surmise, for the young poet in me realised the truth and beauty of *his* words. My astonishment was all the greater, as I did not know of any young poet who had called up such spirit of completeness in his first attempt. I knew the first works of Burns and of Byron, and they could not compare with these first attempts of my friend. Even Chatterton seemed to me inferior in the poetical fire which characterised John Keats."

The circle of friends to which he was introduced was one very different from that to which he was accustomed at home. Whenever Keats was away from Hampstead, however, Severn either ceased to care to go thither or fancied that his visits would be unwelcome, for at that time he was keenly alive to his half real, half supersensitively imagined intellectual shortcomings, and apt to apprehend boredom on account of his company when none existed. Occasionally he wrote to George Keats to this effect, but that plain-spoken individual would promptly reply as follows; for example :—

> "*Hampstead,*
> "Tuesday.
>
> "MY DEAR SIR,
>   "Have the goodness never to complain again about being forgotten. How many invitations have you received from me? How many have you answered? To the former question may be answered 'a dozen'; to the latter, 'not one'! Has Sampson done more execution than the Jews ever wished, or Joseph Severn intended? . . . If you are completely disabled I can do no other than pardon you; but, on the contrary, if you have two fingers left on your right hand, throw pardon to curs. You shall be executed, tortured until your hair turn grey, or I'll pray the fates to direct a thunder-bolt through the broken roof of your Philistine temple, making the destruction of your canvas more dreadful than was the actual event. Unless you behave better I'll do such deeds, what they are I know not,— 'I'll shoe a troop of horse with felt,' and ——. John will be in town again soon. When he is, I will let you know and repeat my invitation. He sojourns at present at Bo Peep, near Hastings. Tom's remembrances, and my best wishes.
>
> "Your friend,
> "GEORGE KEATS."

But before the intimacy became "almost daily," Keats and Severn had many occasions for seeing much of each other : even in London. In the early winter of 1817, Keats, to oblige Reynolds, agreed to act as theatrical critic on the staff of a paper called *The Champion*, and as the work was not of an exigent order he had ample time to spend in the company of friends. Late one evening (in January, 1818) "he burst into my lodging, when I was toiling late at my miniature-painting," and with eager elation described a supper-party, of which an hour or two earlier he had been one. When on a former occasion he had met Wordsworth he had been somewhat chilled by the great man's reception of him, and by his sole comment on his Hymn to Pan (from 'Endymion'),—"a pretty piece of Paganism." He was, therefore, as much surprised as delighted when Wordsworth called and invited him to supper. When he reached his host's lodging he found one or two other friends there, and altogether spent a memorable evening. Haydon has left a vivid account of the supper-party at his own house, the "immortal dinner," as he calls it, when the two poets first met: but he seems to have enjoyed it more than the youngest of his guests, who found Wordsworth serenely frigid, and Charles Lamb "on the down-hill side of tipsydom." Haydon, the irrepressible, at least had the faculty of seeing his friends, as well as his own achievements, in an ideal light; and he was generous enough to believe that the almost unknown young poet was one of the most remarkable of his guests. "Wordsworth's fine intonation, as he quoted Milton and Virgil, Keats's eager inspired look, Lamb's quaint sparkle of latent humour, so speeded the stream of conversation," he declares, that he never spent a more delightful time.

Among the transcripts which Severn made of his friend's early poems was one of a newly-written sonnet which Keats read to him one January evening, beginning "O Golden-tongued Romance with serene lute." He had copied it, from a letter to his brothers, then in Devonshire, for John Hamilton Reynolds. Of all his friends, Keats at this time seemed to delight most in the companionship of Reynolds: thereafter, perhaps, of Severn, whom once he assured laughingly that he was "the most astonishingly suggestive innocent" he had ever met. Severn's love of Art, musical taste, and

genuine if haphazard appreciation of the beautiful in literature had no slight influence in the moulding of his friend's
poetic nature : for even in his own sphere of poetry Keats
occasionally learned from his pupil, as when the urgent
suasion of the latter led him to the study of 'Paradise Lost,'
which hitherto he had neglected or glanced at with indifference.   Keats, on the other hand, every time he went with
Severn to the Sculpture Galleries, or to Picture Exhibitions, learned something or gained some suggestive hint.
One day, early in their friendship, for example, the young
artist waxed so enthusiastic about Titian's 'Bacchus' that
a visit was specially made to the National Gallery.   Keats
was deeply impressed, and soon after read to his friend the
now famous description of Bacchus and his crew in 'Endymion.'   He went again and again to see the Elgin marbles,
and would sit for an hour or more at a time beside
them rapt in revery.   On one such occasion Severn came
upon the young poet, with eyes shining so brightly and
face so lit up by some visionary rapture, that he stole
quietly away without intrusion : less considerate than the
foppish acquaintance who, Keats told Severn, joined him one
afternoon in front of the marbles, viewed them condescendingly through an eye-glass, and, having obtruded his company and his vapid remarks for an unwelcome length of
time, ended by saying, "Yes, I believe, Mr. Keats, we
may admire these works safely."

Keats did not long occupy his post of deputy dramatic
critic, and before the first February spring-days had come
was back at his lodgings in Hampstead.   "It was a delight
to me," says Severn, "to stroll over to Well Walk across
the fields from smoky London, to enjoy and profit by the
brightness of his genius—the more so as he received me
invariably with cordiality, and always found a way of apparently making me equal to himself."   Severn frequently
took his miniatures to finish at Hampstead, nominally so as
to get backgrounds for them, but really for the pleasure of
his friend's company.   "They were my excuse," he adds,
"for obtruding my miniature self on his superior society."

In the same set of reminiscences he tells how he first met Wordsworth: and as this was the famous occasion on which the author of 'The Excursion' damped the ardour of his youngest rival by his indifferent praise, the record may be given in the writer's own words:—

"On these occasions Keats introduced me to many of his friends, mostly literary men, with the exception of Haydon, the historical painter, who, at the same time his work interested me, almost frightened me by his excessive vanity and presumption. It was in his house that, in the company of Keats, I first met the famous poet Wordsworth; when, also, were present Leigh Hunt and Reynolds. The burden of conversation was the fashion of a vegetable diet, which was then being pursued by many, led on by the poet Shelley—enthusiasts who had persevered for some time, to the injury of their constitutions and the artistic appearance of their countenances. Leigh Hunt most eloquently discussed the charms and advantages of these vegetable banquets, depicting in glowing words the cauliflowers swimming in melted butter, and the peas and beans never profaned with animal gravy. In the midst of his rhapsody he was interrupted by the venerable Wordsworth, who begged permission to ask a question. 'If,' he said, 'by chance of good luck they ever met with a caterpillar, they thanked their stars for the delicious morsel of animal food.' [Haydon, it appears, was for a time a vegetarian in practice, and almost a fanatic in his advocacy of the good cause.] "This absurdity," Severn resumes, "all came to an end by an ugly discovery. Haydon, whose ruddy face had kept the other enthusiasts from sinking under their scanty diet—for they clung fondly to the hope that they would become like him, although they increased daily in pallor and leanness—this Haydon was discovered one day coming out of a chop-house. He was promptly taxed with treachery, when he honestly confessed that every day after the vegetable repast he ate a good beef-steak. This fact plunged the others in despair, and Leigh Hunt assured me that on vegetable diet his constitution had received a blow from which he had never recovered. With Shelley it was different, for he was by nature formed to regard animal food repulsively. It was on this occasion [Severn proceeds after his 'aside' about vegetarianism] that Keats was requested by Haydon to recite his classical Ode to Pan from his unfinished poem 'Endymion;' which he forthwith gave with natural eloquence and great pathos. When he had finished, we all looked in silence to Wordsworth for praise of the young poet. After a moment's pause, he coolly remarked, 'A very pretty piece of Paganism,' and with this cold water thrown upon us we all broke up."

Following this account are a few passages concerning Haydon, who was at this time occupied with his picture of 'Christ entering Jerusalem.' When finished, the painter invited many distinguished artists to see it, among them the sarcastic Northcote, who remarked: "Mr. Haydon, your ass is the saviour of your picture"—"which severe critique was actually true, for the animal was most wonderfully painted, so wonderfully as to attract the eye at once."

Wordsworth one day complained that he found no advance in the picture since the time he had previously examined it, on an earlier visit to London. "Mr. Haydon," he said, "if you ever adopt a nickname, as the old painters did, it must be *Tenyears* [Teniers]; for you have been ten years about this work."

In the spring of 1819, Severn, encouraged by the success of his 'Cave of Despair,' decided to send his first oil painting, 'Hermia and Helena,' to the Royal Academy. By this time, also, he had become fairly successful, in a moderate way, as a miniature-painter, and could occasionally indulge in the pleasure of painting one or other of his friends "for love." Naturally, he wished to paint Keats, who willingly agreed; and so, during the winter, the painting was duly made and much admired by Keats's brothers and friends.* Partly to please his friend, partly in the hope of drawing attention to the almost unknown young writer, and partly, no doubt, for his own sake, Severn was anxious to send the miniature also to the Royal Academy. He wrote to Keats, and told him of his intention, and in reply received the following letter, addressed to him at new rooms he had recently taken, situated in Frederick Place, in the Goswell Road :—

" Wentworth Place,
"Monday Afternoon.

" My dear Severn,

" Your note gave me some pain, not on my own account, but on yours. Of course I should never suffer any petty vanity of mine to hinder you in any wise; and therefore I should say, 'Put the miniature in the exhibition,' if only myself was to be hurt. But, will it not hurt you? What

---

* It was about this time [end of 1818 or early in 1819] that the silhouette here reproduced was made.

SILHOUETTE PORTRAIT OF KEATS, MADE *circa* JANUARY, 1819.

To face page 34.

good can it do to any future picture? Even a large picture is lost in that
canting place—what a drop of water in the ocean is a miniature! Those
who might chance to see it, for the most part, if they had ever heard of
either of us, and knew what we were and of what years, would laugh at
the puff of the one and the vanity of the other. I am, however, in these
matters a very bad judge, and would advise you to act in a way that
appears to yourself the best for your interest. As your ' Hermia and
Helena ' is finished send that without the prologue of a miniature. I shall
see you soon, if you do not pay me a visit sooner. There's a Bull
for you.

" Yours, ever sincerely,
"JOHN KEATS."

However, Keats was easily won to consent to his friend's
wish; indeed, by this time, he had, as Severn records,
begun to show a more and more frequent and more prolonged apathy. His immense vitality had enabled him
to withstand, with little apparent discomfiture, the insi-
dious approach of the deadly complaint which, no doubt,
had been induced, or at least hastened, by his undue
exposure to damp and fatigue while tramping through the
West Highlands with his friend Brown. Though a journey
much enjoyed by Keats, and one ever memorable to lovers
of poetry, it was otherwise unfortunate.* Severn was asked

* There may be given here a variant of Keats's poem, ' On Fingal's
Cave.' This poem was written in Oban in July, 1818, when the author
and Charles Brown were on their pedestrian trip in Scotland. The
revised version was interpolated by Keats in his letter to his brother Tom
of 23rd and 26th July; that is, in the latter portion. A copy of the first
draft was made by Brown, and by him sent to Severn.

ON FINGAL'S CAVE.

A Fragment.

Not Aladdin magian
Ever such a work began,
Not the wizard of the Dee
Ever such a dream could see;
Not Saint John in Patmos Isle,
In the passion of his toil,
When he saw the churches seven,
Golden-aisl'd, built up in heav'n,
Gaz'd on such a rugged wonder!
As I stood its roofing under,
Lo! I saw one sleeping there
On the marble cold and bare,

D 2

to join the party, and Haslam also; but neither was able
to .go, the former mainly from lack of funds to assist him

While the surges wash'd his feet,
And his garments white did beat,
Drench'd about the sombre rocks;
On his neck his well-grown locks,
Lifted dry above the main,
Were upon the curl again.'
" What is this? and what art thou? "
Whisper'd I, and touch'd his brow.
" What art thou? and what is this? "
Whisper'd I, and strove to kiss
The spirit's hand, to wake his eyes,—
Up he started in a trice.
" I am Lycidas," said he,
" Fam'd in funeral minstrelsy!
This was architectur'd thus
By the great Oceanus!
Here his mighty waters play
Hollow organs all the day;
Here his d lphins, one and all,
Finny palmers, great and small,
Come to pay devotion due,—
Each a mouth of pearls must strew.
Many a mortal of these days
Dares to pass our sacred ways,
Dares to touch audaciously
This cathedral of the sea.
Here a fledgy sea-bird quire
Soars for ever; holy fire
I have hid from mortal man,
Proteus is my Sacristan!
But the dull'd eye of mortal
Has dar'd to pass the rocky portal,
So for ever will I leave
Such a taint, and soon unweave
All the magic of the place."

*   *   *   *   *

The most notable variation is the absence in this earlier version of the
two lines coming in as thirty-ninth and fortieth in the later :—

I have been the Pontiff priest,
Where the waters never rest.

In the later too, the forty-first line is adapted to the above interpolation
by the substitution of *Where* for *Here.*   The addition of

So saying, with a spirit's glance
He dived ——-

seems to have been an afterthought with Keats. The verse does not
occur in this copy: though it is faintly pencilled below, in another's
writing, which seems to me that of Keats. The other variations, *i.e.*

over even a very short journey, and also from his unwilling-
ness to cut himself adrift from what seemed his only safe
course if ever he were to do anything in Art.

One thing after another, says Severn, wrought at this
time to the undoing of his friend. A fever of the mind,
independent of the slow consuming evil fretting at the
edges of vitality, waxed and waned, exciting soul and body
to fierce activities and leaving them again to prostrating
apathies, "to an apathy that was oftener akin to despair
than to mere dejection."

During the autumn of 1818 Severn saw little of Keats.
When they did meet, he noticed that his friend was distraught and without that look of falcon-like alertness which
was so characteristic of him; and, later, that his face was
often haggard and his eyes strained, as though after prolonged and harassing vigils. Once Keats told his always
sympathetic comrade that not only was his brother dying,
but that with the ebbing tide of life was going more and
more of his own vitality. It certainly seemed as though
the poet were losing strength and energy, for he ceased
to take much interest in intellectual matters, and declared
himself unable to take long walks or even indulge in any
unnecessary exercise. Alarmed by something that Haslam
had told him, as to the frequency of a watcher by the bedside of a dying consumptive patient succumbing sooner
or later to the same malady, Severn did his utmost to
persuade Keats to take rooms near his brother, rather
than actually live with him, or at least to obtain the
assistance of a nurse; and he even volunteered to release
his friend of his night-duties occasionally, but without
avail. Ere long the end came, though not until Keats

---

from the copy printed in Mr. Buxton Forman's edition of "Keats," are—
(line 5) " not *Saint* John in Patmos isle " (and without any comma a'ter
John); (line 7) *heav'n*; (line 8) " Gazed *on*," and with an interjection
after *wonder* !; (line 9) comma after *under*,; (line 10), no comma after *there*;
(line 20) full stop at *brow*.; (line 25) comma and dash after *eyes*,—;
(line 24) full stop at *trice*.; (line 31) " Here *his* dolphins, *one and* all,";
(line 39 MS.) *Here*; (line 40) semicolon only after *ever*; and *Holy*;
(line 44) "*Has dar'd to pass the rocky portal*."

had brought himself to the verge of illness. It was
Severn's intention to persuade his friend to accompany him
on a trip to Cornwall for a few weeks, to distract him after
Tom's death; but that event occurred early in December,
and during a season of inclement weather, and so the
half-formed plan fell through. Nevertheless Keats was
persuaded by Charles Brown to leave the rooms where he
had suffered so much, and where he had seen his dearly
loved brother slowly die, and to reside at his friend's house.*

Early in the spring of 1819, probably about the end of
February or in March, Keats, to all appearances in fair
health again, took Severn to call upon some "valued
friends and neighbours"—a Mrs. and Miss Brawne, who
resided in the other portion of Wentworth Place, and
so were next door to Brown and his fellow-lodger. But
neither then nor till the poet's last days in Rome did
Severn realise the depth and passion of Keats's love for
Fanny Brawne; he was not even aware of any definite
engagement, though of course he knew that the poet was
in love. Keats was very reticent, even with his most intimate friends, and as he could be fiercely jealous, Severn,
as well as the others, thought it wiser to invite no con-
fidences.† Severn, indeed, despite certain contradictory
statements of his own in later life, knew that there was love
on one side at any rate—Brown's letters to him, both before
and during the sad early days in Rome, alone affording
sufficient proof of this—but in any case he was a prejudiced
witness, for to him Fanny Brawne always seemed a cold and
conventional mistress. Reminiscently, he alluded to her
as like the draped figure in Titian's picture of 'Sacred and
Profane Love;' but on the first occasion of meeting her he
does not seem to have been at all deeply, or even favourably,

* Wentworth Place, in John Street, Hampstead. Now known as Lawn
Bank.

† That there was some feeling of this kind on the part of Keats seems
to be borne out by a remark in a letter to him from Miss Brawne, and by
his reply: "I mention a part of your letter which hurt me; you say,
speaking of Mr. Severn, 'but you must be satisfied in knowing that I
admired you much more than your friend.'"

impressed. No doubt Keats noticed that his friend was not enthusiastic about Miss Brawne; possibly, indeed, Severn, with his usual frankness, may have been too outspoken in his strictures upon a style of beauty which had no fascination for him. On the other hand, he conceived a liking for Mrs. Brawne, who was interested in the young artist, and pleased with his gentle and conciliatory grace of manner.

Yet it was at this time, as has been already stated, that Keats and Severn deepened their friendship by frequent long walks into the country; and that the painter found the poet so inspiring and even so joyous a companion. For, notwithstanding the death of his youngest brother, the strain of his secret gnawing passion, his untoward private circumstances, and other causes of disquiet, Keats could in company be as light-hearted as in his pugnacious schoolboy days, and prove himself the most winsome of comrades.

This spring of 1819, which saw the real opening of Severn's art-life, was, moreover, it must be remembered, that wherein Keats's poetic powers reached their splendid maturity. Before the weald of Hampstead had ceased to ring with the cries of the cuckoos—then, as now, more numerous there than anywhere else in the immediate neighbourhood of London—the young poet had written, besides some of his loveliest short poems, five at least of those imperishable odes which to this day remain not only unsurpassed but unequalled. Charles Brown has put on record one charming reminiscence of the poet at this time: of a nightingale having built her nest in a tree in the garden behind Wentworth Place, and of Keats's delight in her mate's song, a delight which found perfect and immortal expression in the Ode with which we are all now so familiar. Severn gives much the same story, but not so well, and more vaguely as to details, so I need not add here his superfluous narrative. On the other hand, Mr. Charles Severn tells me that one night, when Keats was spending the evening with friends at the large house then (as well as the familiar group of pine-trees) known as

'The Spaniards,' he was missed. Joseph Severn, one of
the company, went to look for him, and discovered him
lying on the ground under the pines, and listening entranced to the song of a nightingale overhead; and either
that night or the following morning he wrote his famous
Ode. Severn afterwards painted a picture in exact illustration of this episode.

During the summer and early autumn of 1819 Severn
saw nothing of Keats, who was in the Isle of Wight and
afterwards in Winchester; and as he heard nothing but
good news both from the invalid and his friends, he concluded that there was no need of anxiety about Keats's well-
being. He himself was greatly occupied with his miniature-
painting, and though he was once sorely tempted to accept
Keats's invitation to join him for a few days in Winchester,
he found that he could afford neither the money nor the
time. While he was still deliberating upon a change, he
received a letter from Keats, with " College Street, Westminster," as a heading, and on going thither was delighted
to learn that his friend had definitely returned to London,
and was about to pursue a literary career. At the same
time he could not help seeing that the southern change had
not wrought so much good as he had anticipated. The poet
was in high spirits, and charmed his companion beyond
expression by the odes and other short poems which he
had recently written, and also by ' Hyperion,' against the
discarding of which Severn protested vehemently, though, he
complained, the author " seemed much more taken up with
a rhymed story about a serpent-girl " [' Lamia ']. Severn,
with his love of Milton, and perhaps with a natural pride
in having been instrumental in turning Keats's attention to
the noble beauty of ' Paradise Lost,' delighted immeasurably
in ' Hyperion,' lines of which haunted him ever afterwards.
But by this time the poet had decided to go no further
with his magnificent effort, not because he was dissatisfied
with it itself, but because he thought it too Miltonic in
structure, too artificial to suit his genius for a prolonged
strain, or even to please the highest taste. The very terms

in which Severn expressed his admiration of 'Hyperion' confirmed him in his resolution, for he did not, as he said, want to write a poem "that might have been written by John Milton, but one that was unmistakably written by no other than John Keats."

Severn did not care, at first at any rate, for 'Lamia,' but he promised to return one night ere long and hear it and the rest of 'Hyperion.' In accordance with his promise, though a week or more passed ere he could allow himself a few hours of happy leisure, he called at the house in College Street, but only to find that the late inmate had fled to Hampstead, and for good. When, the following Sunday, he saw Keats there, at his old residence in Wentworth Place, he was perturbed by the change in him. His friend seemed well neither in mind nor in body, with little of the happy confidence and resolute bearing of a week earlier; while alternating moods of apathetic dejection and spasmodic gaiety rendered him a companion somewhat difficult to humour. Yet not even then, in circumstances far more harassing than Severn had any idea of, was Keats otherwise than kindly and generous. "He never spoke of any one but by saying something in their favour, and this always so agreeably and cleverly, imitating the manner to increase your favourable impression of the person he was speaking of."

Except Brown, Severn, and occasionally some other faithful friend (besides George Keats, then in London on business), Keats saw very few visitors in the winter of 1820. Once or twice he was well enough to take a short walk with Severn in the Highgate direction. Now and again he "went into society," but with ever less relish, and at last with so complete a distaste that he vowed to seek entertainment there no more. It was about this time that, with characteristic loyalty, he first expostulated with and then indignantly left a company of acquaintances because Severn was referred to slightingly and unjustly. Long afterwards the artist often recalled the circumstance with pride, and also, it may be added, with a happy gratitude that made his telling of the episode memorably winsome.

But soon after George Keats's departure for America to rejoin his family, his brother endured his first absolute collapse. As Severn gives substantially the same account as the well-known narrative by Brown—from whom, indeed, he learned the details—it is unnecessary to reproduce his record of that first ominous symptom of fatal disease.

During the early spring weeks, when Keats was so much an invalid that he was seldom even out of his room, Severn occasionally went to Wentworth Place to have a chat with his friend, though as he could not see him at night his opportunities were naturally very limited. In May, however, the poet was apparently so much better (though he well knew himself how enfeebled he had become), that he was able to sail as far as Gravesend with Brown, who was bound for another tour in Scotland. So deceptive, indeed, was his appearance that not only were his friends misled, but even the physician suggested the advisability of his again accompanying Brown. The latter, one of the most genial and loyal of friends, started blithely on his trip, not without some lingering hope that he might be joined by Keats later on, certainly without the dimmest prevision that he would never see his loved friend again.

Through May and June, however, Severn saw much of Keats. Their intimacy was furthered by proximity, for after Brown's departure Keats had gone to reside in Kentish Town, so as to be near Leigh Hunt, who was then living in Mortimer Street. But in June, at any rate, the interviews grew shorter and shorter, and there were no more drives or walks. About the 25th Severn received a brief note from Leigh Hunt telling him that Keats had had one or two severe attacks of hæmorrhage, and had been removed to his house in Mortimer Street, so as to be under the immediate care of himself and his wife. Thenceforth, till the elder received through Haslam the sudden and startling news of the younger's complete collapse, the two friends saw very little of each other. Severn, indeed, seems to have been

under the impression that Keats was not more than a
month with the Hunts, and that he had then, feeling
comparatively restored, returned to Hampstead, or gone on
a visit to the Brawnes, whereas the invalid was close on
seven weeks in Mortimer Street, and would have been
longer but for an annoying piece of negligence on the part
of a servant,* which so wrought upon him (particularly as
the Hunts would not look on the matter seriously), that in
a fit of indignant anger he left his hosts, with the intention
of going to his old rooms in Well Walk. Invalid as he
was, however, Mrs. Brawne would not hear of his being left
to his own resources; and, though she was not overpleased
at the engagement which she knew existed, she insisted
upon her and her daughter's rights, in the circumstances,
to have him under their charge.

Although Keats had been told by his doctor, while he
was an invalid under the care of the Hunts, that his sole
chance lay in absence from England during the damp winter
months, he avoided, seemingly, mention of this matter to
his friends. Always scrupulously disinclined to trouble
others with his private affairs, the desperate state of his
health and almost equally bankrupt condition of his finances
no doubt made him still more reticent than his wont. He
hoped against hope, and even when it seemed folly to
refuse further to face the inevitable, he could not bring
himself to severance from her he loved so passionately, and
whose tendance during these summer weeks was to him so
poignantly sweet. Of course, some friends did hear of the
severity of the crisis in his fortunes; and the Leigh Hunts
in particular were kindly and well intentioned in all ways.
As is well known, he received at this time a generous
and most delicately-worded letter from Shelley, who had
heard of his evil straits, urging him to come to Pisa and be
taken care of as an honoured and welcome guest—an offer
which touched him deeply, but which he could not see his
way to accept.

At last the time came when a definite decision as to

* A note from Miss Brawne, delivered open, and two days late.

wintering abroad became imperative. Keats naturally thought of Brown as the one possible companion for him, if he ventured to Italy, as means and occupations stood in the way of any other of his friends whom he could ask or would care to have with him. Least of all did he think of Severn, whose hard struggles he sympathised with, and whose poverty was so pressing.

Early in the autumn he summoned up courage to endure separation from Miss Brawne. He wrote to Brown, unfolding his plans, and urging him, if possible, to be his comrade. But Brown was in the Highlands, and the letters miscarried or followed tardily, and no tidings came from him. Early in September cold and foggy weather set in, and Keats became daily worse. It seemed, if it were to be done at all, as if he would have to make his last venture alone.

CHAPTER III.

So ill had fortune gone with Severn since his signal success in winning the Royal Academy gold medal, that he at last came to wish he had failed. Resentment among his fellow-students, disparaging remarks in art circles, and ill-content at home, made his life at times almost unendurable. If, he wrote a few years later, he had enjoyed better health, and had even had the most moderate resources to fall back upon, he would have had absolutely no fear of winning his way in London; as it was, he was thankful that miniature-painting promised to ensure him at least a living. But even by the summer of 1819, when, following his success of the previous December, he exhibited at the Academy his 'Hermia and Helena,' and his miniature of Keats, his general prospects seemed no whit bettered. From the acceptance and the exhibition of his picture and his miniature he had hoped much. The former was exhibited as No. 267, with the following quotation from 'A Midsummer Night's Dream':*—

> " We, Hermia, like two artificial gods,
> Have with our needles created both one flower,
> Both on one sampler, sitting on one cushion,
> Both warbling of one song, both in one key,
> As if our hands, our sides, voices and minds,

---

* Act III. Sc. ii.

> Had been incorporate.   So we grew together,
> Like to a double cherry, seeming parted,
> But yet an union in partition;
> Two lovely berries moulded on one stem; . . ."

The subject was not in itself one calculated to attract general attention, and in technique the picture was, at most, a promising performance; the young painter, indeed, had worked at it rather as a venture likely to gain the approval of the public and of the convention-loving Academicians, than with free will and enjoyment. On the other hand, the miniature of Keats is an admirable bit of portrait-painting.

But, of course, a miniature is apt to be overlooked by nine-tenths of the visitors to an Academy Exhibition, and if Severn had depended upon the effect the small portrait of Keats would have upon his fortunes, he would have been doomed to speedy and unmistakable disappointment. The miniature was passed over without critical comment, but 'Hermia and Helena' was ill-hung, and unfavourably noticed, and so, if it had any effect at all, brought the young painter no good.

"Not a commission, not a penny came to me in consequence," he writes; "and had it not been that I had some favourably-priced miniatures to do on the occasion, I verily believe this 'great honour' would have killed me, for I should have been stunned by it, and certainly I lost through it most of my student-friends."

Severn, writing long afterwards, somewhat confused his sentiments in the summer of 1820 with those of the preceding year. Having alluded to the loss even of some of his student-friends, he adds: "Indeed, I was reduced to downright despair, and without the courage to go on with another painting [of 'Titania Sleeping'] I had commenced, when an incident turned up which put an end to all this spiteful twaddle and ill-will by snatching me away from the scene—at the same time opening to me a new and glorious world of Art. Fortunately I had the courage to make sure of it at the instant, and so gave a shape and seeming to my new life which otherwise it never could have had." This, however, written retrospectively, applies rather to Severn's state in the summer of 1819. Then he was troubled by many things, distraught by unsatisfactory prospects, and at times almost hopeless. He believed there was no chance for him as a painter of pictures, and that if he could not make sufficient name as a miniature-painter to ensure himself a livelihood, he would have to yield to his father's wish and definitely adopt the craft of the engraver. But by midsummer of the year following that of his first appearance as an exhibitor at the Royal Academy, his prospects had materially improved. He gained greatly, in his miniature-painting, in accuracy of drawing and delicacy of tone, and so much admired were his small portraits that there was every promise of his success in this *genre*. He had, moreover, regained courage, and was looking forward to winning his way even as a painter of historical and poetic subjects. For the first time in his life he had some funds in reserve, and was able to indulge moderately his love of music, the theatre, and books. At last, too, his father had come round to the belief that Joseph had been right in his aspirations, and, with characteristic inconsequence, began to prophesy for him a career of most satisfactory and even brilliant success.

It was at this time, the early autumn of 1820, that " the incident turned up " which " gave a shape and seeming to his life which otherwise it never could have had."

One September evening William Haslam called on him, and announced that the Italy idea for Keats was no longer a vague suggestion, but was about to be carried into effect. Severn was astonished, but was still more taken aback when his visitor, after lamenting the absence in Scotland of Charles Brown, and that individual's unfortunate though understandable delay in replying to Keats's eager letters, remarked that the poet, invalid though he was, would have to go to Italy alone, and in a small vessel, unless he— Severn—would make the venture for friendship's sake.

Writing long afterwards about this important crisis in

his life. Severn is betrayed into one or two minor incon-
sistencies. Thus, in one set of 'Reminiscences,' he relates
the matter thus :—

"* * * Poor Keats was ordered to Italy to save his life, threatened by
misfortune and consumption. He was going alone, in a merchant-ship, to
Naples, and the voyage was all arranged, and he was to sail next day.
Haslam said to me, 'Severn, why s ould you not go?' I answered,
'Why should I not?' He then said, 'How long would it take you to get
ready?' 'If I can have six hours,' I said, 'in that time I'll be ready.'
Straight I went to Sir Thomas Lawrence, who gave me a letter to Canova,
and another to a German artist. On my way I went to my dear angel-
mother, who was not taken by surprise, but approved, and undertook to
get my trunk ready so that I might depart at daylight. During the evening and night I managed to settle all my affairs, and with a solitary £25,
fortunately paid me for a miniature of a lady in a white satin bonnet and
feathers, I returned to my father's house just after midnight, to take farewell of my dear family, from whom I had never till then been (definitely)
separated."

This is a most circumstantial account, and has the ring
of actuality. But when we remember what travelling
arrangements were in those days, how difficult it would
be for even a young man like Severn to disarray his
rooms and put his affairs in order, make calls (particularly
to take 'on the way' a house in distant Hoxton while going
to visit Sir Thomas Lawrence in central London), all in a
few hours, one might be excused for some incredulity.
Still, there would be no just cause for taking the account
"with a difference," especially as an almost childlike
candour characterised the writer, if it were not for the
latter's own conflicting statements recorded at an earlier
date. Here is the other version :—

"Haslam said to me, 'As nothing can save Keats but going to Italy,
why should *you* not try to go with him, for otherwise he must go alone,
and we shall never hear anything of him if he dies. Will you go?' I
answered, 'I'll go.' 'But you'll be long getting ready,' he added ; 'Keats
is actually now preparing. When would you be ready?' 'In three or
four days,' I replied, 'and I will set about it this very moment.'"

The two accounts tally after this, except as to the hurried
calls and sudden departure, and taking Mrs. Severn's house
in Hoxton on the way to see Sir Thomas Lawrence. There

is no evidence to prove which is the true account. However, the matter is unimportant; what is significant is Severn's generous readiness to accompany his invalid friend at whatever cost to himself, and to lose no time in putting his decision into effect. With his sanguine temperament, it is quite likely, as he says, that, as soon as the suggestion was made to him and he realised its significance, he foresaw the possibility of his gaining at Rome the Royal Academy's travelling studentship, as a sequence to the bestowal of the gold medal; but whatever purely personal motive may have affected his decision, he must have all the credit due to him for his generous loyalty. No one who knew Joseph Severn could doubt that he would have gone to Italy with Keats even if there had been no Royal Academy students'-pension in prospect, and if he had had no capital beyond his twenty-five pounds, his industry, his genial temper, good spirits, and winsome manners.

It is certainly not enough simply to say of his action, with Mr. Sidney Colvin, that "a companion offered himself in the person of Severn, who, having won, as we have seen, the gold medal of the Royal Academy the year before, determined now to go and work at Rome with a view to competing for the travelling studentship." This determination was, at most, an afterthought, and, as Severn says, realisation of the hope was just barely possible.

Although Mrs. Severn sympathised with her son's plan, partly because she admired his motive, and partly because she understood plainly that the scheme was a turn in his dubious fortunes which might well be for the better (for she seems all along to have more clearly understood Joseph's chances and prospects in London than even Mr. Severn did, in his range from the most sombre outlook to the most sanguine expectations), the decision was received by Severn's father with the utmost consternation.

"This determination of mine," he writes, "was almost a death-blow to my poor dear father, who reasoned with me in every way as to the rashness of the step, and pointed out that by thus taking matters into my own hands I might

E

even forfeit my chance of gaining the Academy pension. But I had no ear to his arguments, and as I had certainly the virtue of the donkey—obstinacy—in the highest degree, so my plan went on preparing."

It has already been stated that Severn called upon Sir Thomas Lawrence to tell him of his decision to go to Rome, as, presumably, he believed to be the right thing to do. The great man received him kindly, and not only wrote for him a letter of introduction to Canova, "and to an old German artist resident in Rome, who had done a large copy and an engraving from Michael Angelo's 'Last Judgment,'" but invited him to make any remarks he felt inclined to express upon the works in the studio wherein he then stood. Vanity, it is to be feared, must have prompted this complaisance on the part of Sir Thomas, and it is amusing to find that the young and almost self-taught artist calmly criticised a large portrait of George IV. as "unnatural."

Severn does not seem to have seen Keats since his decision to accompany the latter, but to have arranged with Haslam that both should meet on board the vessel, which was a schooner named the *Maria Crowther*, destined to sail from Gravesend on the 18th. The young artist's departure from his home was marred by an untoward event, which seems to have made a strong and painful impression upon him, for twice in late life he gave a detailed written account of the incident, and refers to it in his letters, as he often did to friends in conversation about his early experiences. His father, as there was occasion to mention earlier in this memoir, was subject to violent alternations of temper, and, when crossed, would sometimes remain long in a state of sullen anger or else expend his wrath in spasmodic fits of fury. He was greatly perturbed by Joseph's decision to throw up his chances in London and venture to Rome, and his mingled sorrow and anger had grown to resentment by the time his son was ready to depart.

"It was after midnight [*i.e.* on the 17th] when I reached home, and I found my father sunk down with extreme grief in his armchair. At last, when my mother and sisters had finished packing my trunk, and the time had come for me to leave, my brother Tom and I tried to lift up the trunk, but it was beyond us, and so I asked my father for his help. He rose up in an apparent passion of madness, and swore that if without his touching it the trunk was never to be lifted at all, it should not be touched by him. This was a terrible change in his demeanour, for which I was quite unprepared. No time was to be lost, and so I proceeded to go upstairs to (take farewell of) my younger brother. My poor father, in his abstraction,* stood in the doorway, and when I attempted to pass him he struck me down to the ground. This made a tragic scene of it, for his love for me was unbounded; indeed, his often-avowed delight in my company, and my being his eldest son, conspired to make this blow like the act of madness. My dear mother interposed, as also my sister and friends, to protect me. Tom, then nineteen years old and strong, held my father against the door, but required assistance to do it effectually. With my dear home in this most melancholy plight I had to leave, and did leave with such agitation and trembling nerves that I was obliged to be supported for a few minutes. All this was long before daylight, and the gloom seemed to increase the horror attendant on my departure."

It was certainly a painful and distressing leave-taking, and a dispiriting beginning of a new period in life. It says well for Severn that he bore not the slightest resentment to his father, and that, soon after he had fairly settled in Rome, he wrote a pleasant and affectionate letter, in which no allusion was made to the unfortunate ebullition of temper which had made departure seem tragically sad, and had, indeed, so wrought upon the chief sufferer that, were it not for the deep disappointment and possible peril to Keats, he would even then have renounced the venture. Severn was equally generous in advanced life, when the infelicities of the past are often apt to reappear through an atmosphere more sombre than they ever knew.

Even after leaving the painful scene described above, he says, his mind was filled with thoughts of his "poor dear father,"

"whom I knew to be so devoted to me, and who had lost his senses in our parting. He was always a man of most ardent temperament, and

---

* Severn's use of this word "abstraction" here is interesting, for he does not indicate "absence of mind" as the word now commonly does, but aberration or some equivalent word.

sudden and violent in his anger when it was roused : but, withal, so good a man, so honest and sincere, so benevolent, so generous to all about him, that the good qualities far outbalanced the bad."

Naturally enough the journey to the docks, in the gloom that slowly became the chill morning twilight, was one of the most unhappy episodes in Severn's life. He was haunted, moreover, by a fear that his action had unsettled his father's mind, and that his dearly-loved mother and her children would have to endure sorrow and privation in consequence. But as the Thames was approached, his wonted buoyant spirits rose once more, and by the time his brother Tom had said good-bye he was less despairful and unhappy, though, to add to his discomfort of mind and body, he was suffering at the time from liver complaint. Yet, withal, there was the natural exhilaration of youth in the front of a new if dubious venture.

When he arrived at the wharf on the south side of the river, he found "dear Keats, John Taylor the publisher" (through whose liberality in advancing the poet £100 for the copyright of 'Endymion' the preliminaries of the journey had been expedited and rendered easier in other ways), and William Haslam."* There were other friends besides these, but Severn does not specify them. The *Maria Crowther* was not a very inviting vessel in which to make a lengthy voyage. She was a schooner-merchantman, and but ill-adapted (and, as it proved, ill-provisioned) for the conveyance of passengers. In one account Severn says that he and Keats embarked at Gravesend, but elsewhere (and this seems the fact) they got aboard before the vessel sheered off from the wharf, and slowly swung down upon the tide to Gravesend, where the schooner lay-to till well on in the morning, and where a lady passenger joined the small company. Here Severn, at Keats's special request, went ashore and bought several medicines, some of them prepared according to the direction of the latter, and among them a

---

* By a slip of the pen, Severn mentions Charles Brown as one of those who were present. See below, for the almost tragical by-play of circumstance whereby the two friends missed each other at the last moment, though within hail of each other.

bottle of laudanum. Soon the last good-byes were said, and all Keats's friends were agreeably surprised by his animation and apparently more robust health : though, as a matter of fact, the recovery was but a matter of the moment, and a week or two later he was in a more hopeless state than before.

There is an almost tragic touch of that maladroitness of circumstance which so often wrought cruelly for Keats, in the fact that, all unknown to each other, he and Charles Brown were within hail during the dark hours of that morning. Brown, grievously alarmed by the receipt of one of the urgent letters which had at last reached him in the Highlands, had hurried back with all practicable speed. The nearest port for him to catch a London-bound vessel was Dundee, but on arrival there he found that there was no boat southward-bound save a small coaster, little larger than a fishing-smack. In this he embarked, and on the night of the 17th of September the small vessel came up the estuary, and after midnight brought-to off Gravesend. Severn relates that the two vessels lay within a stone's-throw of each other, and that if Brown had been on the deck of the sloop he might have heard the voices of those on the *Maria Crowther*, and thus been saved the keen regret which he experienced ever after. Almost everything told against Keats from the outset. The start in the chill morning-gloom—and, earlier, from Mr. Taylor's house—wrought him no good, for though he was alert and seeming fairly well during the first days of the voyage, his excitement was really in great part due to a feverish chill, which made him abnormally restless. The food on board was indifferent, and the accommodation bad ; and for the greater part of the voyage the weather was unfavourable. What was perhaps as unfortunate as anything else was the fact that a lady passenger who had joined at Gravesend, a Miss Cotterell, was a consumptive invalid, and in that morbid stage when specification of one's symptoms and ailments becomes, apparently, a burning necessity. While still in the Channel Keats had, indeed, some days of seeming good health, but long before reaching Naples he was much the worse instead of the better for his voyage.

There was only one other passenger besides Keats, Severn, and Miss Cotterell—a Mrs. Pidgeon.

"I could not have made much of a figure," writes Severn, "for before we left Gravesend a lady-friend of one of those on board looked hesitatingly at Keats and myself and inquired which was the dying man. I was suffering at the time from liver complaint, and was very pale and wan. The sea and I have always been enemies, and as this voyage to Naples was long before steam-vessels were in use, I was destined to pass some weeks in sad penance. My dinner was a matter that always came to light: but, as for Keats, he bore the sea manfully. I was continually sea-sick during the fortnight in which we were beating about the Channel—a tedious and disagreeable time with adverse and trying winds. Miss Cotterell was a mere shadow, and although very agreeable and ladylike, it was unfortunate for Keats to have a *vis-à-vis* in such a state, for they were constant companions and always comparing notes. The schooner was often close into the coast, and the captain gave leave to his passengers to go ashore at one or two places"—Dungeness, Studland Bay, Dorchester, and Portsmouth, are specified by Severn. "At Dungeness we scrambled over the gravel; and on the opposite side I was astonished and delighted with the enormous waves, at least ten feet high, rushing in upon the shore. The sight fixed me in wonder and abstraction, until a miserable exciseman appeared and demanded what I was doing. My bewildered explanation only confirmed his suspicion that I was looking out for contraband—which let down all the high romance which the waves had inspired." Off the Dorset coast the schooner one day lay becalmed, and Keats ventured ashore with his friend. "For a moment," says the latter, "he became like his former self. He was in a part that he already knew, and showed me the splendid caverns and grottos with a poet's pride, as though they had been his by birthright. When we returned to the ship he wrote for me on a blank leaf in a folio volume of Shakespeare's 'Poems,' which had been given him by a friend, and which he gave to me in memory of our voyage, the following magnificent sonnet :—

> "Bright star, would I were steadfast as thou art,
>   Not in lone splendour hung aloft the night
> And watching, with eternal lids apart,
>   Like nature's patient, sleepless Eremite,
> The moving waters at their priestlike task
>   Of pure ablution round earth's human shores,
> Or gazing on the new soft-fallen mask
>   Of snow upon the mountains and the moors—
> No—yet still steadfast, still unchangeable,
>   Pillow'd upon my fair love's ripening breast,

Sept 22nd
Friday —

A Flat Day — waiting for a wind in
the Dundee Ness Roads — went on shore
with the Captain — and found it a wide
expanse of Gravel — 2 houses in about
6 miles — and a solitary yard of furze
— Keats appetite increasing —

Sept 23
Saturday

Still waiting for a wind — flat, very
flat — Keats beat me hollow at the
Trencher

1. Sept 22.nd
Friday—

A flat Day — waiting for a wind in
the Dundee Ness Roads — went on shore
with the Captain — and found it a wide

> To feel for ever its soft fall and swell,
>   Awake for ever in a sweet unrest,
> Still, still to hear her tender-taken breath,
> And so live ever—or else swoon to death."

This always remained Severn's favourite among Keats's poems, partly from association, and partly from the solemn calm and beauty of it. It was hurriedly pencilled down by Keats, and shortly afterward read by him to his companion, who eagerly begged the poet to give him a copy—with the result that he obtained both the first transcript of the sonnet and the author's treasured copy of Shakespeare's Poems.

"This," says Severn, "was the very last poetical effort the poor fellow ever made. Thenceforward nothing but letters with pathetic anticipation of approaching fate. But this sublime sonnet inspired me with the hope that he might recover. Indeed this hope was never absent from my mind, and I never once realised the likelihood of our speedy separation by death. At times in his suffering he still retained that elasticity of mind and spirit which was the characteristic of both the man and the poet. Perhaps at times he made a greater effort on my account, as he was painfully sensible of what he called the great sacrifice I was making on his account, and that it might turn out disastrous to me as a young artist. He seemed to feel more for me than for himself, for he had already given himself up for lost. The mysterious power of his genius held him up when he was actually sinking, and held me up in the strained hopes thus inspired."

When the vessel was detained by a strong adverse wind in the Solent, the two again went on shore, and as they were assured that there was no chance of getting forward that day, Keats took the opportunity of visiting some friends at Bedhampton. On his return to the schooner he spent the evening writing a long and most pathetic letter to Brown : and here, again, by a strange perversity of fate, the two friends were near each other without being aware of the fact. Keats thought Brown still in Scotland, and Brown naturally believed that the *Maria Crowther* was by that time, ten days after departure, in or near the Bay of Biscay. When he had discovered how closely he had missed Keats at Gravesend he was deeply chagrined. He did not care to go home just then, and went on a visit to Mr. Dilke at Chichester, where he was on the day when

Keats, having nothing better to do, went to Bedhampton—
when he might more easily have gone to the Dilkes' home—
and where he spent the evening perhaps thinking of his
friend upon the high seas, while that friend was in a ship
riding at anchor in the Solent, and engaged in a long letter
to no other than himself. It is, in truth, an intensely
pathetic letter, and nowhere more so than where the dying
young poet exclaims that he wishes for death every day
and night to deliver him from the pains of his fruitless
and consuming passion. "Land and sea, weakness and
decline, are great separators, but Death is the great
divorcer for ever," he writes, in despairful resignation.

That brief time among the Lulworth sea-caves and fantastic rocks was among the last few relatively happy hours
which Keats knew, for even in his partial rally in Rome
he was always as one moving about under a sentence of
imminent death. He was in his element then, a child of
Nature. His mind, as his friend says of him, " lived on
such things, and whatever may have been his other resources,
certainly the great incentive of his immortal poetry was
his actual converse with Nature, and on this occasion I
could well see how Nature and he understood each other."
But at last, " after about a fortnight's misery," a favourable
wind enabled them to leave Land's End out of sight astern,
and Keats, who, on the whole, had almost enjoyed and had
seemed to benefit by the voyage hitherto, eagerly hoped
for fair and milder weather.

"But in the Bay of Biscay we encountered a three days'
storm. The sea swept over the ship all day and night, and
the rushing up and down of the water in the cabin was a
frightful sound in the darkness. I was afraid that Keats
might die, for we were confined to our berths, without food
and without aid or attendance of any kind; and it was
impossible for me to go to his assistance." Keats, however,
withstood the wretched discomforts as well as Severn, and
even managed to indulge in his old habit of punning.
"After the first dreary night, just when the dawn was
peeping, and the storm temporarily abated, I called to him,

'This is pretty sea-music, Keats, isn't it?' 'Yes,' he answered to my relief, 'it is water parted from the sea' (the first line of a Vauxhall song then all the vogue)."

In the favourable weather which ensued the two friends read aloud 'Don Juan' to each other; but Keats resented the mocking cynicism of the shipwreck canto, and was so wrought upon that at last he flung the volume aside in contemptuous anger. With all his nature craving for sympathy and tenderness (himself the most tender as well as one of the manliest of English poets), and at the same time so near his own life's shipwreck, he could not enjoy Byron's brilliant stanzas.

The storm deeply impressed both:

"On the second morning I ventured up to peep over the cabin door, and was astonished at the grandeur of the sea. The waves were of an enormous length, and so high that the effect was like a mountainous country, and it was a cheering sight to see how nicely the ship met each wave and rode over it diagonally. I lost all fear in this sublime sight, and for the rest of the storm was a continual watcher, even to the lightning. When off Cape St. Vincent the weather changed and a dead calm ensued, and a great relief it was, to the passengers at any rate. Once more we were all in each other's company at dinner, and congratulated ourselves the more heartily when we heard from the captain that he had had fears for the ship, which had laboured heavily in the trough of the seas. Keats was greatly impressed by the beauty of the ocean off Cape St. Vincent. It was smooth as oil, and all one undulating motion, and with the bright sun shining on it we saw many large and strange fish; and once, to our delight and excitement, a whale appeared on the surface. The following day, although the calm still prevailed, we found ourselves in proximity to some Portuguese men-of-war, particularly a large four-decker, the *San Josef*. We were leaning over the taffrail, looking at this unwieldy monster in the distance flapping on the idle waves, when a shot passed close under the cabin-window. The captain, who was shaving, rushed on deck, to discover that a gun had been fired at us for not answering the signals on board the Portuguese man-of-war. While he was still looking seaward bewilderedly (for he had heard a previous discharge, though we had not, and had fancied the commodore was simply signalling to his fleet), the *San Josef* had drifted close enough for communication by speaking-trumpet. Some one shouted in English, demanding to know if we had recently seen any ships, particularly any vessels that looked like privateers. Many semi-piratical sloops were at that time known to be sailing for South America, which was then beginning to emancipate itself from the corrupt and tyrannical dominion of Spain and Portugal. The captain answered that we had encountered no vessels of any kind. We had to approach near to the immen-e ship, and it was a most fearful sight as regards the savage, dirty sailors, who showed themselves at every point, even high up the rigging. After further inquiries and answers, we were allowed to drift on, but not without genuine fear and trembling on the part of our captain, who held the Portuguese in dire mistrust. That afternoon we encountered an English sloop-of-war, clean and brilliant compared with the Portuguese—nay, the very antipodes to it. Its commander, having inquired and heard that we had been stopped by the *San Josef* and other war-ships, promptly turned about in pursuit in gallant style. We afterwards discovered that the Portuguese admiral was not so much on the look-out for South American privateers as cruising about to intercept vessels going to the aid of Spain, which was at that time in a state of civil war, with Don Carlos striving for the crown."

It would be impracticable to follow any one of Severn's three sets of reminiscences in the following narrative; for not only does he indulge in much circumlocution, but is often contradictory, and even, not infrequently, negligent in his statements; as when, for example, he says that, one evening, the *Maria Crowther* came in sight of Gibraltar, and next morning was in the Bay of Naples! Consistently with the plan of this memoir, his own record will be given intact where practicable, and otherwise his words will be woven from his several reminiscences and letters of a later date.

"We passed Gibraltar before dawn, and could but just see the enormous outline; a little later, however, we saw the coast of Barbary lit up by the sun's fiery rays—a scene of great beauty, by which Keats was deeply impressed. Behind us lay the mass of Gibraltar, now all glowing like a vast topaz; around us a wide expanse of ocean, calm and yet full of life and motion with the favouring westerly breeze; beyond us, a sunlit waste of dancing shimmering wavelets; and, seeming close to starboard, so translucent was that fine air, the African coast, here golden, and there blue as a sapphire, stretching away into a pearly haze. Keats lay entranced, and with a look of serene abstraction upon his worn face; while I, glad of the easy motion and the genial warmth, sat near and made a sketch in water-colours. The remainder of our voyage was in favourable weather, and was as pleasant as the unsatisfactory conditions on board permitted. At last, at the end of six weeks,* we entered the beautiful

----

* That is, after four weeks and three days. The *Maria Crowther* reached the Bay of Naples on the 21st of October, and lay in quarantine till noon on the 1st of November.

Bay of Naples. It would be difficult to depict in words the first sight of this Paradise as it appears from the sea. The white houses were lit up with the rising sun, which had just began to touch them, and being tier above tier upon the hill-slopes, they had a lovely appearance, with so much green verdure and the many vineyards and olive grounds about them. Vesuvius had an immense line of smoke-clouds built up, which every now and then opened and changed with the sun's golden light, edging and composing all kinds of groups and shapes in lengths and masses for miles. Then the mountains of Sorrento to the right seemed like lapis lazuli and gold; the sea between being of a very deep blue such as we had not seen elsewhere, and so rich and beautiful that it gave great splendour to all the objects on shore. So lovely was the ever-changing scene that we were not so bitterly chagrined as we would otherwise have been when we were informed that we were placed in quarantine for ten days, owing to the fact that there was then an epidemic of typhus in London, and it was feared that we might have brought the contagion. Keats was simply entranced with the unsurpassable beauty of the panorama, and looked longingly at the splendid city of Naples and her terraced gardens and vineyards, upon the long range of the Apennines, with majestic Vesuvius emitting strange writhing columns of smoke, golden at their sunlit fringes, and upon the azure foreground covered with ships and all manner of white-sailed small craft. It was a relief to me that he was so taken out of himself, for he was often so distraught, with so sad a look in his eyes, with, moreover, sometimes, a starved, haunting expression that bewildered me. Yet at that time I never fully understood how terrible were his mental sufferings, for so excruciating was the grief that was eating away his life that he could speak of it to no one. He was profoundly depressed the day we went ashore at Naples, though he had been so eager to leave the ship and explore the beautiful city; indeed, I was more alarmed on his behalf that night than even during that wretched three days' storm in the Bay of Biscay.

"But, as I have said, the first day or two of our quarantine were delightful, even to the two invalids, though Miss Cotterell had become much worse, and was, indeed, a most trying companion for my poor sensitive friend. It was a delight to hear him talk of the classic scenes he seemed to know so well; he made it all live again, that old antique world when the Greek galleys and Tyrhenian sloops brought northward strange tales of what was happening in Hellas and the mysterious East. He could even be gay before Miss Cotterell, for he seemed to breathe an inspiration from the lovely environment. There was constant entertainment, too, in the people surrounding our ship, as they passed by playing upon their guitars and singing songs, or came alongside to barter with us.

"Our schooner was anchored near the Castell' d'Uovo, and was soon, and constantly afterwards, surrounded by scores of Neapolitan boats with gorgeous heaps of autumnal fruits—grapes, peaches, figs, melons, and many other kinds I had never before seen, all in such abundance that it seemed as though we had arrived at the Enchanted Island—an illusion heightened by the endless array of picturesque skiffs and shallops, with sweet stirring music coming from many of them, the tinkling of the guitars mingling with happy laughter and innumerable shouts, cries, and exclamations of all kinds.   Perhaps the novelty alone was an irresistible charm, and made our haven seem, to me at least, as though it were the shore of Paradise."

It must, indeed, as Severn says elsewhere, have been a delightful experience for the young artist who had seen so little that was beautiful ; and had Keats only been able to enjoy it aright, the time would have passed happily indeed.

" Some company unexpectedly joined us. The English Fleet was then in the Bay, and seeing the Union Jack flying at the mast-head of the *Maria Crowther*, the admiral sent an officer with a boat's crew to inquire who and what we were. Instead of remaining alongside to make his inquiries, Lieutenant Sullivan came aboard with six out of his ten men— and so transgressed the strict rule of quarantine. In consequence, they had to spend the ensuing ten days on board the *Maria Crowther*—the only annoying thing about which was the lack of proper accommodation ; for we were well supplied with innumerable luxuries as well as all the necessities. The men enjoyed their spell of idleness, and the joking that constantly went on ; Lieutenant Sullivan made himself quite at home ; and altogether we had cause to congratulate ourselves upon his thoughtless oversight. His advent, and the constant pleasurable excitement after all our monotony and discomfort, was not only delightful, but had a markedly beneficial effect upon poor Keats, who apparently became much better, and indeed revived to be almost like himself. There was yet another unexpected companion in the person of Mr. Cotterell, a brother to the invalid lady-passenger. Mr. Cotterell, who was a banker in Naples, and knew the strictness of the quarantine regulations, at first contented himself with coming alongside the *Maria Crowther*, and supplying not only his sister but her companions (to whom he expressed himself as most grateful for their unintermitting kindness and attention to Miss Cotterell) with all manner of dainties and luxuries. Keats was never tired of admiring (not to speak of eating !) the beautiful clusters of grapes and other fruits, and was scarce less enthusiastic over the autumnal flowers, though I remember his saying once that he would gladly give them all for a wayside dog-rose bush covered with pink blooms. But after a day or two Mr. Cotterell, concerned about the delicate state of his sister, made his arrangements in Naples, and then came aboard to share our enforced isolation. Not only was he unbounded in his direct kindness to Keats and myself, and a boon to all, for he kept the company supplied with every delicacy in fruit, fish, and fowl that could be procured in Naples ; but he was also most welcome, for he knew Italian thoroughly, and—what was much better so far as our amusement was concerned—the Neapolitan lazzaroni-patois. Lieutenant Sullivan was amusing also, and altogether we had a fund of entertainment to draw upon at all times. The whole day long, after our advent and our boarding by Lieutenant Sullivan and his crew, we were encircled by the joyous Neapolitans; for it seemed that the uncommon accident of having an English naval officer and six man-of-war's men entrapped into quarantine on board a small merchant-schooner, brought hundreds, I am tempted to say thousands, to laugh and be merry at the expense of the blunderers. Mr. Cotterell translated the jokes and gibes, and caused us and our visitors continued roars of laughter. All kinds of chaff went on, and Keats was not behind either Mr. Cotterell or Lieutenant Sullivan in witty puns and remarks. The fun, the laughing, the singing, all contributed to increase the brilliant holiday scene, so much so that at the expiry of our 'isolation' I could not help feeling regret—for, altogether, it was to me a scene of such splendour and gaiety as I had never imagined and did not expect to realise again. Moreover, we were told, as was the case, that once on land the disenchantment would begin, that all the wonderful charm would vanish. Even after half a century, it is all still vividly before my eyes, as vividly as though it were present. Keats was very brilliant in the midst of this gay scene, and his ready wit always forms a part of it in my memory.

"But at last the day came when we had to say good-bye to our worthy Captain and to Lieutenant Sullivan, though not to Mr. Cotterell, who kindly conducted us to the Hotel d' Inghilterra, as he could not manage to accommodate others besides his invalid sister, and insisted upon our promising to let him be our friend and cicerone during our stay in the city. Indeed, we were almost persuaded into promising to make that stay indefinitely long; though, as a matter of fact, it came to an end even sooner than we ever intended. Despite the warnings which had been given us, when we landed in the city that looked so beautiful from the sea, we were quite taken aback by the dirt, the noise, and the smell. Everything seemed offensive, except the glorious autumnal atmosphere, and the sense of light and joy of the vintage, which was everywhere in evidence. With songs and laughter and cries, and endless coming and going, the whole city seemed in motion. The men ran to and fro with their baskets of grapes, bawling and screaming with mere delight apparently, not one here and there, but everywhere and all at once. The city itself, with its indiscriminate noises and bewildering smells, struck us as one great kitchen, for cooking was going on in every street and at almost every house—*at*, not *in*, for it was all done out-of-doors or upon the thresholds. At every corner was a barelegged Neapolitan devouring macaroni and roaring for more; mariners in red caps were hawking fish at the tip-top of their voices; and everywhere beggars were strumming guitars or howling ballads. The whole occupations of the citizens seemed to be done in the streets, and never ceased, for, as we soon experienced, it went on all night, so that at first we could not sleep for the continued row. We were amused, too, by the exaggerated appearances of liberty, for shortly before there had been a revolution in Naples, and so we found ourselves in the midst of a constitutional government, with the people intoxicated and almost crazy with their unwonted liberty, which was, however, of the most gingerbread kind, or rather all gilt and no gingerbread. The King had sworn fealty to the new Constitution, but at the same time had secretly intrigued with the Austrians. Two days after we landed, the perjured tyrant, called His Majesty, escaped in an English man-of-war and got safe to Vienna, so the Neapolitans were left in the lurch. On the afternoon of the same day we came ashore we saw a grand review of the Neapolitan troops. The men had a fine martial appearance I thought, but Keats would not allow that they had any backbone in them, and ere long events proved how right he was."

That night, at the Hotel d' Inghilterra, both were very fatigued after their exciting day, though Keats yielded also to a profound dejection. There is something dramatically affecting in the contrast between the joyous pictures outlined by Severn and the bitter wretchedness of spirit shown by Keats in the letter he wrote that night to his friend Brown, his sole confidant in that cankerous trouble which was eating away his life. Severn also wrote home, heading his letter simply "Naples. November 1st." It was addressed to his sister Maria, and contained little beside the following :—

"I have arrived here in perfect health, much of it gained in this sea-voyage. I have been frequently sea-sick, but it has done me much good, improved my appetite and given me strength. Oh! that I could say all this of poor Keats. He suffered most severely; many times I expected him to die; but at present in this city he is better—most certainly there is hope of his recovery. I still think to bring him back well. It is a source of the greatest consolation that I am with him."

While Severn was writing that "certainly there was hope of Keats's recovery, and that he was somewhat better," his friend was sitting in an adjoining room, overcome by physical weakness and sore distraught by bitter anguish of mind and heart. In burning words he wrote to Brown, not about his late pleasant experiences or the new and wonderful city in which he was for the first time, but about his ruining love and all the disastrous end of his brief dream of happiness :—

"I can bear to die—I cannot bear to leave her. . . . Oh, God! God! God! Everything I have in my trunks that reminds me of her goes through me like a spear. The silk lining that she put in my travelling-cap scalds my head. My imagination is horribly vivid about her—I see her. . . . I hear her. . . . Oh, Brown, I have coals of fire in my breast. It surprises me that the human heart is capable of so much misery."

Keats—to return to Severn's record—

"was but so-so, and scarcely strong enough to go about, but yet he picked up for awhile with the excitement all around us. In the morning we strolled about, and later on I went out by myself, and, I remember, stood waiting at one place in order to see the King pass. When he came I was dismayed, for he had the face of a goat, and I said to myself, 'if ever I might have to do with legislation I'd make a law that sovereigns should be good-looking people at least.' The sight of this King Ferdinand—Bomba, as he was called in mockery—with his goat's countenance, let down my loyalty fifty degrees. He was true to his countenance, for, as I have already said, he stole away the following day, and notwithstanding his most solemn oath to the Constitution, played the part of a traitor. He had waited till he had received the Pope's absolution, and then went over without shame to his country's enemies, the Austrians. There was silence in Naples on the morrow when it was first discovered that the King had fled, and that the people were betrayed.

"We went that evening to the San Carlo Theatre, and much admired the fine scene-painting, though the singing was not good, and the acting indifferent. We were particularly struck by the admirable painting or clever representation of two sentinels on the stage, one at either side. To our astonishment—an amazement which gave way to indignation— we saw, at the end of the act, the painted sentries became suddenly animated and move about. They were, in fact, real men, and such was the debasement of the Neapolitan national character that this outrage was actually permitted to pass without indignant challenge. This gross instance of tyrannical despotism was more than either of us could stand, so we rose and forthwith left—though not till Keats had exclaimed in a frenzy, 'Severn, we'll go on at once to Rome, for as I know that I shall not last long, it would make me die in anguish if I thought I was to be buried amid a people with such miserable political [debasement?].' Next morning he received a letter from Shelley, then in Pisa, urging him to come northward, and be the guest of him and his wife; a most generous letter, and the second he had received from that fine poet and noble man. But our plans were already fixed, and all our arrange- ments made for an immediate departure for Rome. Before we left Naples Mr. Cotterell would have a farewell dinner-party for us. Poor Keats made a special effort and was very entertaining; and he did not appear to suffer much. All the time we were at the Hotel d'Inghilterra he read 'Clarissa Harlowe,' in nine volumes I remember, and finished it just before our departure.

"Next day * we were on our way to Rome. The journey was made in

---

* Severn says "next day," but it is not clear whether he means the 4th or the 5th. The context indicates the 4th; but probably they left early on the 5th. With his customary heedlessness as to dates, Severn in one place specifies the date as 31st October—the day before they were free from quarantine.

a small *vettura* (carriage), and in many respects was pleasant, though the roads were bad, and the accommodation at the wayside inns villainously coarse and unpalatable, from which Keats naturally suffered much more than I did. The season was delightful, and as the carriage did little more than crawl along, I was able to walk nearly the whole way, and at frequent intervals delighted Keats by gathering the wild flowers which in some parts grew in profusion. The scenery, always near the sea, combined with the pure air, was most exhilarating, the former not only in its novelty, but in richness of colour and freshness at the same time. I gained strength by my pedestrian trip, and got to Rome considerably stronger than when I left England. Keats, on the other hand, had become very listless, and seldom seemed even relatively happy, except when an unusually fine prospect opened before us, or the breeze bore to us exquisite hill fragrances or breaths from the distant blue seas, and particularly when I literally filled the little carriage with flowers. He never tired of these, and they gave him a singular and almost fantastic pleasure that was at times almost akin to a strange joy. But there was nothing sufficiently out of the common to impress us till we reached the Campagna, whose vast billowy wastes, Keats said, were like an inland ocean, only more monotonous than that we had lately left. Soon after we had entered the Campagna, my attention was attracted by a large crimson cloak, and on approaching nearer I discovered it to be around no less a dignitary than a cardinal, engaged in what seemed to us the extraordinary sport of shooting small birds. He had an owl tied loosely to a stick, and a small looking-glass was annexed to move about with the owl, the light of which attracted numerous birds. The whole merit of this sport seemed to be in not shooting the owl. Two footmen in livery kept loading ·he fowling-pieces for the cardinal, and it was astonishing the great number of birds he killed. At last we came within view of Rome, a memorable sight in its grandeur and seeming deserted solitariness. As we drew nearer it became evident that we were approaching a great town of the living. We were both much excited as well as impressed by the absolutely unique environment of the Eternal City; and it was indeed an eventful moment. We entered Rome by the Lateran Gate, and almost immediately came upon the Colosseum, superb in its stupendous size and rugged grandeur of outline. It is the best way to approach and enter Rome, and far more striking than the route from the north—at least, such was the effect on my mind, an effect never since erased or diminished by all I have seen. Naturally, there was more to interest us in Rome than in Naples, but the sight that, in the circumstances, was the most welcome of all, was the genial face of the eminent physician Sir James Clark, or rather, as he then was, plain Dr. Clark. Keats had had a special letter of recommendation to him, and had written from the *Maria Crowther*, just before we were out of quarantine, apprising him of his arrival, and again from Naples just before we left that city, and the excellent doctor had already taken an apartment for him on the first floor of the house on the right hand of the steps leading up from the Piazzi di

Spagna to the church of Santa Trinità dei Monti. This had the great advantage not only of good situation, but of being opposite to the physician's own house, which, indeed, was a pre-arrangement, so that Dr. Clark might have his patient near at all hours. We both found accommodation in the same house, and Keats's bedroom was the one which looked over the steps on the side of the house.

"To be in Rome with Keats was in itself an event, independent of Rome and all it meant for me; for at last there seemed a chance of his being saved, and his restoration in so famed a place would surely secure his recovery. But the good doctor also thought of me, when he heard that I knew no one and had introductions to none, except that of Sir Thomas Lawrence to Canova. He went and spoke of me to John Gibson, the great sculptor; and poor dear Keats, though at the moment he could ill spare me, insisted on my going straight to Gibson's studio. On my arrival I found a great man, the eminent connoisseur Lord Colchester, just entering, and so I thought it expedient to retire: but Gibson caught me by the arm and insisted on my entering along with my lord. Throughout the visit and during inspection of his works, he showed me the same attention as he did to Lord Colchester, and I was so much struck by this generous consideration towards a poor and unknown young artist like myself, that I thought, 'if Gibson, who is a great artist, can afford to do such a thing as this, then Rome is the place for me.' Indeed, the act, slight as it may seem, was like sunshine to me: it was literally a revelation, for as the profession of Art in London was, in my experience, limited to the making of money, so my little career had been very painful, for I had not then, and have never since had, the power of uniting trade and Art to the advantage of the former. On my return Keats was delighted with this first 'treat to humanity,' as he called it, and discussed the plans he had devised for me during my sojourn. To staff with, he wanted me to begin at once upon a picture, to commence that very day with at least a sketch, particularly as I treasured some hope of a chance of the Royal Academy's granting me the three years' pension of travelling-student, of which the unfavourable aspect was that I had already got to Rome on my own account, and, as Keats suggested, I might thereby have offended the touchy pride of the Council. It required a greater amount of prudence than I possessed to make a too obvious clutch at the pension. Keats then told me confidentially some of his reasons for thinking that my chances were very slight. One was that my having obtained the gold medal after it had been withheld so many years had created such an amount of envy and even malice against me that I had to fight against a host of tradesmen in Art. He recounted his being at a dinner with Hilton and some other artists at the house of Hilton's brother-in-law, and the subject of conversation was the Royal Academy's having given me the long unawarded gold medal. Some one scornfully explained that the picture was very inferior, but that as the artist was an old fellow, and had made frequent attempts for the prize, the Council had given the medal out of pity and not for any merit. Keats, after a few moments, expressed his disgust at

F

such a mean lie, having first awaited a flat contradiction from one of the three artists present besides Hilton, who knew it to be a lie; and he declared that he would not any longer sit at the same table with such traducers and snobs; that he knew me intimately, had seen my picture and recognised its merits; that, as they well knew, I was a young man, and that the picture was my first attempt for a prize of any kind. He then rose from the table and abruptly left the party. This fact he had not communicated to me before, he said, from the fear that it might disturb me and lead me astray. But now, he urged, it was most expedient that I should lose no time in contending with my artistic enemies, and to confront them before they could do me further harm. He became much excited as he recounted this villainy, for with his ready sympathy he placed himself in my position. Although small of stature, yet on these occasions of acts of meanness, he seemed to rise to a larger stature, and the effect was a marvellous contrast to his charming manner when he was tranquil. Yet though thus ever ready to speak of my small worries, he said little of his own. While in Italy he always shrank from speaking in direct terms of the actual things which were killing him. Certainly the ' Blackwood's ' attack was one of the least of his miseries, for he never even mentioned it to me. The greater trouble which was engulfing him he signified in a hundred ways. Was it to be wondered at that at the time when the happiest life was presented to his view, when it was arranged that he was to marry a young person of beauty and fortune, when the little knot of friends who valued him and believed in a future for the beloved poet, and he himself, with generous, unselfish feelings, looked forward to it more delighted on their account— was it to be wondered at that, on the appearance of consumption, his ardent mind should have sunk into despair? He seemed struck down from the highest happiness to the lowest misery. He felt crushed at the prospect of being cut off at the early age of twenty-four, when the cup was at his lips, and he was beginning to drink that cup of delight which was to last his mortal life through, which would have insured to him the happiness of home—happiness he had never felt, for he was an orphan, and which would be a barrier for him against a cold and (to him) a malignant world."

Earlier, in the article which he entitled ' The Vicissitudes of Keats's Fame,' he wrote :

"Now that I am reviewing all the progress of his illness, from his first symptoms, I cannot but think his life might have been preserved by an Italian sojourn, if it had been adopted in time, and if circumstances had been improved as they presented themselves. And, indeed, if he had had the further good fortune to go to America, which he partly contemplated before the death of his younger brother, not only would his life and health have been preserved, but his early fame have been insured. He would have lived independent of the London world, which was striving to drag him down in his poetic career, and adding to the sufferings which I consider one of the immediate causes of his early death."

On Keats's urgent request, Severn agreed to go on with his art-work in such leisure as he could command.

" I proceeded forthwith," he says, " to make the sketch of the ' Death of Alcibiades.' Keats continued to be anguished on my account, for he knew as well as I that my prospects in great measure depended on my producing another picture in competition for the student's pension; but with my agitation for the poor fellow it seemed impossible that I could execute such a work for such a purpose, in what were then my circumstances. Nevertheless it was a great consolation to Keats to see that I was building up the ' Alcibiades.' About this time he expressed a strong desire that we had a pianoforte, so that I might play to him, for not only was he passionately fond of music, but found that his constant pain and o'erfretted nerves were much soothed by it. This I managed to obtain on loan, and Dr. Clark procured me many volumes and pieces of music, and Keats had thus a welcome solace in the dreary hours he had to pass. Among the volumes was one of Haydn's Symphonies, and these were his delight, and he would exclaim enthusiastically, ' This Haydn is like a child, for there is no knowing what he will do next.'

" In our first Roman days we got very odd and bad dinners sent in, as the Roman custom is, from a *Trattoria*, or restaurant. This was the more intolerable as we paid a crown for each meal, and as each, for all their cunning disguises in sauces and spices, was more unpalatable than the other. We put up with this annoyance for more than a week, although we made daily complaints to the *padrona di casa*, but one day we both pronounced the dinner to be unfit to eat. Keats hit on an expedient by which we always got good dinners afterwards. He would not tell me what it was to be. When the porter came as usual with the basket, and was beginning to set out the dinner, Keats stepped forward, and smiling roguishly at me, with a ' Now, Severn, you'll see it,' he opened the window, which was over the front steps, and taking up each dish one after the other he quietly emptied the contents out of the window and returned the plate to the basket—and thus disappeared a fowl, a rice pudding, cauliflower, a dish of macaroni, &c. This was all done to the amusement of the porter and the padrona. He then quietly but very decidedly pointed to the basket for the porter to take away, which he did without demur. ' Now,' said Keats, ' you'll see, Severn, that we'll have a decent dinner;' and sure enough in less than half-an-hour an excellent one came, and we continued to be similarly well treated every day. In the account, moreover, the padrona was discreet enough not to charge for the dinners thrown out of the window."

Slowly, but, as Severn thought, surely, Keats seemed to improve in health; and though he was forbidden to go to the Colosseum, or indeed to indulge in any sight-seeing, he sauntered along the Corso to the Porta del Popolo, or rested upon the upper terrace of the "Spanish Stairs," or lounged among the olives and ilexes upon the Pincio. He himself thought that there was at least a more definite chance for him, or at least he pretended that there was the shadow of a hope; and Severn joyfully wrote to common friends in England that they might reasonably expect further encouraging news. So with a lighter heart the young artist betook himself to the Colosseum, the Palace of the Cæsars, and elsewhere, to sketch the ruins, or to the Vatican Galleries—and particularly, at last, to study "at the feet of Michael Angelo." Keats, on his part, not only read a good deal in English, and studied Italian (with such nimbleness and industry that he could soon read with some enjoyment), but began to dream of again taking up the pen and of writing a long poem upon the story of Sabrina. He was, even in this short-lived rally, subject to swift moods of dejection—to moments, rather, when the phantoms he strove to keep at bay suddenly sprang forth from the wayside coverts where they lurked, and overcame him. Severn has recorded one such episode, when he tells how Keats began to read a volume of poems by Alfieri, but could read no more, and threw the book away, when he came to the following words, with their, for him, too poignant significance :—

> "Misera me! sollievo a me non resta
> Altro che 'l pianto, *ed il pianto è delitto.*"

But this Indian summer of the poet's life was destined to be pathetically brief. In a few weeks after his arrival in Rome a serious relapse happened, and the invalid sank at once from a condition of promise to the very frontiers of death. Terrible hæmorrhages led to a fierce wasting fever, and the fever and renewed hæmorrhages to a deathly weakness.

"Dr. Clark was very kind and considerate, and was most ardent in his attention on Keats, and at times arose in the night to watch him, when any serious change took place or seemed imminent. This bitterly painful position for me (and so it was in a high degree, when nothing seemed to help my unfortunate friend) was not without a redeeming point—I mean that it was not utter misery, for I was at least the nurse of Keats, however unworthy and whatever my deficiencies; and, moreover, I was sustained by the delightful hope of my beloved friend's recovery, if God so willed. This hope reconciled me to every difficulty and supplied the place of sleep at times, and even food, for I was obliged to devote myself wholly to him both day and night, as his nervous state would not admit of his seeing any one but Dr. Clark and myself. And yet, with all his suffering and consciousness of approaching death, he never quite lost the play of his cheerful and elastic mind. Yet these happier moments were but slight snatches from his misery, like the flickering rays of the sun in a smothering storm. Real rays of sunshine they were, all the same, such as would have done honour to the brightest health and happiest mind: yet the storm of sickness and death was always going on, and I have often thought that these bursts of wit and cheerfulness were called up o set purpose—were, in fact, a great effort on my account. I could perceive in many ways that he was always painfully alive to my situation, wholly dependent as I was upon my painting. His wit, I should add, was seldom exercised but upon unpleasant things, for he was essentially chivalrous and tender-hearted; and, too, it never failed to call up something pleasant."

On December 14th, four days after the disastrous collapse, Severn wrote to Mrs. Brawne :

" My dear Madam,

"I fear poor Keats is at his worst. A most unlooked-for relapse has confined him to his bed, with every chance against him. It has been so sudden upon what I thought convalescence, and without any seeming cause, that I cannot calculate on the next change. I dread it, for his suffering is so great, so continued, and his fortitude so completely gone, that any further change must make him delirious. This is the fifth day, and I see him get worse.

" *Dec. 17th,* 4 A.M.—Not a moment can I be from him. I sit by his bed and read all day, and at night I humour him in all his wanderings. He has just fallen asleep, the first sleep for eight nights, and now from mere exhaustion. I hope he will not wake till I have written, for I am anxious that you should know the truth; yet I dare not let him see I think his state dangerous. On the morning of this attack he was going on in good spirits quite merrily, when, in an instant, a cough seized him, and he vomited two cupfuls of blood. In a moment I got Dr. Clark, who took eight ounces of blood from his arm—it was black and thick. Keats was much alarmed and dejected. What a sorrowful day I had with him! He rushed out of bed and said, 'This day shall be my last;' and but for me most certainly it would. The blood broke forth in similar quantity the next morning, and he was bled again. I was afterwards so fortunate as to talk him into a little calmness, and he soon became quite patient. Now the blood has come up in coughing five times.   Not a single thing will he digest, yet he keeps on craving for food.   Every day he raves he will die from hunger, and I've been obliged to give him more than he was allowed. His imagination and memory present every thought to him in horror; the recollection of 'his good friend Brown,' of 'his four happy weeks spent under *her* care,' of his sister and brother.   Oh! he will mourn over all to me whilst I cool his burning forehead, till I tremble for his intellect. How can he be ' Keats ' again after all this?   Yet I may see it too gloomily, since each coming night I sit up adds its dismal contents to my mind.

"Dr. Clark will not say much ; although there are no bounds to his attention, yet he can with little success ' administer to a mind diseased.' All that can be done he does most kindly, while his lady, like himself in refined feeling, prepares all that poor Keats takes, for in this wilderness of a place, for an invalid, there was no alternative.   Yesterday Dr. Clark went all over Rome for a certain kind of fish, and just as I received it, carefully dressed, Keats was taken with spitting of blood.

"We have the best opinion of Dr. Clark's skill : he comes over four or five times a day, and he has left word for us to call him up, at any moment, in case of danger.   My spirits have been quite pulled down. Those wretched Romans have no idea of comfort.   I am obliged to do everything for him.   I wish you were here.

" I have just looked at him.   This will be good night."

CHAPTER IV.

It was not till after Christmas—"the strangest and saddest, yet not altogether the least happy I had ever spent"—that Severn was able to write home, and then but a brief note, addressed to his sister Maria. After some remarks on the journey from Naples to Rome, with an "old England for ever" chorus throughout, he adds:

"Yet I can but little judge, for I never leave my friend Keats. He continues in this last attack so bad that I fear he never can recover. 'Tis nearly three weeks since his relapse, and yet no signs of recovery. He has kept in bed all this time, nor dares move, from the fear of the blood-vessels on his lungs breaking out again. His suffering is great. He wishes night after night he may die, for if he recovers from his present attack he must yet succumb to consumption. Heaven look down upon him. . . . . I am finishing a journal of our voyage so that you shall have every particular, and I will try to send you my picture. The treatment we meet with here is very kind, that is, from the English."

It was during the most trying period of Keats's relapse, when he faintly rallied from the edge of the grave and then slid slowly backward, and so alternately hovered between life and death, that Severn had the pleasure of hearing from William Haslam in England.* It is a pathetic revelation of how deep was the feeling entertained towards Keats by his friends. The letter, moreover, affords a somewhat

---

* Severn had written to Haslam from the *Maria Crowther*, and posted the first or second day after entering Naples.

amusing insight into Severn's character, as viewed by one of his early friends.

" *Greenwich,*
" 4th Dec., 1820.

" MY DEAR SEVERN,

"Your letter from shipboard when under quarantine gave me an extent of anxiety such as my heart hath not known since I parted with Keats at Gravesend. It hung about me intensely for days, and at nights I dreamt of you, but I did not, could not, show it to a soul. I could not bring myself to give occasion to that grief to any man that the perusal had forced on me. Do not, however, mention in any of your letters home that I have acknowledged the receipt of a letter of that date, for altho' I should not forgive myself if I had shown it—still friends will not acquit one—for that I did not show it, but I hoped you would write, and you ought, Severn, to have written within three days again. Why have you not kept your diary? I ask you solemnly, for no one thing on earth can give such satisfaction at home as such minute detail as you set out with. If you have discontinued it, in God's name resume it, and send it regularly to me, only that, however, I may see fit to circulate it. I will zealously preserve each section (number each, or letter it, that I may do this unerringly, and write on *bank post paper*), so that you may possess the entire diary whenever you call upon me for it. Do THIS, Severn, tho' at some sacrifice of your inherent dislike of order and of obligation to do a thing—do it, if but because I ask it.

"Your letter came to me but last Friday (to-day is Monday, and our mail goes out to-morrow); you will hardly think that the receipt of it relieved me, and yet, sorrowful as are its contents, it did, so deeply had the letter of which I have been speaking distressed me—'that Keats this morning made an Italian pun;' these, Severn, are the things that do one's heart good. 'Water parted from the sea,' was another of them. But, the fact of the return of Keats's spitting of blood stands! and yet I did not but expect the voyage would have the effect of inducing its return; the climate, however, will, I trust, avail him. Keep him quiet, get the winter through; an opening year in Italy will perfect everything. Ere this reaches you, I trust Doctor Clark will have confirmed the most sanguine hopes of his friends in England; and to you, my friend, I hope he will have given what you stand much in need of—a confidence amounting to a faith. Study to gain this, Severn, for trust me, that much, very much with invalids depends upon the countenances of those about them. Omit no opportunities that present themselves to induce Keats to disburthen his mind to you. I know (tho' since he left England it has come to my knowledge) that he has much upon it. Avoid speaking of George to him. George is a scoundrel! but talk of his friends in England, of their love, their hopes of him.* Keats must get himself well again, Severn, if but for us.

---

* Haslam wrote this remark about George Keats under a misapprehension. He and Charles Brown were always harsh in their judgments of

I, for one, cannot afford to lose him. If I know what it is to love, I truly love John Keats. I sent your letter (the last) to Brown. Brown read it, with omissions and additions, next door, and returned it to me to-day. I send by this post a letter from Brown to Keats, sent to me on Saturday before he saw the last-mentioned, also one from your sister Maria, who called and left it with me to-day. Your family, she tells me, are all well. Tom has several times called on me, and I understand your father has at last become tolerably reconciled. I continue miserably oppressed, I mean as regards my executorship; 'tis now near three o'clock that I am closing this for you. My wife and child are well, and I, at least in them, am happy.

" Your attached friend,
" WM. HASLAM."

But while the friends in England, who had been alarmed by the first news that had come home, were gratified by a more hopeful letter which Keats wrote to Brown on the 30th of November, some eight or ten days before his relapse began, and when he was slowly gaining strength and almost hope, the poet was lying in what nearly proved the pains of dissolution. Unaware of Keats's evil plight Brown wrote the following cheery letter immediately after receipt of the welcome note from Rome, which reached the invalid during his last deceptive rally, and brought a look of pleasure to his face for the rest of the day. It is addressed to " John Keats, Esq., Poste Restante, Rome."

" *Hampstead,*
" 21st Dec., 1820.

" MY DEAR KEATS,

"Not two hours since your letter from Rome, dated 30th Nov., came to me, and as to-morrow is post-night, you shall have the answer in due course. And so you still wish me to follow you to Rome? and truly I wish to go; nothing detains me but prudence. Little could be gained, if anything, by letting my house at this time of the year, and the consequence would be a heavy additional expense which I cannot possibly afford, unless it were a matter of necessity, and I see none while you are in such good hands as Severn's. As for my appropriating any part of remittances from George, that is out of the question, while you continue disabled from writing. Thank God, you are getting better! Your last letter, which I so gravely answered about 4th Dec., showed how much

---

their friend's brother. It is not easy to discover the truth. But the unbiassed reader will note that Brown to the last maintained his point, and that whereas he had certain puzzling documents and facts, Dilke had nothing save asseverations.

you had suffered by the voyage and the cursed quarantine. Keep your mind easy, my dear fellow, and no fear of your body. Your sister, I hear, is in remarkably good health. The last news from George (already given to you) was so far favourable that there were no complaints. Everybody next door is quite well. Taylor has just returned to town. I saw him for a few minutes the other day, and had not time to put some questions which I wished, but I understand your poems increase in sale. Hunt has been very ill, but is now recovered. All other friends are well. I know you don't like John Scott, but he is doing a thing that tickles me to the heart's core, and you will like to hear of it, if you have any revenge in your composition. By some means (crooked enough I dare say), he has got possession of one of 'Blackwood's' gang, who has turned king's evidence, and month after month he belabours them with the most damning facts that can be conceived; if they are indeed facts, I know not how the rogues can stand up against them. This virulent attack has made me like the 'London Magazine,' and I sent the first chapter of my tour for Scott to publish, if he would pay me ten guineas per sheet, and print the whole chapters monthly, without my forfeiting the copyright in the end. This would have answered my purpose famously, but he won't agree to my stipulations. He praises my writing wondrously, will pay the ten guineas, and so on; but the fellow forsooth must have the chapters somewhat converted into the usual style of magazine articles, and so the treaty is at end. . . . . I dined with Richards on his wedding-day—he had just recovered from breaking his leg. How could he be so brittle? And it was done in a game of romps with his children! Now, I've something to make you 'spit fire, spout flame.' The batch of brag-players asked me to town, hoping to fleece me; it was at Reynolds' lodging, and I carried off £2 10s. When will they be sick of these vain attempts? Mrs. Dilke was next door yesterday; she had a sad tumble in the mud (you must not laugh). Her news was that Martin is to be married this year; that Reynolds and Mrs. Montagu correspond sentimentally, and that Barry Cornwall is to have Miss Montagu. There's some interesting small-talk for you. Oh! Barry C——— had a tragedy coming forth at the theatre, christened Mirandola—Mire and O la! What an odd being you are: because you and I were so near meeting twice, yet missed each other both times, you cry out 'there was *my* star predominant;' why not *mine* (C. B.'s) as well? But this is the way you argue yourself into fits of the spleen. If I were in Severn's place, and you insisted on ever gnawing a bone, I'd lead you the life of a dog. What the devil should you grumble for? Do you recollect my anagram on your name? How pat it comes now to Severn! My love to him and the said anagram, '*Thanks Joe!*' If I have a right guess, a certain person next door is a little disappointed at not receiving a letter from you, but not a word has dropped. She wrote to you lately, and so did your sister.

" Yours most faithfully,
" Chas. Brown."

Some three weeks later, after Brown had heard of the disastrous relapse following so suddenly upon the improvement, he wrote to Severn in a very different strain. The letter, notwithstanding its exaggerated language against George Keats, indicates what deep feeling " the exuberant Brown " could show. It is satisfactory to know that in the course of time George Keats was found guiltless of any fraud, at any rate by all save two of his acquaintances.

" Your letter of 17th December arrived here last Tuesday, the 9th. I cannot dwell on the subject of it. Either I am shortly to receive more favourable accounts, or to suffer the bitterest news. I feel—and I cannot help it—all your attentions to my unhappy Keats as if they were shown to myself,—yet how difficult I have found it to return you thanks, until this morning it has been utterly out of my power to write on so melancholy a story. He is present to me everywhere and at all times— he now seems sitting by my side and looking hard in my face, though I have taken the opportunity of writing this in company—for I scarcely believe I could do it alone. Much as I have loved him, I never knew how closely he was wound about my heart. Mrs. Brawne was greatly agitated when I told her of —— and her daughter —— I don't know how—for I was not present—yet she bears it with great firmness, mournfully but without affectation. I understand she says to his mother, ' I believe he must soon die, and when you hear of his death, tell me immediately. I am not a fool!'

" Poor girl! she does not know how desolate her heart will be when she learns there is no hope, and how wretched she will feel, without being a fool. The only hope I have rests on Dr. Clark not considering the case in so gloomy a light as you do—for his kindness ask him to receive a stranger's thanks. But you and I well know poor Keats's disease is in the mind; he is dying broken-hearted. You know much of his grief, but do you know how George has treated him? I sit planning schemes of vengeance upon his head. Should his brother die, exposure and infamy shall consign him to perpetual exile. I will have no mercy: the world will cry aloud for the cause of Keats's untimely death, and I will give it. O Severn, nothing on my part could stop that cruel brother's hand —indeed I knew not, till after he quitted us the second time for America, how cruel he had been. I have already written to him. Not a penny remitted yet! not a word in excuse for not remitting! I authorise you to open my letters to Keats; if he is still alive, you may perhaps cull something to cheer him, if not it is no matter, but take care you do not open a letter with *my* handwriting on the address which *contains another* handwriting; there is such a letter, and you can avoid opening it by peeping inside. I hear your family are well, but I suppose you are by this time satisfied on that score. Take care of your own health. While attending a sick-bed, I know by experience, we can bear up for a long, long time, but in the end we feel it severely. God bless you!

"Yours sincerely,
"CHARLES BROWN."

A fortnight later Brown wrote again, having heard from George Keats. He is still as embittered against the latter, though less rhetorical in his denunciations.

"This morning a letter from Mr. George Keats, dated Louisville, November 8th, addressed to Keats, arrived. I took the liberty of opening it, for it might have contained notice of a present remittance. It, however, does not, though he says, 'I hope to be able to send you money soon.' As for the rest, he writes very cheeringly; everyone is in good health, and there is this sentence, 'By next autumn I hope to live in a house and on ground of my own, with returns at least three times my expenses; my gain now is double my expenses.' It appears the only hindrance against remitting is a perverse want of the circulating medium. Tell Keats all this. As for the remainder of the letter, it is full of happy prospects and good hopes. So far, my dear Severn, you may read to our poor friend, if yet alive; it may do him more good than anything else. Though the above extracts are really culled from the Louisville letter, and though the whole of it is composed of the kindest expressions, my opinion of the writer remains unaltered. He is a canting, selfish, heartless swindler, and shall have to answer for the death of his brother, if it must be so. Three days since we heard, by a letter from Dr. Clark to one of his friends, that there was no hope and no fear of a lingering illness. I have no complaint except 'in my indignant feelings against Mr. G. Keats—they keep me up. Miss Brawne does not actually know there is no hope, she looks more sad every day. She has insisted on writing to him by this post, take care of the letter—if too late, let it be returned unopened (together with the one with *my* handwriting on the address and *her's* inside) to *Mrs.* Brawne. God bless you! take care of your own health—so much do I feel for your kindness towards Keats, that I cannot bear the thought of your being a sufferer by it, and therefore regret I did not, at all hazards, and in spite of apparent difficulties, follow you both to Italy, and relieve you in your distressing attentions.

"Yours truly and affectionately,
"CHARLES BROWN."

Keats's rally in January partially deceived Mrs. and Miss Brawne as well as Severn. The latter, thankful to have good news to communicate, wrote hopefully, and even hinted at the prospect of accompanying Keats back to England in the summer. It is difficult to understand

Severn's exact intention in this matter, for he must have known how irrecoverable was his friend's health. Even had he been blind to the almost unmistakable heralds of death, and deaf to Keats's own calmly judicial survey of his case, Dr. Clark had already made it clear that the end was inevitable, however delayed by the slow surrender of a strenuous life battling to the last. Possibly he thought it kindest to give Miss Brawne some shadowy hope as long as possible, or he may really have conceived the possibility of the invalid holding out for many months, long enough to die at home and more happily than in a remote and alien city. Hope annihilated is perhaps better than hope tortured in a slow, lingering death, with heart-sickening fluctuations; yet even tortured hope is hope, and it may be that the letter by which Severn slightly lightened the grief of Keats's "widowing love," was the best that could be written.

> "*Rome,*
> "Jan. 11th, 1821. 1 o'clock morning, (finished 3 A.M.)

"MY DEAR MADAM,

"I said that 'the first good news I had should be for the kind Mrs. Brawne.' I am thankful and delighted to make good my promise, to be able at all to do it, for amid all the horrors hovering over poor Keats this was the most dreadful—that I could see no possible way, and but a fallacious hope for his recovery; but now, thank God, I have a real one. I most certainly think I shall bring him back to England—at least my anxiety for his recovery and comfort made me think this—for half the cause of his danger has arisen for the loss of England, from the dread of never seeing it more. O! this hung upon him like a torture: never may I behold the sight again, even in my direst enemy. Little did I think what a task of affliction and danger I had undertaken, for I thought only of the beautiful mind of Keats, my attachment to him, and his convalescence. But I will tell you, dear madam, the singular reasons I have for hoping for his recovery. In the first fortnight of this attack his memory presented to him everything that was dear and delightful, even to the minutiæ, and with it all the persecution, and I may say villainy, practised upon him—his exquisite sensibility for everyone, save his poor self—all his own means and comfort expended on others—almost in vain. These he would contrast with his present suffering, and say that all was brought on by them, and he was right. Now he has changed to calmness and quietude, as singular as productive of good, for his mind was most certainly killing him. He has now given up all thoughts, hopes, or even wish for recovery. His mind is in a state of peace from the final leave he has taken of this world and all its future hopes; this has been an immense weight for him to rise from. He remains quiet and submissive under his heavy fate. Now, if anything will recover him, it is this absence of himself. I have perceived for the last three days symptoms of recovery. Dr. Clark even thinks so. Nature again revives in him—I mean where art was used before; yesterday he permitted me to carry him from his bed-room to our sitting-room—to put clean things on him—and to talk about my painting to him. This is my good news—don't think it otherwise, my dear madam, for I have been in such a state of anxiety and discom-fiture in this barbarous place, that the least hope of my friend's recovery is a heaven to me.

" For three weeks I have never left him—I have sat up all night—I have read to him nearly all day, and even in the night—I light the fire—make his breakfast, and sometimes am obliged to cook—make his bed, and even sweep the room. I can have these things done, but never at the time when they must and ought to be done—so that you will see my alternative; what curages me most is making a fire—I blow—blow for an hour—the smoke comes fuming out—my kettle falls over on the burning sticks—no stove—Keats calling me to be with him—the fire catching my hands and the door-bell ringing : all these to one quite unused and not at all capable—with the want of even proper material—come not a little galling. But to my great surprise I am not ill—or even restless—nor have I been all the time; there is nothing but what I will do for him—there is no alternative but what I think and provide myself against—except his death—not the loss of him—I am prepared to bear that—but the inhumanity, the barbarism of these Italians. So far I have kept everything from poor Keats; but if he did know but part what I suffer from them and their cursed laws, it would kill him. Just to instance one thing among many. News was brought me the other day that our gentle landlady had reported to the police that my friend was dying of consumption. Now their law is—that every individual thing, even to the paper on the walls in each room the patient has been in, shall without reserve be destroyed by fire, the loss to be made better than good by his friends. This startled me not a little, for in our sitting-room where I wanted to bring him, there is property worth about £150, besides all our own books, &c.—invaluable. Now my difficulty was to shift him to this room, and let no one know it. This was a heavy task from the unfortunate manner of the place; our landlady's apartments are on the same floor with ours—her servant waits on me when it pleases her, and enters from an adjoining room.

" I was determined on removing Keats, let what would be the conse-quence. The change was most essential to his health and spirits, and the following morning I set about accomplishing it. In the first place I blocked up their door so as they could not enter, then made up a bed on the sofa, and removed my friend to it. The greatest difficulty was in keeping all from him; I succeeded in this too, by making his bed, and sweeping the room where it is—and going dinnerless with all the pretensions of dining, persuading him that their servant had made his bed and I had been dining. He half suspected this, but as he could not tell the why and the wherefore, there it ended. I got him back in the afternoon, and no one save Dr. Clark knew about it. Dr. Clark still attends him with his usual kindness, and shows his good heart in everything he does; the like of his lady—I cannot tell which shows us the most kindness. *I* even am a mark of their care—mince-pies and numberless nice things come over to keep me alive. But for their kindness I am afraid we should go on very gloomily. Now, my dear madam, I must leave off—my eyes are beginning to be unruly, and I must write a most important letter to our president, Sir Thomas Lawrence, before I suffer myself to go to sleep. Will you be so kind as to write Mr. Taylor that it was at Messrs. Torlonias' advice Mr. Keats drew a bill for the whole sum £120?—this was to save the trouble and expense of many small bills, he now draws in small sums. I have the whole of his affairs under charge, and am trying the nearest possible way. Mr. Taylor will hear from Dr. Clark about the bill; it will be well arranged.

"Present my respectful compliments to Miss Brawne, who I hope and trust is quite well. Now that I think of her, my mind is carried to your happy Wentworth Place, where all that peaceful English comfort seems to exist. O! I would my unfortunate friend had never left your Wentworth Place—for the hopeless advantages of this comfortless Italy. He has many, many times talked over ' the few happy days at your house, the only time when his mind was at ease.' I hope still to see him with you again. Farewell, my dear madam. One more thing I must say— poor Keats cannot see any letters, at least he will not—they affect him so much and increase his danger. The two last I repented giving, he made me put them into his box—unread; more of these when I write again, meanwhile any matter of moment had better come to me. I will be very happy to receive advice and remembrance from you. Once more farewell.

"Your obedient and affectionate servant,

"JOSEPH SEVERN."

"3 o'clock morning.

"P.S.—I have just looked at him—he is in a beautiful sleep; in look he is very much more like himself—I have the greatest [hope] of him——"

Mrs. Brawne replied just as Keats's final death-agony had begun :—

"*Hampstead,*
"February 6th, 1821.

"MY DEAR MR. SEVERN,

"Your letter afforded me great consolation, if it were only hearing Mr. Keats was in a tranquil state of mind. How much I feel for you! how unfortunate his being out of England! how happy should I have been to have assisted you in nursing him! After the distressing accounts we have heard I scarcely dare have a hope of his recovery, but I will trust to what you say. When you talk of bringing him to England it cheers us, for, believe me, I should consider it among the happiest moments of my life to see him here in better health. You do not say whether he has a cough, which I fear he has. Your voyage, everything, has been unfortunate; the only comfort you have had has been in meeting with kind friends in Dr. and Mrs. Clark, but we must hope for better prospects. Mr. Keats has sincere friends in England who are most anxious about him. Should he be recovering in the slightest degree, entreat him for their sake to look forward, and not dwell upon the past, as I feel assured it would add greatly toward it. I saw Mr. Haslam last week; he appears much distressed for Mr. Keats and yourself. I must beg you to take care of your own health. Do not omit taking nourishment, as it is absolutely necessary to support yourself during the fatigue of body and mind under which you must be labouring. Mr. Taylor sent me the miniature [*i.e.* of Keats], beautifully set, for which I return you many thanks. I received your letter on February 1st, and the next morning sent your message to Mr. Taylor. Whenever you are allowed to mention Hampstead, tell him we all desire to be kindly remembered to him, and shall feel happy to pay his sister every attention. Fanny and she have constantly corresponded since he left England. Should there be anything I could do or send for you, pray write, as I shall take a pleasure in doing it. Mr. Brown desires to be remembered to Mr. Keats and yourself; he wrote to you the 30th of last month. For the future, any letter with the initials ' F. B.' at the corner, we will leave to your discretion to give to Mr. Keats, but we entrust them to your care. Your account of Italy would not induce me to visit it, if I may judge by the feeling of those you have had to deal with; their want of it annoys me beyond description. Fanny desires to be particularly remembered to you. With love to Mr. Keats,

> " I remain, my dear Mr. Severn,
> " Your sincere and obliged friend,
> " FRANCES BRAWNE."

In his December attack Keats seems to have reached the crisis the day after Christmas, when, though still in desperate straits, he visibly began to mend. I have before me an unfinished letter by Severn, probably intended for Mr. Taylor. It is dated the 24th of December, and is as follows :—

> " *Rome,*
> "December 24th, 1820.

"MY DEAR SIR,

" Keats has changed somewhat for the worse—at least his mind has much, very much—and this leaves his state much the same and quite as hopeless. Yet the blood has ceased to come; his digestion is better, and but for a cough he must be improving, that is, as respects his body. But the fatal prospect of consumption hangs before his mind's eye, and

Rome Dec. 24th 1820—

My dear Sir

Keats has changed somewhat for the worse—at last
their high hopes of him—his certain success—his experience
he will not hear a word—then the want of some kind
..le to feed in voracious imagination

Rome Dec. 24th 1820—

My dear Sir

Keats has changed somewhat for the worse—at last his mind has much, very much—and this leaves his state much the same and quite as hopeless—yet the blood has ceased to come his digestion is better and but for a cough he must be improved very that is as ~~far~~ respects his body—but is the fatal prospect of consumption hangs before his minds eye—and turns every thing to despair and wretchedness—he will not hear a word about going, nay I seem to lose his confidence in keeping the ~~~~ from this hope, for his knowledge ~~~~~~~~ ~~to grasp of every change around him—and add largely to his torture~~ he will not think his future prospects favorable he says the continued stretch of his imagination has already killed him—and were he to recover he ~~never~~ would write another time—he will not hear of his good friends in England, except for what they have done—and this is another load—but of their high hopes of him—his certain success—his experience he will not hear a word—then the want of some kind able to feed in voracious imagination

turns everything to despair and wretchedness. He will not hear a word
about living—nay, I seem to lose his confidence by trying to give him
this hope [for his knowledge of internal anatomy enables him to judge of
every change accurately, and adds largely to his torture].* He will not
think his future prospects favourable. He says the continued stretch of
his imagination has already killed him. He will not hear of his good
friends in England, except for what they have done—and this is another
load; but of their high hopes of him, his certain success, his experience,
he will not hear a word. Then the want of some kind hope to feed his
voracious imagination——"

In this brief unfinished letter alone there is revealed to
the close student of Keats's life and character the true secret
of the misery of the last year of his life. "The continued
stretch of his imagination has already killed him "—" the
want of some kind hope to feed his voracious imagination."
These two phrases bear out Keats's own poignant remarks
about himself. With a constitution undermined by organic
weakness, partly inherited and partly induced, and with an
intellect so ardent, so fiercely alive, that it never rested,
consuming itself if defrauded of the objects of its eager
pursuit, he was unable to withstand, in the last straits
of prostration, the devouring flame of an incontrollable
imagination; and above all he was tortured by the image
of the woman he loved, whose features, voice, and bodily
presence were conjured up by his mind by night and by
day, the woman whom he would fain forget for a little while,
since she could never be his, and was already irrevocably
removed from him, surrounded, to his imagination, by all
the vanished hopes, dead ambitions, and impossible ideals
he had erewhile cherished.

Before New Year's Day the fever had abated, and each
succeeding day Keats, to the astonishment of those about
him, rallied more and more, till, as we have seen, Severn
was able to send encouraging news to expectant friends in
England.

"By the beginning of the month he had rallied wonderfully. He was
able not only to get up, but to go out and enjoy the warmth in the
sunlight, although not for a moment was he to be once more deluded by

---

* The words within brackets are scored through in the original.

even the meagre hope of any other cessation to his pains than that of
death.   We went out in a quiet way, not to see sights, but just for him to
breathe the sunny air, which invariably made him pleasant and witty.
The fine public walk on the Pincio was our principal place of resort,
particularly as it was sheltered from the north wind, and was warm like
summer, with a balmy air.   By this time we had made the acquaintance
of a Lieutenant Elton, a gentlemanly young officer, tall and handsome,
though consumptive, yet, despite his complaint, always an excellent
companion for Keats.   He regularly joined us for our stroll on the Pincio,
and at first we were invariably a trio, for, until Keats seemed to be
really gaining in resistive power, I could not bring myself to leave him
even for my art.   On the fashionable promenade we frequently met the
celebrated beauty and *grande dame*, the Princess Buonaparte, sister of
Napoleon, who was the wife of the great Roman seignior, Prince Borghese.
She was still very handsome, both in countenance and person, and had
a very haughty air, save that it was at times unbent by such coquettish
glances that we all agreed the sight was uncommon, and that it quite
realised the Armida fame of the lady.   There was a degree of likeness
to her brother Napoleon.   This gay lady lived at the Villa Paulina in
great splendour, of course quite separated from her husband, the Prince
Borghese, and made herself notorious in many ways peculiar to herself.
Canova had just done a nude statue from her, which we went to see, and
thought it 'beautiful bad taste.'   It was Keats gave this statue its lasting
name, 'The Æolian Harp.'   But among other virtues which distinguished
this eminent lady was a quick eye for a handsome figure and fine features,
and hence it came about that she cast languishing glances upon Lieutenant Elton each time we encountered her.   At last this so jarred upon
Keats's nerves, though he thankfully acknowledged that he was not the
attraction, that we were obliged to go and take our walk in another place.
Elton gladly enough acquiesced, for, as I have said, he too was consumptive, and shunned all excitements; and to be with us was a pleasure,
for he was quite alone in Rome.   He more than once assured me that his
first symptoms of decline were caused by his bolting his food at his meals.
I may add that he survived Keats nearly a year.

" 'Twas a joy to me to see the latter improve from day to day.   The
winter being very fine he was able to walk out every day, and at times
was even like his own self.   Erelong I proposed that my two friends,
who always went at a snail's pace, should try the effect of riding together.
Both found that they were quite able to go on horseback, though their
rides were never anything else than slow walks.   In this way I was
able to get some glorious strolls at my own pace, and indulge in uninterrupted speculations, and these remain in my mind amid the most agreeable and fascinating reminiscences of dear Rome.   The season was more
like the lovely Italian spring than winter, and as I had had few opportunities in my continued London life of seeing nature in her beauty, or
even in her vigour, it was with no small delight that then and later I saw
this burst of vegetation, this early festival of Flora.   How well I remember

risking my life in getting a wallflower on a ledge of the Colosseum, for Keats to feel how all the air could be scented by its keen perfume! The eye was doubly charmed with the grandeur of antiquity in its noblest forms, and with the sweet freshness of nature exulting over all its lofty walls and precipitous ledges. The huge ruins, consisting of massive boulders, amazed me, for I wondered how the latter were ever lifted and joined. . . . In this way I saw many of the finest ruins at the most favourable moment, and was able to entertain Keats with my descriptions. His rides did not extend far, and of course he could walk but the shortest distance; besides, Dr. Clark was afraid of the excitement which might be caused by his beholding stupendous and world-famous sights. But he was able not only to ride at a slow walk about the Pincio, but also along the banks of the Tiber, beyond the Porta del Popolo; and such was the good effect on his mind, as well as his body, that he seemed to be recovering, and I was even rash enough to again cherish a faint hope. These bright moments were sadly counterbalanced by the sad and pathetic poignancy of his mental sufferings and forlorn hopes. It was a hard task to keep him even outwardly soothed, and still harder to hazard any encouragement. What made it still more severe was the fact of his surgical education having prepared him to judge correctly of his own case, so that, whatever sympathy I might evince, I was not allowed to entertain in his hearing a hope of his living. He always explained his own case so clearly and convincingly, and so calmly described just how he would die and when, that I had no answer but silence, and he knew it. Often, even in those latter days, he showed his charming wit and humour, which a stranger might easily have mistaken for gay spirits and natural fun. He wrote nothing, but we talked on many themes, and even on poetry. Once, when I was talking of Tasso, my great favourite, he said that he anticipated 'he should become a greater poet if he were allowed to live;' but immediately he shook his head, and bewailed his cruel fate that he was about to be cut off before he had completed anything great."*

But this calm was not to last. At the end of January a new disaster befel him, for he had another most alarming attack—a spitting of blood in such quantity that he declared it to be the forerunner of his death.

On the night of Keats's fatal relapse Severn, though worn with fatigue and anxiety, perplexed himself with vagrant thoughts as to how best to occupy himself, for he could not venture to fall asleep lest the swoon-sunken invalid should awake and need immediate attention, or perhaps die

* It is not quite clear whether Severn means that Keats compared himself with Tasso, or merely meant that if his life were prolonged he should do something excelling anything he had hitherto accomplished.

G 2

unobserved. Sometimes he had passed his lonely vigils in writing to friends in England, as when in the early morning of January the 11th he wrote to Mrs. Brawne between one and three o'clock. But on this anxious night he could not put pen to paper. Suddenly, touched to tears by the wan face of Keats upon the pillow, with deathly dews upon the forehead, the idea occurred to him to make a drawing of his friend while life yet remained. To this happy inspiration we are indebted for the well-known and lovely drawing reproduced on the opposite page, though this "facsimile" necessarily loses much in delicacy of tone.

"Dr. Clark was taken by surprise at the suddenness of the collapse, as he had a favourable opinion of his patient, and had encouraged me in thinking that Keats would recover. But now I saw that the doctor no longer had any hope, for he ordered the scanty food of a single anchovy a day, with a morsel of bread. Although he was thus kept down in a starving state, yet there was always the fear of his ulcerated lungs resuming their late dangerous condition. This shortly happened, and at once threw him back to the blackest despair. He had no hope for himself save a speedy death, and this now seemed denied to him, for he believed that he might be doomed to linger on all through the spring. His despair was more on my account, for, as he explained, his death might be a long and lingering one, attended with a slow delirious death-stage. This was in apprehension his greatest pain, and having been foreseen had been prepared for. One day, tormented by the pangs of hunger, he broke down suddenly and demanded that this ' foreseen resource' should be given him. The demand was for the phial of laudanum I had bought at his request at Gravesend. When I demurred, he said to me that he claimed it as his own and his right, for, he added with great emotion, 'As my death is certain, I only wish to save you from the long miseries of attending and beholding it. It may yet be deferred, and I can see that you will thereby be stranded through your lack of resources, and that you will ruin all your prospects. I am keeping you from your painting, and as I am sure to die, why not let me die now? I have now determined to take this laudanum, and anticipate a lingering death, while emancipating you.' Of course I was horrified, and tried in every way to explain the madness of the act, and to urge the cruelty it would evince to all his friends, and indifference to their efforts for him. Again and again I urged this, affirming my right as the principal of these friends, and assuring him that I should never be tired of him or of my ministrations, and that even on the score of my immediate prospects I was in no fear of perdition, for I expected the student's pension from the Royal Academy. This somewhat calmed him, but as I still refused to let him have the laudanum he became furious. He even supplicated me with touching pathos, and

God bless you, my dear
Brother & Sister. Your ever affectionat
Brother John Keats.

with equally touching eloquence described the manner of his death by
continued diarrhœa ; but on my persistent refusal he grew more and more
violent against me, and I was afraid he might die in the midst of his
despairing rage. And yet in all this there was no fear of death, no want
of fortitude or manliness, but only the strong feeling on my account to
which he regarded himself and his dying as secondary. So for long we
contended—he for his death, and I for his life. I told Dr. Clark about
the bottle of laudanum, and he took it away with him. This was on
the second day of our sore contention, and when he learned what I had
done Keats became silent and resigned, and sank into a solemn seriousness.
'Twas evident the physician was powerless to mislead the great intelligence the invalid had of his own case. Dr. Clark came to see him many
times a day, and it was an awful sound and sight to see Keats look
round upon the doctor when he entered, with his large increasing hazel eyes
(for as his face decreased his eyes seemed to enlarge and shine with
unearthly brightness), and ask in a deep pathetic tone, ' How long is this
posthumous life of mine to last ? ' Ever after the loss of the laudanum he
talked of his life as posthumous. When, on the day following my surrender of the bottle to the doctor's care, our kind friend called, and was
abruptly and sternly asked, ' How long is this posthumous life of mine to
last ? ' he was unable to answer, and afterwards assured me that he could
not withstand the intense expression of Keats's eyes. Now that his face
was so sunk and pale, those hazel eyes became more prominent and less
human ; indeed at times, owing to the intelligence of Keats when he was
questioning Dr. Clark, his eyes had the abstract expression of a super-
natural being, and he evidently knew well all that was passing in the
doctor's mind, although the latter was unable to venture a word. After a
week of those tragic scenes (and daily Keats asked Dr. Clark the same
question as to how long his posthumous life was to last) he became somewhat more calm, and harrowed me by recounting the minutest details of
his approaching death. As I was so fortunate as never to lose my patience
or my temper on the most trying topics—and in his sore weakness he
was often regardless of my feelings—he at last became sensible of his own
want of dignity, such as he said 'every man should have in his dying
moments.' I had made him some coffee, and he threw it away. I then
made some more, and he threw that away also. But when I cheerfully
made it a third time, he was deeply affected, and confessed 'that he had
no agony but what he felt for me,' and that he was sure my endurance
of his 'savageness' arose from my long prayers on his behalf and from my
patient devotion to him. ' Severn,' he said to me one day, ' I now understand how you can bear all this—'tis your Christian faith ; and here am I,
with desperation in death that would disgrace the commonest fellow !
How I should like it if it were possible to get some of Jeremy Taylor's
works for you to read to me, and I should gain consolation, for I have
always been a great admirer of this devout author.' "

Although only the first of the following letters reached

Severn before Keats's death, it seems opportune to include them here. One from the poet's publisher, Mr. Taylor, did arrive before that event, and was welcome on account of what it said concerning certain financial matters. Mr. Taylor's letter was, indeed, a great relief to Severn, who had been in profound anxiety on Keats's account.

About a week later, Mr. Hessey also wrote to Severn. It is a long letter, the kind of epistle one would expect from a clergyman of the most pronounced evangelicalism. It is unnecessary to print Mr. Hessey's well-meant sermon, or even the equally earnest though more interesting epistle despatched a fortnight later, wherein there is " a regretful remembrance of having heard poor Keats utter the most extraordinary and revolting opinions."

Though this letter was written four days after Keats's death, the news of that event did not reach the friends in London till the 17th or 18th of March. So when Leigh Hunt wrote the following letter to Severn he had no idea that " the great poet and noble-hearted man," as with characteristic generosity and enthusiasm he calls Keats, had been dead for more than three weeks.

" Vale of Health, Hampstead,
" March 8th, 1821.

" Dear Severn,—

" You have concluded, of course, that I have sent no letters to Rome, because I was aware of the effect they would have on Keats's mind; and this is the principal cause; for besides what I have been told of his emotion about letters in Italy, I remember his telling me on one occasion that, in his sick moments, he never wished to receive another letter or even to see another face however friendly. But still I should have written to *you*, had I not been almost at death's door myself. You will imagine how ill I have been, when you hear that I have but just begun writing again for the ' Examiner ' and ' Indicator ' after an interval of several months, during which my flesh wasted from me with sickness and melancholy. Judge how often I thought of Keats, and with what feelings. Mr. Brown tells me he is comparatively calm now. If he can bear to hear of us, pray tell him; but he knows it all already, and can put it in better language than any man. I hear he does not like to be told that he may get better, nor is it to be wondered at, considering his firm persuasion that he shall not thrive. But if this persuasion should happen no longer to be so strong upon him, or if he can now put up with such attempts to

Vale of Health — Hampstead. March 8. 1821

Dear Severn,

You have concluded, of course, that I have sent no letters to Rome, be-
cause I was aware of the effect they would have had on Keats's mind; and this is the principal cause,
for besides that I have been told of his emotion about letters in Italy, I remember his telling me on one occasion,
that, in his sick moments, he never wished to receive another letter, or even to see another face however friendly.
But still I should have written to you, had I not been almost at death's door myself. You will imagine how
I have been, when you hear, that I have had moreover, on my own account, the worst news I could have — judge
I have seen, when you hear, that I have had just begun inquiring again for the soul, I believe, after so —
relieved of several months, during which my flesh wasted from me with sickness & melancholy. Judge
how often I thought of Keats, & with what feeling. Mr Brown tells me he is to be in comfortably calm now, or
rather quite so. If he can bear to hear of me, pray tell him — but he knows it already, & can put
it in better language than any man. I hear he does not like to be told that he may get better; nor can only regard it as
is it to be wondered at, endeavouring his firm persuasion that he shall not survive. Out of this persuasion if possible
happen no longer to be so strong upon him, or if he can now put it off with and attempt to console him, remind
him, & what I have said & done a thousand times, & what I will (upon my honour, Severn) think always, that I have
seen the many instances of recovery from apparently desperate cases of consumption, not to indulge in hope,
to the very last. If he still ceased before this, tell him — tell that good poet & noble-hearted man, that
we shall all bear his memory in the most precious part of our hearts, & that the world shall bow
their heads to it as our loves do. And if this again will trouble his spirit, tell him that we
shall never cease to venerate & love him, & that, Christian or infidel, the most sceptical of
us has faith enough in the high things that nature put into our heads, to think that all
who are of one accord in mind or heart are journeying to one & the same place, and shall unite
somehow or other again, face to face, mutually conscious, mutually delighted. Tell him so in any
... before us on the road, or be us in any thing else: or whether you tell him the latter or
no, tell him the former, & add, that we shall never forget that he was us, & that we
are coming after him... The tears are again in my eyes, & I must not afford to shed them,
The next letter I write shall be more to yourself, & more refreshing to your spirit,
which we are very sensible must have the pretty traced. But whether our friend dies or not, it all
... is among the best gifts of your recollection, by & bye, that you helped to soothe the sick bed
of so fine a being. God bless you, dear Severn. Your sincere friend Leigh Hunt.

Vale of Health – Hampstead – March 8. 1821.

Dear Severn,

You have concluded, of course, that I have sent no letters to Rome, because I was aware of the effect they would have had on Keats's mind; and this is the principal cause, for besides what I have been told of his emotion about letters in Italy, I remember his telling me on one occasion that, in his sick moments, he never wished to receive another letter or even to see another face however friendly. But still I should have written to you, had I not been almost at Death's door myself. You will imagine how it has been, then, with you, that I have but just begun writing again for the news of which I have seen, — the interval of several months, during which my flesh wasted from me with sickness and melancholy. Judge how often I thought of Keats, and with what feelings. Mr. Brown tells me too it is comparatively calm now, or rather quite so. If he can bear to hear of us, pray tell him — but he knows it all already, and can put it in better language than they can do. God bless you, dear Severn. Your sincere friend

Leigh Hunt.

console him, remind him of what I have said a thousand times, and what
I still (upon my honour, I swear) think always, that I have seen too
many cases of recovery from apparently desperate cases of consumption,
not to indulge in hope to the very last. If he still cannot bear this, tell
him—tell that great poet and noble-hearted man that we shall all bear
his memory in the most precious part of our hearts, and that the world
shall bow their heads to it as our loves do. Or if this [   ] will trouble
his spirit, tell him that we shall never cease to remember and love him,
and that, Christian or Infidel, the most sceptical of us has faith enough in
the high things that nature puts into our heads, to think that all who
are of one accord in mind or heart are journeying to one and the same
place, and shall meet somehow or other again, face to face, mutually
conscious, mutually delighted. Tell him he is only before us on the
road, as he was in everything else; or whether you tell him the latter
or no, tell him the former, and add, that we shall never forget that he
was so, and that we are coming after him. The tears are again in my
eyes, and I must not afford to shed them. The next letter I write shall
be more to yourself, and a little more refreshing to your spirits, which we
are sure must have been pretty taxed. But whether our friend dies or
not, it will not be among the least lofty of your recollections, by-and-by,
that you helped to smooth the sick bed of so fine a being. God bless you,
dear Severn.

" Your sincere friend,
"LEIGH HUNT."

This is in every way a memorable letter, and readers
will be glad of the accompanying facsimile. It occupies
a single page of a quarto sheet. The two inside pages
are filled up with a letter from Charles Brown, to whom
Leigh Hunt took his letter to be supplemented by that
common friend if he had anything he wished to say.
The third page is much torn at the width-margin, and so
certain words can only be guessed at. The lection is given
as it stands :—

" *Wentworth Place*,
"9th March, 1821.

"MY DEAR SEVERN,—

    "Upon the whole your letter ending 14th and 15th Feb. gave com-
fortable news. Keats, though without hope of recovery, was calm ; and your
health was reinstated. Ever since I first read your account of his dreadful relapse, I have never been able to hope. It was then his death took
place in my mind—and inwardly I mourned for him as lost. That he
should have so long lingered, and in pain of body, and in irritation of
mind, was a new distress. The hearing of his sufferings was worse than
of his hopeless state. I have sat and eagerly wished and prayed to learn
he was no more. Yet I was full of fears as I read over your letter, that

my wishes had become realized. Let me have a lock of his hair—should it end as my despair tells me it will. Taylor and Haslam have had your letter. I expect it back again to-morrow, when Mr. and Mrs. Richards will be here. You refer to Keats's enemies, cursing them as his friend,—I suppose you mean the villains of the 'Quarterly' and 'Blackwood.' I understand (as indeed Keats told me) how he intended to treat Lockhart. Now Lockhart was violently attacked in the 'London' by John Scott for his atrocious libels on Keats and others. Lockhart challenged Scott, but was (it seems to me) afraid to fight. From this affair arose a quarrel between Scott and one Christie, Lockhart's second. They fought near Chalk Farm, and Scott is killed. Keats never liked Scott, but in such a cause, how hard that he should die. I tell you this, as it is in a degree part of Keats's history, and possibly you have not heard it. They are in good health next door. Mrs. Brawne saw your letter, but her daughter did not, from whom the worst is kept back, in (to my mind) a very ill-judged way. Meanwhile she fears perhaps worse than is supposed. I observe her gaiety is become boisterous,—fitt
one start rather than laugh ; and, at
seems sinking under apprehension.
getting better,—he has been extremely
asked to fill a page, and you will be
I heard of your friend Holmes two days
about to meet him (hearing he was walking
Hunt on the heath), to ask what he had to
to you, and how your family are ; but I
missed him. I have just been next
Mrs. Brawne sends her remembrance to you—Miss Brawne said not a word, and looked so incapable of speaking, that I regretted having mentioned my writing to you before her. I have so many dull thoughts coming across me at every line, that I confess it is an irksome task to write [even] to Severn. Yet had I anything more to say, I would not spare myself for your sake ; for, my dear Severn, I feel towards you as a brother for your kindness to our brother Keats.

" Yours most sincerely,
" CHAS. BROWN.

" P.S.—Dilke is at my elbow, and desires to be remembered to you."

" Mrs. Brawne saw your letter, but her daughter did not, from whom the worst is kept back," &c. This may refer to a letter which Severn wrote to Brown by the English Mail leaving Rome on the 15th (the contents of which would be similar to those in the letter next printed here), or, more probably, to the letter to Mrs. Brawne herself, directed (as Severn was once requested to do) to her to Brown's care—a precaution taken on Miss Brawne's behalf.

" Rome,
" 12th February, 1821.

" My dear Mrs. Brawne,—

"I have just received your letter of the 15th—the contrast of your quiet friendly Hampstead with this lonely place and our poor suffering Keats brings the tears into my eyes. I wish many, many times that he had never left you. His recovery must have been impossible whilst he was in England, and his excessive grief since has made it more so. In your care he seems to me like an infant in its mother's arms—you would have smoothed down his pain by varieties, his death might have been eased by the sight of his many friends. But here, with one solitary friend, in a place else savage for an invalid he has had one more pang added to his many, for I have had the hardest task in keeping from him my painful situation. I have kept him alive by these means week after week. He had refused all food, but I tried him every way—I left him no excuse. Many times I have prepared his meals six times over, and kept from him the trouble I had in doing it. I have not been able to leave him, that is, I have not dared to do it, but when he slept. Had he come here alone he would have plunged into the grave in secret—we should never have known one syllable about him. This reflection alone repays me for all I have done. It is impossible to conceive what the sufferings of this poor fellow have been. Now he is still alive and calm. If I say more I shall say too much. Yet at times I have hoped he would recover, but the Doctor shook his head, and Keats would not hear that he was better—the thought of recovery is beyond everything dreadful to him. We now dare not perceive any improvement, for the hope of death seems his only comfort. He talks of the quiet grave as the first rest he can ever have. I can believe and feel this most truly. In the last week a great desire for books came across his mind. I got him all the books at hand and for three days this charm lasted on him, but now it is gone. Yet he is very calm—he is more and more reconciled to his fortunes.

"Feb. 14th.—Little or no change has taken place in Keats since the commencement of this, except this beautiful one that his mind is growing to great quietness and peace—I find this change has its rise from the increasing weakness of his body, but it seems like a delightful sleep to me. I have been beating about in the tempest of his mind so long. To-night he has talked very much to me, but so easily that he at last fell into a pleasant sleep—he seems to have comfortable dreams without nightmare. This will bring on some change—it cannot be worse, it may be better. Among the many things he has requested of me to-night, this is the principal, that on his grave shall be this—

' Here lies one whose name was writ in water.'

"You will understand this so well that I will not say a word about it, but is it not dreadful that he should with all his misfortunes on his mind and perhaps wrought up to their abisme, end his life without one jot of human happiness? When he first came here he purchased a copy of

Alfieri, but put it down at the second page—'Misera me!' He was much affected at this passage.

> 'Misera me! Sollievo a me non resta
> Altro che 'l pianto, ed il pianto è delitto.'

*   *   *   *   *

"Since, a letter has come. I gave it to Keats, supposing it to be one of yours, but it proved sadly otherwise. The glance of that letter tore him to pieces. The effects were on him for many days—he did not read it—he could not, but requested me to place it in his coffin together with a purse and letter (unopened) of his sister's, since which time he has requested me not to place *that letter* in his coffin, but only his sister's purse and letter with some hair. Then (?) he found many causes of his illness in the exciting and thwarting of his passions, but I persuaded him to feel otherwise on this delicate point. In his most irritable state he sees a friendless world with everything that his life presents, particularly the kindness of his friends tending to his untimely death. I have got an English nurse to come two hours every other day ; so that I have quite recovered my health, but my nurse after coming three times has been taken ill to-day—this is a little unfortunate as Keats seems to like her. You see I cannot do anything until poor Keats is asleep : this morning he has waked very calm—I think he seems somewhat better. He has taken half a pint of fresh milk ; the milk here is beautiful to all the senses —it is delicious—for three weeks he has lived on it, sometimes taking a pint and a half in a day.

"You astonish me about . . . poor Keats is a martyr to the tricks of these infernal scoundrels, others besides G. . . his is rather the fault of his (   ) than his heart. I can understand him—but the others—ten thousand curses light upon them. Not only our friend's life, but his very nature has been torn to pieces by them—that he is here a thousand miles from his dear home, dying without one comfort but me when— I cannot bear to think of it. The Doctor has been—he thinks Keats worse. He says the expectoration is the most dreadful he ever saw— never met an instance where a patient was so quickly pulled down. Keats's inward grief must have been beyond any limit—his lungs are in a dreadful state. His stomach has lost all its power—Keats says he has fretted to death—from the first drops of blood he knew he must die. He says no common chance of living was for him."

If Keats, to the regret of Messrs. Taylor and Hessey, died without the benefit of those gentlemen's spiritual exhortations, he at least had the pleasure of gratification in his wish as to temporary possession of one of Jeremy Taylor's works.

The first allusion to this in point of date is in one of Severn's February letters to Brown :—

"Poor Keats has just fallen asleep. I have watched him and read to him to his very last wink; he has been saying to me, 'Severn, I can see under your quiet look immense contention—you don't know what you are reading. You are enduring for me more than I would have you. O! that my last hour was come!' He is sinking daily; perhaps another three weeks may lose him to me for ever. I made sure of his recovery when we set out. I was selfish, I thought of his value to me; I made my own public success to depend on his candour to me. Torlonia, the banker, has refused us any more money; the bill is returned unaccepted, and to-morrow I must pay my last crown for this cursed lodging-place: and, what is more, if he dies all the beds and furniture will be burnt and the walls scraped, and they will come on me for a hundred pounds or more. But, above all, this noble fellow lying on the bed and without the common spiritual comforts that many a rogue and fool has in his last moments: if I do break down it will be under this; but I pray that some angel of goodness may yet lead him through this dark wilderness. If I could leave Keats every day for a time I could soon raise money by my painting, but he will not let me out of his sight, he will not bear the face of a stranger. I would rather cut my tongue out than tell him I must get the money—that would kill him at a word. You see my hopes of being kept by the Royal Academy will be cut off unless I send a picture by the spring. I have written to Sir T. Lawrence. I have got a volume of Jeremy Taylor's works, which Keats has heard me read to-night. This is a treasure indeed, and came when I should have thought it hopeless. Why may not other good things come? I will keep myself up with such hopes. Dr. Clark is still the same, though he knows about the bill; he is afraid the next change will be to diarrhœa. Keats sees all this—his knowledge of anatomy makes every change tenfold worse; every way he is unfortunate, yet every one offers me assistance on his account. He cannot read any letters, he has made me put them by him unopened. They tear him to pieces—he dare not look on the outside of any more; make this known."

In the 'Recollections,' the incident is thus introduced :—

"Dr. Clark succeeded in obtaining a copy of Jeremy Taylor's 'Holy Living and Dying,' and thereafter I read daily to poor Keats, both morning and evening, from this pious work, and he received great comfort. When he became restless, and when he was willing, I prayed by him, and so a great change and calmness grew upon him, and my task was much lightened. If I had no longer any hope in the prolongation of his life, yet the gentle Christian spirit beginning to soften the rigour of his dying, relieved me more than I can well account for.

"He kept continually in his hand a polished, oval, white cornelian, the gift of his widowing love, and at times it seemed his only consolation, the only thing left him in this world clearly tangible. Many letters which he was unable to read came for him. Some he allowed me to read to him; others were too worldly—for, as he said, he had 'already journeyed far beyond them.' There were two letters, I remember, for which he had no words, but he made me understand that I was to place them on his heart within his winding-sheet.

"Those bright falcon eyes, which I had known only in joyous intercourse, while revelling in books and nature, or while he was reciting his own poetry, now beamed with an unearthly brightness and a penetrating steadfastness that could not be looked at. . . . ."

Throughout the long and trying period of Severn's unflagging ministry to his dying friend he had been fertile in expedients, in trivial matters as well as in pecuniary troubles. He has himself told us how, overcome with fatigue, he would sometimes fall asleep in the night-watches, and, awaking, find himself enveloped in total darkness.

"To remedy this, one night I tried the experiment of fixing a thread from the bottom of a lighted candle to the wick of an unlighted one, that the flame might be conducted, all which I did without telling Keats. When he awoke and found the first candle nearly out, he was reluctant to wake me, and while doubting, suddenly cried out, 'Severn, Severn! here's a little fairy lamplighter actually lit up the other candle.'"

Certainly no one had a more loyal friend and tender nurse than Keats had in Severn. There is a touch of deep pathos in the latter's simple yet eloquent words :—

"Poor Keats has me ever by him, and shadows out the form of one solitary friend; he opens his eyes in great doubt and horror, but when they fall on me they close gently, open quietly and close again, till he sinks to sleep."

This passage occurs in one of the most pathetic of all Severn's letters to his friends. It was addressed to Haslam, and was written the day before Keats's death.

" Feb. 22nd.

"My Dear Haslam,—

"O, how anxious I am to hear from you! I have nothing to break this dreadful solitude but letters. Day after day, night after night, here I am by our poor dying friend. My spirits, my intellect, and my health are breaking down. I can get no one to change with me—no one to relieve me. All run away, and even if they did not, Keats would not do without me. Last night I thought he was going, I could hear the phlegm in his throat; he bade me lift him up on the bed or he would die with pain. I watched him all night, expecting him to be suffocated at every cough. This morning, by the pale daylight, the change in him frightened me; he has sunk in the last three days to a most ghastly look. Though Dr. Clark has prepared me for the worst, I shall be ill able to bear to be set free even from this, my horrible situation, by the loss of him. I am still quite precluded from painting, which may be of consequence to me. Poor Keats has me ever by him, and shadows out the form of one solitary friend; he opens his eyes in great doubt and horror, but when they fall upon me they close gently, open quietly and close again, till he sinks to sleep. This thought alone would keep me by him till he dies; and why did I say I was losing my time? The advantages I have gained by knowing John Keats are double and treble any I could have won by any other occupation. Farewell."

"At times during his last days," says Severn in a memorable passage,* "he made me go to see the place where he was to be buried, and he expressed pleasure at my description of the locality of the Pyramid of Caius Cestius, about the grass and the many flowers, particularly the innumerable violets, also about a flock of goats and sheep and a young shepherd—all these intensely interested him. Violets were his favourite flowers, and he joyed to hear how they overspread the graves. He assured me 'that he already seemed to feel the flowers growing over him.'

"During the last few days of his life he became very calm and resigned. Again and again, while warning me that his death was fast approaching, he besought me to take all care of myself, telling me that 'I must not look at him in his dying gasp nor breathe his passing breath, not even breathe upon him.' From time to time he gave me all his directions as to what he wanted done after his death. It was in the same sad hour when he told me with greater agitation than he had shown on any other subject, to put the letter which had just come from Miss Brawne (which he was unable to bring himself to read, or even to open), with any other that should arrive too late to reach him in life, inside his winding-sheet on his heart—it was then, also, that he asked that I should see cut upon his gravestone as sole inscription, *not his name*, but simply 'Here lies one whose name was writ in water.'"

Throughout Keats's latter days Severn was much cheered by the sympathy and constant attention of Dr. and Mrs. Clark, and of Mr. William Ewing, an English sculptor, who had a profound interest in the dying poet, and was eager to be of any service to him or his devoted friend. But at last the inevitable moment came.

"He remained quiet to the end, which made the death-summons more terrible. It happened about half-past four on the afternoon of Friday, the 23rd. He held my hand to the last, and he looked up at me until his eyes lost their speculation and dimmed in death. I could hear

---

* Already familiar in various wordings. Here I follow the text of his MS. 'Recollections.'

the phlegm boiling and tearing his chest. He gasped to me to lift him up, and in a short time died in my arms without effort, and even with deadly rejoicing that it had come at last, that for which he had so ardently longed for months. And I confess that his pallid dead face was for awhile to me a consolation, for I had seen it express such suffering. I had seen it waste away in that suffering, and I had seen that suffering long and in loneliness, and it was a happiness to think that the poor fellow's misery was over."

And so the long tragic episode came to a close, and with the relaxation of the severe strain Severn gave way completely. Even four or five days later, he could not at first sufficiently control his grief to finish a letter he began, intended for Brown. The fragment remains among his papers.

"My dear Brown," it begins, and then goes on without further preamble, "He is gone. He died with the most perfect ease. He seemed to go to sleep. On the 23rd, Friday, at half-past four, the approach of death came on. 'Severn—I—lift me up, for I am dying. I shall die easy. Don't be frightened! Thank God it has come.' I lifted him up in my arms, and the phlegm seemed boiling in his throat. This increased until eleven at night, when he gradually sank into death, so quiet, that I still thought he slept—but I cannot say more now. I am broken down beyond my strength. I cannot be left alone. I have not slept for nine days, I will say the days since—— On Saturday a gentleman came to cast the face, hand, and foot. On Sunday his body was opened; the lungs were completely gone, the doctors could not conceive how he had lived in the last two months. Dr. Clark will write you on this head. . . . ." ;

The letter is scrawled, and as though written by a tremulous hand. It breaks off just over the second page, and on the third is a roughly drawn but suggestive figure of one mourning—reproduced on the opposite page.

It is not surprising that, with all his fortitude and philosophical way of looking always at the best side of things, Severn was utterly prostrated. He was, truly enough, glad to see the calm of death upon the features he had so often beheld distraught by bodily and mental agony: and yet the final loss of so dear a friend was a bitter grief: "one so dear that up to his death I knew not how to trace its value, one so fascinating, not only in the power of his genius, but also in the charm of his manners, and one I had

MOURNING FIGURE, FROM THE THIRD PAGE OF UNFINISHED LETTER
ANNOUNCING THE DEATH OF KEATS.

To face page 94.

known so long in the constant and sincere communion of
our two arts of Poetry and Painting—this great loss, the
loss of all these, came upon me, and I sank under the
blow most painfully; with difficulty, and only, indeed, by a
great effort, recovering sufficiently to be present at the
funeral."

"The first thing Dr. Clark did when he arrived too late to see Keats
again in life was to feel my pulse, to command me to keep perfectly quiet,
and to order an English nurse to take charge of the sick-room. Mr.
Ewing also kindly came to aid me in my new harassing trouble, for, on
the head of my partial collapse, came an unlooked-for sore annoyance.
The vile indiscriminating Roman law required that all the furniture
should be burned, and the rooms refurnished and everyway restored. In
this new disaster Dr. Clark was a true friend in need, and managed to
reduce the heavy charges down to one-half the amount demanded from me.
Ultimately, too, the sitting-room was left untouched, mainly on account
of the hired pianoforte, which I refused to be allowed to be touched; and
as in connection with my protesting guardianship of it I was able to
prove that I had never carried my dying friend into the room, it followed
that nothing else therein could be touched. But the expenses were
heavy enough otherwise, and the whole affair most distressing and
shameful."

In a letter written eight days later (March 3rd) Severn
returns to this matter, which evidently caused him profound
annoyance. To judge from this unsigned and unfinished
note, the delay on the part of the persons deputed by the
municipality to see to the demolition of 'infected furniture'
must have been unduly prolonged.

"Those brutal Italians," says Severn, "have nearly done their monstrous
business. They have burned the furniture—they have done their meetings—and I believe, at least hope, no more of these cursed cruelties will
take place. They have racked me in my most painful moments, and I
have suffered so much that my nerves are sadly affected. Four days
before poor Keats died the change was so great that I passed dark
moments of dread. He was aware of it himself. He made me lift him
up in the bed many times. The apprehension of death was strong upon
him, but its effect was only that of giving him comfort. He seemed only
affected when the morning came and still found him alive, and he grieved
inwardly until some further change made him hope that the night would
bring death. Each day he would look up in the doctor's face. . . . . .
This look was more than we could ever bear. The extreme brightness of
his eyes with his poor pallid face were dreadful beyond description. These
our last nights I watched him; on the fifth the doctor prepared me for

his death—this day I cannot dare think on. Some future time I will write of it, now I cannot but say little."

"The burning of the furniture in the death-room," says Severn elsewhere, "took place in the Piazza di Spagna. Then the walls were all done up afresh, and I had scarcely paid the shameful demand when the brute of a landlady sent for me to pay for the crockery broken in our service, and I was at once indignant and amused to find a long table covered with the broken crockery of what must have been the *débris* of the whole parish. I assumed to be in a mad rage, and with my stick I dashed and smashed everything that was on the table, and singularly enough I frightened the vile creature of a landlady, with the result that I never heard any more about the crockery."

But before this the funeral of the poet had taken place, almost unnoticed by the English visitors in Rome. Lieutenant Elton was away, and there was no one else among those who had known Keats, besides Severn, Dr. Clark, and William Ewing, to follow in the meagre procession to the grave.

"Keats was laid to rest under the sods of a grassy slope in the old ground of Monte Testaccio, where all Protestants and others outside the pale of the Roman Catholic Church were interred. He had the noble pyramid of Caius Cestius over him—in all, so beautiful a scene that it formed one of the few pleasant things on which he liked to dwell during his last days. It was a real consolation to him that he was to be laid in so lovely a place of rest, and in the companionship of so many sons of misery like himself, men of genius and enterprise who had found an early grave at Rome. This was the only theme on which he tried, in the midst of his anguish, to be once more the poet—since that of his 'having one poor friend to close his eyes'—though on this he spoke only with his eyes.

"Ill, and almost prostrated and grief-stricken as I was, it was all I could do to attend the funeral, but was aided by my friend Ewing. Several English visitors who, since his death, had suddenly become interested in his pathetic story (or such of it as was known), attended at the final ceremony. I was deeply affected at this last closing scene, particularly as I was the only personal friend present from among the little band of devoted friends whom the poet had left behind in England. After my recovery I visited this sacred spot continually until the advent of the Italian summer."

In that beautiful graveyard, doubly sacred as enshrining also the ashes of Shelley, Keats was laid among the flowers he loved best, which he had "almost felt growing over him"; "and there they do grow," writes Lord Houghton,

"even all the winter long—violets and daisies mingling
with the fresh herbage, and, in the words of Shelley,
'making one in love with death to think that one should
be buried in so sweet a place.'"

A few weeks after Severn, ill and lonely in his great
sorrow, was left to begin his career anew : the tide of welfare
had turned. The first welcome boon was the recovery of
health ; and among the earliest "luxuries" he allowed
himself were hours of contemplation and rest in the valley
of Monte Testaccio.

In the early summer, writing to Haslam, he says : " Poor
Keats has now his wish—his humble wish : he is at peace in
the quiet grave. I walked there a few days ago, and found
the daisies had grown all over it. It is in'one of the most
lovely retired spots in Rome. You cannot have such a
place in England. I visit it with a delicious melancholy
which relieves my sadness. When I recollect for how long
Keats had never been one day free from ferment and torture
of mind and body, and that now he lies at rest with the
flowers he so desired above him, with no sound in the air
but the tinkling bells of a few simple sheep and goats, I
feel indeed grateful that he is here, and remember how
earnestly I prayed that his sufferings might end, and that
he might be removed from a world where no one grain of
comfort remained for him."

At this point it is opportune to return to some of Severn's
correspondence belonging to the period immediately succeeding the death of Keats. In answer to his already quoted
letter to Brown, announcing the end of all their hopes and
fears, that loyal friend of both wrote, on March 23rd, as
follows :—

"From the first account you gave of Keats's relapse in December, I
never had a hope, as you may have perceived by the constant strain of
despair in my letters. At last your news, passing from bad to worse, and
from worse to worst (I will confess it), became too distressing to make me
congratulate myself he was yet alive. Had I been with him I could have

borne all this with an equal mind, and, perhaps, as you did, hoped. Still when the blow actually came, I felt at the moment utterly unprepared for it.' Then *she*,—she was to have it told her, and the worst had been concealed from her knowledge ever since your December letter. It is now five days since she heard it. I shall not speak of the first shock, nor of the following days,—it is enough she is now pretty well,—and thro'out she has shown a firmness of mind which I little expected from one so young, and under such a load of grief. To-morrow I shall be expecting the promised letter of mournful particulars; and, what I am now most anxious about, a true account of your health. My solicitude seems transferred from him to you. Under Dr. Clark's friendly care everything I feel confident will be done towards reinstating your strength of body as soon as possible. Ah, I write this idly,—for before you read these lines you will be well and cheerful,—you ought to be so. The hand of God took our friend away, and to God, in all His behests, am I ever resigned. I never yet lost any one by the hand of man, though that (you will say) is still by the will of God, but certainly with a difference,—I mean by a violent death, and know not how I could bear the loss of any one in that manner; but here, though enemies have preyed upon him, I am quite resigned, for those very enemies knew not what they were doing, whose heart they were breaking. The highest praise that mortal can have belonged to Keats: no one ever saw him without loving him, no one could know him and treat him unkindly: so convinced am I of this that I acquit his brother of malevolence. There is no more news from that same brother. I wrote to Haslam to call on Abbey, and if Abbey will permit it, Mrs. Brawne and Mrs. Dilke will call on Miss Keats. They are in mourning next door. As for myself, though such things are a mere form, I mourn for him outwardly as well as inwardly; as for a brother. My last letter was dated either ten or fourteen days ago, one side had a letter from Hunt. Mrs. Richards called on your sister nine days ago, and gave the good account you had then written of yourself. When I hear you are cheerily again, she shall again hear of you. All our friends in common are well. John Scott's death has made some noise, and seems to threaten Mrs. Christie and the seconds seriously; they certainly behaved most foolishly. What is melancholy, and almost incomprehensible, is that Mrs. Scott advertizes for a subscription. Hazlitt is to be chief man of the 'London Magazine,' Hunt will likewise write for it; he has put a stop to his 'Indicator.' I have not yet seen Haydon's 'Agony in the Garden;' it does not appear to create a very great enthusiasm, some find fault with it for being a little melodramatic. It is surely a great mistake to represent Judas as a palpable villain in his countenance, which I understand he has done in the extreme; he ought to possess a good taking face, one whom an honest man might trust. There, I have given you a page of chitchat, such as it is.

"God love you, my dear fellow, and believe me ever

"Yours sincerely,

"CHARLES BROWN."

This letter, one of interest and value, was not written immediately on receipt of Severn's (as indicated in an early passage), but about five days later and in time for the Italian mail. The next letter given here, that from Mr. Taylor, has also special interest, particularly for students of Keats's ' Life ' in its fullest details.

"London,
"3rd April, 1821.

" My dear Sir,
"Your first interesting letter since our dear friend's death has just reached me, but I was previously aware of the melancholy issue of this deplorable trial to which you have been subjected, by your short letter to Brown about three weeks ago. To us here who had sympathised most sincerely with you in all our poor friend's afflictions, it really came like a relief at last to hear that all was over . . . . . You will greatly oblige me by continuing to relate as often as you can find time and inclination, any particulars of our friend's life and conversation, giving me as nearly as possible the identical words used by him. I have been requested by several of our friends to write a short account of his life, and for this purpose the most valuable of my materials will be those communications which you are able to make me. Did you ever remember my wish to have a portrait of him? I hope you have one for me.

"That which Mr. Brown has is an admirable likeness, and will do better than any perhaps to engrave from, but as a picture I would rather have a sketch in anything taken from the life than a copy merely. If there are any papers left by our poor friend which you think will be interesting, please to take care of them, as well as of his books. In a little *will,* or memorandum of what he wished to be done after his death, which he sent me in a letter previous to leaving Hampstead, and which, so far at least as this one particular goes, constitutes me a kind of executor, he desired me to divide his books among his friends, and states in which order his debts are to be paid if ever there should be money forthcoming to discharge them. I have written to George to ask him for some of that money which John lent him. In the meantime I was compelled to try among a few friends here to raise money after that was gone, which we proposed to advance. Five of those who had seen poor Keats sufficiently to feel much interest for him have told me to apply to them for £10 each whenever it is wanted, and the Earl Fitzwilliam, to whom I wrote on the same subject, sent me £50. For this £100 you will please to draw if you have not done it already. Should it prove enough to defray the expenses of the funeral, &c., and to repay the kind Dr. Clark, I shall be very glad. When I wrote to you before on this subject, I did not state how this money was to be collected, for fear of poor Keats being aware of the circumstance, and I knew it would so hurt his feeling as to accelerate his death. I have told George of the manner in which it has been raised,

and I hope he will enable me to retu[rn it]. Reynolds, I find, did not
send the £50 after all. I did not know that till very lately; he wrote
[to me of his] desire Keats would draw upon him for that sum. [You]
will oblige me by sending me an account of what is still owing beyond
what the £100 above mentioned will enable you to pay . . . . . Will you
make me a drawing of the spot where Keats is buried? And the mask,
hand and foot will you also send me?

"Believe me, my dear sir,
"Your truly obliged and sincere friend,
"JOHN TAYLOR."

This letter might easily be taken as in some respects
unwarrantable, but an unprejudiced judge would probably
exonerate Mr. Taylor from any underhandedness, as
Brown and others persisted at a later date in asserting
of him.

As to the request to Severn, begging him at his convenience, and if not disinclined, to send all particulars of
Keats's life and conversation, there is of course nothing to be
said, except that Taylor had full right to make it if he saw
fit. He had no right to expect compliance, of course, and
good taste would prevent his insistence upon his claims to
be the biographer of Keats if any of the friends of longer
standing who had been nearer and dearer to the poet had
announced his intention of writing a biography. But the
request, such as it was, and in the circumstances, was certainly
not an inexcusable liberty. No doubt Taylor honestly
believed that he was as able as any one else to write a good
biography or short memoir of the poet whom he thought he
knew so much more intimately than he really did; and in
any case he may be credited with an unselfish wish to preserve everything relating to Keats, and not least effectively
by warning Severn, whose happy-go-lucky nature he probably knew, and of whose careless memory he had possibly
some acquaintance. But as to his having been requested
by several friends to write an account of Keats's life—this
is probably mere fiction. It is, at any rate, scarcely likely
that any other than his partner, Mr. Hessey, suggested his
taking this task upon himself. Again, however, in justice
to Taylor, it must be noted that he alludes to the writing of

a short account only—perhaps, at most, for an article in some important magazine, and possibly only with intent to put together a *mémoire pour servir*, invaluable to the biographer to be. Further, the fact that Keats had in some measure appointed him "a kind of executor," would naturally seem to him to warrant his application to Severn.

It is pleasant to know that Keats's dear friend, John Hamilton Reynolds, set aside £50 from his not very ample means for the relief of the invalid, if necessary, though, with characteristic carelessness, he omitted to remit the draft.

As to the news of personal import to Severn, he was greatly encouraged and stimulated by learning that Mr. Hilton, the Academician, believed he had a good chance of obtaining the foreign pension ; and he determined to go on at once and with all expedition upon his ' Alcibiades ' picture.

Yet even when several weeks had succeeded the quiet funeral of one of the foremost poets of England, Severn was unable to recur to the subject of Keats's death without emotion.   Writing to his mother to reassure her about his health and way of living, he says :—

"Thank God, I have perfectly recovered my health, for it had suffered. I am now better and stronger than ever I was. This place, the manner of living, everything seems to agree with me. I don't know how it is, but the example of poor Keats has made me take great care of myself. Including the time spent at my meals, I walk two or three hours every day, paint eight hours, and read two, or study Italian. Have you now, my dear mother, any cause to fret about my coming here? If I go on as I do now, you will *not* very soon have me back again. Did I not think the good God above would never let me suffer for serving my poor friend ? Poor Keats, I cannot get him out of my head, and never shall out of my heart, never ! I often drop a tear to his memory. You ask me word about him, but he must have been dead and buried before Maria wrote. His case was real consumption. His lungs were entirely destroyed. I cannot write anything about my poor friend's death. I cannot bear to think of it."

CHAPTER V.

Keats-reminiscences—"The Death of Alcibiades," and other Art-work—
Wm. Ewing, Seymour Kirkup, and Sir Geo. Beaumont—Chas. East-
lake—*Keatsiana*—Letters from Severn and Taylor—Letter from Charles
Brown—Brown's reasons for opposing Taylor—Severn gains the travel-
ling-pension—Severn and Samuel Rogers—Reminiscences of Shelley—
Shelley's influence on Keats—Shelley, Keats, and Severn—The
' Adonais ' Preface—Edward Trelawny—Burial of Shelley's ashes.

In his diaries, his several ' Reminiscences,' and again
and again in his letters, Severn gratefully acknowledges
the great change for the better wrought in his fortunes
through the circumstance of his having accompanied Keats
to Italy, and there so long and unselfishly ministered to
him.

When his friend had been laid in the grave and he found
himself alone in Rome, with no friends except Dr. and
Mrs. Clark and Mr. Ewing, with painfully uncertain prospects, and with scarce any money in hand, his courage
almost failed him. At one time he thought of obtaining a
loan from one or other of his English friends, for the purpose
of returning to London, where he could at any rate support
himself by miniature-painting. Then came the strongest
disinclination to leave the city which he already loved so
well, and which had for him so many tender associations, and
where, moreover, he had opportunities of study and self-
improvement in Art such as he could not have in London.

But scarcely had he recovered from the prostration to
which for several days after Keats's funeral he succumbed—
and for a week at least he seems to have been dangerously
weak and feverish, during which period he was constantly
visited by Dr. Clark as a friend, and supplied by Mrs. Clark
with various delicacies, while he was saved from all other
worry and responsibility by the hospital-nurse whom the

kindly physician had obtained for the young painter in whom he was so interested—scarcely had he pulled himself together to renew the struggle of life when he found to his surprise and pleasure that the tide had already turned, and that, with care and tact, he might be able to stay for a time, and possibly prosper sufficiently to reside permanently in Rome.

"After the death of Keats," he says, "my countrymen in Rome seemed to vie with one another in evincing the greatest kindness towards me. I found myself in the midst of persons who admired and encouraged my beautiful pursuit of painting, in which I was then a very poor student, but with my eyes opening and my soul awakening to a new region of art, and beginning to feel the wings growing for artistic flights I had always been dreaming about. In all this, however, there was a solitary drawback; there were few Englishmen at Rome who knew Keats's works, and I could scarcely persuade any one to make the effort to read them, such was the prejudice against him as a poet. . . . 'Here lies one whose name was writ in water, *and his works in milk and water*'—this I was condemned to hear for years repeated, as though it had been a pasquinade; but I should explain it was from those who were not aware that I was the friend of Keats."

Severn now set himself to work in earnest at his picture, 'The Death of Alcibiades,' with which he hoped to win name and fortune, and their first practical manifestation, "the travelling pension."

He had now gone to reside at No. 18 Via di San Isidoro —though there, at first at any rate, he had no studio.

With the advent of summer* only one of his acquaintances remained behind indifferent to the warnings of the hot weather, Mr. Campbell the sculptor. This gentleman had been left in charge of the studio of Charles Eastlake,

---

* Early in May, William Ewing left Rome for England, and Severn gave him the following note to Charles Brown:—"I have great pleasure in introducing to you this gentleman—Mr. William Ewing—for his kind services to our poor Keats and myself. Altho' we came here strangers to him, he gave us all the attention of an old friend, and that of the most valuable kind. . . . I had no other soul to help me. Except Dr. Clark and myself, he saw more of Keats than any one—he will inform you on many points, as yet, too dreadful for me to write. I am still compleatly unnerved when I look upon poor Keats's death; it still hangs upon me like a horrible dream. You will find this gentleman to possess extraordinary skill as a Sculptor—his works in ivory are to me the most beautiful things of the kind I ever saw."

who had left Rome with the intention of not returning till
the following winter. Acting with brotherly friendli-
ness, he installed Severn in the large and almost wholly
unutilized studio. Here 'Alcibiades' proceeded to die
dramatically with all due expedition, and all was going well
and quietly (particularly as the young painter had received
a note from Mr. Howard, the Secretary of the Academy, to
tell him that he had no competitors, there having been no
gold-medallists for several years past, and that all he had
to do was to send a painting of an historical kind by a
specified date), when news came that Eastlake was about to
return to Rome.

"I had to quit, almost 'with my tail between my legs,' for Mr. Campbell
was severely reproved for thus letting a stranger into the *sanctum sanc-
torum;* but in a short time Eastlake became friendly. I returned to my
lodging in the S. Isidoro, where I was able to finish my 'Alcibiades,' which
had been for me a great effort. I had nominally ended my work upon it
by the beginning of May, but as there was, as I understood, no hurry for it
to be sent off, I kept it by me for a little to rework upon."

Referring to the comparatively lonely months of March
and April, he writes in 'Incidents of My Life':

"And, perhaps, I too might have been cut off like Keats, for my health
was but very indifferent; but I had the help and the consolation of my
new picture, and was fortunately able to abstract myself with it. Then
the early execution of it was imperative, as my future well-being in art—
indeed, my very existence—depended thereupon; so that the necessity of
hard and continuous work not only occupied my mind, but fed and nursed
my melancholy spirit. Then the magic charms and all the enchantment
of spring at Rome soothed me, when I was not painting, into poetic delights.
It was a miracle of nature such as I had never even dreamed of; for it
seemed to me when I wandered out in the early morning that I could almost
see the wild flowers grow—such progress they made in a single day. There
was endless pleasure for me in watching the contrasts with the old antique
walls and marbles of all this vegetation in its Italian abundance of brilliant
freshness and perpetual novelty. All this had the most wonderful effect
in restoring me to health, but might not have been effective had not another
unlooked-for ally arrested my feeble step and helped both my painting and
my loving understanding of nature, for I was soon awakened to a still
higher aspect of nature, 'where dawns the high expression of a mind.'
The Englishmen and English ladies who now crossed my path were of
an order much higher and more intellectual than any I had been acquainted with before. There was an ease and elegance in their manners
and ideas that most singularly accorded with the beautiful aspects of nature

that were then constantly disclosing themselves to me. These accomplished ladies and gentlemen now often crossed my path and offered me their sympathy and friendly aids in all the gentle offices of life, as well as the essential. The death of Keats, although he was unknown, and my devoted friendship, had become a kind of passport to the English in Rome, and I soon found myself in the midst of not only the most polished society, but perhaps the most Christian in the world, I mean in the sense of humanity, of cheerfulness, of living rather for others than ourselves. This was a 'treasure-trove' to me as a young artist, invaluable, as it was my introduction to my future patrons, and the foundation of those valuable and lasting friendships which not only extended through my first lonely Italian sojourn, but has become the inheritance of my children."

The chief friend who brought about this change was Seymour Kirkup, to whom Severn had been introduced by William Ewing at Keats's grave on the day of the funeral. He was at once an artist and a most accomplished and excellent man. Moreover, he had the means wherewith to indulge his love for rare and beautiful things, and he did indulge in a true and generous spirit.

" To him even more than to Dr. Clark I was indebted for my introduction to the leading English then in Rome, and particularly to Lord and Lady Ruthven, the Countess of Westmoreland, and Lord William Russell, who all delighted me with their love and understanding of art, and who opened to me so many new sources of information and progress. They invited me to charming parties, *al fresco* dinners (for the season was advancing), rural excursions to the neighbouring villas, to the Campagna, and the hill-resorts about Rome. . . . . Then there were excavations and a perpetual round of intellectual novelties, to me the source of all I was aiming at. And when it is considered how great were my gains in thus suddenly coming across numbers of individuals who knew more about art than I did—many of whom, moreover, made me valuable presents of books, prints, casts, &c.—it will be allowed that I was very fortunate. All this was the more agreeable to me as I was conscious that I had achieved little to merit it. . . . By the time of their departure by the end of May I was sufficiently recovered to be able to endure my own society, and even to enjoy my existence in the new delightful symptoms of returning health, and to find my pencil moving gaily and with artistic enthusiasm. . . . I stayed a week at Tivoli with Sir George and Lady Beaumont " (*Vide* p. 114, *post*), " and had the pleasure of his conversation the whole time. He was always recurring to the great artistic days which had passed. His accounts of Gainsborough, Romney, Lady Hamilton, Nelson, and so forth, were delightful, but all were made to centre round the pivot of Sir Joshua Reynolds, who was the top of his admiration, both as a man and an artist. . . . . I used at times stop to regret that poor dear Keats was not alive to participate in these scenes. What a world would have been open to him. Boy-poet as he was, he would have soon risen into the philosopher. . . . . His illness and death were pioneered by despair. He was hurried down a sea of troubles to death."

Severn contentedly enough made up his mind to a summer in Rome. Several of his friends urged him not to do so foolish a thing as to remain throughout the hot months; but he had not the wherewithal to take up summer quarters, and, with his very uncertain prospects, did not care to saddle himself with even the least burdensome of debts. Before the end of July, however, he recognised the advisability of a change to the neighbouring hill-country. Before he left Rome, he wrote to Charles Brown:

"You see on the approach of the hot and dangerous weather I shall be obliged to go away, and that without placing a stone on poor Keats's grave. All his papers I have sent to you, packed for safety in a box of divers things belonging to my old friend and master Mr. Bond. I chose this from many as the safest way—they will arrive in London about August or September. Mr. Taylor has written me of his intention to write some remembrances of our Keats. This is a kind thought of his, and I reverence this good man—nothing can be more interesting than to have the beautiful character of Keats described and appreciated. If it can be made known to the English, his memory will be cherished by them, not more for his genius than for his English nature. I begin to think of him without pain —all the harsh horror of his death is fast subsiding from my mind. Sometimes a delightful glance of his life about the time when I first knew him will take possession of me and keep me speculating on and on to some passage in the 'Endymion.' (I am fortunate to have a copy of this—it is Dr. Clark's—the last also.) Here I find many admirers—aye, real ones— of his poetry. This is a very great pleasure to me. I have many most agreeable conversations about him—but that only with classical scholars. The 'Lamia' is the greatest favourite. I have been most sadly harassed about my picture for the Royal Academy, for this reason—I have received notice to send it by the 10th of August. Now, this is a month sooner than I expected . . . so that I have sent it unfinished without any delay. Now, this has been an unfortunate point, more particularly as I am ill, out of spirits, and friendless—most of the kind fellows here have gone to Naples or elsewhere—so that I am left to brood over the loss of poor Keats's company, and above all his advice.

"You will recollect, my dear Brown, a mention of me (not with the greatest kindness or charity), at Mr. Hilton's house. Keats spoke several times of this with very great pain, from the fear that something of the same spirit might keep back my pension. He told me it was one of the

meanest said things he ever knew, and at the same time made me promise
that I would explain to Mr. Taylor the whole affair—that I would write
in such a manner as to persuade Mr. Taylor to use his greatest influence in
my behalf with Mr. Hilton. He said: 'I am sure Hilton will take up
your case on my account. Now promise me you will do this. I have been
long brooding over it, and think this damned H. will keep you without
your pension—or try to do so—I know he will—so that this cursed dying
of mine will have been to your loss.' This was but a short time before his
death. I have written to Mr. Taylor about my present concern, but not of
the affair past—I have still thought it better not mentioned—nor would
I say about it now, but it seems hard I must run the risk of my picture's
non-arrival in time from the notice sent me by Hilton. Keats foresaw most
keenly, and his words come strong upon me. [Now] How, my dear Brown,
shall I do in this? . . . Above all things pray answer [*paper torn*] letters.
Tell me how the sad finish of poor Keats affected his enemies—tell me
about his friends—tell me about Miss B. I have been once or twice almost
writing to her. Only think, my dear Brown, I have known nothing from
England since poor Keats's death—O, yes, one very kind letter from Mr.
Taylor, which I answered. Haslam does not write me. . . . I have likewise got in [hand] a small whole-length of my poor Keats; it is from a
recollection of him at your house, I think the last time I saw him there—
he was reading, the book on his knee."

Late in August he heard from Mr. Taylor about his
missing 'Alcibiades,' and concerning certain Keats details.

"On the subject of a gravestone for our poor friend, I said something in
a letter to Dr. Clark, which was to serve as an introduction of Mr. Horace
Smith to him, but the dread of being in Rome in the hot weather will
probably prevent Mr. Smith from delivering it till Xmas, and therefore
this letter will possibly arrive the first. I find by your letter to Mr. Haslam
that you have designed a tomb in the form of a Grecian altar, with a lyre,
&c. This is said to be executing, I think, by some English sculptor, but
you want an inscription. I can conceive none better than our poor friend's
melancholy sentiment, 'Here lies one whose name was writ in water.' It
is very simple and affecting, and tells so much of the story that none need
be told. Neither name nor date is requisite. These will be given in his
life by his biographer. So, unless something else is determined on, let this
line stand alone. I foresee that it will be as clear an indication to posterity
as the plainest, every-day inscription that one may find in Westminster
Abbey. I imagine the expense will not be great at Rome. You must
excuse me that I have not replied sooner to your letter on this latter subject. I am harassed beyond my strength by a multitude of different
avocations which not only take up all my time, but rob me of all inclination to write even a letter. I shall be very glad to receive the portrait, &c.,
of poor Keats. In the course of the winter I hope to get on with the
Memoir."

When he wrote this, Taylor had quite made up his mind to be Keats's biographer, and clearly relied upon Severn's collaboration. Severn, however, with wise and generous discretion, instead of yielding to Taylor's importunities, thought of the likeliest course which Keats would wish, and sent the most valuable literary remains to Brown. This and other episodes are alluded to in the latter's letter, the first part of which is occupied with what the writer has to say concerning the missing picture, and Severn's fluctuating chances in the matter of the " travelling pension."

" As affairs stand," he concludes, " look to the worst. Believe that your pension is lost, and if the contrary happens to be the case, it will be a joy. And supposing it to be lost, let it not fret you. Take heart, and laugh at an irreparable misfortune. I would do so were it my own case, better than if it were my friend's. Place your regret chiefly on the disappointment of others, and, surely, with your abilities, you can put your shoulder cheerfully to the wheel, and retrieve the loss. I am a fit one to give you comfort on this score. Over and over again have I to Keats and others lamented your reliance on a band of Academicians, where there is nothing but envy, jealousy, intrigues, and squabbles, in preference to the pursuit of the art on your own account, independently, and at freedom from all conventional laws. The English like to be flattered, but in fact they are not enthusiasts in art,—they neither understand it, nor are they generous enough to reward a man during his life. Can you not read a lesson in the fate of our unhappy Keats? The English are too proud and selfish to acknowledge living merit in art and literature. If you continue to study portraits, both in miniature and in oil, crowds will be led by vanity to your door, and you be rich and at ease in your mind; but if you were to paint a work like the ' Transfiguration,' lo! now—you must be poor in purse, and (what is worse) poor in spirit, and kick your heels in a great man's antechamber, and be fevered thro' your life with broils and anxieties. Look to facts. Who has succeeded in historical painting since Sir J. Reynolds? None, save West, and he most undeservedly. I repeat, the English understand it not. Think of this, my dear Severn—think of the choice you are now to make. Do not let hopes destroy your happiness. What was Sir T. Lawrence's advice? Truly, it was wise. You are now the best miniature-painter we have. This is no compliment; you know it yourself. Still, you need not debar yourself from the pursuit of the historical,—only make portraits your sheet-anchor for profit, and when your purse is swollen, sit down for awhile to the other. I could write a quire full on this theme—but enough.

" *14th Aug.*—If my memory does not deceive me, I have sent three letters since I received your last; one of them had a page filled by Leigh Hunt; none of them, however, is of late date. Mr. Ewing has not yet called, nor sent the letter from you which, I understand, is in his hands; I shall be glad to see him. You asked Mr. Taylor to consult with me about Keats's epitaph—or, I believe, to let you know what epitaph I wished. He did not allow me to see that letter for a long time; I then talked to him about it, and he behaved as if he thought it was no concern of mine, changing the topic as soon as he could. It was not till the other day that I discovered he bears me no goodwill for claiming, in return for MSS. and information, a sight of his memoir before it went to press. I confess I could not trust him entirely; now and then he is a mere bookseller—somewhat vain of his talents, and consequently self-willed. My anxiety for poor Keats's fame compelled me to make this request; for, in my opinion, Taylor neither comprehended him nor his poetry. I shall always be the first to acknowledge Taylor's kindness to Keats; but towards me his conduct has been ungracious and even unmannerly. Reynolds is the secret spring; it is wished he should shine as the dear friend of poor Keats—(at least I suspect so)—when the fact is, he was no dear friend to Keats, nor did Keats think him so.* This, however, might be borne, but there are other points where I fear Taylor may do Keats an injustice—not knowingly, but from the want of knowing his character. He has sent no answer to my yesterday's note. Either by the next or the next but one post I will write again, and give you my ideas of an epitaph for our beloved Keats. The health of every one of your family is excellent, but they are sadly perplexed about this R.A. business. Mr. Bond sends his remembrances, and desired me to say his brother is in better health, and will soon arrive here from Paris. Richards is well, and asks continually about you; I shall insist upon his writing. I thank you for intrusting me with Keats's papers—the sight of them will renew many painful thoughts. My next-door neighbours are quite well; Miss Brawne had been growing (I thought alarmingly) thin, but of late she has looked more cheerful and better. I delivered your messages to them, and they sent some of the same nature. Do not imagine I am in a peevish mood about Taylor; to give my aid to a thing of so momentous a description as the fame of Keats without being satisfied on every point is more than I can do in duty to the memory of the dearest friend I ever had. Still I promised Taylor my aid, provided I might be allowed to approve or condemn in particular passages, which he assented to, and praised my solicitude; but lately I have heard that having got the chief things from me, he resolved to laugh at my opinion. I am afraid it will be made a job—a mere trading job—and *that* I will lend no hand to, further than what I have done. You must feel with me that I should be culpable, as Keats's friend, even to run a risk. If Taylor choose,

---

* This is a new light upon the friendship of Keats and Reynolds. Brown seems to have been prejudiced against Reynolds, and so may have written rashly: on the other hand, he was not the man to hint at disagreements where none existed. If he wrote with assured knowledge, there need be no further regrets that Reynolds did not undertake the biography of Keats. The general drift of evidence, however, points to some misapprehension on the part of Brown.

on my conditious (which he himself has approved of) my assistance will be
given most willingly.   I heard yesterday that Clark is thinking of writing
a memoir—to tell the truth, I would rather join him, but at present I am
(conditionally) bound.*   God bless you, my dear Severn.

" Yours truly,
"Chas. Brown."

On September 19th Severn replied to this and Brown's
next letter (August 21st).

" Why, my dear Brown, what sad affair is this?   I know not what to
say in it, except this, that you are the only one to write Keats's Memoir—
at least to describe his character.   I have the greatest respect for the talent
and good heart of Mr. Taylor—his exertions for poor Keats when all was
hopeless—the publication of his books, &c., set him down as a most noble
friend—[that] he loved Keats is certain, to have made all these sacrifices,
but did not feel the delicacy of his mind.   I hope and trust you will reconcile this dispute.   It seems to me your seeing the memoir is the only way
to compleat it—that Mr. Taylor's and your own idea of Keats's character
will be compleat, but certainly not one without the other. · I would say
consult Richards too—he was inferior to no one in the estimation of Keats.
He will give some valuable scraps.   Keats's genius and character must
make a most beautiful book, as a book alone—not in making a compleat
poet, or even comparing him to others, but in describing and tracing the
progress of Genius from nature to art, and then to their union.   I can see
all this with immense pleasure.   I can recollect him before he had that
delicate perception for art, when he talked and felt only nature—and I can
recollect his knowledge of art to have been greater than any one *I* ever
knew.   Then his English nature is a subject most grateful.   I don't know
whether to prefer his heart or his soul—but pardon me ; I can only think
of him and paint him.   You must not ask me for contributions for this
work, except it be from my painting.   I am not master of words to show
what I feel or think.   I recollect a point which may be known to you,
perhaps.   Keats mentioned to me many times in our voyage his desire to
write the story of Sabrina, and to have connected it with some points in
the English history and character.   He would sometimes brood over it with
immense enthusiasm, and recite the story from Milton's ' Comus ' in a
manner that I will remember to the end of my days.   Do you [know] the
sonnet beginning—

' Bright star, would I were stedfast as thou art ! '

He wrote this down in the ship—it is one of his most beautiful things.   I
will send it, if you have it not—at present I have lent the book in which
he wrote it, or I would send it.   Why how singular that none of you can
lament out his Epitaph.   I agree with you that more should [be] written

---

* It is not clear whether Brown wrote *Clark* or *Clarke*, but his
allusion is to the memoir projected by Charles Cowden Clarke.

than the line he desired. This morning my friend and myself visited poor Keats's grave. It is still covered with grass and flowers, and remains quiet and undisturbed. The place where he lies is one of the most romantic I know—but I won't send you my bungling descriptions, but I will send a small picture of it. On our return home I thought of another ' record ' to him—a Greek seat, with his solitary lyre standing against it, but I will draw it. You see this is a seat vacant, such as the Greeks used in their [*paper torn*]. It would say—Here is his seat and his lyre, but [*paper torn*] not beneath. Tell me how you like this. I am delighted with it.'

A week later Brown wrote again to Severn, and still without good news of the missing picture. The main interest in the letter is what it has to say concerning the vexed question as to Keats's biographer.

"When I mentioned to you my fears about Mr. Taylor's memoir, I omitted to make known the original cause of those fears. It was this. Immediately on receipt of your letter announcing poor Keats's death, almost in the same newspapers where there was a notice of his death, even before Mrs. Brawne's family and myself had got our mourning, in those very newspapers was advertised ' speedily will be published, a biographical memoir of the late John Keats, &c.,' and I, among others, was applied to by Reynolds to collect with all haste, papers, letters, and so on, in order to assist Mr. Taylor. This indecent bustle over (as it were) the newly covered grave of my dear friend shocked me excessively. I told Mr. Taylor it looked as if his friends had been collecting information about his life in expectation of his death. This, indeed, was the fact. I believe I spoke warmly, and probably gave offence. However, as I was jealous of my own feelings upon such a subject, I took the precaution to sound those of Hunt, Dilke, and Richards, who were all equally hurt with myself at such an indecorous haste. I then came to this conclusion, that Messrs. Taylor and Reynolds, who could show such a want of feeling at such a moment, ought not to be confided in by me unreservedly, and since I came to that conclusion, I have had cause to believe myself correct. I will not consent to be a party in a bookseller's job. Perhaps it may turn out otherwise, but in justice to the memory of Keats, I dare not run a risk. Mr. Taylor expected to be trusted implicitly, and takes dudgeon. Now, on such a point I know of none whom I could trust implicitly. He says no one understood Keats's character so well as himself; if so, I who knew him tolerably well, and others of his friends, greatly mistook him, judging from what has dropped from Mr. Taylor—for he is one from whom things *drop* —he cannot utter them boldly and honestly, at least he never did to me, and I have heard Keats say the same of him. What I have written, I have written, and I leave you to judge if you think me right or wrong. I rejoice you sent *me* the papers, and under the circumstances, I think you will rejoice likewise. He is welcome, according to *my* promise, to any information I can afford, provided he, according to *his* promise, allows me a voice on the occasion. In my opinion, Taylor would rather decline the information. If you differ from me in my claim of having a voice, still I have Dilke, Richards, and Hunt on my side. Hunt has some poems, &c., of Keats, and offers them unreservedly to *me*, stipulating, however, that Taylor must not be possessed of them without the memoirs passing under my eye. Why should it be denied to me? Any sort of hesitation will make the business suspicious. Hunt was very kind to Keats last summer, and I cannot forget it. If Keats could not like his wife, that is nothing to the purpose. . . . .

"I had written thus far on 21st, expecting every minute a knock by Hunt at the door with an epitaph for Keats. He did not come till the evening, and then with an apology, promising, however, to let me have it on the following post-day (Friday last), and then he again disappointed me. I can wait no longer, but am resolved to send you this letter without it. Why, you will ask, set Hunt about this affair? The truth is, I have tried, but can do nothing for the epitaph to my own satisfaction, and Hunt is one, if I am not mistaken, who could word it with feeling and elegance. He has sadly disappointed me, but the trouble he is in must be his excuse. I like your idea of the lyre with broken strings. Mr. Taylor sets his face against that, and against any words except what Keats himself desired to be put on his tombstone, viz.: 'Here lies one whose name was writ in water.' This I contend is scarcely proper, insomuch as an epitaph must necessarily be considered as the act of the deceased's friends and not of the deceased himself. Still, in obedience to his (Keats) will, I would have his own words engraven there, and *not* his name, letting the stranger read the cause of his friend's placing such words as 'Here lies one, &c.,' somewhat in the following manner :—'This grave contains all that was mortal of a young English poet, who, on his death-bed, in bitter anguish at the neglect of his countrymen, desired these words to be engraven on his tomb-stone: "HERE LIES ONE WHOSE NAME WAS WRIT IN WATER."' * Something expressive of this, and surmounted by your emblem of a Grecian lyre, I think would be proper. But mind, I am not satisfied with *my* wording, and therefore pray delay the epitaph for a while. If, however, you are of the same opinion as Mr. Taylor, I give up mine instantly. I find it a difficult subject. Two or three days ago Richards called. He and family are very well. He was in the midst of a long letter to you. . . . ."

Even by the end of September there was no word of the missing picture. At the beginning of October he heard from William Ewing: a long letter full of pleasant gossip of temporary interest. One sentence may be quoted :—"I called with your letter on Mr. Brown, at Hampstead, who

* Many years later Brown regretted he had even to this extent advised anything beyond strict adherence to Keats's own words. (*Vide* his letter of 26th November, 1836, *post*, p. 178.)

received me very kindly. I have dined with him twice; he appears a very friendly man. He procured me a sight of your miniature of poor Mr. Keats, and I really think it the best performance I ever saw. It is admirable."

When September and the greater part of October had passed, and there were still no comforting tidings about the unfortunate canvas which was to have won for the artist the coveted travelling-pension, of which he stood in urgent need, Severn began to lose hope either of the picture turning up at all, or of his success with the Council, though now and again he solaced himself with the belief that "friends at Court" would accomplish what his own efforts would never achieve. About the end of the month he wrote to his sister Sarah : "Tell father I have heard in answer to Lady Westmorland's letter to Sir Thos. Lawrence, and most favourably of the Council towards myself. She says I am sure of the most kind treatment. I have just discovered I have the Marquis of Anglesea speaking for me, and many other powerful individuals, so that [in any event] I shall be no loser. . . . . . I am now occupied on a miniature of Lady Westmorland, and for the finishing of it I am going with her ladyship to Civita Vecchia, about thirty miles from Rome."

At last one day a search at the Royal Academy was ordered, "and a tin case, all bent double and without any direction or intimation as to whom it belonged, was found. It was opened, and lo, my 'Dying Alcibiades'!"

The Council had postponed its decision till the end of November, and no doubt at the final meeting the vicissitudes of the picture and the artist's sore tribulation about its fate—backed up by the influential recommendations to which allusion has already been made—had distinct effect in bringing the Academicians to a decision altogether favourable to Severn. They not only awarded him the pension of £130 annually for three years, and intimated that it would date from the 1st (of the preceding) August, but also remitted a draft in payment of the sum he had expended in going to Rome. It was a welcome Christmas card, for he received it on December 25th.

I

But before leaving this ever-memorable year of 1821, there are one or two important things in Severn's life to chronicle. As far as may be, the words of the artist's Journals shall be given intact.

"In the spring I became acquainted with a person of great interest to me; this was the famous amateur artist, Sir George Beaumont. I was making an oil sketch at the Capitol from Rubens' 'Romulus and Remus,' and doing it with outrageous boldness that I might try to rectify my great want. He spoke to me and admired my daub most indulgently, and told me who he was, and talked charmingly of Sir Joshua Reynolds and his contemporaries, all of whom he had known personally. He told me about Reynolds' art, how he painted, how many hours, and indeed everything I asked him, and finished by inviting me to dine with him, telling me that he expected Mr. Samuel Rogers amongst his guests. I was as greatly pleased at this kind compliment as I was at the manner of it. Although our acquaintance was so sudden, and without the least introduction, he spoke with so much ease, and had such a lively, benevolent expression of countenance, that I was lost to the value of the incident in the actual fascination of it. At dinner the subject of Keats's death and misfortunes were discussed, and I became aware for the first time that these were very well known, and the continued source of conversation, although both Keats and myself were personally unknown. Mr. Rogers ventured to say that he believed he had been twice applied to by Keats for money, and that there were so many of these needy poetic aspirants that he could only shut his door. This made me flare up, as I knew it was a falsehood, or a mistake; so I asked him more particularly, but he stuck to his point that it was Keats himself; and then I opened upon him, and indirectly showed him the slanderous way of talking he was indulging in, and that Keats was not only far removed from such 'uncanny acts,' as he called them, but also that he had no occasion, having been in possession of a small competence; and I finished by expressing my regret that one poet should thus speak of another, and appealed to Sir George Beaumont's generosity, who had that very day spoken to me at the Capitol and invited me to dine only because I was also a 'pittore.' Mr. Rogers felt the reproof, made me ample apology on the ground of carelessness, and became ever after a most attached friend."

Elsewhere Severn gives another account of this now celebrated meeting, effectually convincing even the staunchest of Rogers's admirers, who affected to discredit the truth of the rumours which spread abroad concerning his disparaging remarks about Keats.*

---

* In 'The Vicissitudes of Keats's Fame' (*vide The Atlantic Monthly* for 1863).

"I soon discovered," adds Severn, "that it was the principle of Mr. Rogers' sarcastic wit not only to sacrifice all truth to it, but even all his friends, and that he did not care to know any who would not allow themselves to be abused for the purpose of lighting up his breakfast with sparkling wit, though not quite, indeed, at the expense of the persons then present. I well remember, on one occasion afterwards, Mr. Rogers was entertaining us with a volley of sarcasms upon a disagreeable lawyer, who made pretensions to knowledge and standing not to be borne; on this occasion the old poet went on, not only to the end of the breakfast, but to the announcement of the very man himself on an accidental visit, and then, with a bland smile and a cordial shake of the hand, he said to him, ' My dear fellow, we have all been talking about you up to this very minute;' and looking at his company still at table, and with a significant wink, he, with extraordinary adroitness and experienced tact, repeated many of the good things, reversing the meaning of them, and giving us the enjoyment of the *double entendre*. The visitor was charmed, nor even dreamed of the ugliness of his position. This incident gave me a painful and repugnant impression of Mr. Rogers, yet no doubt it was after the manner of his time, and such as had been the fashion in Walpole's and Johnson's days.

"I should be unjust to the venerable poet not to add that, notwithstanding what is here related of him, he oftentimes showed himself the generous and noble-hearted man. I think that in all my long acquaintance with him he evinced a kind of indirect regret that he had commenced with me in such an ugly attack on dear Keats, whose fame, when I went to England, in 1838, was not only well established, but was increasing from day to day; and Mr. Rogers was often at the pains to tell me so, and to relate the many histories of poets who had been less fortunate than Keats."

It was at the first advent of winter, and at a time when Severn had begun to fear that the fame of Keats, such as it was, was about to be eclipsed, that he was deeply affected by Shelley's magnificent tribute to his fellow-poet and by the unexpected dedicatory eulogy of himself. At that time he knew little of Shelley's work, and did not take any real interest in the poet, for, like most of his contemporaries who were aware of Shelley's existence, he was prejudiced against "the atheistical writer and licentious man," as it was the vogue to call the rarest singer of the age.

In his annotations on some MS. selections from the ' Adonais,' after the lines—

> "Why linger, why turn back, why shrink, my heart?
> Thy hopes are gone before: from all things here
> They have departed; thou should'st now depart"—

I 2

he writes :*

"I first became known to Shelley in 1817, through Leigh Hunt. The poet's fine presence is still vividly before me: his tall, elegant, but slender figure: his countenance painfully intellectual, inasmuch as it showed [traces of his] struggle with humanity, and betrayed the abstract gift of a high mind in little relation with the world. His restless blue eyes seemed to dwell more on the inward than the outward aspect of nature. His manner, aristocratic though gentle, aided his personal beauty. Fine, classical features, luxuriant brown hair, and a slightly ruddy complexion, combined with his unconsciousness of his attractive appearance, added to his fine exterior. He expressed himself in subdued accents, which commanded attention from their select mental character."

The remark about Shelley's "classical" features, and still more that about his "subdued accents" in conversation, afford interesting evidence at first hand to set against the statements that have been made as to the irregularity of the poet's features, and as to his shrill and almost strident voice.

"The common charge against him of moral unworthiness," Severn resumes, "I cannot but think was very unjust. But it was the tendency of the time, and the charge attached itself to all liberals who strove to fight with the conservative party. I remember with pleasure a remark on Shelley's cruel fate made me by the late Lord Chancellor, Lord St. Leonards, that he thought Lord Eldon was in error in taking away Shelley's children, when he could so easily have conciliated the fond father through various literary men—whereas the act of deprivation drove the poet to utter despair, who finished by attacking religion itself instead of the Chancellor. I can judge clearly on this, as Shelley, in our first interview, went out of his way to attack me on my Christian creed.† He repeated to Leigh Hunt the plan of a poem he was about to write, being a comparison of the Blessed Saviour with a mountebank, whose tricks he identified with the miracles. I was shocked and disturbed, and breaking in upon his offensive detail, I exclaimed, 'That the fact of the greatest men having been Christians during the Christian period placed the religion far above such low ridicule.' Shelley immediately denied this fact, and we at once began enumerating on our fingers the great men who were Christians, and the few who were not. When we got to

---

* In later life Severn once stated to Lord Houghton that he was introduced to Keats by Leigh Hunt in 1817; but he was confusing that incident with his introduction to Shelley.

† Shelley, then quite a youth, was in the habit at that time of saying things calculated to shock unwary hearers. Severn accepted all he said in dead earnest, and judged accordingly.

Shakespeare he attempted to deny the great poet's belief, and quoted the sailor in 'Measure for Measure.' My counter quotations were from the utterances of Portia, Hamlet, Isabella, and numerous others; so that Leigh Hunt and Keats declared I had the best of the argument—whereupon Shelley declared that he would study the subject and write an essay upon it. I am not aware if he ever wrote that essay, but among his posthumous works there is an unfinished essay on Christianity, of the most ardent and beautiful nature, showing his belief and expatiating on the sublimity of Christ and the Creator. I do not know when this was written, but most certainly no one but Shelley could have written it, and it proves to me that his assumed paganism was a monomania—an assumption borne out at a later date by the 'Young England' party declaring Shelley to be the only religious poet of the age! The transition is immense, but there cannot be a doubt that 'Young England' was right, as now every one thinks so. The 'Prometheus Unbound' was explained to me by Mr. Gladstone as a Christian poem, if but the name were changed; and I have met several distinguished clergymen, both Protestant and Catholic, who have expressed the same opinion, and even that the greater belief in the Christian religion now apparent was owing to the poetry of Shelley—indeed, one Papist went so far as to infer the conversion of England through it."

In surprising discrepancy with these remarks are some written at an earlier date in the MS. 'Incidents of My Life.'

"About four [eight] months after his [Keats's] death I received from Shelley the beautiful poem to Keats's memory, 'Adonais.' Great and touching as it was, and filled, as I thought, with greater beauties than Milton's 'Lycidas,' yet I could not be reconciled to the author when I reflected that in so great a degree he had been one of those friends who had most helped to take away the means of hope from Keats, when despair was so shortly to kill him. Shelley, in his poem, is wholly unconscious of what I mean, nor do I think even now after thirty-nine years are there many who would comprehend what I feel."

It is a pity that all readers of Severn's words are also left in ignorance of his exact meaning. The most likely inference is that Keats's faith in the Christian religion had been undermined by Shelley, and that in his last year or two of mental and bodily anguish his sufferings were greatly increased by a kind of nostalgia for the faith he had left behind, a longing for the old believing prayers, the answering God—even for the symbols of worship. On the other hand, Severn's solemn emphasis (all things considered) does not seem quite natural from him; while the closing sentence would seem to indicate some meaning less obvious than the above inference.   It is to the last degree unlikely that Keats sheered off from Christianity at the suggestion or under the influence of Shelley, or, indeed, of any man ; moreover, the two poets were never intimate, and Keats was, as we know, unmoved by his comrade's eloquent denunciations of Christianity, whether in conversation, prose-essays, 'Queen Mab,' or 'The Revolt of Islam.' Probably there is nothing behind Severn's remark, beside the natural inference : and in all likelihood it was inspired by his regrets that Keats did not share to the full his own enthusiastic sentiment for the Christian faith, and his strong prejudice against Shelley's general views—a prejudice that affected the man, in his estimation, only a degree less.   Moreover, he changed or modified his views about Shelley several times in his life.

But it may readily be imagined how keen was his gratification when he received the first copy of the 'Adonais,' and with it the following letter from the author :—

" *Pisa,*
" Nov. 29th, 1821.

" Dear Sir,

"I send you the elegy on poor Keats—and I wish it were better worth your acceptance.   You will see by the preface that it was written before I could obtain any particular account of his last moments ; all that I still know, was communicated to me by a friend who had derived his information from Colonel Finch; I have ventured to express, as I felt, the respect and admiration which your conduct towards him demands. In spite of his transcendènt genius, Keats never was, nor ever will be, a popular poet ; and the total neglect and obscurity in which the astonishing remnants of his mind still lie, was hardly to be dissipated by a writer, who, however he may differ from Keats in more important qualities, at least resembles him in that accidental one, a want of popularity.

" I have little hope, therefore, that the poem I send you will excite any attention, nor do I feel assured that a critical notice of his writings would find a single reader.   But for these considerations, it had been my intention to have collected the remnants of his compositions, and to have published them with a Life and Criticism.   Has he left any poems or writings of whatsoever kind, and in whose possession are they ?   Perhaps you would oblige me by information on this point.   Many thanks for the picture you promise me : I shall consider it among the most sacred relics of the past.   For my part, I little expected, when I last saw Keats at my friend Leigh Hunt's, that I should survive him. Should you ever pass through Pisa, I hope to have the pleasure of seeing you, and of cultivating an acquaintance into something pleasant, begun under such melancholy auspices. Accept, my dear sir, the assurance of my highest esteem, and believe me,

"Your most sincere and faithful servant,
"PERCY B. SHELLEY."

It is interesting to learn from this letter that Shelley at one time thought of writing a Life of Keats, and that, by his inquiry as to the destination of the literary remains, the idea was one that really occupied his mind.

A little later Severn wrote to Brown concerning the 'Adonais.'

"*Rome,*
"Jan. 1st, 1822.

"I have received a copy of the Monody on Keats. I find many beauties in it, but is it not a pity so much beauty should be scattered about, without the balancing of lights and shades, or the oppositions of colours? In this poem there is such a want of repose,—you are continually longing to know what he will be at. It gave me great pleasure as a tribute to poor Keats's memory. The picture of poor Keats is in a fair way. I have put in your accurate drawing, but I seem to want that beautiful cast of him there is in London. I cannot finish without, and have named it amongst many things to be sent out to me. The gravestone is advanced, but not up yet. I cannot well recollect the Greek Lyre, so that they wait for the Drawings from London. I liked the Inscription much, and it shall be done exactly. I have some hair of our poor Keats, and have been waiting for a friend to bring it to London. I have thought of a little conceit, as a present to poor Miss Brawne—to make a Broach in form of my Greek Lyre, and make the strings of poor Keats's hair, but I cannot find any workman to do it. . . . . I shall not send a drawing of poor Keats I intend for you, but reserve it until I have the happiness to meet you."

In this connection there may be added here another "Keats" letter, though it was not sent to Brown till nearly ten months later.

"*Rome,*
"Oct. 26th, 1822.

". . . . I am just about putting up the grave-stone to our Keats. This delay has been occasioned by the want of the drawings of the Greek Lyre. I could not proceed without them—they are accurate outlines I made from the beautiful Lyre in the Museum of London, and they have at last arrived. I am sorry, my dear Brown, that you are not here with me to share this deep-thinking office. I would have been gratified, for I still long to talk with some one friend about our poor Keats. Yesterday I visited his grave, which is still covered with Flowers and Grass. I was in company with some German Artists and Poets—they seemed much affected with my recital of Keats's fate—and of Shelley's too.

"This stone is to have simply the Greek Lyre, with half the strings not tied. On the upper part will be a bit of Oak and Myrtle, and under, his name, the date when he died, and his age. I say it is to have these, but it is only my own idea. To say the truth, I did not like yours—you seemed to have anticipated so. By (but?) tell me if you approve of this of mine, though I fear it will be accomplished before you write. It will be rather an expensive concern, though the friends here of mine, mostly Artists, who are delighted with Keats's works, offered to subscribe, but this I won't allow. I shall make it out somehow. Yet I will have it handsome, even for my own credit as an artist, as well as my other feelings. I understand that the Life is advertised. I wrote to Mr. Taylor, but have never received any answer—tell me if you know as to this. I would like to know if I have given offence to Mr. Taylor—tell me if you correspond with him. . . . . I am now occupied on a picture for the Somerset House Exhibition . . . . I shall also send Keats's portrait. . . . .

"I have not heard of Shelley's ashes—how shall I do? Tell me on this point, and you shall find me apt . . . . I have not shaken hands with one mutual friend of mine and Keats's since I left England. You can't think of this, my dear Brown, at least not feel it. . . . ."

What memories must have been stirred in Severn's mind when, in the ' Adonais' Preface, he came to the now famous words, "It might make one in love with death to think that one should be buried in so sweet a place."

"The following words," he says in one of his letters home, "I have read again and again, till I can read no more for the tears that rise and obscure my sight: 'The circumstances of the closing scene of poor Keats's life were not made known to me until the Elegy was ready for the press. I am given to understand that the wound which his sensive spirit had received from the criticism of "Endymion," was exasperated by the bitter sense of unrequited benefits; the poor fellow seems to have been hastened from the stage of life, no less by those on whom he had wasted the promise of his genius, than those on whom he had lavished his fortune and his care. He was accompanied to Rome, and attended in his last illness by Mr. Severn, a young artist of the highest promise, who, I have been informed, "almost risked his own life, and sacrificed every prospect to unwearied attendance upon his dying friend." Had I known these circumstances before the completion of my poem, I should have been tempted to add my feeble tribute of applause to the more solid recompense which the virtuous man finds in the recollection of his own motives. Mr. Severn can dispense with a reward from "such stuff as dreams are made of." His conduct is a golden augury of the success of his future career—may the unextinguished Spirit of his illustrious friend animate the creations of his pencil, and plead against oblivion for his name !' "

In a later letter Severn says that, "as a source of inspiration for high effort," he chalked upon a blank space on the wall, where his eyes would often see them, the memorable closing words : "May the unextinguished spirit of his illustrious friend animate the creations of his pencil and plead against oblivion for his name !" His gratification, however, was somewhat damped by the reception of ' Adonais ' in England, and though in late life he recognised at its true value Shelley's generous tribute, he was often, throughout the months succeeding the publication of ' Adonais,' unpleasantly reminded of his " association with the detestable school of republicans, atheists, and free-livers."

"When it was published in 1821," he writes in his reminiscences, "it occasioned a great stir in London among my friends and my family, for in the preface his mention of me—though written with such fine taste and feeling—was by them taken in a quite contrary spirit, and I was written to immediately with warnings and prayers that I would break off all acquaintance with a man of such vile reputation as Shelley, or it would be ruinous to my standing and prospects. How singular are the changing manners of the changing world ! Ten years later I was sought at Rome by members of the young aristocracy, as the friend of Keats and Shelley—and this arose from the very preface which had the contrary effect on its publication. To that preface, indeed, I owe some of my proudest and most valuable associations and friends, including William Ewart Gladstone, who all consider Shelley the only real religious poet of the age. However, it was not long that I had to be 'in danger' of Shelley, for in less than a year after Keats's death he was drowned, and I had the melancholy task of placing his ashes (his body was burned) by the side of Keats, where an infant of Shelley's had been already buried." *

After quotation of the closing stanza of ' Adonais,' ending—

> " I am borne darkly, fearfully, afar ;
> Whilst burning through the inmost veil of Heaven,
> The soul of Adonais, like a star,
> Beacons from the abode where the Eternal are!"

---

* Originally, Shelley's son William was buried beside Keats.

Severn writes :—

"'Tis thought that the poet is also a prophet, and certainly in the case of Shelley the saying is strikingly borne out—for in this stanza he foretells his own speedy death, which occurred six months after he wrote these prophetic lines. He was drowned in the Gulf of Spezzia by the upsetting of his boat, and his body was identified by the volume of Keats' poems in his pocket. By the quarantine laws it was not permitted to remove the body from the sea-coast, and therefore the poet's friend, Mr. Trelawny, adopted the alternative of cremation. The bones and ashes were conveyed to Rome to be placed by the side of his infant son William, and there under the old wall of Rome is his tombstone, shaded by a group of cypresses, planted at the time by Edward Trelawny. The inscription 'Cor Cordium' was the suggestion of Leigh Hunt, and the plain stone adjoining that of Shelley was placed there by Trelawny, who purchased the ground that he might finally be laid beside the poet. In order to mark the occasion and the locality with an apt epitaph, Trelawny wrote to many of his literary friends. Several consented and composed inscriptions for the tomb, but the mourner was not satisfied with any of them, and after his waiting and tribulating a whole month, a friend who was present at the interment proposed to supply the deficiency as follows :—

"'Here lies Edward Trelawny, for he is still living.'"

It is noteworthy, by the way, that Severn more than once, in enumerating the few friends who were present at the interment of Shelley's ashes in Rome, omits mention of Leigh Hunt, who is frequently stated to have been present. The following letters afford conclusive proof that Leigh Hunt was absent at the ceremony, and are, at the same time, full of a painful interest. The first is addressed to Hunt, the second to Charles Brown.

" Jan. 21, 1823.

"My dear Hunt,

"I have just returned from poor Shelley's funeral, the accumulating delays which have taken place having prevented me writing [earlier]. I had hoped from day to day to give you the finish of this melancholy task; but these droning Italians threw everything in the way. The delay has been unfortunate—it has given me great pain and much fruitless endeavouring. You must know that the Government here has made a new Burial Ground for us heretics—well walled in to protect us from the Catholics who destroyed the Protestant Tombs, and shewed us every indignity—this was some years back. The old ground, which contains our dear Keats and the son of Mr. Shelley, stands against the Pyramid of Caius Cestius—the English have often petitioned to have it walled in ;

but no, the Government thought it would spoil the view—and perhaps it is so—it is the most lovely spot I know. They have now made this new ground only twenty feet from it, and it is well protected by walls and soldiers. Now here was the difficulty : they had ordered that no more should be deposited in the old place, and we could not get permission to inter the ashes in the same spot, so we were driven to the alternative of removing them both to the new ground. Here another difficulty faced us. The grave was opened immediately under the stone, and we found the skeleton of a grown person! The stone had been placed in a wrong place, so that we had horribly disturbed a stranger's grave. I could search no further—we were surrounded by respectful, but wondering Italians, and so we proceeded to the interment of Mr. Shelley's ashes alone. This was distressing after what you had said; but I know that you feel and think with me, that it could not be otherwise. . . ."

" Rome,
" Jan. 21, 1823.

" My dear Brown,

"I have just returned from the Funeral of poor Shelley. Much delay had taken place from the difficulty of placing the remains together. You must know a new Burial Ground has been made, well walled in, to protect us heretics against the Catholics, who had most wantonly defaced many of the Protestant Tombs. The old Ground they would not wall, because it would spoil the view of the Pyramid of Caius Cestius, so this new one is given, and the old one protected with a Ditch, and with an order that no more shall be buried there. Now here was the difficulty. Shelley's ashes were not permitted to [be] placed in the Old Ground where his Child lay, so that we were driven to the alternative of the new place, and of disinterring the Bones of the Child and placing them together ; but even this was frustrated, after I had got permission to do it, for, on opening the grave, we discovered a skeleton of 5½ feet. Yet it appeared to be under the Stone, so that some mistake must have been made in placing the Stone. To search further we dare not, for it was in the presence of many *respectful* but wondering Italians : nay, I thought it would have been a doubtful and horrible thing to disturb any more Strangers' Graves in a Foreign Land. So we proceeded very respectfully to deposit poor Shelley's ashes alone. There were present General Cockburn, Sir C. Sykes, Messrs. Kirkup, Westmacott, Scoles, Freeborn, and the Revs. W. Cook and Burgess. These two gentlemen, with myself, wished it to be done solemnly and decently, so the Box was inclosed in a coffin, and it was done altogether as by the hands of Friends. My next sad office is to place poor Keats's Grave Stone, which is not yet done. I hope this week it will be finished. I shall put some Evergreens round it—of course it is in the Old Ground. I was going to make a proposition to you. There is now here, living with me, a young English Sculptor named Gott, of most rare and delicate genius, who from his first coming to Rome (seven months) has been ill with the Fever. He had a Gold Medal with me in the R.A., and is now sent here (pensioned like myself) by Sir T. Lawrence. Oh *his* account I am going to ask your advice about a little Monument to Keats, more worthy him than ours, to be placed (if it is thought better) in Hampstead Church. What gave me this. Idea was the applications of several gentlemen to subscribe twenty guineas, &c., for this purpose. I have no doubt it might be done. The Subject of a Basso-rilievo was this which I thought. 'Our Keats sitting, habited in a simple Greek Costume—he has half strung his Lyre, when the Fates seize him. One arrests his arm, another cuts the thread, and the third pronounces his Fate.' Gott is very pleased with this Idea and thinks he could make a fine thing of it. Another thing—I know his works would have pleased so much Keats's taste. It will give him spirits, also, since he finds his income too small to support his Wife and 2 Children. Tell me how you take this—think of it charitably. If any further than the plain stone is placed over Shelley (*sic*), pray let him do it. . . ."

CHAPTER VI.

SEVERN, notwithstanding the warnings he had received about the unhealthiness of the city during the great heats, contentedly spent the summer in Rome. He had been invited to Florence, but, as he says in one of his home-letters, "I preferred to remain and study from the divine pictures of Raphael." Already he had fallen into the bad habit—from which, in the following year and for some time afterward, he preserved himself—of trusting to memory or observation of other pictures for his presentation of nature. Drawing, composition, and artistic verisimilitude, the qualities wherein he had most need to improve, were too often indifferently studied by him.

"The Roman summer—my first—found me," he says in his 'Reminiscences,' "in its solitude waiting in hopes of my pension, and the result of many other things then existing only in experiment. My health kept improving, and so I had no fear of malaria. I liked the loneliness, as I had so much to commune with myself as regards the future. Among many visits I made to Keats's grave at Monte Testaccio was one of a very striking nature. In the twilight of the full moon I found a young Italian asleep, his head resting against the gravestone, his dog and his flock of sheep about him, with the full moon rising beyond the Pyramid of Caius Cestius. One long moonbeam stole past the Pyramid and illumined the outline of the young shepherd's face, and to my eye realised the story of Endymion. What would Keats—who, as I have already said, made me go once and again during his lingering illness to see the place where he was to be buried, and who was so pleased with what I told him of it that at times it seemed almost his only consolation—what would Keats have said had he seen this Endymion vision?"

Nearly forty years after this episode, Severn painted it for Keats's biographer, Lord Houghton, then Monckton Milnes.

In the early autumn Severn set himself to the painting of two pictures of classical subjects. Although, as he says, "my passion was for Italian pastoral nature, yet I felt bound to study academically, and so began my 'Alexander the Great reading Homer,' and of 'Greek Hill-Shepherds rescuing a Lamb from an Eagle,' founded upon a passage in Keats's 'Hymn to Pan.'" Neither of these, he admits, was in any way successful, but, no doubt, they were eminently serviceable in teaching him to seek at the fountain-head what he was vainly striving to gain from alien tributaries.

On the return of the English residents in September Severn's solitude was soon broken in upon. His acquaintances grew in number steadily, and some of them were people of high rank and influence, among them the Duchess of Devonshire, who was exceptionally kind, but died not very long after her acquaintanceship with Severn had begun. Chief among these new friends, in after-influence upon his life, was the Countess of Westmorland.

The winter was for him one of hard work, with intervals of novel and delightful social enjoyment. The new year opened favourably, for the Academy pension ensured a sufficient income for at least a period of three years.

Early in the year Severn was gratified to receive a letter from Edward Holmes, one of his oldest and most intimate acquaintances, valued for his own sake, and also because he had been the schoolfellow and dear friend of Keats. They had, moreover, one strong bond in common—music. Keats owed much pleasure to both, and particularly, in the early London days, to Holmes. It is pleasant to find the latter writing so sensibly about Shelley.*

---

* Edward Holmes (1797–1859). Holmes's chief writings are a 'Life of Mozart' and a 'Memoir of Purcell.' He wrote some excellent papers on the English Glee and Madrigal Composers, and was himself a composer of songs, of which 'My Jenny' was popular. It was he who went with Vincent Novello to Germany, in 1828, to present to Mozart's widow the subscription they had raised in England. Of this trip Holmes wrote an account, 'A Ramble with some of the Musicians of Germany,' which passed into three editions.

"London,
" February 23rd, 1822.

" DEAR SEVERN,

"… . . I was delighted at hearing that you had obtained the allowance from the Academy, which will enable you to work away at your painting with such a gusto. All your future fame seems to me to depend on your application now, and with such advantages and inducements as you have to work, I am sure great performances may be expected from you. I was half afraid those old devils at the Academy meant to humbug you out of the money; but it has happened very fortunately, and I give you joy. I think if you were suddenly transported to England you would scarcely know the place again, it is so strangely altered; not only are all the buildings and streets different from what they were, but none of our old acquaintances and friends live where they did; they seem all to have been suddenly whisked away by the four winds, the Lord knows where, and they seem to have lost many of their inclinations and feelings in the hurry of the change. This is what has made me wish for you back many hundred times, and I assure you, without sending a compliment all this way, that if I had known the sacrifice I was making of your society and neighbourhood, at the time you left, half as well as I do now, it would have cost me a devilish deal more to have given you up than it did. Mr. Hunt has left London on his way to Italy, and hopes to join Lord Byron and Shelley at Pisa by the spring or soon after; I advise you, if possible, to join him there, as he told me that he would introduce you to Lord Byron and Shelley, and you know of what consequence the society of men like these is to a person of your pursuits; besides, you are personally indebted to Shelley for the very handsome manner in which he has mentioned your name in his elegy on Keats. It is as honourable a testimonial to your friendship as could be made publicly; just such a thing as you deserved, and I was delighted beyond measure when Mr. Hunt read it to me. I know you have some old prejudices against Shelley, but you may depend upon it that he is a much abused person, and the world has from time immemorial chosen the most amiable people and its greatest benefactors for the subjects of its spite and malignity—witness your own favourite Christ. If you should go to Pisa you will most probably meet Mr. Brown, who leaves this place in March, and I wish I could make the same promise for myself, but I must be content to remain a Barbarian of the North. Having now given you a faithful account of all the people who leave for Italy, I must tell you something about those who remain at home. The message that you sent by me to Richards I have not delivered, as we never meet now, and he is one of those men whom I should have thought could never have fallen in my esteem, but some of those strangest unaccountable things have happened, which sometimes do fall out, and we are no longer friends—you shall have my reason at another opportunity. . . . ."

From a long letter written in March to his father, there

is a detailed account of Severn's doings and surroundings, and of his progress with his picture of ' Alexander the Great.' On the same day—with the same letter, in fact—he wrote as follows to his brother Tom, giving a vivid account of an amusing episode. The idea of going to Venice with Eastlake was not fulfilled; but it is interesting to note that Severn and Eastlake had become so friendly.

"It is my intention after I have finished my ' Alexander,' or on the approach of the dangerous season here, to go to Venice. I am going with Mr. Eastlake, a painter of great talent. We intend to work very hard in copying from the many fine pictures there. I make small copies in oil. This Venice is the most choice place in the world for pictures. I expect to derive great improvement from the visit. The spring has set in here at last, and most divinely; for six weeks the sky has scarce had a cloud; one fine day beats another, until it will be Paradise.

"We had a droll affair here the other night. Soon after our Academy had met, my old servant tapped at the door and said there were thieves in the house. In an instant our model (who is a very strong and honest man) leaped down from the throne, seized a large stick, and, *stark naked*, went in pursuit of them half-way down the street. It turned out to be a mistake; but the family who live under me were much alarmed, and a lady, a countess, who is a beautiful musician, stood at the door wringing her hands in great fright and crying, when at the moment returns the model from the street, *stark naked*, and suddenly the lady and her sisters forgot their fears and set up a laugh that I thought would have killed them—but I assure you the model had a droll effect."

Instead of going to Venice Severn left Rome in the middle of May for Naples, having been advised to do so after a sudden and severe illness that had prostrated him. It was a pleasant journey, he writes, though haunted by pathetic memories of the circumstances in which he had previously made it. There was no dying poet now for him to tend and delight with wild flowers, and cheer with sanguine hopes and bright conversation ; in turn, he was the invalid, and Keats was asleep below the violets under the old Roman wall.

"I got through the pleasantly tedious journey without similar attacks, though I had to be very careful. I was more than once in peril. Thus, soon after our start, we were stopped in the Pontine marshes by the breaking of a wheel, and had to stay about seven nocturnal hours in the most deadly malaria. The air was heavy with a damp fog exuding from rank vegetation and a poisonous soil, with a heavy vapour from the neighbouring canal. In the latter, the largest toads I ever saw were crawling up and down the banks in great numbers, most loathsome looking creatures, at least thirteen inches in length. We had to keep ourselves awake by drinking tea, for sleep would have been fatal soon or late."

He returned in October, well in health, and having accomplished a great quantity of work in pictures, studies and sketches. In the early autumn he received from Charles Brown the welcome news of the latter's arrival in Italy.

"*Pisa,*
"5th Sept., 1822.

" My dear Severn,

"Here I am at last. I arrived here six days ago with my little boy. In London I could not learn in what part of Italy you intended to pass the summer, and one of my first questions with Leigh Hunt was touching your present abode. He believes you to be at Naples, so at Naples I address this letter. Yet I will not venture till I hear from you to send three letters from Holmes, Ewing, and Richards, which were entrusted to my care. From Turin to Genoa I had a tedious process to go through, and in the felucca, which was to carry us to Leghorn, we were favoured with a storm and contrary winds, and everything that was abominable, till my patience at the end of four days was exhausted, and landing at Lerici, I came here by carriage, with an English gentleman. You have heard, I suppose, of Shelley being drowned near Lerici. I am really grieved for him. I believe he was a good man, and, certainly he was a good friend to Keats, and to his memory. His body has been burnt, and I understand his ashes are to be deposited near his child at Rome. A Captain Williams was also drowned with him. Lord Byron is moving off to Genoa, and so is Hunt with his family. Hunt introduced me to his Lordship two or three days ago, which is considered (not by me) as a prodigious favour. I was prejudiced against him, but somehow he got the better of my prejudice, and I hear he has taken a liking to me. I should like to keep house with you at Florence for a twelvemonth ; my brat, in the hands of a servant, will not annoy either of us. Now I wait for an answer, and then I shall send your letters. Good-bye, my dear Severn, and believe me ever

" Yours sincerely,
" Charles Brown."

K

Severn wrote at once in reply, and though regretting his inability to go to Pisa, promised to meet his friend the following year in Florence, if not in Rome.   In December he heard again from Leigh Hunt.

("*Direct to me,*

" 'Ferma in Posta,' Genoa.)

"16th Dec., 1822.

"DEAR SEVERN,

"You and I have gone through hard tosses and trials since we saw each other last, too terrible at present to dwell upon; but these things at all events bind the survivors the closer, and if I had not had a regard and respect for you on your own account I should have had them both after what you did for Keats, and what my late beloved friend said and thought of you.   Pray tell me if I can in any way help to further any of your views.   Brown tells me that you say you shall regard me here as standing in the same light to you as Shelley did.   You do not know how that compliment goes to my heart.   Write to me, pray, and tell me about your pictures, your prospects, and all that you can afford time to write about.   You are naturally, I believe, no greater lover of letter-writing than myself; but you must know I am mending in this respect, and I will give you a reason for writing to me speedily, which I am sure you will think a good one.   I am very uneasy about a circumstance, which I wish you to inquire into for me.   You know, I believe, the way in which my friend's remains were finally consigned to their coffin after being rescued from the sea.   They were burnt, collected into it or rather into a small funeral-box, and sent to Rome for interment near his little boy in the same ground as dear Keats.   Now some difficulties, it seems, have started with respect to their consignment to the ground.   The gentleman to whose care they were sent is a Mr. Freeborn, a merchant, correspondent of a Mr. Grant at Leghorn, to whom they were first consigned.   The friend, who is the medium between these gentlemen and Mrs. Shelley (who is at present living here with us), is not a man of business, though a very good fellow; and altogether the delay, which has now been long, is a very distressing one, and without further explanation not very intelligible.   There is a talk of some difficulty on the part of the Government; but everything has been conducted regularly through the other Government, the Sardinian, in whose territory the remains were found, and if any interference is wanted on the part of the English ambassador no doubt it could be obtained. Now will you be kind enough to go to Mr. Freeborn's, as the friend of Mr. Shelley's nearest friends, and let us know exactly how the matter stands?   When we know this we may know what to do finally.   You have nothing, dear Severn, but funeral tasks put upon you; but they are for extraordinary people and excellent friends, and I hope all our prospects will brighten again before we join them.   Yours, I trust, have been doing so, as well as mine; but Italy, the most cheerful of all places to me when

I first came, is no longer the Italy it was, and never again can be. Its brightest sunshine will always have a shade in the very core of it. Again, what are you painting? what doing? what expecting? Your sketch of Keats is always over my shelf, and Mrs. Hunt, notwithstanding her long and terrible illness, which is however better upon the whole, never omits to be proud of showing the sketch you made of me to every stranger.

> "Yours sincerely,
> " LEIGH HUNT.

" P.S.—Lord Byron says he shall be happy to do anything that lies in his power to serve you. I wish you had rescued him out of the hands of an Italian sculptor and Raphael Morghen, who have conspired to make a vile *unlikeness* of him."

Earlier in the same month Severn wrote to Brown:

". . . . I had just given my directions about poor Keats's gravestone. Your mention of your still-existing wish for the epitaph as it stood made me all consent. I saw the superiority of it—it is doing so (*sic*). I am all anxiety to know about poor Miss Brawne. Pray tell me this, if you have more accounts. I shall be most ravenous by May to have a sight of you. What must regulate the time is the finishing my 'Alexander,' after the 'Greek Shepherds' now going on. This, with 'Falstaff,' and I hope Keats's portrait, will be in the Exhibition next summer in London. . . . . Did you ever have poor Keats's papers? Know you about the Life? Taylor is going to publish, after all. He has never written to me [again]—is this kind? . . . . Poor Shelley's ashes have arrived. When I get out, I will conduct them to the grave, with the respect due to the Friend of Keats. I have not yet heard from Hunt or Lord Murray. . . . .

"Have you got a spare copy of the 'Lamia' or the 'Endymion'? I have been cheated out of mine, and I am so vexed to be without. My friend Mr. Gott (the sculptor who had a gold medal with me) is doing something from 'Endymion,' and I have a drawing going on from 'St. Agnes' Eve.' Pray think of us."

Shortly after his arrival in Rome from Naples Severn had heard again from Charles Brown, in reply to a letter of his own concerning the inscription for Keats's tomb. From this and other letters of Brown's of this period, it is clear that he was steadily engaged in literary work: and, no doubt, from his standpoint, he had reason to be proud of his measure of success.

> " *Pisa*,
> " Nov. 7th, 1822.

" I got your letter yesterday. If not too late pray reflect a little more on the inscription for our Keats. Remember it was his dying request that his *name* should *not* be on his tombstone, and that the words 'Here lies one whose name was writ in water' should be there. I thought you liked my inscription, for you said so. All his friends, Hunt, Richards, Dilke, and every one I showed it to, were greatly pleased with it. You seem to imagine it does not honour him enough, but, to our minds, it says more in his praise than if his name were mentioned. You have done right in not accepting of any assistance from strangers to his worth, in erecting this gravestone; but I insist on bearing my share, and I will pay it you when we meet in Florence—you shall not have all the pleasure—a mournful one—but still a pleasure. I told you all I could, all that Hunt could tell me, about Shelley's ashes—Mrs. Shelley had then set off to Genoa. As for Mr. Taylor, I have no correspondence with him whatever. When we meet, if it live in my remembrance so long, and it is hardly worth it, I will tell you the whole story. Even my friends allow, and that I have found a rare thing, that he has behaved badly towards me, and, to my mind, unfeelingly towards the memory of Keats. . . . .

"I cannot give you any account of Lord Byron's and Leigh Hunt's work, except that it is called 'The Liberal,' and that the first number came out on the 14th of October. To write in such good company I feel a great honour. What I shall be paid I know not; but it can't be less than what the 'New Monthly' paid me, twelve guineas per sheet. I hear they are much pleased with my article 'Les Charmettes and Rousseau'; and they have another which Hunt saw in Pisa, and said was very good indeed."

Severn certainly at one time entertained the idea of living with Brown in Florence, but only while the prospect was a distant one. With the spring of 1823 he had come to the conclusion that even the pleasure of his friend's companionship, and the economy involved in a joint expenditure, would not make up for the advantages he enjoyed in Rome.

About the beginning of 1823, he received the following letter from Sir Thomas Lawrence, President of the Royal Academy, in response to a communication wherein he had recounted his artistic doings and set forth his progress, and had at the same time hoped that the Council might see its way to assisting him in his effort to establish and extend an English Academy in Rome.

"*Russell Square,*
"Dec. 23rd, 1822.

"Sir,

"I am sorry that the pressure of much business, and the propriety of laying the subject of your letter before a general meeting of the Royal

Academy, prevents me at present from sending a satisfactory answer to your gratifying communication. I must not pretend to conjecture the degree or mode of assistance that can be offered to you by this Institution, and I must previously request of you to bear in mind that, from the common distress of the times, there are many afflicting claims on its finances, that exceedingly limit its general power of service, and I fear, with the necessary expenses of the establishment, may deny it the pleasure of affording you such enlarged assistance as otherwise would be the prompt determination of each individual member.

" The difficulty of presuming to legislate for you at this distance, and in ignorance of many local circumstances which must materially influence the arrangement of any defined plan, at once deters me from the attempt. I trust you, however, to convey to your friends my strong sense of their flattering attention to me, and of their too poetical deference to my opinion.

" If I may venture to suggest anything, it is that of a policy of great prudence and moderation, in the first outset of the undertaking—that you limit your views as strictly as possible to the absolute necessities of study, and suffer the comforts of full convenient accommodation to be the gradual result of your success. My sincere wishes prompt me to offer the unauthorised hope, that but little may be left for other subscription, but such as may neither be wounding to rational pride, nor affect your independence; and that in some way or other, though on more limited scale, the English Academy at Rome may yet vie in real usefulness and dignity with the other foreign institutions of that beloved city.

" I cannot sufficiently admire the patriotism and liberality of Mr. Hamilton's conduct. His letter speaks him as fine a gentleman as he is a generous benefactor, and his name, I have no doubt, will always be remembered in the Academy with the warmest affection and respect. If the convivial ever presumes to break in on the sacred severities of study, it must be justified by the grateful satisfaction of establishing that name as the first standing toast.

" You may rely on my communicating to you the result of the opinions of the next general meeting of the Royal Academy, and their decision on your letter. I take the liberty of offering for the present funds of your Academy the sum of £50, yet entreating the society not to consider it as contribution from the President of our own institution, although I take advantage of that character, for the freedom of presenting it. I will give directions for its being placed in the hands of Messrs. Torlonia, payable to the order of my greatly esteemed friend Mr. Eastlake, to whom I beg the kindness of you to present my best regards.

" Believe me to be, Sir,

" Your obliged and obedient servant,

" THOMAS LAWRENCE."

Unfortunately, it cannot be said that then or later the English Academy in Rome ever got within reach of " vying in real usefulness and dignity with the other similar foreign institutions."

The spring of 1823 quickly passed. Severn was so busy with his Art-work that he saw few friends; refrained from his then spasmodic diary-keeping, and let his not very large correspondence drop into long arrears. He finished his 'Greek Shepherds' and his 'Death of Alexander,' and sent them to England, and though much engaged upon his other canvases, found time to paint several miniature portraits.

Early in the year, as we know (p. 123, *ante*), he wrote to Brown, upon the subject of the erection of a monument in England, in London or Hampstead preferably, to the memory of Keats. Having suggested that Mr. Gott, the young sculptor who shared his abode, should be entrusted with the commission, and spoken warmly of his powers; and referred to the establishment of the so-called English Academy in Rome, in which he had taken an active part, and to the several artistic projects he had in view, as well as the pictures upon which he was actually engaged; he ended with an account of the burial of Shelley's ashes, and of the disturbing of other remains in the making of the grave. There can be little question as to the good sense and wise discretion of Brown's answer to Severn's plea for the erection of a monument to Keats in London or Hampstead. No one loved and revered the memory of the young poet more than Brown did, but his was no feather-brain affection that could be blind to all save the fulfilment of its own immediate desires; moreover, he knew, as Severn had no means of knowing, the virulence and spite of the small fry in "the wretched literary world;" and, indeed, at that time the jealous ill-will even of men who might be supposed superior to pettiness of mind and meanness of judgment.

" Pisa,
" February 7th, 1823.

"My dear Severn,

"There is one subject in your letter that has employed my consideration, and that to the best of my ability—I mean the erecting of a monument to Keats's memory in England. In one word, I cannot but disapprove of it. The fact is this: his fame is not sufficiently general; with the few and the best judges it stands high, but his name is unknown to the multitude. Therefore I think that prior to his name being somewhat more celebrated, a monument to his memory might even retard it, and it might provoke ill-nature, and (shall I say it?) ridicule. When I quitted England his works were still unsaleable. For that cruel word *ridicule* I must explain myself. There apppeared, some time after his death, in one of the Government newspapers, an article scoffing at him and joking at his death. I did not read it, I could not, but I heard of it, and it put me in a fortnight's irritation. In prudence we ought to wait awhile. First, let his merit be undoubted. Let it not be said that not only bad men have costly tombs with flattering inscriptions, but that nowadays bad poets have the like. This will be as unpleasant as irksome, as discordant for you to read as it is for me to write; but I must tell you the truth, his name is yet scarce anything in England; it becomes, and will become, more ennobled every day, while a monument might throw that happy time back. Ten years hence, to my mind, will be time enough. You, in your affection for him, think nothing can be done too much. Alas! I, knowing the wretched literary world, think otherwise. Yet still all this is but one man's opinion, and one as likely to err as yourself, and from the same motive, though our opinions are contrary. I regret that I am against the interest (in this instance) of your friend the sculptor, whose *name* I cannot make out in your letter; but if you mention my reasons to that gentleman, he will surely understand me. I could say much more on this head, but why?—you with this already written can fill up the rest. I thank you for the particular account you give of the ceremony of depositing Shelley's ashes; that disturbing of other bones—though I am by no means scrupulous about such matters—made me start, for it might happen that some living friend of the skeleton should hear of it."

In April Severn wrote again to Brown :

"There is a mad chap come here, whose name is Trelawny. I do not know what to make of him, further than his queer, and, I was near saying, shabby, behaviour to me. He comes as the friend of Shelley, great, glowing, and rich in romance. Of course I showed all my paint-pot politeness to him, to the very brim—assisted him to remove the ashes of Shelley to a spot where he himself (when this world has done with his body) will lie. He wished me to think, myself, and consult my friends, about a monument to Shelley. The situation is beautiful, and one and all thought a little basso-relievo would be the best taste. I was telling him the subject I had proposed for Keats, and he was struck with the propriety of it for Shelley, and my friend Mr. Gott (whom I mentioned to you) was to be the doer of it. I made the drawing, which cost us some trouble, yet after expressing the greatest liking for it, the pair of Mustachios has shirked off from it, without giving us the yes or no—without even the why or wherefore. I am sorry at this most on Mr. Gott's account, but I ought to have seen that this Lord Byron's jackal was rather

weak in all the points that I could judge, though strong enough in
stilettos. We have not had any open rupture, nor shall we, for I have no
doubt that this 'cockney corsair' fancies he has greatly obliged us by all
·this trouble we have had. But tell me who is this odd fish? They talk
of him here as a camelion (*sic*), who went mad on reading Lord Byron's
'Corsair.' He told me that he knew you."

About the middle of May, Severn heard from Leigh Hunt,
in reply to a request which he had made as to the use, for
the Keats Memoirs, of the letter which Leigh Hunt had
written before he knew of the poet's death. The "royal
news" alluded to in the postscript probably concerns the
promise of Byron to be an active collaborator with Hunt in
his ill-starred journalistic venture.

> " *Genoa,*
> "May 10th, 1823.
>
> " . . . . As to the letter concerning dear Keats, pray do with it as
> you wish. It was very scrupulous in you to ask my permission, yet I
> thank you for doing so, as it affords me another specimen of a nature that
> I like. Gilby is a very good fellow, and so is Trelawny. Roberts I do not
> know enough of to say what he is, but Trelawny likes him, and that is
> something. Thank you for your attentions to them all. Trelawny will
> be here in two or three weeks, and then, my dear Severn, I will write to
> you further respecting those other interesting matters. I am sorry I
> cannot join you at Florence in June, but at any rate we shall not be there
> till autumn, if then. It will depend upon circumstances when we are to
> move. My wife (who begs her best remembrances) is singularly well, for
> her, and considering how dreadfully her health has been shaken; the
> doctors say that she is about to have the best possible chance for the
> recovery of her health. She expects to be confined in a month. Judge of
> my anxiety. Good God! when shall we have an end of anxieties? I
> have been very unwell myself since I wrote last, with a low fever, but it
> is gone again, and I am returned as usual to my literary warfare upon
> earth, pen in hand. God bless you, dear Severn.
>
> " Yours very truly,
> "LEIGH HUNT."

As the spring advanced into summer, the likelihood of
Severn's visit to Florence seemed to lessen. He had hoped
for a remunerative commission, but as it had not reached
him, he feared to involve himself in money troubles by
leaving his work in Rome and going to a city where social
and other attractions would be numerous, and where his
expenses would be more than he could afford, even as the

partial guest of Brown, at the latter's residence in an old palace, part of which he had rented at an almost nominal sum. But about the end of May he received a commission from a Mr. Crauford to paint a replica of Raphael's 'Madonna della Sedia,' in the Pitti Gallery at Florence; and though at first he was uncertain as to the amount he was to be paid, and thus whether the venture would be worth his while, he wrote hopefully to his friend as to his probable imminent arrival. Almost immediately afterwards he was able to write again with the good news that all was satisfactory.

By the middle of June, Severn had temporarily settled in Florence, well content to enjoy Brown's companionship again; and, besides getting on with his replica of the 'Madonna della Sedia,' glad of the opportunity to make studies for his ambitiously conceived picture of the 'Rescue of Lorenzo di Medici from Assassination.'

Notwithstanding the summer heats, Severn remained in Florence till the latter part of August, when he went, on what proved a delightful and memorable visit, to Venice.

"To-morrow morning at four Brown and I set off to Venice, where next to Heaven I long to go. He goes entirely on my account, good fellow—how happy I am in his fellowship! His learning, his candour, his experience, but most his good heart, are comforts to me that I have never known since I left England. At Venice I shall make many studies in oil-colours from the chief pictures. We return to Rome in five weeks. I have painted nineteen pictures (copies) here in Florence, and made sixty drawings, for I have been blessed with real health during this summer, which is all sun and heat. The great part of these pictures are preparations for my large picture, which I begin on the 1st of January. The subject is 'Lorenzo di Medici rescued from Assassination by his Friends.' This Lorenzo was the great Florence merchant about the time of our Henry VIII. He revived the arts, literature, &c.; everything is owing to him. This picture represents an attempt on his life by some enemies who were jealous of his greatness; he was saved by his friends, who devoted their lives to him. Why I take this subject is—first, I am, and everybody is, sick of sacred ones; next, I am fond of Gothic architecture, times, and people, and in the picture I shall show what is the feeling of my own heart—a human being, who has raised himself to such a pitch of goodness and greatness, that his friends devote their lives to save him. The scene is in the Gothic cathedral of Florence; Lorenzo is encircled by friends, his wife and son clinging round him; his brother is just dying from the assassins' wounds, who rush forward to finish their deed; but they are stopped, and Lorenzo's life is saved. Among the large group of friends I introduce the portrait of Raphael, the greatest painter that ever lived ; Michael Angelo, Leonardo da Vinci, and many others of this great time—as Lorenzo's friends, for they were 'protected' by him. The assassins chose the time when the High Priest raised the Host, and the people were all praying. This subject is well known and admired by the English nobility. It is found best told in Roscoe's 'Life of Lorenzo di Medici,' which is read and admired by everybody. It is a subject quite new and very splendid in the dresses ; the background is from the actual spot. My picture is 12 feet by 18, and I hope it will quite establish my fame. I shall be all next year at work upon it."

There has already been occasion to allude to Severn's intimate love of music, one of the accomplishments of the young artist which had helped to endear him to Keats. The following letter, which he wrote to his brother Tom some eight or ten weeks after his Venetian holiday, is interesting in this connection. His remarks upon Purcell, and upon the artistic requirements of the art of song-writing, are excellent. Severn's home-letters are generally of a chatty nature, and sometimes the only reference to some important picture, incident, or undertaking, is to be found casually interpolated in one of his many epistles. From the present letter we learn that about this time he had composed both the words and the music of a glee ; elsewhere there are allusions to his having frequently composed songs, sometimes to his own words, but generally to those of others.

'The Mother and Child' picture referred to is not the same canvas as that of the same name which, painted a little later, was bought by Prince Leopold of Saxe-Coburg, afterwards King of the Belgians, and is still in the Royal Palace at Brussels. Whatever may be the view now held as to Severn's work in Art, there can be no question as to the high opinion of him entertained by many good judges, including Calcott, Westmacott, and the Academician alluded to in the following letter :—

"Your music has been a feast to me. My love for you has made me think it equal to Purcell's. You have been very fortunate in finding such very fine words (mind I am speaking of the song): it is certainly a very poetical subject. The originality of your musical setting has struck me more than the excellent and even learned Harmonies. One thing strikes me as a defect, that the accompaniment is made too much of. It sometimes is independent and even interrupts the subject. Now, an accompaniment should be to assist the theme, by clothing its nakedness. Since I came to Italy I have been more than ever convinced that the accompaniments to a song should be very simple. Are not Mozart's? Perhaps Haydn's are not in such a good taste, they are too complex. Your song in this respect has too much the character of a symphony or overture. Look at Purcell in his songs, and you will find that he does not put forth all his strength in harmony. It strikes me that the symphony or chorus is where all this knowledge is to be shown, but a song is to be beautiful in its simplicity. I sometimes think that a musician might *now* be very original, by writing quite in the early simple style, because that style is still very much admired, and would be also in the works of a modern composer. In painting it is so, and it is the most difficult thing to acquire. All the effect produced by bravery in the art—such as great knowledge of the mechanism, violent contrast, and strong expressions, are easily produced, and what all can and do produce—but to accomplish that gentle loveliness of expression, touching most by simplicity, and that simplicity always touching the heart—this is the true thing, and what few, and none but those who by great striving against the ostentatious display of all their knowledge, can produce. Yet those are the works that all love, that belong to all ages, that are the chief works in every art, where they primarily address themselves to the heart and not the head.

"Now, my dear Tom, I am saying all these things because I know it is the case with you musicians to make your beautiful pursuit only for your own comprehension, that is, in its highest parts. I have heard musicians continually say that the Fugue is a thing (and many other parts of music) that was never meant to be relished but by those very learned in the science. This must be a mistake. It cannot be good if it does not affect those who may be ignorant of the science and yet have very great feeling. Of the finest kind are Haydn's Symphonies—they affect all, the unlearned and learned equally. There are subjects in them for the delight of the most common mind, yet are not less estimated by the musicians.

"You must tell me if you know the gentleman who wrote this fine song. Mr. Brown seemed very much struck with it. If you do know him personally I would advise you to set the highest value on his acquaintanceship, for he is a man not only of genius but of most beautiful taste. I am most anxious to hear that you do know him.

"So now I have had my say about *you* I will say something about *myself.* First, I have been rather ill from a cold which brought on a jaundice; now the yellow is gone, and I am nearly recovered, for I have such a fine fellowship in my good friend Mr. Brown, who is living in my house. We cook, and are completely at home; perhaps this has tended to keep away those horrid attacks of indigestion, which have ceased since October twelvemonth. In my painting I have made great progress, thank God! owing to my journey to Venice. My large picture of 'Alexander' is just completed, and I think seems to be liked. It has been a great labour. The subject I mentioned for my next—of Lorenzo di Medici—I must give up for the present. I have now been studying a long time, and got to a profound knowledge of the most difficult and essential parts of painting, and when I painted the 'Alcibiades' I found myself so deficient in almost every point that I have since set to most seriously. I felt that my pension was given me for this purpose, and that although I could paint pictures and be getting on, yet I was determined to make myself equal to the execution of works with facility.

" Now I have chosen the subject of a Mother and Child. They were occupied in making wreaths; the child, gathering flowers, had strayed to the very edge of a precipice, when, had the mother spoken, much less have reached forward, the infant would have dropped. The mother, in this dreadful moment, shows her bosom, and the infant involuntarily wants to go to her. I shall have in this picture a beautiful landscape. Mr. Cook, the R.A., has visited me many times, and the other day in my absence he told Mr. Brown that I should certainly be one of the greatest English artists, and he said this without hesitation. This has given me courage, as Mr. Cook is one of the Council of the Royal Academy. He seems very much satisfied with what I have done. We are going together to [paint?] in the Vatican. Now they are beginning to talk to me about commissions. I daresay this winter I shall receive some order to paint a picture. I send you a glee which was done for Christmas Day; both the words and music are mine, but if you like to try your master hand do. Mind the bass is the drunken man moving, except when he speaks. So now, my dear Tom, good-bye, and may God bless and preserve you.

" Your affectionate brother,

" J. S."

CHAPTER VII.

THE year 1824 found Severn thoroughly at home in Rome,
and determined to remain there at any rate for some years.
There was reasonable prospect, by this time, of his making
enough by his brush to support himself; if he failed, he could
return to London, he wrote, and take to musical criticism,
and even undertake what Keats called "the theatricals."

The spring was mainly occupied by him in love-making
and work. The former came to nothing, though he seems
to have had a genuine, if not very deep attachment to
the young English girl who had fascinated him. A few
months later, however, she left Italy for England, and he
never saw her again. It does not appear that there was
more than one "wounded heart."

In May he heard from Richard Westmacott Jr., who was
then paying his first visit to Venice.

"Venice,
"May 20th, 1824.

"MY DEAR SEVERN,

"*Eccomi quà* at last—full of wonder and admiration of the famed
tho' fallen spouse of the Adriatic. I have always studiously avoided looking
at views, or reading, or listening to descriptions of Venice, wishing to

come upon it at once without any prejudice, and if possible to save myself
a disappointment upon seeing the original, after reading some account of
it, like Eustace's and Piranesi's of Rome, which we all agree are humbugs,
and only lead one astray. I have been well repaid for waiting for the reality
—any description must fall short of it—my imagination sometimes gets
upon stilts, and I had, of course, *fancied a sort of a city* in the water, with
latticed windows, orange trees, gondolas, &c., &c., but I had not neared the
original. I came from Ferrara by water, and I think few things can be
more beautiful than the scene that presented itself as soon as we entered
the principal canal of Venice. It was about four o'clock in the evening,
and the weather—tho' the sky was not quite Italian—very fine. I can't
tell you how I felt as we cut through the water. I was full of Desdemona,
Shylock, Pierre, Belvidere, old Dandolo, and fifty other delightful and
interesting associations; but you have seen it all, and are just the sort of
chap to enjoy it, so I need not tease you with any details of the *what* nor
the *why* I admired. As soon as I could I saw the Rialto, then S. Mark,
then the Bridge of Sighs, 'on either side a Palace and a Prison;' in fact,
from the time of my arrival I have been running about devouring whatever came in my way. I am now driven in by darkness and fatigue, but
before going to my couch have resolved to keep my promise of writing to
my dear Giuseppe. Mr. Brown told me he had written to you. I
suppose he told you of my having proceeded almost immediately on my
arrival at Florence to Carrara. I returned in a few days, and was glad to
avail myself of his kind offer of an introduction to Leigh Hunt. I saw but
little of him, unfortunately for me, but that little made me regret that our
acquaintance was so lately made and so soon to be interrupted. I spent
much of my last day in Florence with him and Mr. Brown in the Vale of
the Belle Donne, which we all enjoyed very much—could I have remained
longer in dear Tuscany we should have spent many pleasant days
together I daresay, for Mr. Brown is just the man to be happy with, and
I feel I should have liked Mr. Hunt more and more every time I met
him. I saw the *Brunino*, and think him a very fine little fellow; your
miniature is certainly very like him. He spoke nothing but Italian, and
his papa—like all papas—is not a little proud of him. I thought our old
plague, Johnny Hunt, looked very ill. I think he must be improved, for
altho' he tried to bolt up to me with his *taking, innocent*-sounding 'Ah!
how d'ye do, Sir?' I saw he made himself scarce as soon as possible—poor
child! or, rather, poor parents! I suspect a bad child is a curse of which
we single gentlemen can't even *imagine* the bitterness. God save us from
it if ever we become Benedicts! I wrote to Mr. MacDonald a week or ten
days ago, on business; I begged him to deliver two or three messages from
me to you, Kirkup, and others; of Kirkup I requested some information
of poor Eastlake. I shall go to the Post Office to-morrow to see whether
there is any letter for me. Knowing how bad E. was when I left Rome,
I feel extremely anxious to hear something of him. I meant to stay here
seven or eight days, in which time they tell me I may see Venice pretty
well. I am still with Mr. Critshell, and it is probable we may make a
long journey together. I wish I had a brother artist here, such as your-

self or Kirkup; a sculptor ought not to go picture-hunting alone, he loses half the things worth seeing, or frequently passes by a *non è male* work just for want of knowing where and how to take it. I, however, think myself very fortunate in having found so gentlemanly and agreeable a companion as Mr. Critshell. I never could feel happy nor enjoy anything alone, *solus*. Had I not had companions from Rome I don't know what I should have done. You recollect what a weeping, miserable, mourning day we had to start on by way of helping me to recover my *spirits*, Gesu Maria! but Mr. Brown made us all merry, after a fashion, in spite of ourselves—well, I won't imagine I am not to return to Rome next year. A letter lately received from my father is neither one thing nor the other, but in my mind full of *unintelligibles*. *Sto sperando.* God bless you.*

"Yours truly,
"RICHARD WESTMACOTT."

About the same time he received a joyous and characteristic letter from Brown, of which a portion may be quoted.

" *Maiano (Florence)*,
" May 20th, 1824.

"MY DEAR SEVERN,

"Do not think me unkind for not having until this time made you acquainted with a matter of the utmost moment concerning myself. Indeed, it would have been useless in me to ask your advice on such a point, as no opinion of yours could have changed my resolution. You, who know me well, must be aware that though I have heedlessly, perhaps too heedlessly, gained among my friends and associates a character at times approaching to folly and buffoonery (for which I am now as repentant as I ought to be), yet that I have always, beneath that trivial behaviour, entertained the most serious reflections; you, I say, know this well, and ought not to be surprised at the step I have taken. My future happiness has been the constant idea in my mind ever since I left you; and hating as I do the vain and gaudy glitter of this world, and feeling that nothing but a religious retirement can give ease to my soul, I have determined to enter a convent. I am now bound by law to remain there for five months, and at the end of that period I cannot believe I shall once desire to bid adieu to so blissful a habitation. Before this reaches you I shall have entered within its holy walls. Hunt speaks very kindly to me under the circumstances—I know he means kindly—but nothing he can say shall make me waver; indeed, it is now too late. My Italian friends, Gianetti and Magini, when I first acquainted them with this change in my situation, not only refused to believe me, but when I assured them of the fact, they began—would you credit it?—to jeer me;

---

* The reader may care to turn from this letter, recording first impressions of Venice, by the sculptor, Westmacott, in 1824, to that by the painter, Richmond, in 1839 (pp. 189–191, *post*), and to that by the critic, Ruskin, in 1843 (pp. 205–7, *post*).

yet, what was their astonishment when I let them into the secret that I was going to live in a Convent of Nuns! Tol-de-rol-lol! Fal-lal-lal-la! Yes! you rogue, I have taken half a suppressed Nunnery for a villa, with four rooms and a pantry and a kitchen on the first. I am buying furniture at a swinging rate. By-the-by, I occupy the Abbess's apartments. Charlie and I intend to be as merry as grigs here. Leigh Hunt talks of taking the other half of the Nunnery next October. I pay only 31½ crowns per annum. I forgot to tell you I've a glorious romping place, as big as a ball-room, at the top of the house. Did I take you in as you read the former page? Yes, Severn, thoughts of my future happiness make me retire to this convent."

A letter written by Severn about midsummer to his father gives the origin of his ‘King Lear,’ certainly one of the best pictures the artist ever painted. It was a fortunate year for him, for he received another and very generous commission from his friend Mr. Crauford, who had previously enabled him to go to Florence by commissioning him to paint the ‘Madonna della Sedia’ at the Pitti. Moreover, from a letter to his sister Maria, written about the same time, it appears that he was asked by Lady Westmorland to paint six pictures illustrative of scenes or episodes in ‘Quentin Durward.’

When the summer heats made residence in Rome no longer a pleasure, he began to make ready for his long-projected expedition to the Alban slopes, in order to paint his ‘Italian Vintage.’ He was aware of the reputation of the women of Genzano and L'Ariccia for beauty and grace, and he decided to reside at one or the other for a time. Ultimately he chose L'Ariccia, as the healthier and more picturesque.

In that lovely country which stretches along the flanks of the Alban Hills, from Frascati to Velletri, every one must feel as a poet and see as a painter. There is a beauty about the lakes of Albano and Nemi, and the wooded valleys and volcanic uplands which environ them, of a fascination absolutely unique.

It was to this ideal country that Severn prepared to betake himself, and though then as now either Frascati or Albano offered the most obvious advantages, he believed he would be freer in the pursuit of his work, more fortunate in

PORTRAIT-STUDY OF A LADY OF GENZANO, MADE IN 1824.

To face page 144.

results, and at less expense to his purse, if he settled at Genzano or L'Ariccia. Genzano was the better known and the larger : but, despite its lofty seat, it had a bad reputation for fever, and it had neither the quietness nor the distinctiveness of its neighbour. Severn had already made a sketch in oils of his proposed picture. The latter was to be a large upright canvas, with vines growing up an elm ; the men on the branches of the tree to be severing the grape-clusters and lowering them to the women standing below, with outspread aprons to catch the grape-drift.

When he had first gone thither, he writes that he found the handsome Genzano peasant-women obdurate ; and that he was driven to the expedient of making known secretly that his picture was only a pretence, and that in truth he had come to select a wife from among them. The expedient was successful. Every girl and unmarried woman wanted to be painted by the young *Signor Pittore Inglese.* " In this happy turn of affairs, I did twelve figures for my picture— and these were afterwards considered in Rome to be the most striking studies that had ever been done of Roman peasants by any contemporary."

At L'Ariccia Severn became acquainted with an Italian gentleman who then and later showed him much kindness. This was the Marchese d'Azeglio, who ultimately invited the young artist to reside in his house till he had finished his work upon or for the ' Vintage.'

"This is the same nobleman," writes Severn, " who has since become so famous as a politician, in forming and perfecting the Constitutional Government of Sardinia.* He was then a most gentlemanlike and

---

* Massimo Taparelli, Marquis of Azeglio, best known simply as Massimo d'Azeglio, was five years younger than Severn, and so in his twenty-sixth year when the two met. His father had come to Rome in 1813, as Ambassador from the King of Sardinia, and he had accompanied him. In 1822 he returned by himself, and spent some seven or eight years in or near Rome, devoting himself to painting and literary study and composition. It was during this period that Severn knew him. Later, he married the daughter of the illustrious Manzoni. His famous national romance, ' Ettore Fieramosco,' was published in 1833, and was followed by many other important and widely influential writings. After a long and noble career as painter, author, soldier, patriot, and statesman, he became Prime Minister to the King of Sardinia.

accomplished companion, and I passed some weeks in his company most
agreeably and profitably. We seldom talked politics, and our conversations were mostly on history, poetry, or art—for in painting he himself
excelled, and was indeed at that very time engaged upon an historical
landscape. He was a tall, dignified man, rather fair for an Italian, and so
far as I could judge more English than Italian in his sympathies and
tastes.* He was well learned in our history, and, indeed, in that of every
other country, and it was one of the fascinations of his conversation that
he could with ease and elegance go at once from ancient to modern
history, or *vice versâ*, and in this enviable range could combine the history
of any country in a most charming and illustrative way. One thing
struck me as characteristic of him, a marked dislike of Popery—indeed,
his whole mental attitude was founded upon this dislike and distrust; not
that he confessed to Protestantism, but simply that he could not but
regard Popery as the source of modern Italian misery."

Naturally, this acquaintanceship meant much to Severn,
and it was one he was wont to recall with pride and pleasure
when in after years the name of Massimo d'Azeglio was in
every one's mouth.

The 'Italian Vintage' occupied the greater part of a year
before it was finished. It was purchased for the Duke of
Bedford by his brother, Lord William Russell. The general
idea at that time as to the monetary value of modern pictures
was neither flattering to Art nor encouraging to artists.
Severn was asked by Lord William Russell, after his large
picture (the sixteen figures in which were half life-size, and
with what the painter calls a background of extensive landscape) had been bought by agreement, to name his price.
The moderate sum of £150 was asked. Lord William Russell
wrote that he thought the price extravagant, and declared
that from his long acquaintanceship with young artists, he
could say that the price bore no comparison with what was
generally asked.

"I answered that I had no knowledge of other artists' prices, but I
wished and was obliged to live by my profession; that I had carefully
reckoned the length of time which I had been engaged upon the picture,
and the many expenses to which I had been put; and that, in a word,

---

* Severn at this time knew nothing of the anti-papal, or rather
patriotic Italian party, and for long after the rising of Victor Emmanuel's
star, he practically adhered to the Papal dominion, notwithstanding his
indignation with and even abhorrence of its incapacity, weakness, and too
frequently conspicuous iniquity.

the price would barely cover all. He was satisfied, and even pleased, with my answer, and the Duke himself wrote that he thought the price moderate."

While still in the hill-country he heard again from Brown :—

"George Keats has written a very long letter to Dilke, to exculpate himself from the charge against him, and expressing himself as very angry that ever it was made. Dilke thinks his letter conclusive in his favour, and sends me the heads of it. I am sorry I cannot agree with him, as his assertions are directly in opposition not only to what John Keats said (who might on money affairs be easily in error) but to what Mr. Abbey told me. Therefore I have asked Dilke, in order to clear up all doubt, to call on Mr. Abbey, and procure his further explanation. Should it appear that George is guiltless, I will not only inform you, but endeavour to do him justice with every one in my power. He owns, for the sake of John's feelings, that he voluntarily deceived him ; making him believe he was at times richer than he was, and also that he was borrowing money from him ; John's consequent destitution of course made others acquainted with this, and therefore how can George, however innocent, be surprised at the charge having been made against him, grounded, as it was, on his own words and deeds? This I think so strange that it is only possible. Indeed, he makes out that when he first went to America John had not a penny, and that he (George), under pretence of adjusting accounts, gave him £300, without John knowing anything of such a gift. When he went for the second time to America, he says he took from him only £170, so that, by his account, John had been the better for his brotherhood to the amount of £130. Mr. Abbey's story to me differed in *sums* and *facts* from George's. What think you of this ? "

In October he was still at L'Ariccia, for on the 4th he wrote to his sister Maria ; and from his record of his doings he certainly seems to have been indefatigable. He there turned his musical faculty to account, and appears to have fulfilled the part of organist at the church to his own and others' satisfaction. It is interesting to learn that at this early date, "Keats's name was rising," for though the 'Adonais' had drawn attention to him, it cannot be said that in England he was at all widely known, while there is evidence that the sale of his writings flagged sometimes to nothing for months. The unexpected reward which his devotion to Keats had won him was not long delayed in the coming, and it is pleasant to know that, as one instance, so good a judge of art and literature as Mr. Erskine of Linlathen first took an interest in the young artist, and commissioned a picture from him, on account of his connection with the poet, whose early death was even then regarded by not a few as a disastrous loss to English literature. Later on, he won the friendship of Mr. Ruskin, Mr. Gladstone, and other eminent men, primarily on the same account. "You would be surprised," he writes, "how often I am pointed out here as the friend of Keats."

The year 1825 was a memorable one for Severn. In that year he formed a friendship with Thomas Uwins,* the painter, which lasted unbrokenly for thirty-four years, and was fruitful of much good as well as pleasure. Another friendship, also, he gained, that of the Countess of Westmorland, of whom he had already seen a good deal; yet it was one that, though it brought him no little pleasure and advantage, was, later, the source of infinite pain and distress; and in this year, also, he came to know the lady whom, in 1828, he married.

In the summer of this year he went with Lady Westmorland and other friends to Mola di Gaeta, in the Neapolitan kingdom, and thence, later, he accompanied them to Naples. There he made some further acquaintanceships, one or two of which proved advantageous to him later on; and there he was glad to see much of Mr. Cotterell, the friend who had shown so many courtesies to Keats and himself from the time when the *Maria Crowther* arrived in the Bay of Naples till the day when they had set forth on their journey to Rome. He found to his regret that Miss Cotterell, who had at first benefited by the change of climate, had died of consumption. She had heard of Keats's sufferings and death, and with surprise as well as regret, for she had believed the young poet had a far better chance for his life than

---

* Thomas Uwins, R.A. (1782–1859), was, in early life, like Severn, an apprentice to an engraver; but at the age of sixteen he became an art-student. In 1814 he went to live in the South of France, and in 1824 to Italy, where he stayed till 1831. He was elected R.A. in 1838; and Keeper of the National Gallery in 1847. He was an able and successful painter.

she had for hers. She had been much attracted by Keats during the long voyage they had made in company. As for Mr. Cotterell, he shared her admiration and liking, and not to the exclusion of Severn. He was one of the few people at that time who were fully aware of the treasure possessed in ownership of the first editions of Keats's books.

In the autumn Severn returned to Rome and assiduously began to make up for lost time. There is no doubt that he gained much at this time from his frequent intercourse with Gibson, Westmacott, Seymour Kirkup, and others. In reply to a long chatty letter about what was happening in Rome, in his own circle rather,—how in addition to his sculptor-friend Gott and his family, a Captain Baynes had joined their company ; some gossip about a new 'relationship' of Kirkup's in Rome; about the despatch, to Brown's care, of his twenty-guinea " man on horseback, brother, and dog ; " and, chiefly, a request for his friend's advice upon one or two moot points in the problem of what constitutes Art and artistic selection,—he received the following letter from Brown, with its excellent response on the main point.

*   *   *   *   *

"I must tell you Hazlitt is here, and will shortly, so he says, proceed to Rome, where he is to study your favourite Raphael and Michael, and write a book on them. He will be accompanied by his wife. It is his wish to have a letter to you, which he certainly shall have. Don't let this news cause trepidation among the artists, though, it must be confessed, an Edinburgh reviewer is a formidable sort of person, and his pen is not one of the finest nibbed. I think you will like him extremely, and, between ourselves, he may be of the utmost service to you in your profession, as far as its patronage is concerned; and already he has a high opinion of your talents.

"What you ask about your painting, I think is easily answered. Painting is as poetry, where the art is to concentrate ideas, and to embellish common events through the medium of the imagination. Your naked boys treading the ripe grapes form a beautiful subject, sufficiently natural, because it is not too far removed from possibility. A man *soiling* the grapes, as I should call it, is an unworthy object for painting, purely because it is unpleasant, however undoubtedly in nature. In poetry and painting, things are not to be represented as they positively exist, for there is not an entire pleasure in them in that view ; but they should be embellished to the utmost, always however in taste, and in the feeling of the subject. Those who object to your boys, should, on the same principle, object to so many beautiful women assembled at the same moment in the same vintage—both are improbable, only the boys are less so. God has given us a real world and an imaginary one— both lovely and both perfect; and He has also given us the power to relieve our minds by flying from one to the other, and by mingling them at our will for our delight. The last belongs especially to the poet and the painter; when they fail to take advantage of it, they become matter-of-fact gentlemen, who use their fine words and their fine colours to no purpose. Your man is a matter-of-fact; your boys a touch of poetry. The former a disagreeable reality, the latter a brilliant probability, a threading of the imagination through the dull course of common events. Your own natural feeling led you to the beautiful, the poetic, and your fear of infringing on the *usual* mode, the *common one*, has startled you. Have I satisfied you ? "

It was about this time that Severn met, and was at once strongly attracted by Miss Elizabeth Montgomerie, Lady Westmorland's ward. In one of his ' Reminiscences ' he speaks of this events as having occurred towards the end of 1825, but other evidence, together with an allusion in a letter from Brown, written in August of the same year, and hints in his home-letters, prove that he must have met Miss Montgomerie during or shortly after the Christmas season of 1824–25, if not, indeed, earlier.

"It was [in the early winter of] 1825," he writes, "that I had the first sight of my future wife, during a visit of respect which, in company with [Sir] Charles Eastlake, I was making to the Countess of Westmorland, who was then residing in the Palazzo Rospigliosi. This young lady, ostensibly the adopted daughter of Lady Westmorland, was the orphan child of General Lord Montgomerie, who had died in 1803, while the army of which he was in command was in Sicily. Miss Montgomerie, who had come to Rome with Lady Westmorland, or had joined her there, soon interested everyone among the Countess's friends; and this perhaps, not so much by her highly born beauty and a certain gentleness of manner, as by her position as protégée of such an animated specimen, or rather fiery particle of womanhood, as the Countess certainly was—as the adopted daughter of the most remarkable Englishwoman then resident in Rome.

"This impulsive, arrogant, dictatorial, but witty and brilliant woman was cursed with another turbulent tendency; namely, to pay no regard to times and seasons. Night would sometimes be day, and day night, to her too compulsive mind. A natural consequence was that this *un*-commonplace lady was often asleep when everybody else was awake or tried to be. Hence arose her custom to make Miss Montgomerie act

GROUP FOR "THE FOUNTAIN," PAINTED AT L'ARICCIA, 1825.

One work so-named belongs to the King of the Belgians, and one to
the Marquis of Lansdowne.

To face page 151.

entertainer (and detainer) to any guest who should make an informal call, while she hurriedly or leisurely made her toilette."

Severn enters into full and prolonged details about the charms of the lady who was to become his wife, about his sensations when he first met her, about the growth of his regard to affectionate sympathy and thence to love: with, incidentally, an occasionally entertaining but irrelevant *chronique scandaleuse.* Most of all this may be omitted from this narrative. Miss Montgomerie was really a beautiful girl, and certainly unhappy with her intolerant guardian. She was attracted by the handsome young artist (and Severn at this time must have been exceptionally winsome and good-looking) and won by his courtesy, sympathy, and admiration. He, for his part, though he confesses to "a gay and elastic temperament which had led me to suppose marriage was not altogether my forte," was touched by the girl's real loneliness, by her evident unhappiness under Lady Westmorland's tyrannical rule, and by her beauty. It was, with him (though he does not seem to have quite realised it for some time), a case of love at first sight.

"When I left this lovely vision after that first brief interview," he says, "my life seemed to have taken on a new form, and I was impelled to shape it anew; it was like the lump of shapeless clay in the sculptor's hands, and I was the sculptor filled with vague conceptions of fresh creation."

A lengthy period, however, was to pass before Severn asked Miss Montgomerie to promise to be his wife, a request which was granted on condition of the betrothal being kept secret till the marriage could be arranged. Miss Montgomerie feared Lady Westmorland's displeasure, and it is quite clear that Severn was by no means willing to incur it, if honourably avoidable. The fears of both were, as a matter of fact, well founded.

But meanwhile Severn was not idle at his easel. Besides another 'Fountain'—with the landscape background taken from a grotto and a grove of trees in the Giugi Park at

L'Ariccia—he was busy with several important undertakings.

Writing to his brother Tom on the last day of 1825, he concludes his long letter with these notable words :—

> "I have now been in Italy five years—it seems impossible. Betwixt you and me, certainly I gained more from poor Keats, who is dead and gone, than from any other source. He introduced me to all the learned men I know, and helped me on in my painting by his own great mind ; and then my name is so interwoven with his friendship and death that it will ever be an honour to me."

A few weeks later he received a visit from Walter Savage Landor, who on going to Rome bore a special letter from Brown to Severn. Landor and Severn at all times enjoyed each other's society.

Room must be found for the following amusing anecdote about Turner, from one of Thos. Uwins's many letters of this date to Severn.

> "The impression that Turner's pictures seem to have made on the English travellers as well as the foreign artists, appears very unfavourable, if I may judge from the reports. How is all this? are they deficient in the high qualities that used to distinguish his former works, or is he trifling with his great powers? The following simple account of him has amused me not a little. It is written me by a merchant travelling towards Bologna, a young man who knows nothing of art, and nothing, as you perceive, of the reputation of artists.
>
> "'I have,' he writes, 'fortunately met with a good-tempered, funny little elderly gentleman, who will probably be my travelling-companion throughout the journey. He is continually popping his head out of window to sketch whatever strikes his fancy, and became quite angry because the conductor would not wait for him whilst he took a sunrise view of Macerata. "Damn the fellow!" says he, "he has no feeling." He speaks but a few words of Italian, about as much of French, which two languages he jumbles together most amusingly. His good temper, however, carries him through all his troubles. I am sure you would love him for his indefatigability in his favourite pursuit. From his conversation he is evidently *near kin to*, if not *absolutely* an artist. Probably you may know something of him. The name on his trunk is J. W. or J. W. M. Turner!'"

During the summer Severn wrote to his brother Tom, that his picture of 'Lear and Cordelia' was wanted by three would-be purchasers, one of them the Duke of

DOLCE FAR NIENTE.

One of several finished studies for " A Pastoral."

To face page 153.

Bedford; and adds that he was then painting nothing but
what was commissioned. A little later he wrote again:

"Amongst my best news, you will be glad to know that I have made a
good friend and patron in Prince Leopold. He has just sent me a most
kind letter from Paris, offering me his services and assuring me of his
esteem, and, what is better, ordering me to paint him another picture, and
what is better still, telling me I may receive the money when and how I
please. Now all this is most princelike. My works are to be placed in
Manchester House; there now, think of that! If you, my dear Tom,
think that being introduced to the Prince Leopold would be of service to
you, nothing can be easier for you. As my brother, you will find
him receive you well and speak of me like my other friends, for I have
known him well here through my friend the Countess of Westmorland,
and he seems very desirous to serve me. My friends here tell me that I
shall get an order from our King through these means. Think of that!
Am I not a lucky dog? Who would have thought all this of such a poor
fellow as I was? why, I am like to become downright illustrious!

*   *   *   *   *   *

"I am living very well here. If only Keats was here it would be
delightful—for by this time I am quite accustomed to the place."

I may close this account of the main incidents in Severn's
life in 1827, by extraction from one of his MS. 'Reminiscences' of a vivid and strange account of a terrible event
that happened at that time in Rome, an event which had
important consequences both in Rome and upon the Papal
policy, and would have created excitement throughout the
civilized world had not extraordinary precautions been taken
(at the time of the priest's confession) to prevent any definite information getting into the Foreign press. Even
letters, it was asserted, underwent a rigorous scrutiny. I
give Severn's account practically in his own words.

"A marvellous and horrible execution took place in Rome in 1827,
which I beheld most unwillingly. I was returning from the Vatican
across the fields,* and had just crossed the Ripetta ferry, when an immense
crowd which was moving onward to the Piazza del Popolo irresistibly bore
me with it. I discovered that the cause was a criminal going to execution, and although I had long determined never to be witness of such a
scene, yet the wild fury of the crowd carried me along off my feet: and on
finding myself at the Piazza del Popolo, bewildered with the scene, I got

---

* The Prati di Castello, now alas! ruined by the jerry-builder.

into a booth which was being erected for the Carnival, and so had a complete command of the whole Piazza. It was soon made known to me that the culprit was a lad of eighteen, accused of the murder of a Monsignore, which by the Roman law is punishable by death by the hammer. There was a universal feeling of pity in the crowd, and it was evident that the Roman people did not think it possible that such a youth could have committed such a crime, for. he was described to me as a simple, harmless lad, employed as an under-servant in the murdered Prelate's house, and physically and morally unequal to such an atrocious deed. He was conveyed in a cart, handcuffed, with two priestly confessors holding a crucifix close to him, and apparently in close and intense communication with him in the hope of forcing his confession of guilt. This he steadfastly refused to make, and with tears and solemn protestations declared his entire innocence. All this interested me in his favour, and when he was led forward and up to the scaffold blindfold I felt assured that he must be innocent, for everything, even to his general appearance and terrified and almost convulsed features, overwhelmingly pointed to that conclusion, and unmistakably he was a lad of the most simple character. The executioner was provided with a long square piece of iron about two inches thick, also a large knife. He began by forcing the poor screaming lad down on his knees, and then I just saw.him raise the iron bar to strike and hammer the boy to death, when I was unable to behold more, and involuntarily turned round. But one tremendous blow I did hear, and knew that the skull was dashed in, for the convulsive groans of the multitude declared it. The agitation and fainting of some and the dismay of all was a sight so superhuman, inasmuch as I saw an expression on the single face of the crowd as it were, such as I never saw before or since, that I could not but conclude (if such an ordeal could *possibly* have any moral good in it), that only the fact of the victim being indisputably an atrocious assassin could warrant even a shadow of excuse for such a criminal abuse of legal authority. After some minutes, when I recovered sufficient strength to turn round, the executioner had thrown down the lad's body and was kneeling on it. His left hand was thrust in the broken skull and scattering the brains from it on to the scaffold; while in his right hand he had the large knife and was cutting off the head. On and on he proceeded deliberately to amputate the limbs, the arms and the legs, while the scaffold was streaming with blood, and the whole figure of the executioner also. When his bloody work was done he packed all the parts together, each in its place, and finished by covering the frightful remains with a mat. Of course I took particular notice of the executioner, his face, his hands, his dress, his top-boots, all I remember vividly up to this moment. The moral impression on the Romans was the very contrary of that meant by the Pope. From the outset they had doubted the lad's guilt, as he had been condemned wholly on circumstantial evidence, a doubt that became a conviction because of his simple youthful appearance, and known gentleness of nature. It was everywhere declared, moreover, that at the utmost the execution should only have been by the usual guillotine. The result was a general execration of the Pope's harsh cruelty and ignorant bigotry.

"About a fortnight later I was crossing the same ferry and fields to go to the Vatican, when I heard a guitar and some singing at the door of an *osteria*. When I approached I was astonished to see the very executioner in the identical dress and boots tho' clean from blood : further, that this was the man who was gaily playing and singing to women and boys at the table. There was a total abstraction from the atrocious scene of blood that had passed a fortnight before, although the savage strangeness of the execution continued to be the subject of conversation. And here I would stop to remark that in all my Anglo-Roman experience, and all my enquiries about the various executions, no Italian criminal is ever known to confess. The answer after an execution is invariably ' that he died like a dog,' and this I find extends to most Catholic countries, and is a singular characteristic in the contrast it affords with like episodes in our own country, where it is a rare circumstance to find a criminal dying impenitent; indeed the confession is the interesting part of an English criminal's end. I don't stop to reason about this fact, as the tremendous finale of this murderous ordeal will speak for me. Some six or seven months after the execution, the whole Roman people were convulsed again by the astounding fact, that the attendant-priest on the murdered prelate had just died, and had confessed the fact that he himself was the murderer. He admitted on his dying oath that he had contrived to put all the appearances of the guilt on the simple lad, had seen his execution, had dined afterwards, and in no way betrayed himself. But he had not lived a comfortable life, for it seems his conscience had helped to hasten his death. The Pope, Gregory XVI., was so struck down that it was admitted he fainted at the news, and he certainly shut himself up for some days in absolute seclusion. For the remainder of his reign he would never allow another execution. Most certainly at the time everyone was against the presumptive guilt of the lad on the scanty evidence, but for the crime of murdering a Prelate the Church imperatively required a victim. Officially, in the Papal Rome of that day, vengeance was importunate, and such a crime could not be left unexpiated, as reverence for the Princes of the Church was regarded as even more essential than reverence for God. I remember Admiral Sir William Parker once saying a striking thing on my asking him about the execution of Admiral Byng, who was shot for presumptive cowardice. Sir William replied, 'Certainly 'twas a most atrocious act of injustice, but it was the act of a political party, and however it is to be condemned, it has certainly made good admirals of us ever since': and he added, 'there cannot be a doubt that the world is so callous about the reform of any bad principle or custom that at last it requires the sacrifice of an innocent individual to bring it about. Then for the first time society becomes sensible of the evil, and of the imperative necessity of doing away with it for ever; but without a martyr nothing is ever done, and so it was that with the execution of poor Admiral Byng the whole system of the British Navy was changed.'

"This striking remark I have often thought of since the Roman murder and mutilation. Up to that time the Church had held it as a principle of power to punish with unchristian severity any agression done against it, and particularly any affront or violence to its high dignitaries; but now these matters are treated like other worldly things, and society is improved by the change, and even perhaps somewhat more inclined to the Roman Church. This principle of the martyrdom of an innocent individual," adds Severn in his MS., "may not only be traced through the history of every country, and of every experience and improvement, but also supremely in the sacrifice made by the blessed Christ himself: for the pagan principle of inhumanity and hard wickedness was such that nothing less was required than that He should die guiltless on the Cross, in order to impress the cruel world with a fact that would call up the novel tenderness of human nature, the feeling of repentance, the consciousness of our united nature, the dependence on a benevolent Providence against our pagan pride; all these matters were new to the world and necessary to its present well-being as well as to its ultimate salvation. Sceptics may say that the Christian principle has been abused, that greater cruelty has followed Christ, that the world has only become more cunning; but no doubt they shut their eyes to the truth that there is far more humanity in the world, as all subsequent history will prove by facts. Even the works of Shakespeare will prove it, for there cannot be a doubt, that the charm he gives us in the noble and elevated principle of his chief personages, the reward he finds for virtue, the moral he shows in patience and suffering—contrasting so strikingly as it all does with the Pagan authors of Greece and Rome, is all derived from the glorious Christian principle. The play of 'Hamlet' is altogether like the story of Orestes, save that the ghost forbids Hamlet to raise his hand against his guilty mother—'Leave her to Heaven, and to those thorns that in her bosom lodge.' This elevated principle may be found in the contrast of classic Pagan authors with those of the Christian era."

By all which, it may be added, Severn's familiarity with Epictetus, Marcus Aurelius, and other "classic pagans," was evidently of the most superficial kind, if it existed at all.

The year 1828, memorable to Severn as that of his marriage, was a prosperous one for him. He had been fortunate in obtaining several good commissions, and, as he wrote home, among the many canvases upon which he was then engaged there was not one but what was "to order." Among these was a picture of a 'Warrior and Lady,' which was painted for the Marquis of Lansdowne, and is now in the present Lord Lansdowne's collection.

In a letter from Brown, though written on the last day

of September, there is, strangely enough, not only no allusion to Severn's approaching marriage or even any apparent knowledge of that event as likely to be immediate, but he persuades his friend to come to Florence in October to recruit his health. Severn had succumbed to an attack of fever, severe though fortunately short, and he seems to have himself had some idea of going to Florence for a change; yet, at that time, his marriage was already arranged to take place in October. There is nothing in Brown's letter calling for quotation: it is mainly occupied with the news of the death of his brother Septimus, with messages to Severn from Landor and Kirkup, and from the writer to Eastlake and Gibson. At the end he adds: "Lady Westmorland is here: I trust that's no hindrance to your coming."

It is unnecessary to go into full detail on the subject of Severn's rupture with Lady Westmorland, and his marriage with Miss Montgomerie.

He declares that he long endured with the best grace he could Lady Westmorland's autocratic ways with Miss Montgomerie. The latter was often placed in unpleasant, if not even humiliating, positions, the only redeeming point in their favour being the frequent opportunities thereby afforded to the lovers to see each other away from Lady Westmorland's jealous scrutiny.

The result of the announcement of his coming marriage was that a complete break occurred between Severn and his old-time friend. He saw that it would not do to postpone the wedding: and as at the same time Miss Montgomerie declined to be married from the Palazzo Rospigliosi, and as Lady Westmorland had set nearly every one against her, it was settled that the event should take place in Florence. Severn wrote at once to Brown and other friends, and soon all needful arrangements were made. Till the last moment both he and Miss Montgomerie half anticipated some act of violence or interference on the part of one whom they could not but look upon as their enemy. But as a matter of fact the latter subdued her ill-will for the time being, sufficiently to allow her to be present at the ceremony, and to give Miss Montgomerie away : though once the celebration was over she refused to have anything to do with either. The young people were married by her son-in-law, Lord Burghersh.

Later on, some weeks after the turn of the year, Severn had a long letter from Seymour Kirkup, from which, among other things, we learn that Severn had no fewer than seventeen commissions on hand. No wonder that he had at last felt justified in marrying. There is an allusion to Trelawny as living with Chas. Brown : and, in a postscript, "they were all lies about his marriage in Greece, &c., &c."

Trelawny must have left Florence before midsummer. however, for on the 21st of June he wrote to Severn from Ancona. The letter gives exact indications as to the age of his little " Greek daughter," Zella :

" Ancona,
" June 21st, 1829.

" Dear Severn,

"It's long since we have communed by letters, and longer since we have met, yet now that we are resident in the same land, I hope to again shake hands with you, and that speedily ; more particularly as I am told you are matched with a gentle and most sweet lady ; now the mystery of alchemy, the discovery of longitude, the phœnix, the philosopher's stone, or the Duke of Milan with his enchanted island, old Sycorax, Caliban, and the rest (I say do you mark me), that I have thought any or all of these were less difficult to find than a woman whom a husband, after a year's possession, really thought perfect, as I am told you do your wife, and have felt no compunctious visitings of the conscience, or chew'd the cud of sweet and bitter memory of their days of freedom. Well, I wish you joy, and thinking it worth a journey, though to the Antipodes, shall certainly make a pilgrimage to the shrine where you have garnered up your heart, as doubtless will others from the four quarters of this bale of earth. Mecca, Loretto, and the hoary temples of India will lose their wonted worshippers, and even St. Peter's toe be left green with mould ; all worship being transferred to Mrs. Severn, and Shelley's creed of universal love become the sole creed on earth.

" But the object of my writing, though principally to congratulate you, is in some degree to serve myself, by requesting you will either through Freeborn and Smith, or Colonel Finch, or in what other manner you in your wisdom think meet, make or get made application to the proper authorities at Rome to commute the period of quarantine which my little daughter Zella will otherwise be condemned to pass in the Lazaret here, on her arrival from Corfu, from whence I expect her hourly on board an

Ionian vessel. In your application to the authorities at Rome who preside over the Quarantine regulations you must say the child is only three years of age, and in perfect health now, and insist on the danger of losing her health by long confinement at her delicate time of life, incarcerated in a comfortless Lazaret.

"Giving four or five days' grace on application where there is any grounds to go upon, or what is better, where interest is made, is an every-day occurrence, and not a favour that is often refused, so I pray you look about you, for it will be doing me a great favour; and address me here, to the care of H. Kain, Esq., English Consulate, Ancona, and so farewell.

"Yours and truly,
"J. E. TRELAWNY."

Within the first year of his marriage Severn was put to infinite annoyance and heavy expense by an iniquitous conspiracy to extort money from him for services that were never rendered. A long trial conducted with absolutely grotesque parody of justice, and characterised by shameful perjury and bribery, ensued. The whole affair, he writes, tended much to lower the small remaining prestige of the Pope's temporal government, and was often quoted against His Holiness.

But long before the final result of the trial, shortly after the shock and worry consequent upon the first gross miscarriages of justice, indeed, Severn, though still determined to fight his case and thwart his enemies, broke down in health. Ere long he became seriously indisposed. It was at this juncture that he received from the Hon. Henry Edward Fox, Lord Holland's eldest son, an invitation to occupy his vacant villa at Frascati, a welcome suggestion gladly acted upon. Thither the Severns went again in 1829, and there, late in the summer, a daughter was born to them and was christened Claudia.

Towards the end of December, 1829, Brown wrote to Severn, begging for his practical aid in the Keats Memoir, to which Severn replied on the 17th January. Late in February Brown wrote again, on the subject of the responsibility of George Keats in his financial relations with John. It would seem that it was about this time that Brown began in earnest to prepare the long-projected Memoir of Keats. Severn, of course, already knew of his project, and had offered to engrave his own miniature portrait of

Keats, though he had expressed a wish to engrave the
original in Miss Fanny Brawne's possession rather than a
replica of it. Brown wisely refused to take the responsibility of this suggested loan from Miss Brawne, and offered
the fine copy by himself in his own possession—and this
is the one that was ultimately engraved. The generous
proposal as to the prospective profits is eminently characteristic of the writer.

* " It was about four years and a half ago that George Keats sent to
Dilke a defence of himself, refuting the ' cruel charge ' (as he called it)
which I had made against him. Dilke sent me the purport of it, with a
request that I should make you and others acquainted with it. I did so,
for I had no evidence by which I could contradict his bold assertions;
though, as I told you in Rome, when you put the question to me, I had
no faith in his defence. Now, see the danger of villainy, and by what
unlooked-for chances it is laid bare. Having a bundle of papers which
belonged to Keats, part in his own handwriting, I lately opened it, on the
supposition the papers might assist me in the Memoirs. They were
chiefly letters between Keats and his brothers. I threw George's and
Tom's aside; but, after awhile, as if by an invisible hand, a passage in
one of George's own letters was turned towards me, which gave the lie
direct to the groundwork of his defence! I then searched further, and
found an Acc^t. Cur^t. of Abbey's; when, by these two documents, I was
instantly enabled to prove that every tittle of his defence was false, most
impudently and atrociously false. I have sent these proofs to Dilke,
requesting him to promulgate them among our acquaintances, that I may
be no longer suspected as a rash accuser. How he, who has been so
positive in George's favour from the first, will take it, I know not. I
expect his answer every day. You may rely on my obeying your orders
respecting the papers you have promised. You knew Keats before I did,
and perhaps you can give me some account of the development of his
mind as a poet. He himself has talked to me a little on this subject;
but, if possible, I would have further information. When did your
acquaintance with him begin? Nearly two months since I wrote to
Richards for assistance; no answer. If I knew how to direct a letter to
Haslam, I would apply to him; can you tell me his address? or will you
write to him? When I asked you about the terms for engraving, it
never entered my head that you would offer to engrave his miniature; if
you can spare time, this offer of yours is admirable. Respecting the
original, in Miss Brawne's possession, I am afraid you cannot have it.
Were I to ask her for the loan of it, I believe she would send it; and that
belief makes me the more delicate in asking for it; besides, I cannot run
the hazard of its being lost on the way. No, Severn, I do not feel myself

---

* Written after receipt of the letter from Severn given overleaf (p. 161.)

authorised in making that request. I will send you my copy, and the
drawing I made from your representation of him a little before his death,
together with that foolish little painting I have promised in a short while.
I have been very much occupied in Mrs. Medwin's affairs, battling with
bankers, and lawyers, with my hands day after day full of documents in
Courts of Law; let this be my apology, especially when I tell you I have
been of service to that ill-treated lady, with whom every one in Florence
sympathises. I have had much conscientious responsibility on my head,
little able to think of anything else. To return to Keats: Dilke urges
me, as a proof to the world of my friendship for Keats, and as the only
proof that I am not book-making, to declare, from the first, that I will
not accept of one penny of the profits which may arise from the Memoirs.
I never thought of profit, rather of loss, as I expected to pay a large sum
for the engravings. To my mind Dilke's advice is good; and I intend,
you willing, to set out with a declaration that the book is an offering to his
fame by you and me, both refusing to partake in the profits. The only
question then is, who is to have them? Should there be any, ought we
not to present them to his sister? It is true she does not *want* them, and
therefore we might dispose of them in some other way, something still
conducive to his fame, what say you?—what have you to propose? Give
my love to Mrs. Severn, and say I am eternally obliged to her for the
copy she is making. I am equally surprised and rejoiced to hear of her
excellent painting. Carlino also sends his love, with ten kisses to Claudia.
Shall we make up a match between them? Their ages are suitable,—ask
Mrs. Severn what she thinks of it. Kirkup is very well—all very well.
Did I tell you Marina is married? I cannot, literally *cannot*, answer
your question about Trelawny. I'm turned whist-player.

" Yours most sincerely,

" CHARLES BROWN."

Severn's earlier letter of the 17th January may now
be given, for convenience' sake, together with several
" Keatsian " letters addressed to Brown, though written at
considerable intervals apart. Each deals either with the
question of the Memoir of, or a monument to, the poet.

" January 17th, 1830.

" Your letter found me in all the glorious confusion of moving. I
recognized it as from you, and so put it into my pocket to read in the
first quiet moment. I am glad I did so, for its contents affected me much,
altho' it was agreeable news, for everything about poor Keats is melancholy. I am content that this reverse in the fate of his works gives you
the occasion to pay a true tribute to his memory, such as I have ever
long'd should be done, and such as I know you quite able to do.

" I feel, that if you can get over my defective writing, and promise me
(which I know you will) not to expose it to the public as mine (for I
am not a little proud of Keats as my friend), that I can supply you with

ample materials, which I will write spontaneously, not only as to facts which I have witnessed, but also as to my own feeling and impression of his beautiful character. I will not expect or oblige you to use anything I write but as you see fit, but I shall expect that you destroy these papers when you have used them, as I feel they *must* contain invectives against many persons whose enmity, or even notice, I am little anxious to have.

" Respecting the portrait I feel differently, and shall be proud to make my appearance before the public as the unchang‹d friend of Keats, loving his memory now he is dead, as I did himself and his works when he was alive, and this is an honour that no one shall share with me, not even the engraver, for I will take up the graver once more and fancy myself inspired to give his resemblance to the world, faulty as it may be, yet done with all my heart and soul. I think the miniature will make a good engraving, and have already imagined the style of the thing, and long to be about it. It would be necessary to have the one in colours to engrave from, which can soon be had from England, as it is such a trifle,—not that I think yours defective in any respect, but it is a great advantage always to engrave from colours when it [is] possible. I take it one great reason why the Italian engravings are so stony and lifeless is because they are copied from mere black and white drawings, whereas there exists a singular power in engraving in the insertion of colours. So pray write immediately for the original in colours, and I will commence the moment I receive it. It may come by the Courier quite safe. . . ."

" Rome,
" April 15th, 1830.

" . . . . You ask me what shall be done with the profits of our work to poor Keats's memory. Now I have thought a good deal of it, and am going to propose *that we erect a monument to his memory here in Rome* to the full extent of the money arising from the sale of the work. I have consulted Gibson, who says that for £200 something very handsome may be made. I have a subject in my mind for the Basso Rilievo, which I think I once mentioned to you before. It is Keats sitting with his half-strung lyre—the three Fates arrest him—one catches his arm—another cuts the thread—and the third pronounces his end. This would make a beautiful Basso Rilievo, and as the gravestone is so unworthy him, and so absurd (as all people say), and as the spot is so beautiful, I hope you will agree to it. Gibson seem'd very much taken with the idea of placing a work of his on this spot.

" I knew Keats as far back as 1813. I was introduced to him by Haslam. He was then studying at Guy's Hospital, yet much inclined to the Muses. I remember on the second meeting he read me the Sonnet on Solitude, in which is the line

' To start* the wild bee from the foxglove bell.'

He was at that time more playful in his manner, the world seem'd to have

---

* A misquotation for " startles."

nothing to do with him. Poetry was evidently at that time his darling hope. He disliked the surgery, and complained that his guardian, Mr. Abbey, forced him to it against his will. He was introduced to Mr. Hunt, I think, in 1814 or '15, which wrought a great change in him. It confirmed him in his future career, and I think intoxicated him with an excess of enthusiasm which kept by him four or five years, perhaps until you knew him. This was injurious to him, as Hunt and others not only praised his works and spoke of them as faultless, but even advised him to publish them. Now, merit as they then had, they were not fit things to offer to the world, and I have always thought that that publication was in a great measure the reason poor Keats did not sooner acquire the power of finishing his works. At the same time, he got a kind of mawkishness also from Hunt, which to my thinking was a fault, and which he got rid of when he came to live with you. Yet that first volume gives a good idea of his beautiful character—of one who, on his death-bed, acknowledged that his greatest pleasure, in almost every period of his life, had been in watching the growth of flowers and trees—and it [was] thro' this medium that he was so profound in the Greek Mythology. At my first acquaintance with him he gave me the compleat idea of a Poet—'twas an imagination so tempered by gentleness of manner and steady vivacity, that I never saw him without arguing on his future success. At that time he had no morose feeling, or even idea. He never spoke of any one, but by saying something in their favour, and this always so agreeably and cleverly, imitating the manner to increase your favourable impression of the person he was speaking of. At that time he was not well acquainted with painting, but soon acquired a very deep knowledge of it. Indeed, I used to observe that he had a great power of acquiring knowledge of all kinds, for, after a few years, he used to talk so agreeably on Painting and Music, that I was charmed with him, and have often spent whole days with him devoted to these things. The only difference in his personal appearance at first was that he had not that look of deep thought, but, as I said, his look and manner were more playful.

"How long shall [you] be occupied on this work? I would like to know, that I may be ready with the Engraving. The original miniature I should like to have had, for yours, good as it is, will render my engraving a mere copy from a copy—yet I am content and anticipate that I shall succeed. I think the picture well calculated for an engraving . . .

"I do not know Haslam's address. He knew Keats before I did."

"*Rome,*
"March 14th, 1834.*

"Now I don't know what you'll say to the request I am going to make, that you come off to Rome without a moment's delay and bring Keats's

---

* Brown at this time was still living in Florence, though illness and financial embarrassments were soon to lead to his departure for England.

M 2

tragedy with you. There are here five Englishmen, who have all been together at Cambridge. They are devoted admirers of Keats, and as they are really clever fellows I must confess myself gratified with their attentions to me as the friend of Keats. Now you must know that they have been acting—two of them are first-rate—and they made me join them iu the 4th Act of the 'Merchant of Venice,' as Gratiano, when I was so much struck with one (Mr. O'Brien) as the very man for Ludolph in Keats's 'Otho.' His voice and manner of reading remind me most forcibly of Keats himself. When I mentioned to them the tragedy, they were all on fire to be at it, but I did not see any hope until I heard from Capt. Baynes, who is also an actor, that we could easily have the beautiful private theatre here. I then recollected how much some years since you would have liked to have had the tragedy acted in Rome, when there were private theatricals, and I think how much more you would like it done now by *devoted admirers of Keats, good actors, and handsome young men* into the bargain. I assure you that I think it would be well done, and as they are all young men of rank, it would certainly be a good report to its forthcoming. Should you not be able to come yourself, nor even Charley, to play the Page, cannot you send me the MSS. by the return of post? I will be particular that no copies be taken in any way.

"Now I wonder what you will say to all this. Is there any possibility that you throw cold water upon it?

"And now I am going to wrangle with you. Here I have heard and heard of Keats's Life which you are doing; *I* have written and written to you about it, and now I hear nothing more, now, when the world is looking for it, and the tragedy. Why, you would be astonished, were you to know the many who come to me as the friend of Keats, and who idolise him as another Shakespear. 'Tis an injustice to withhold these two works any longer. I remember you said 'the public should never have the tragedy until they have done justice to Keats's other works.' *The time has come, and* I FEAR THE TIME MAY PASS. These young men read and recite Keats to me, until I think him more beautiful than ever. (I am dying for them to see the tragedy.) Then there is another point—the Public is wrong about Keats himself. L⁴. Byron and L. Hunt have most vilely led them astray. I persuade myself that Keats's life will be a most interesting subject. If you will go on, I will send you everything I can think of, and I am sure I can supply much. If you will not, I mean to defy you, and try and write his Life myself, which I am sure will make you look about you . . . . Now tell me what you have to say by way of excuse. It cannot be, save that you do not know how high Keats's fame has risen—that if he is not the Poet of the million, he is more, for I would say that, judging of the talents of his admirers and their rank as scholars, that his fame is a proud one. So now, my dear Brown, I send this off Saturday ev⁵—you'll hear Tuesday morn⁵—and I shall receive the tragedy Saturday."

" *Rome,*
" July 10th, 1836.*

" . . . . I inquired about the new edition of Keats, and I was invited to embellish it to any extent, and have some nice ideas for it. Be sure you tell me what movement it makes. Many kind lovers of Keats's poetry offer to subscribe to make him a monument. Gibson made a liberal offer to do it for whatever might be subscribed, which I made known to poor Woodhouse without receiving any answer. Now I have come to the determination *that I will accept these subscriptions,* and let Gibson make a beautiful monument, either to be placed here or in England. Tell me what are your thoughts, but don't tell me you set your face against it, for *so I will have it. I can collect a handsome sum. I am an artist myself, and a fine work I'll have.* As you have called me an old man, I'll e'en do something to grace my years . . . .

"I am just going to write to Mr. Milnes about Keats's tomb. I feel sure that £500 could be easily got, and this, let me tell you, would be useful and even honourable to his reputation. The present gravestone, with its inscription, is an eye-sore to me and more, for as I am sought out and esteem'd as his friend something is look'd for from me, and something I will have. I have thought to have the beautiful profile of Girometti's on the upper part, surrounded with architectural flowers in the Greek style—underneath a bas-relief (the subject of which I have not determined, and will not until you give your ideas, for I'll do nothing without you except your denial—with that I'll have nothing to do). George Keats ought to subscribe, but I have the right, as Keats's last friend, and also as an artist, to the management. After the Monument is up, I'll plant the most beautiful laurels and cypresses ever seen, and attend to the keeping them fresh to the extreme days of my old age, for I feel that I owe much to the name of Keats being so often linked with mine. It has given the public an impression which has ensured me a good career, much as it was denied to him.

"Now I dare say you will think all this very vain on my part, and throw cold water upon me and that; but no, I am too old to be damped by you. You may encourage me to anything, but I won't be put down. *Keats shall have a fine monument,* and I will produce fine historical works, worthy of his friend. . . ."

" 19, *Brook Street,*
" August 21st, 1838.†

" . . . .What are you doing about Keats's Life? If you have printed, pray let me have it. I am stirring up here for a new edition of his and Shelley's works. It is shamefully unjust that you all on the spot do not pull together and catch this nice moment for Keats. Tell me the difficulties in the way of a new and compleat edition of him. —— and I talk it

---

* Brown had by this time left Italy (1835), and had settled at Laira Green, near Plymouth.

† In the summer of this year Severn made a flying visit to London.

over, and determine on having beautiful engravings in it. I have got very pretty ideas for it. Gibson will give us many things. I assure you Keats stands so high with all the aspiring young men, particularly the aristocrats, that a book would take. I'll do anything to help it on, even for my own sake, as I am so proud of having been Keats's friend, seeing how people are disposed to caress me for his sake.

"We are about a new project: —— and I, of course. It is to let the good feeling go on, and have a group in marble by Gibson of Shelley and Keats together, to be placed somewhere in London. Isn't this a beautiful idea? What a subject for sculpture! What a fine tribute to the men, friends as they were, and making greater—both Greek poets, and both with fine and young poet-looks. Now don't throw cold water upon it. I'll raise plenty of money to do it, and Gibson made a liberal offer. That stir in Parliament about Lord Byron's statue was my doing, and now I'll be an agitator about Keats's. Tell me about George Keats, and also about Taylor, and poor Woodhouse's papers. I knew he had the tragedy copied, he told me so himself—it was from the love he bore Keats, and foreseeing there might be difficulties in the way of bringing his works together for a new edition."

Severn was very busy throughout 1830, partly with pictures which have already been mentioned, and partly with others.* Of these, among the most admired were,

* There may be given here the list of the more important copies made by Severn from the pictures by the Old Masters in Rome, Florence, and Venice :—

1. Doge of Genoa	Vandyke		Florence.
2. Presentation of Virgin.	Titian		Venice.
3. Pope Julius II.	Raphael		Florence.
4. Knight of Malta	Giorgione		"
5. Battle of Cadore	Titian		Venice.

Sketch from the original, which was burnt.

6. Musicians.			
7. Lady from picture of Prodigal Son	Bonifaccio		Venice.
8. Duke of Urbino	Titian		Florence.
9. Pope Paul III., who set up the Inquisition	"		Naples.
10. The Father of Titian, or Doge Grimani	"		{Arical Pal. {Venice.
11. St. Agata Martyr	P. Veronese		Florence.
12. St. George and the Dragon	Rubens		Naples.
13. Madonna and Child	Correggio		"
14. Angel from	Guercino		..
15. Sibyl	M. Angelo		Rome.
16. Madonna (Assumption)	Titian		..
17. Peter Martyr	"		Venice.

From the picture which was burnt.

18. Miracle of the Hammer	Tintoretto		"
19. Head of Saviour: an original or old Oriental copy	Cimabue?		..

To face page 167.

' Vintagers at Eve,' the ' Sicilian Mariner's Hymn,' ' Godfrey and the Crusaders in sight of Jerusalem,' ' Rienzi in the Forum,' and ' The Falconer and Lady '; the first two bought respectively by Sir Matthew White Ridley and the Marquis of Northampton, ' Godfrey ' and ' Rienzi ' by Sir Thos. Redington, while ' The Falconer ' was sent to the British Institution in 1831, and sold to a Sir Charles Lamb.

But the chief event of the year, for him, was the birth of his first son and second child, Walter, an event which happened at Frascati on the 12th of October.

Early in 1831 it seemed as though at last the protracted civil suit in which Severn had been so long and distractingly engaged was about to be brought to a definite end. As a matter of fact the business, so discreditable to all concerned, save the unfortunate person chiefly implicated, was concluded in the early summer of this year. It was now the turn of Mrs. Severn to become seriously indisposed as well as her husband, whose ill-health had become chronic during these trial-years. as he calls them; but fortunately Mr. Fox again happened to offer the use of his villa at Frascati, and so there Mr. and Mrs. Severn, with their daughter Claudia and the little Walter (upon whom, by the way, his father often regretted not having bestowed ' Keats ' as. at any rate, a second baptismal name —as both Brown and Kirkup suggested).

At the end of the preceding December, or early in January of this year, he had sent to London his picture ' The Falconer,' for exhibition at the British Institution, a

20.	Elizabeth and Mary	Albertinelli (Mariotto).	Florence.
21.	Confession of Saul	Rubens	..
22.	St. John the Baptist	Titian	Venice.
23.	Jeremiah	M. Angelo.	Rome.
24.	Head, Rubens' Wife	..	..
25.	Entombment	Spagnoletto	Naples.
26.	Romulus and Remus	Rubens	Rome.
27.	Briseis and Achilles	"	"
28.	La Fornarina	Raphael	"
29.	Sacred Subject	Spagnoletto	Naples.
30.	Landscape	Claude.	Florence.
31.	Crucifixion	Tintoretto.	Venice.

work of additional interest from the fact that the falconer is a portrait of Severn himself, and the lady an exact likeness of his wife.

When Severn again returned to Rome, he had not only recovered from the incessant worry of the trial and his own prolonged and sometimes serious indisposition, but was in the best of health and the highest spirits.

"What with my Altar-Piece for Cardinal Weld," he writes, "and other works on hand or in prospect, and with other matters to my great content, a fortunate turn in the tide of my affairs had again come. When we returned to Rome we had the most complete happiness and enjoyment that it is possible for human creatures to know—prosperity, friendship, the best and most entertaining society, no end of brilliant gaieties when we wished them, our love for each other and our children, and above all we had both by this time good health to enjoy all. Thus, despite everything connected with that ugly trial, and all the anguish and exhaustion for which it was directly and indirectly responsible, I have never ceased to think with pleasure of this time."

If I were to edit, however concisely, from Severn's papers, the account of his friendly relations with Cardinal Weld and of the painting and placement of the picture he was ever wont to regard as his *chef d'œuvre*, it would occupy more space than can be spared. The whole question of the destination of this sacred picture, painted by a Protestant artist for a Catholic church, excited at the time a great amount of controversy and high feeling. To this day it is the chief precedent when any similar difficulty arises.*

This, Severn's most ambitious picture, 'The Infant of the Apocalypse caught up to Heaven,' was commissioned by Cardinal Weld, as a present to the Pope, and to be placed as an altar-piece in the Cathedral Church of 'St. Paul beyond the Walls,' and was the most fruitful result of the long and unjust trial through which the English artist had to maintain his stand for the right against overwhelming

* The essential part of Severn's narrative will be found in the Appendix (No. II.). As Cardinal Weld had a singular influence on the fortunes of Roman Catholicism in England, all Severn's remarks about him will be read with interest.

falsity and injustice. During that period and till the too early death of the excellent prelate, the most friendly feelings existed between Cardinal Weld and his injured countryman.

During the progress of the altar-piece Severn, of course, painted many other pictures, among them 'The End of a Venetian Masque' and 'The Abdication of Mary, Queen of Scots,' bought by the Earl of Eglington, and still at Eglington Castle; 'Angelica,' bought by the Duke of Manchester; 'Temptation' and 'Ophelia,' bought by the Duke of Devonshire, and still at Chatsworth, and other equally important works. For Cardinal Weld himself he painted another picture besides his great Apocalypse subject:

"A small picture of the Roman *Ave Maria*, with the Pantheon in the background by twilight, with the full moon rising beyond, and with a third light in the glow of the numerous candles with which the Madonna was illumined. This small canvas, however, brought me great credit; and some years afterwards I had to paint a duplicate for the present Emperor of Russia [that is, the Czar Nicholas], who when visiting Rome, gave me the order himself."

The chief account of the several episodes arising out of Severn's projecting this picture, its being commissioned by Cardinal Weld, and its presentation by that Prelate to the Pope for the Cathedral Church of St. Paul, then being restored, and the jealous ill-will and many difficulties which had to be overcome before ultimate success, is given in a special chapter in Severn's MS. 'Incidents of my Life.' But it is not necessary to give this detailed record here. Briefly, it may be said that it covers succinctly the years between Severn's marriage and those of his departure from Rome and return to London (1828–1841). This was, in the main, a happy and prosperous time for him. Other children were born, and one was lost through a tragic mischance. There is not much else important to chronicle beyond the visit of Sir Walter Scott to Rome, and Severn's significant interview with him concerning the Keats-article in 'Blackwood's;' this, and some correspondence. It may be added here that he did not make his often projected flying visit to England till 1838, and that over twenty years elapsed between that " sad and despairing night " when he sailed from Gravesend with Keats, a young and unknown artist without money or definite prospects, and when he arrived [1841] at Dover with his wife and family, with ample means, good prospects, an assured reputation, and having among his patrons an emperor, a king, a prince of the Church, and several of the greatest and most influential nobles of England.

To return now, briefly, to the year 1832. The quotation of part of an autumn letter from Brown, from a villa near Florence, will save occupation of the reader's time with unnecessary details. The allusions are to Woodhouse's medallion portrait of Keats by Girometti and to Tre-lawny's 'Adventures of a Younger Son,' much of which had been written during the author's stay with Brown, to whom, indeed, the opening portions were submitted, and for most of which he chose the mottoes—the majority of them from Keats's then unpublished poems, particularly his and Brown's joint tragedy 'Otho.'

" . . . . I am wonderfully happy among my flowers, watching their growth. Woodhouse lived with me here for seven weeks, and he got so well in health, he was quite a credit to the place. He left me about a fortnight since for Venice and England. I like him much, and hope he will come back again. The bas-relief he gave me of our Keats delights me; never was anything so like, it seems quite a piece of magic. Trelawny went to England in the spring. Every one ascribes 'The Younger Son' to him, but I believe he still denies it. Have you read it? I am told it runs off like wild-fire. At the head of every chapter are one or two quotations from Byron, Keats, and Shelley,—from *no one else* ; and Woodhouse and I think his lordship does not look over grand in such company. Woodhouse also thinks that these quotations, in so popular a book, will be of great service to the fame of Keats ; and indeed they are chosen, in number fifty-three great and small, with much care,—some great friend of Keats's must have done all this, don't you imagine so? Woodhouse has promised to send me certain dates and other particulars, which no one would ever send me, and further, has made me promise to write the life of Keats in my quiet country nook during this winter. Now I have changed my mind about his portrait; it must be from that medallion. What a pity it is you know nothing of flowers,—how can you

be so ignorant and live?—otherwise I'd talk to you of my perfection of a
volkamoria, perfuming half my garden with its hyacinth scent, with its
second crop of blossoms on it at this moment; and of my noble metro-
sideros now in full bloom; of my verbena splendour, in bloom for these five
months back, with a scarlet that would cut out all your painter's shops!"

The only letter of this year which need be quoted is one
from Westmacott, written from London in June. It will
be read with appreciation by all interested in the history of
English Art.

" London,
" June, 1832.

" My dear Severn,

"I have been so busy and so bothered lately that I have not had will
or time to write the usual bulletin on our Exhibition; but I have had my
conscience quieted in some respects by finding that Eastlake has already
sent you an account. After his, I hardly think it necessary to go into the
business, for he will have given you just the opinion you ought to have—
a painter's. The *tout-ensemble* is very good and highly creditable to the
country. Historical works of course are lacking. There are fewer
portraits, both in quantity and quality than usual, but in the works that
do tell there is, to my mind, a great deal of right stuff—very careful drawing
and finish, which we don't always get, and no falling off in the other
qualities for which the English school has been blamed and praised—colour
and effect. (Blamed for sacrificing too much to obtain it, and praised for
having hit it better than any other modern school.) Wilkie's ' Knox
Preaching,' ' Leslie's ' Grosvenor Family,' and ' Katherine and Petruchio,'
Calcott's Landscapes, ' Hilton's ' Una entering the Cottage with the Lion,'
and Landseer's various pictures, Collins in two pictures, and others whom
I need not name here,—all contribute to prove what we have in us. Turner
is splendid, and excepting in one picture, ' The Burning Fiery Furnace!',
charming and intelligible. His ' Italy ' is the most magnificent piece of
landscape poetry that was ever conceived. It is like nothing but itself,
so I cannot compare it with Claude or any other painter, to help your
notion of it. Landseer has a very fine picture called ' Hawking.' It is a
largish picture and almost all sky. The hawk and his prey, the sign of
life, are rolling down together, and have almost reached the ground—they
seem to live; they are full of fury, bustle, and expression. They are
magnificently painted, yet still so carefully that they might be examined
with a magnifying-glass. The hawk has such an eye! In the distance
over a bit of heath or common are seen two or three figures on whose
wrists are hawks; just sufficient to explain the subject. Collins's favourite
picture is of some children opening a gate to a shady lane—*the spectator*
being the person riding through and into the picture; the horse and rider
cast their shadow before on the foreground. The Duchess of Devonshire
has purchased this. Uwins has a very clever picture of a Neapolitan

Saint-maker's workshop. Partridge is strong in a portrait or two. Phillip's I have forgotten—who is at the top of the tree this time—in spite of Beechey's and Wilkie's ' Kings.' A costume picture by Williams is the delight of us all, and though I mention him last I am glad to assure you that our President helps on his own and the Academy's honour ; he has two or three capital pictures. Your picture is in the ante-room, on the right hand of the entrance into the Great-room,—is in good company, and light. Eastlake will have told you what struck us in it. With my usual candour, at which you will not be angry, I tell you honestly I think it very unfinished in parts, and *that* is hardly compensated for to the public by its agreeable composition, appropriate expression, and warm good tone, all of which it possesses, but which artists who care to look for them alone appreciate—perhaps, too, your figures are a little thick or short. I do wish you would come over here, if only to see the calibre of some of our chaps whom you have forgotten. To our great annoyance we hear nothing of Gibson. He tells us in a letter that Lord Yarborough was to have sent a work ; he has not done so. The composition and feeling in Wyatt's group are much admired. *We* here, don't like your [? his] treatment of Portrait heads. Wyatt's boys and his lady have not what we think should exist in that class of art. I speak with deference, because I think so highly of Wyatt, and even if you tell him this I know he will take it well and without attributing any unworthy feeling to my criticism. The sculpture-room is full—too full. I daresay Eastlake has served us up to you, so I will run the risk of it and leave ourselves out. We go on grumbling about our wretched den of a room ; perhaps we may do better by-and-by, for they now talk of building the National Gallery, and it is expected that an Academy of Arts may be joined with it. It is a consummation devoutly to be wished. The British Gallery was kept open an unconscionable time, in the hope, I suppose, of forwarding the sale of the works, but there has been no great deal done— people will not spend their money this year—or they are thinking of something else. I have not been to the Water-Colour Exhibition yet. I hear that it is, as usual, excellent. A new Society has not been deterred by the badness of the times from starting an extra Exhibition speculation. There is a new Water-Colour show in Bond Street. I have not visited it, but Uwins and other clever fellows belong to it. Your ' Falconer' still sticks on hand. It has an excellent place in my house, everybody can see it, and all who do, stop and admire it—but no buying !

"Mr. Ridley Colborne, who is much looked up to, stood before it a long time lately and enquired all about it—whether with any view to purchasing it I know not, but be assured I shall not lose sight of your interests and wishes. We are doing German Operas with a German Company on the *off* nights at the Italian Opera House. I think the singers want ' *voce*,' but they perform very *charily*, and the Chorusses are excellent—time and tune perfect ; an accomplishment which the usual corps of singers do not possess. ' *Der Freischütz* ' and ' *Fidelio* ' have been the two given us up to the present. They draw immense houses.

How are you all going on in Rome? Gibson writes us that he likes your composition for the picture ordered by the Cardinal. I wish you well through it—it's an awful work and will want every power that you can bring to bear upon it. I am delighted to hear you are pleasing yourself in your progress with it. You are becoming a sad idle correspondent, but I suppose a wife and children are to be the breaking up of all *vagabond* vagaries. The better for the aforesaid vagabond, I daresay; but the survivors miss their old companions without finding any substitute, as they do, for the loss. I should like to drop into the midst of you, but that may not be. Will you tell Gibson I received his letter, and thank him for it? It was very gossipy and pleasant, and I wish he could bring himself to send me one oftener. Pray oblige me by giving old Barbara three or four dollars out of our account. I don't think I have sent her a *regalo* for a long time. Remember me to all my old friends.

> " Believe me, dear Severn,
> " Yours truly,
> " WESTMACOTT."

" June 15.—It is not generally known yet, but Sir Walter Scott is arrived—very bad—so bad indeed that his death would be hailed as a blessing compared with the living on in a state of almost imbecility. Shocking, is it not? to see this wreck of mind.* Death has been busy with great names lately—James Mackintosh—Butler—Jeremy Bentham—Cuvier—and now Walter Scott falling! Mr. Bentham's body was publicly dissected by his own desire—for the advancement of science. *Come va la famiglia?* Are you still playing a *Crescendo* movement? Gibson seems to have come to a conclusion on non-matrimony, for himself!"

In Severn's single published writing of a personal nature, the article on the ' Vicissitudes of Keats's Fame,' which appeared in ' The Atlantic Monthly' for 1863, there is a memorable account of his meeting with Sir Walter Scott, an account varied in no essential particular in another written at a later date. It is, however, not only so well known, but was written in such radical misapprehension of the nature of that great man, that it need not again be set forth.

I have already given an outline of Severn's life in the years immediately following his marriage and before his return to England, and it is unnecessary to dwell at length upon details of artistic labours or to repeat the merely local and transiently interesting gossip of the Rome of his day, enough of which has been already given, conformably with

* Sir Walter Scott died a little over three months later.

the scope of this memoir.   A few personal details can best
be reproduced in his own words.   But first I may find
room for one or two letters which will be of interest to some
readers at any rate.

Charles Brown made his visit to England alone, though
he did so in 1833 instead of 1832.   Before he went he
formed an acquaintanceship at Landor's house on the hill-
slope below Fiesole, which, though he had no idea of any
particular outcome from it, was an event of singular importance for English biographical literature, and particularly
for lovers of Keats.   It was to this fortunate meeting,
indeed, that we owe one of the most charming biographies
that we possess ; a book, moreover, which will preserve the
memory of a genial and delightful man, himself too a poet,
when his other writings as well as the personal tradition of
him shall be forgotten.

" It is now fifteen years ago," writes Lord Houghton (then R. Monckton
Milnes), in the Preface to the ' Life, Letters, and Literary Remains of
John Keats,' " that I met at the villa of my distinguished friend Mr.
Landor, on the beautiful hill-side of Fiesole, Mr. Charles Brown, a retired
Russia-merchant, with whose name I was already familiar as the generous
protector and devoted friend of the Poet Keats. . . .

" . . . . Few of these [unpublished productions and letters of literary
interest] had escaped the affectionate care of Mr. Brown, and he told me
that he only deferred their publication till his return to England.   This
took place two or three years afterwards, and the preliminary arrangement
for giving them to the world were actually in progress, when the accident
of attending a meeting on the subject of the colonisation of New Zealand
altered all Mr. Brown's plans, and determined him to transfer his fortunes
and the closing years of his life to the Antipodes.   Before he left this
country he confided to my care all his collections of Keats's writings,
accompanied with a biographical notice, and I engaged to use them to the
best of my ability for the purpose of vindicating the character and
advancing the fame of his honoured friend."

Brown, however, returned from his first visit to England,
and was settled again by the autumn of 1833 at his villa
outside Florence, whence he wrote to Severn on the 17th of
September.   By this time two more children had been
born to Severn, the elder named Arthur, and now, like his
elder brother Walter, a distinguished artist.

In a following letter, written a few months later, there is the first warning of that disastrous change in the writer's fortunes as well as in his bodily health, which was the indirect cause of his leaving Italy, and afterwards England, for New Zealand; for the lecture on colonization, alluded to by Lord Houghton, was only the secondary, if determining cause of his emigration.

A letter from Leigh Hunt, introducing a friend, may be given here for the sake of its fine and characteristic remark about Rome.

> "*Upper Cheyne Row*, *Chelsea*,
> "*Aug. 1st, 1834.*
>
> " MY DEAR SEVERN,
>
> "I snatch a moment, though it be but a moment, after a hard day's work, that I may have the pleasure not only of introducing to you a young artist, Mr. Dallas, a friend of my eldest son's and highly esteemed by him, but of asking you under my own hand how you do, and pretending to myself that I am standing for an instant in the thick of Rome! I cannot look even upon this bit of paper without something like respect as well as envy, to think that it will be really there, when I, the sender of it, and the human soul, cannot find a way to it. I repeat the word to myself like a fine bass note—Rome—mixing it up with the murmuring of the great sea of ages, and with tenderer voices of the departed, and long indeed to be with you. God bless you.
>
> " Your sincere friend,
> " LEIGH HUNT."

The many troubles which beset Brown in his later years, the first hint of which was given in an earlier letter already quoted, had their serious beginning in an apoplectic seizure which overcame him one day when he was in Vieusseux's Library in the Via Tornabuoni in Florence, then as now the only institution of the kind in Italy of any importance.

He had always enjoyed robust health, but after this attack he was more or less an invalid, though one of the most dauntless and energetic sufferers among literary workers since Defoe. Though in his last few years the victim of epilepsy as well as apoplexy, from dyspepsia and what he calls again and again a " hell of nervousness," and from financial embarrassment, he actively interested himself as a Librarian, as a committee member of an art institution, as a lecturer, and as an author, and ultimately even ventured upon what was then a far more hazardous enterprise than now, emigration to New Zealand, at that time a virgin colony. His restless activity of mind and body kept him busy even after his first serious attack of apoplexy. Not content with gardening in addition to his usual literary and artistic undertakings, he tells Severn in one of his letters that he has also taken up the study of astronomy.

But his illness materially added to the home-sickness which Brown had felt for some time, and this longing, combined with the advisability of his going to England to attend to his monetary affairs, with his son's education, and with his uncertain health, determined him to break up his home in Italy and return to his own country. He decided to go at the end of March, and expected to arrive in good time to take a house in Plymouth by Midsummer day. He travelled more leisurely than he had at first intended, for he did not arrive till about the end of April or early in May. With characteristic enjoyment of persiflage, he assured his Italian acquaintances that he was returning to England, as it was necessary for him to seek a milder climate than that of Italy, a remark which had point in it from the fact that the winter and spring of 1835 had been, for Italy, a severe one. His account of the expenses of living in England about the year 1835 shows what a radical difference has taken place since then. A Vicar of Wakefield could not nowadays exist under his famous predecessor's régime; in Brown's time he could at least have managed to make both ends meet.

CHAPTER VIII.

The Keats-memorial—Brown's memoir of Keats—The " Great Plague "
in Rome—Severn-correspondence—Tragic death of Severn's child—
Charles Dilke and Charles Lamb—Letter from Sir Charles Eastlake—
Letter from George Richmond, R.A.—Letter from Charles Brown—
Keats's possible biographers—Last news of Charles Brown—His death
in New Zealand—Letter from Mr. Dilke—Keats and "fame."

Brown's next letter is from his new home, a cottage at
Laira Green, near Plymouth, and is the first written under
its roof, though he had been a tenant for some weeks. His
new illness, the serious one of epilepsy, did not interfere with
his projects of lecturing on Shakespeare's sonnets and other
subjects, nor his undertaking to be one of the Hanging
Committee at a local Art Exhibition. This little exhibition
is certainly the first where any prominence was given to
portraits of Keats. It comprised the medallion which Signor
Girometti made for Woodhouse, and two replicas of Severn's
portrait of the young poet, besides his sketch of him in
the hour of death. In a letter of later date Brown gives
further particulars, though in this communication the
chief interest is in what he has to say concerning George
Keats's legal injunction against his using any of John's
literary remains in his possession for his projected Memoir,
already in part done. He consulted Monckton Milnes on
this awkward point, and though at first Mr. Milnes disputed
George's legal power of interdict he found on enquiry that
such power did exist. This, for a time, caused Brown to
fear for his Memoir an indefinitely prolonged delay in
publication.

Another letter by Brown, written in this year, which
should be quoted, is that bearing date the 20th of November.

N

Severn had mooted, to friends in Rome as well as to Brown
and others in England, yet another proposal as to the erection
of a monument to Keats in the Protestant Burial-Ground at
Rome. To this Brown was strongly opposed, and there
are probably few who do not approve his attitude rather
than that of Severn. Not only, he writes, does he thoroughly
disapprove of the scheme as unnecessary and in every way
undesirable, but he repents of even having allowed, so far as
his approval was a matter of concern, anything else on the
tombstone but the words which Keats himself had wished to
be placed there. Indeed, he hopes that the Roman authorities will permit the erasure of every word beyond those to
which the poet himself limited his epitaph. There is, he
well declares, "a sort of profanation of adding even a note
of admiration to [Keats's] own words."

"*Laira Green,*
"26th November, 1836.

"When I received your last letter, nearly three months ago, I resolved not
to answer you in a hurry, though now, upon looking back, I am astonished
at so much time having passed. How could I write to disturb the pleasant
dreams in which you then were? You were resolved on a fine monument to
Keats, and I utterly disapproved of it. If his Poems should induce
his countrymen, otherwise uninfluenced, to erect a monument to him,
my joy would be great; but I cannot approve of such an honour,
in a questionable shape, by his *personal* friends, paid to him *as a poet.*
Still, looking on the intention in its best point of view, I do not perceive
it can do his fame any harm,—which, at first sight, I thought I did
perceive. The impropriety of a relation or a friend as a subscriber to or
furtherer of national feeling, of a national tribute, I feel so strongly, that I
am afraid thousands of others will feel the same. On this ground, while I
sincerely thank you for referring the subject of a bas-relief and other
matters to me, conjointly with yourself, I must decline having anything
to do with the monument,—except on one point. This point is that not
one word shall be there except those contained in his dying request—
'Here lies one whose name was writ in water,' Swayed by a very natural
feeling at the time, I advised more, but now I am convinced of the error,
the sort of profanation of adding even a note of admiration to his own
words. If a dying friend, a good man, leaves strict orders for the wording
of his epitaph, he should be obeyed, if good faith is in the world. I have
long repented of my fault, and must repeat what I said to you in Rome,
'I hope the government will permit the erasure of every word, with the
exception of those words to which he himself limited his epitaph.' The

[The child, in this group from "The Roman Ave Maria;" painted early in 1837 (a replica of an earlier picture), was drawn from the Severns' eldest son, Walter, then some months over six years old. The mother is a rough study from Mrs. Severn. The picture was commissioned by the Czar Nicholas (then Czarovich), and is now in the Imperial Gallery in St. Petersburg.]

To face page 179.

memory of Keats has been one of my greatest pleasures, but lately it has been mixed with pain,—for I have been occupied in writing my life of him, and, consequently, been turning over letters and papers, some full of hope, others of despair, and my mind has been compelled to trace one misfortune to another, all connected with him. I knew this task was my duty, and, from the beginning I had from time to time made, I found it a painful one. Therefore to compel me to my duty, I boldly put down my name at our Institution for a lecture, on 27th December, on 'The Life and Poems of John Keats.' Now that it is advertised, the card printed, the members looking forward to it, there is no retreating: it must be done. About one half is done. Probably I shall afterwards print it in a Magazine, there to rest as a voucher for his admirers; possibly I may print it in a small volume by itself; in either shape you must have it. My first lecture was given about a fortnight ago, 'The Intellectual History of Florence.' I was aware of the interest of the subject, but the unusual hand-applause and the high compliments bestowed on me were unexpected. After the 'Life of Keats' I shall give no more lectures this season." . . .

The year 1837 was that known throughout Italy, and nowhere with more horror of remembrance than in Rome, as "the cholera year." To the Severns it was further unforgettable as the year wherein by a tragic misadventure they lost their youngest and best beloved child. Severn's own record of this period of individual and general suffering and horror is too lengthy and too discursive to quote here: but it may be said it was a time that old Romans speak of yet with shudderings. The ignorance of the people and the selfish attitude of the rich, including that of the Pope and his satellites, induced almost unparalleled misery; and unfortunately, though many of the monks and humble clergy strove heroically, there were among the Italians few if any potent workers of the stamp of the Catholic English noble, Lord Clifford. Room may, however, be found here for one of Severn's reminiscences of this period.

"The cordon was drawn round nearly all the towns, and with such vigour that it was impossible to enter any of them.

"At Palestrina I slept outside the town at a miserable inn, but at last I got safely to Rome, saw a few alarmed friends, got together all we wanted, and returned to Olevana the following day. My re-entering the town was agreed on before I left, provided the cholera was not officially declared at Rome. Very soon after, in the month of June, the cholera broke out at Rome with unlooked-for fury.

"There had been heavy rains during two days, when the damp chill produced double effect on the people, owing to the superstitious ceremony in vogue in time of the plague, of going at night barefoot to pray to a certain Madonna, a ceremony on this occasion attended by upwards of ten thousand people. The result was that the next day about three hundred persons died! What made their death and cholera more dreadful was that the victims were almost all young and hale persons. Death had proudly and scornfully refused the old and infirm. How, when I heard this terrible news, did I reflect on the arrogance of the Roman people in assuming that the cholera would not dare to enter Rome on account of the holiness of the place, and how the Roman pride was at last struck down by the fact that the number of the deaths was greater than in any other place, and with the victims all young and hale people. It was to us like living anew the period of the plague as described in Boccaccio's 'Decameron,' shut up as we are in the Apennine town, where no cholera ever approached, and where we received every kind of hospitality, and that almost daily, and where the scenery was of the most romantic nature and the people, in addition to being finely made and handsome, were so amiable and good and indulgent to all our wants. After a short time our money became exhausted, and as I had just made a loan to Chevalier Bunsen for his hospital on the Capitol, and as I could not get at the banker in Rome, nor at Bunsen, who was also shut up by the Frascati cordon, our case would have been very deplorable had not these people been of the best kind of Italians. But with all their great hospitality and fondness for the few strangers visiting them, and their generosity as far as their means went, they had little or no money amongst them. Yet they lent sacks of corn, bags of salt, baskets of potatoes, and so on, and in this way we paid for what we had and got on most pleasantly. But, oh! the contrast of our most charming and quiet, healthy and beautiful retreat, when we received the fumigated letters from Rome giving us frightful accounts of the deaths of friends and acquaintances of all ranks, and even in our own house, for the old General Braci died, and our English friend Barlowe the sculptor, and under very painful circumstances. Then we heard of a state of almost public anarchy. Contagion being the order of the day, all the nobles, and even the Pope himself, had bricked up their palaces, and selfishly left the rest of the city to destruction from plunder and murder; anarchy indeed, had it not been that the cholera arrested the one and the other by its impartial and severest judgments.

"It was an astounding fact that a body of assassins, some hundred and twenty in number, had planned to sack the city and murder all the wealthy inhabitants. The police had got [information of ?] all their men, but were unable through fear to arrest any of them. The cholera lasted three months. At the end of that time, when the police began to gain power and confidence and were at last able to arrest these assassins, out of the six score they found only six alive. Such justice had the plague wrought! Yet in the midst of all this horror were episodes of such beauty and loveliness that it seemed almost impossible at such a time there could be any more enduring. Among other things, I heard continually of the doings of Lord Clifford who, at the moment of the most frightful public perversion on the subject of contagion, and when the plague was devastating the city without there being any practical public effort to save it, pursued a calm and even tranquil career in medically attending some fifty to a hundred people a day. By his fearlessness and reasonable procedure he must have done great good, and helped to clear away the prejudice about apathy to contagion. When the disease was nearly over, he generously opened the English College as a convalescent hospital. He surprised me by his statement that more persons died from the sudden return of life during artificial restoration than of those who died from the malady. This, latterly, he obviated by giving patients from twenty to twenty-five grains of aconite, which so retarded the return of life that it saved the attack on the brain, but of course it involved a much longer convalescence.

" There were acts of Lord Clifford that, unless they were in harmony with his whole career in Rome at this time, would appear as the acts of a heroic madman. For instance, there was in Rome, at this period a very old English Roman Catholic lady with her two daughters, Devonshire people and old friends of Lord Clifford. This old lady was taken ill, and died at the age of 84, but not of cholera. The cart which went round daily for all the dead took the body of the old lady, to the great grief and horror of the two daughters, as thus their dear old mother would not have individual burial or even the service of the church. The burial-place outside the walls, at the Church of San Lorenzo, was made by forming immense long fosses into which, without any service of the church, were thrown each evening all the dead of that day, and this, at the worst time, took from sunset to sunrise. Lord Clifford was accustomed to visit these ladies every evening, and, on that following the day of the old lady's death, he was dismayed to find her dead, and her body taken to San Lorenzo. He soon found a consolation for the daughters by assuring them that he would in the morning get an order from the Governor of Rome to disinter the body, and that he would then cause to be performed all the funeral offices of the church. All this he accomplished. He assured me that the sight after sunset at San Lorenzo was the most awful that could be imagined. Carts were arriving continually, filled with naked dead bodies, which were at once on their arrival thrown into the fosse. These death-carts came in unbroken procession from sunset until two and three o'clock in the morning. There were innumerable torches to light up the dismal work. During a month, this rude interment was at the rate of 300 corpses a day. Of course, to return to my anecdote, the men were unable to attend to Lord Clifford's request to disinter the body of his old friend until they had buried all of that day. About dawn they commenced digging into the trench of the day before, and after the work of a whole hour they found the old lady's body, and got it up and placed it in the coffin

on the bier his Lordship, with all the San Lorenzo priests, had prepared.
The body was taken to the church, and the service for the dead chanted,
and then he saw it quietly placed in the tomb which had been hastily
prepared for it.

"This being done, he returned at seven o'clock to breakfast with
the two ladies, and consoled them with the news that their mother's
body was placed in a Christian tomb. There was no funeral ceremony
whatever over those dead of cholera, and of course at such a time there
was no chance of distinction, as death levelled all. The details were
awful; for instance, people threw the dead bodies out of the windows into
the streets to save perilous handling of contagion, and I was informed
that it was an appalling thing to see the continued falling of the corpses.

"The one extraordinary fact of all was that of the numerous men employed
to receive and convey the dead bodies to San Lorenzo, *not one died of
cholera!* Yet they were guilty of acts of levity and even atrociousness
that cannot be believed. The population of Rome was reduced by
15,000, and these mostly young people. When I went back to Rome
for a day in the month of October it amazed me to see all the poor old
miserable beggars and invalids with whose appearance I was familiar
still there. At that time I was occupied on a difficult pictorial subject:
'Godfrey and his Army in sight of Jerusalem;' for the background of
which I had set my mind on a scene with olives at Tivoli. This place
had been one of the worst visited by the cholera, notwithstanding that
a cordon had been drawn the whole time. To accomplish this study at
Tivoli, I had to cross the mountains with a guide, and make a retrograde
movement. On arriving at dawn, I soon found what I wanted to paint,
and having had my breakfast, and all being ready, I sat down and
began. I had painted for about an hour, when I heard the sound of
drums and trumpets and bands of music, and soon saw a procession
advancing from the town, which slowly came to where I was painting.
In this spot there was a little open chapel, and I was agreeably surprised
to find that the whole procession stopped, while all knelt on the very
spot I had chosen for my background; so that I had the singular
gratification of seeing just the real effect of figures and landscape
which I was trying to paint. The dresses were very rich, there
was even armour, with many banners, and moreover a cardinal in his
scarlet robes. When I got to Rome and was able to go on with my
picture I changed all the composition to the effect of what I saw at
Tivoli, and so this picture of mine of 'Godfrey and his Army in sight of
Jerusalem' was really a record of this incident. I got back to my family
again at Olevano the following day, having travelled all night with a
guide over the mountains. To walk in, I wore a white jacket over a
flannel one during the cool of the night.

"It was with some regret that we left this most lovely sojourn. The
romantic beauty of the scenery had grown upon us during our stay, and
there being no cholera and no illness we were as it were in a Paradise,
and had the happiness to see our children thrive in the Apennine air.

I was also able to paint four small pictures, which produced me £100; two of these are now in Eglinton Castle, and another was bought by Lord Northampton ('Isabella and the Pot of Basil').

"We returned two years later in the month of November, and then I painted the Fountain picture, now in the possession of Lord Lansdowne. The kind people had kept the grapes on the vine for me, and during three days' heavy rain I sat and painted this pergola, knowing that my constitution would pay for it. I went on painting all the figures of this picture until Christmas, always drooping and drooping a little more, and on my return to Rome, before I had finished my picture, I had an attack of rheumatic fever, and for two months was scarce able to turn over in my bed."

Of course during all the visitation of cholera to Rome, Brown was naturally most anxious on account of his friends, and particularly for the Severns. But the chief reason for inserting the following letter is its interesting information concerning his difficulties with the Keats Memoir, and his idea of leaving the MS. with the authorities of the British Museum for ultimate publication. The letter also contains news of his improved health; of his forthcoming lectures; of his theory as to the amount of Shakespeare's means, and of Shakespeare having been in Italy in 1597; and his opinion as to the dominant quality of the great dramatist's genius. Though in it he writes upon subjects already alluded to, room may be found immediately afterward for Severn's letter written on his return to Rome, after the cholera had left: particularly as few letters of his, from 1835 to 1860, seem to have been preserved. Thereafter follow two letters from Brown, which hardly require comment. Mr. C. W. Dilke, heartily disliked by others than Brown, does not appear in a pleasant light in either. I think that Charles Lamb's epithet for "a particular kind of blockhead" is new to us. It is pleasant to learn that Haslam, who, some time after Keats's death, was far from prosperous, seems to have been so in his later years. It appears from what Brown says of Dilke's communication with him, that the chief difficulty with George Keats, in the matter of the injunction against Brown, was a money one. Once he was satisfied on this point, there was to be no more opposition from George.   In connection with this letter the reader should turn to Dilke's letter of 1841, quoted later.   Brown, however, was unwilling to diverge from what he elsewhere called the straight line of his duty to Keats's memory, and wished to be responsible for nothing unless it were likely to be properly as well as loyally and pleasantly done.

" Laira Green, near Plymouth,
"26th October, 1837.

"My dear Severn,

     "It is now ten months since I wrote to you, and all this time I have had no news of you or yours.   My faculty of hope is tolerably strong; but when I found the cholera had ceased in Rome, and still you did not write, I became uneasy, till last night I tossed about in bed in downright fear.   Pray write immediately.   Keats's ' Life ' remains unpublished till called for; I am sorry to say there is no call for it at present, so it may remain quiet till I am ' quietly inurned.'   1 have done what I conceived my duty, and I can leave it to another generation, if, after my death, he should be then more considered by the many.   I cannot bear the thought of its being printed and received as of little interest except among a few.   Sometimes, however, I think of printing a limited number, and of not selling one; and sometimes my purpose is to lodge it in the British Museum, to be referred to at any time, by anybody.   It is, of course, short, as I am not permitted to use for publication his posthumous poems. . . . Last Thursday I gave one lecture on Shakespeare, and to-night I am to give another.   In that one already given I brought forward very strong circumstantial evidence from his works that he must necessarily have visited Italy, about 1597, I having first proved that he had sufficient means, with prudence, to meet the expense of such a journey.   By the bye, from some late discoveries, irrefragable ones, I can calculate that, at the age of forty-four, he was possessed in lands and money, of £6500 in our present money, or £1300 of his time.   I was listened to with deep interest; but neither that, nor the question of his learning in the classics, could raise a general discussion.   Every man would have it understood he knows a great deal about Shakespeare, but if he is led into deep water, he is silent." . . .

" Rome,
"November 21st, 1837.

"My dear Brown,

     " You surprise me greatly in the fact of ten months having passed away without a letter from me.   Except that I had nothing very good or agreeable to tell, I know not what to say.   Your letter is delightful, as it brings all good tidings, when I am glad to grasp at anything cheerful.   Your having embraced a life and habit so congenial to your health and character is very gratifying to me.   Really you give me such a lively picture of your lecturing that I can almost hear you and fancy myself in a good place, considering what a full assembly you have got. Does the Institution ever publish? if so, I may hope to have the pleasure of reading some of yours. We have during the cholera been in a beautiful retreat at Olevano, forty miles from Rome, where we have passed the time as happily as it was possible for people bringing with them a load of grief. You have not heard of our horrible misfortune, and were you only a man of feeling, I would not oppress you with it; but as you are also a useful member of society, I feel it my duty to relate the whole sad tale. My youngest boy, a beautiful and lively infant nearly a year old, was cut off by a most calamitous death. I confess that he was our loving pride. He had never had a moment's sickness; his vivacity was such that he played with everybody, and was known everywhere. I mention these things as they helped to make our loss still greater. His mother had just put him to bed in the daytime, and in the next room was relating the pretty way in which he had gone to sleep, for everything he did was spoken of. She was absent some few minutes, when on returning to the room she found him hanging dead from the bed. We had instant aid, but to no purpose. It is supposed he got his dear little feet under the rail of his bed whilst he slept, and by passing down the bed on one side by degrees he slipt quite down to his head, and then the rail, made to prevent him, caught the back of his neck and was the cause of his death; and so my poor wife found him. He seemed still asleep, and the surgeon supposed that he must have died sleeping. You can imagine the state this threw us into; indeed, on my return to Rome after a week's absence, I found all our part still in tears for our lovely boy. We had arranged to go to the mountains a week before, and the carriage came by appointment two days after this frightful accident. I thought it a providence to save us all; we had forgotten all about the journey; the cholera had begun, and our danger would have been great. In Olevano we stayed till the middle of November, and now we are returned to our house, which within presents every painful remembrance of our dear angel, and without doors reminds us of friends snatched off by the cholera. You will easily imagine how pleasant your letter must have been. Our return to Rome seems after an absence of twenty years instead of a few months,—for the number of deaths, some fifteen thousand, the pallid countenances all seemingly sunk in years, the vacant streets and the gloom, it all seems as though after an absence of years. I have been also unfortunate in the sale of my pictures, having by me some thousand pounds' worth; this is from the persons who ordered them not being able to pay me. My last commission I am now at work on, 'The Crusaders in sight of Jerusalem.' The future may turn up some good fortune. I have done many small works in the country which are saleable. Thank God, I am in good health, and also my family. I shall strive hard, but have great enemies, as I believe there is no one who has had commissions in painting of historical subjects but myself. I have numerous friends who are, I think, good and useful. Farewell, my dear Brown. Believe me ever

" Sincerely yours,
" J. SEVERN."

" *London,*
" 2nd June, 1838.

"My dear Severn,

" Here am I, lured from my quiet cottage to the turmoil of a city, for the sake of publishing a volume, which may, in its consequences, bring disquiet into my cottage. One good thing, however, has accrued :—I have seen your four pictures in the Exhibition. My praise is worth nothing, as I am an interested party; but they are much praised by those who know nothing about you. They are well placed. Your ' Crusaders ' seems to be the chief favourite ; though I prefer the Venetian scene. The composition of the former is most striking. Imagination, which we rarely see now-a-days in painting, is in your painting; not a dreamy one, like Fuseli's, but one that makes your treatment of a subject gain imperceptibly on the beholder. The colour fully keeps its purpose with any of the best around them. Wilkie must be merely painting for money,—his are sad fallings off. Turner is like a kitchen-fire in the dog-days. Going from the Exhibition to the National Gallery, I became intoxicated with admiration ; and I endeavoured to account for part of their—the old masters'—superiority. Beyond any modern they contrived to give a roundness to the figures ; somehow, it seems as if, by turning the frame, we could see the other side of the limbs. How this is managed I know not, but occasionally I perceive they adopted a bold, harsh outline, which, I thought, contributed to the magical effect. This, together with the depth they gave to their pictures, seems to me the grand secret : reflect on how it might be done. . . . Dilke is altogether unpleasant towards myself. He is dogmatical, conceited, and rude. Success has turned his brains. For the last fortnight I have kept from his house, except in paying two visits of mere civility ; and though I will not again quarrel with him, I would rather not henceforth be in his company : it is a nuisance to my better thoughts. My forthcoming volume is on Shakespeare. It is printed at my own risk. I say nothing of its contents, as I shall send you a copy by Mr. Crawford, who will set off for Florence in about two months. Charles Richards prints it. I have dined with Haslam, who lives like a most prosperous man. He has a wife and daughter, the latter a nice girl of about sixteen ; he sends remembrances, and no reproaches for not writing. In this town, this city of humbug, I am hurried and flurried in all sorts of ways. I am sick of the eternal wheels, sick of the eternal streets, and abominably sick of the process of printing. Away I go to-morrow, leaving the last proofs to the care of the printer."

" *Laira Green,*
" 23rd August, 1838.

"My dear Severn,

" You puzzle me with your unadvised comings, your threatened goings, and your unthought of stayings. I enter heart and hand into all your good purposes about Keats. You do me injustice in thinking I am remiss or lukewarm. His memoir has been long ready, and I am anxious it should be published. Here are the difficulties in publishing the whole of his poems. Moxon told me that Taylor, like a dog in a manger, will neither give a second edition, nor allow another to give one. But now, I believe, his copyright is out. George Keats threatened anyone with an injunction who should publish the posthumous poems; this indeed stopped me in the intended publication of the Memoir. Dilke, George's agent, however, told me, when I was in town, that George wished to obtain from me those posthumous poems, by purchase, if they could not be otherwise obtained. My reply was most conciliatory on this point, putting all thoughts of profit aside. I desired to publish a few here. Dilke told me he knew of no objection *now* to my publishing the whole. Thus it stands. A publisher, whoever he may be, would desire explicit allowance, lest he might subject himself to an injunction; and he, a stranger, would be the fittest party to apply to Dilke and, if necessary, to Taylor. I know not where Woodhouse's papers are, but I have everything, from which a proper selection should be made, as some poems are trivial, or some parts are, and some were written when he was unskilled. The former difficulties may now be easily overcome, and I hope soon to hear from you that a respectable publisher is taking it in hand. Perhaps mine, Bohn in King William Street, will be glad to enter on it. When in town I doubted the behaviour of Dilke, as he is subject to violent fits of ill-temper. I doubt nothing now. It was all *malice prepense.* My fault has been in not lauding his literary talents, which was out of my power. I could praise his talents in obtaining success, but no more. My conscience has undone me with him. Two days since I wrote him a declaration of war, because I would not be treacherous like himself; and I told him plainly he was generally regarded as a blockhead, quoting Charles Lamb's adjective—for a particular sort of blockhead—a Dilkish blockhead. Thus, during the winter I can, without remorse, draw him at full length in a novel. He is a capital character for one. Because I rarely show my teeth, he thought I was unable to bite. Mind you come here on your way to Paris. You can go every mile of the way by steam. Give me warning of your approach, lest I should be flitting on some little excursion. I wrote to you at Rome a kind message from Haslam. You have seen him of course. Thomas Richards, the eldest son of our old friend, wrote to you at the Academy in order to learn your address for me. He writes he has neither seen you, nor heard from you.

" Yours most sincerely,

"CHAS. BROWN."

The last quoted letter was addressed to its recipient at a house in Brook Street in London. Severn had thought it best, apart from his wish to see his people again, to go to London before arrival there with his family for good. His stay was a brief one, however, nor did he spend any time of it in the house of his parents: indeed, he seems to have encountered few even of his old friends. In August he left England again for Italy, and up to the beginning of 1840 remained uncertain as to the date of the family's migration from Rome.

A chatty Art-letter from Eastlake, which he received in June 1839, will be read with interest. 'The Ancient Mariner' alluded to in it is one of Severn's best as well as most imaginatively conceived pictures. It is now in the possession of Lord Coleridge, to whom it was presented by its previous owner, the late Mr. Walter Halliday.

"13, Upper Fitzroy Street, London,
"June 12th, 1839.

"MY DEAR SEVERN,

"I have to thank you for your letter and the kind promise to send me some engravings. Hewitt has not yet made his appearance.

"I fully expected to see you here or I should have written to you some time ago. What was then in my mind, however, is now like an old or forgotten story, and I turn to matters of more immediate interest. I am glad to hear that you are going on with your altar-piece.

"Am I to understand that this is the work for the Emperor of Russia? Perhaps his is a distinct work, if so, 'tanto meglio,' as your practice in history will be the greater.

"Thank you for your news about Cammuccini, &c. I suspect your impression of the Munich works is quite just, but fresco is always a little more removed from nature than oils—not, however, so far as to excuse a total absence of good colour, which you seem to think is the case with the Munich artists.

"In asking me to give an account of the Exhibition you ask me to do what might be barely possible in the first moments of surprise, and if then done might afterwards be regretted. I never feel inclined to say anything of the works exhibited; a just and discriminating criticism is a very difficult and should be a long considered undertaking, and as to private opinion, it is not only the opinion of a particular person but of that person at a particular time. What therefore is it good for? You have generally applied to Uwins for a critique on the Exhibition, and if I do not regret that you have not done so now it is only because he could not say so distinctly as I can, that he himself has succeeded in this year's Exhibition in a very remarkable manner. Since his election into the Academy he had (as is often the case) been attacked very violently (I learn from himself) in the papers, and hence it was an object with him to muster as strong and as well as he could in this Exhibition.

"He sent eight pictures, but reserved one to make room for others.

The seven exhibited were disposed of, but he has had numerous applications for them all. The tide of public favour has in short turned effectually towards him, and his position has never been so prosperous or promising as it now is. This news at least will be gratifying to you. Of the other Exhibitors I should mention Maclise, and say he is as great as ever, but as we differed about his talent last year it will be useless to describe and extol what you can imagine and might condemn. Landseer is also I think as great as ever, but because he is not *more* great than ever the public is beginning to be fastidious.

"The impression you made last year has made people ready to carp at you too. Had you not exhibited your ' Ancient Mariner,' which is greatly admired, you would hardly have held your own, for the ' Rienzi ' is not so great a favourite.

"Tell Gibson his ' Venus ' is very much admired indeed. His other works and Wyatt's figure may be as much praised, but I have heard most of the ' Venus.' There is a marble statue by the daughter of a sculptor which has great merit—but I forget, all this and more will be better told by Theed, who shortly returns to Rome. I am writing in some haste for I am going out of town, indeed out of England, for a fortnight. Do not, however, think this is an excuse for not saying more of the Exhibition. I could not now say more if I had a whole day to write. I believe I before mentioned, in a former letter to Rome, that some comparatively new men have greatly distinguished themselves, viz.:—Redgrave, Cooper, and others, but these two especially. The arrangers, of whom Uwins was one, did themselves credit by placing the works of these contributors in good places, and they (the latter) are all in a fair way in consequence, but their merit deserved every consideration.

"Your ' Rienzi ' is hung where your ' Godfrey ' was last year, the ' Ancient Mariner ' a little to the left and rather lower. Wishing you all success, and with best remembrance to all, I am dear Severn,

"Yours very truly,

"C. L. EASTLAKE."

In the following July Severn received a letter from another artist correspondent, one of the chief friends of his later life, George Richmond, R.A. It is an account of that distinguished artist's impressions when he first went to Venice. The reader may be interested to turn from this letter to one (*vide* p. 205) written by Mr. Ruskin on the occasion of one of *his* early visits to the beautiful city.

" *Venice*,

"July 24th, 1839.

"MY DEAR SEVERN,

"I promised you a letter, so here goes, but you must not expect a fine critique on Venetian Art, ravings about their glazing, or any wonderful discoveries about grey grounds; for I am sorry to say I have made none, but have looked when I have not been at work (which has been seldom), with much such eyes as others I expect bring, quite willing to be pleased, and therefore have not been disappointed. Here nature has triumphed over art, or rather nature and art have combined in the evening of every fine day to beat everything that ever was or will be for splendour and gorgeousness of effect in the view from the water at sunset of St. Mark's, and all the rich accompaniments about it. I pay you an honest compliment in saying it has often reminded me of the beautiful sketch you made of this as a background to your picture of Venice. Well I must say I have not been so surprised as I expected by the works I have yet seen, for the Palz° St. Marco I have not yet visited. In Rome I was thunderstruck at the first view of its treasures: in Venice, I have been less astonished than delighted, and I find its treasures grow on me daily. One thing is to be said in explanation of this, that out of Rome one can hardly know Raffaello or Michael Angelo at all, but out of Venice one may be perfectly acquainted with Titian and Paolo Veronese. Tintoretto is the man whom one sees for the first time here, and truly I have been astounded by the magnificence and daring character of his works, both in design and colour. He puts me often in mind of Rembrandt, but he is immensely stronger in invention, indeed some of the works in the Scuola of San Rocco rank him with the great designers of the Roman and Florentine schools. What a group of women that is, in the great picture of the Crucifixion, at the foot of the Cross. I very much doubt if Volterra's so much celebrated one in S. Trinita dei Monti surpasses it. Art seems but a plaything in his hands, and this over-boldness has often betrayed him into errors, not to say signal failures for such a man.

"The 'Assumption' of Titian's is a surprising picture, full of greatness of intention and in the execution, but the figures strike me as no more or less than picturesque books, excepting the children and angels, some of which equal anything I have seen. But the picture of pictures, to my taste, is the large Paolo Veronese, which for vivacity and freeness of execution united to a most enchanting tone over the whole, is one of the wonders of art. I don't think anything can be finer or more simply painted. It strikes me as a far more agreeable whole than the large picture in the Louvre. I have just begun a copy of two figures the size of the originals. They stand before a pillar something such [sketch follows], and I think for intensity of character nothing I ever saw surpasses them. The great fat fellow with the hanging-looking moor beside him is worthy of Michael Angelo. Do you not think for style that Paolo is even better to study than Titian? By-the-bye what curious works the latter ones of Titian, [?] put me something in mind of old Northcote's painting. They look so muddled and pottered over, just what one would look for as the result of extreme old age. A work they show of his early youth gives promise of all that followed. To have been in order, I should have told you that we stayed a whole day at Bologna, so that I had at least one hearty good look at the Gallery there, which surprised me by its riches; although small, it is very perfect. All the pictures are good, and many of them are first-rate specimens of the masters. What a sober, subdued, and grand tone pervades the works of their school. I certainly think they went very far towards achieving their object of uniting to the tone and colour of Venice the gusto in design of Rome and Florence. I made a number of little sketches while I stayed, just taking the plan of some of the finest works, and I shall do this now wherever I go. Since I came here I have made ten water-colours of the best pictures in the Belle Arti, which I think will be of use to me. I am sure you are right in recommending a sketch whenever it may be got, for it remains, while mere impressions are fugitive as the day. What rascally cheats these Venetians are, and yet very good people in their way, wonderfully civil, and at the Galleries (oh! what a contrast to Rome) they are perfection. One has but to apply and entrance to study is obtained instantly. Pray give my love to the illustrissimo blackguard Agricola when you see him. I speak of his maldirection wherever I can, for such a man ought to be removed from his post."

A long period of silence intervened in Severn's and Brown's regular correspondence, which was at length broken by a letter from Brown, the last but two which Severn was to receive from him, one announcing his departure for New Zealand and the reasons for that adventurous step, and the other (written shortly before his death) from the settlement of Taranaki. The letter is dated from Chichester, near which town Brown had gone to see his son, there in training for his intended career as a civil engineer. Despite his broken health, he is as indefatigable as ever, and writes that in addition to his literary vocation and many avocations he is engaged to contribute weekly a political article to a Liberal Plymouth paper.

In the spring of 1841 a letter was received from George Keats, waiving his legal rights, and agreeing to the publication of a ' Memoir, and Literary Remains ' of his brother John. But shortly before this, Brown happened to take great interest in the new El Dorado for the colonist, New Zealand. In a letter to Trelawny he mentioned that if he were a younger man he would certainly embark for the new country : and in another to Kirkup he referred to Carlino's future, and said (alluding to New Zealand) " that way fortune lies." Still, all this was merely in the air. One day, however, he went to Plymouth to hear a lecture on the

subject of the colonization of New Zealand. The result was
that he was convinced, charmed, irresistibly attracted by
the idea of emigration. With all his prudence and scrupulous heed of common sense, he was, *more Scotico*, impulsive
and enthusiastic. Before he reached home that day he had
practically made up his mind to emigrate, despite the
uncertainties thus opened before him, his time of life and
very indifferent health, and Carlino's interrupted studies
and dubious prospects. Further reflection confirmed his
first intention. With characteristic promptitude he made
at once all necessary arrangements, even to his outfit and
the engaging of two berths in a ship due to sail towards the
end of May.

The cottage at Laira Green, where, and amid his flowers,
he had hoped to live quietly for the remainder of his days,
unless Carlino's prospects should make it advisable for him
to live elsewhere, was sold. Carlino had already left his
manual work at Midhurst, and the two spent a brief time in
London, visiting Leigh Hunt and other friends. Brown's
chief regret was in leaving his long projected 'Memoir and
Literary Remains of John Keats,' unfinished and unpublished. It had been his great hope, particularly latterly, to
be the biographer of his beloved friend : and this not so
much from eagerness to be associated with the illustrious
poet as from a loyal regard for his memory and genius, and
a fear lest the work should inadequately be undertaken by
some one else. He had, however, great confidence in
Richard Monckton Milnes, and decided that he could not do
better than leave his MSS. with him. Mr. Milnes was
himself a man of letters, and though unfortunately he had
never seen Keats, he was a fervent admirer both of the man
and the poet. In two letters to Severn, addressed to him
after his arrival in England, in which he alludes again to his
decision to emigrate, and sets forth his reasons, he also
relates his reasons for entrusting the Keats 'Memoir' to
Monckton Milnes, and those for his objection to its being
handed over to one or two other friends and acquaintances.

The second is torn : the first is as follows :—

"*Laira Green,*
"21st March, 1841.

"My dear Severn,

"Welcome to England! An impudent congratulation, you will say, from one about to go to the other hemisphere at the beginning of May. I knew you were coming, knew it from others, though I have been strangely kept in the dark by yourself. How could I well reply to your letter of September? Scarcely was it received, when I was cogitating on New Zealand; and when I had made up my mind, and was about to tell you the news, I heard you were expected in England. Did I not tell you that your Coronation visit might come to this? I am certain you have done right, not only for your wife's health, and your boy's education, but for your profession. You press me, with your wonted kindness, to go and live with you, instead of pursuing my plans. You tempt me, but I cannot, must not. Had I thought of such a course, while making up my mind to be or not to be an emigrant, I might have concluded otherwise—certainly I should have paused. As it is, the die is cast. Yesterday I took leave of Carlino, who precedes me—he is at present wind-bound in the harbour. Though chiefly for his benefit, it is fair to state that our going was by no means at his suggestion, for he was, at first, very averse to it. Of course I have weighed the consequences of this step with all the ability in my power, and I ought to have the credit of proper deliberation. You *blame* me; but are you acquainted with the country by the best report, with the probable great advantages (not so much, perhaps, in money getting at my time of life, but in happiness), and with the scheme in detail or generally? I think you are not; for those of my friends who have most withstood me have known nothing—nay, they will confound one country with another, one colony with another, one purpose with another. Some friends of this sort have withstood me, and, indeed, teased me. Do not you, my dear Severn, join them, or rather *follow* their example, for they are silent at last. There is doubtless some risk of happiness in any course a man may pursue, however promising; but as it is now too late, pray do not repeat your objections, because you throw a gloom over my cheerful hopes. Your letter, though dated on 18th, did not arrive till last night, when I had taken leave of Carlino. I almost wish you had not arrived so early, because I am now strongly induced to visit London before I go; you need not press me to this, for my inclinations are of themselves enough; you may rely on my going to see you, if I can get rid of business matters and other matters here in time.

"I resolved not to leave England and carry away with me the 'Life and Remains of Keats.' They will be confided for publication to Mr. R. M. Milnes, M.P., whom, I believe, you know. At the close of the 'Life' I leave your letters, written at the time, copied verbatim, to tell the sad story of his sufferings. I have attempted to make a selection from his poems, but I find myself too partial to reject any, so Mr. Milnes must exercise his judgment on that point; for I am well aware that a poet's fame is more likely to be injured by the indiscriminate admiration of his

O

friends than by his critics. Mr. Milnes is a poet himself, an admirer of
Keats, and, in my mind, better able to sit in judgment on a selection for
publication than any other man I know.

"The greater part of this letter is for your wife as well as for yourself;
so, with my love to her,

"I am yours, ever truly,

"CHAS. BROWN."

The two among all Keats's friends whom Brown thought
best qualified—everything, from friendly intimacy to literary ability, considered—were John Hamilton Reynolds
and Leigh Hunt. Either of these might have been safely
trusted to produce what would at once be adequate and
satisfactory to Keats's friends, though the elder and better
known author could not have given so many personal
details, as he had never enjoyed that varied intimacy with
Keats with which the younger was privileged. Unfortunately there were, in each instance, imperative reasons
against acceptance of the trust, or rather against undertaking its accomplishment: and this apart from any action of
George Keats or the jealous ill-will of Mr. Dilke, and perhaps
Mr. Taylor. Again, Brown would gladly have entrusted the
'Memoir' to Benjamin Bailey, not only because Keats had
loved and admired him, and that the love and admiration
had been reciprocal, but on account of Bailey's literary
faculty, scholarly taste, and poetic insight, combined with
his very high estimate of Keats's place in our literature.
But by this time Bailey, who had won high preferment in
the Church, had gone abroad. Again, there was Charles
Cowden Clarke, who doubtless would have undertaken the
task aright, though Brown does not seem to have thought
of him in this connection. He did think of Edward Holmes,
but as a sympathetic friend rather than as a biographer.
With all his liking for Severn as a man, admiration for him
as an artist, and gratitude to him for his unforgetable
services to Keats, Brown was well aware, and frankly told
Severn, that a literary task of such importance could not
possibly be entrusted to him. Nor did he consider
Woodhouse's qualifications sufficient. He had thought

of Trelawny, of whom he had a very high opinion, but wisely had entertained the idea only to dismiss it. There remained, then, only George Keats, Charles W. Dilke, and Mr. Taylor to be considered. The last-named was almost out of the question : and all lovers of Keats must rejoice that the work did not fall to that no doubt worthy Evangelical publisher. As for Mr. Dilke, Brown not only disliked him but shared Charles Lamb's opinion as to his lack of real discrimination and taste. Finally, the ill-feeling that existed between George Keats and Brown, particularly on the part of the latter, made an arrangement which would be mutually agreeable out of the question. Brown was prejudiced, but he was not unfair, and still less was he disloyal. He was willing to do what was best for Keats's sake, even to surrendering entirely to George Keats, to collaborating with or assisting even Dilke : indeed, he was willing to admit that his judgments both of George Keats and his sole English defender might be based upon supposition and misunderstanding rather than unfavourable facts, though he could not do so on the evidence before him. The last letter he received from Dilke annoyed him greatly, not so much by anything personally affronting as by the writer's arrogance, or what seemed to Brown his arrogance, in assuming that he knew more about Keats and Keats's concerns and the Keats family and circumstances generally than Brown, and Severn, and George Keats, and indeed all concerned, put together. Dilke, it may be added, wrote later on to Severn in somewhat the same strain.

Brown rightly concluded that Monckton Milnes, over and above his literary qualifications, was the right man to whom to depute the undertaking. If he could come to an arrangement with George Keats, so much the better : in any case, he would be assured of the assistance of the more important members of the Keats circle. Brown wrote to Hunt, Holmes, and others, and also formally deputed his responsibility to Mr. Monckton Milnes. Mr. Milnes willingly undertook to carry out loyally his friend's wishes.

With the death of George Keats in 1842 disappeared the

chief difficulty. Consent was in due time gained from his widow and from Fanny Keats, then resident in Madrid as the wife of Señor de Llanos, a Spanish gentleman of high mental and literary attainments. Four or five years elapsed before Mr. Milnes had collected from various sources all the then available information, and before his readiness and the occasion coincided. The 'Life, Letters, and Literary Remains' was published in the autumn of 1848.* In the Preface, from which a partial quotation has already been made, the following further words about Brown appear. "Before he left this country he confided to my care all his collections of Keats's writings, accompanied with a biographical notice, and I engaged to use them to the best of my ability for the purpose of vindicating the character and advancing the fame of his honoured friend."† It seems that after Brown's departure from England, Monckton Milnes was seized with sudden qualms as to his fitness for the task which had been entrusted to him, and that he would, indeed, have resigned it after all but for the earnest advice, strong encouragement, and promised aid of Severn, who by that time had, with his family, arrived in London.

* There may be given here Lord Houghton's (R. Monckton Milnes) letter which was sent to Severn together with the first copy of the ' Life ' which was issued.

"Dear Severn,
   "The proofs of Keats's ' Life ' was sent by Moxon to Lord Jeffrey, to try and get him to review it for the ' Edinburgh.' This is literally the first copy made up. I did not show you the proofs, because I felt if I once did so to any one of Keats's friends, and thus exposed myself to their criticism, there was an end of the book, for I could not undertake to please them. Even Reynolds, without whom the thing could not have been done at all, has not seen a word in print.
                                    " Yours always,
                                       " R. M. Milnes.
"P.S.—The book is Moxon's, not mine."

† After acknowledgment of indebtedness to Leigh Hunt, C. Cowden Clarke, Reynolds, Holmes, Felton Mathew, Haslam, and Dilke, he adds: "I have already mentioned Mr. Severn, without whom I should probably have never thought of undertaking the task, and who now offered me the additional inducement of an excellent portrait of his friend to prefix to the book: he has also in his possession a small full-length of Keats sitting reading, which is considered a striking and characteristic resemblance.

From that time forward there is no record of Brown beyond the letter he wrote to Severn shortly before his death. No doubt he wrote several times from New Zealand, but none of his letters seems to have been preserved: strange, so far as Severn is concerned, as he had, almost since his first arrival in Italy, carefully kept all his friend's communications.

Brown was bitterly disappointed with his experience of New Zealand, and in particular believed that he and others had been grossly deceived as to the advantages of New Plymouth (Taranaki), whither he had gone. Late in January of 1842, he wrote to Severn complainingly of these matters.

" New Plymouth, Taranaki, New Zealand,
" 22nd January, 1842.

" MY DEAR SEVERN,

" The Plymouth New Zealand Company have grievously disappointed us, and I intend to proceed, as soon as I can, to return to England viâ Sydney (as the cheapest way), perhaps leaving Carlino behind me, at least for a short time. Our letters, it is surmised, have been opened, and, if found to be unfavourable to the New Zealand Colonies, they never reach their destination. We now entertain better hopes of our letters, and should this arrive at your hands, you will be of essential service in causing it to be printed in the public papers as a caution to others not to put faith in representations made by New Zealand companies. No one letter can contain our grievances; but it is enough to tell you at present that this place has not a port except Port Hardy, 100 or 110 miles off, in D'Orville's Island, nay, has not a roadstead, and is so dangerous to approach that, after wrecks and various disasters, ships no more attempt it, and we are left unsupplied, possibly, at last, to live on the fern root, which would soon kill me. *I was promised a Port by the Company for my money*, and I intend to protest against receiving any sections of land on this coast, and to bring an action against the Company for their non-fulfilment of the contract between us, I claiming a return of my money paid to them, together with every expense to which I have been put, and damages of all sorts which the law will allow. In the meantime, though much injured in ' mind, body, and estate,' I shall not be a pauper, and, looking at your hearty invitation just before I quitted England, it is my intention, should my health and time of life permit me outlive the voyage, to offer myself at your threshhold as your guest,—at any rate, for a moderate period. My health and strength are certainly improved since last month, when I feared I was irretrievably sinking under my grievances; but since that time I happily discovered a document from the Company, perhaps inadvertently granted to me, though a very common one, and that seems to promise me the fullest justice.   Without it, I had not anything but verbal promises, verbal representations—which are nothing in a legal point of view.

"Think of our being compelled to take shipping to go to our *Port!* the impudence of such an attempt to fulfil a contract is scarcely imaginable. But I have proof that my sections of land were engaged to be at the *Port* of New Plymouth.   Accordingly I demand to be conveyed to Port Hardy (the declared Port), and there to take any sections of land ; but first the Company must carry land thither, as it is little more than a naked, steep rock ; enough of land, at least, for our 201 acres : but though I expressed our willingness, at a public meeting, to go thither, no answer was returned, all looking aghast at the unexpected though reasonable turn I gave to their discussion as to the best means to be adopted for obtaining a Port.

Carlino, 1 am glad to say, is well and in good spirits.   1 have written much of my 'New Zealand Handbook ;' not 'New Zealand Guide,' because I cannot conscientiously guide any one to it.

"Remember me most kindly to Mrs. Severn, and

"Believe me, ever yours truly,

"CHAS. A. BROWN."

The hope expressed in this letter, of again seeing Severn in England, was not to be fulfilled.   Ere long he was overcome by another and more serious apoplectic fit, which proved fatal.*

Thus died, in comparative isolation and disappointment, one of the kindest and most genial of men, beloved by nearly all who knew him, the most intimate of all the friends of Keats till the poet went to Italy on the hazard of life. On his grave in distant New Zealand one may believe that, among the tall grasses which surround it, are a few evergreen leaves from the laurel-wreath of the illustrious friend whom he loved so deeply, and to whose memory he was so scrupulously loyal.†

Shortly after his arrival in England with his family,

* His son, Mr. Charles Brown ("Carlino"), remained in New Zealand, and became a prosperous colonist.

† The reader interested in Charles Brown should turn to the letters of Alfred Domett and Jno. Geo. Cooke, particularly the second, quoted at pp. 262 and 264, *post.*

Severn took up residence at 21, James Street, Buckingham Gate. At first, however, he found accommodation at a house in Burlington Gardens, and it was there that he received the following letter from Mr. Dilke, in reply to one from him concerning the Keats 'Memoir.' The truth of the matter seems to be that Mr. Dilke acted, throughout, the part of one who would neither do a thing himself nor allow any one else to do it. In any case, it is a matter for congratulation that he "had not sufficient leisure to attend to anything" of the kind.

"9, Lower Grosvenor Place,
" Sunday Evening. 1841.

" Dear Sir,

"I forward a dozen copies of the paper on Fresco. I am not even sure that in my haste last night I thanked you for your intention of sending me a second. Such papers are welcome, and I think serviceable to the good cause. If you will let me know beforehand what number of copies you would wish to have, they shall be reserved and sent. I have directed the printer to return the MS., and will then add the address of George Keats in Louisville, Kentucky. Your note touched on other matters to which I was unwilling to reply on the spur of the moment. I have no doubt Mr. Milnes will do justice to the subject :—whether a stranger can do justice to the man is a question open to consideration. I have never seen Brown's ' Memoir,' but the spirit of it was foreshadowed in his letter, and that led to a quarrel—the ' be all and the end all' of which was a refusal on my part to reply elaborately to sixteen pages of charges against George, conjured up out of the ambiguous givings-out of poor John, and George's letters, who had intentionally mystified his brother for the peace and quiet of his vexed and wearied spirit. You may say how could I know this—do I pretend to know more of Keats's affairs than Keats himself! Yes, I assuredly know more than all the Keats [*sic*] put together. How I acquired my knowledge would be a tedious story. It cost me years of anxiety, the benefit of which Miss Keats had and enjoys, and even George benefited by it, the only one among them that affected to be a man of business, having given his guardian a receipt in full. To be sure, Brown promised further to vindicate John from the attacks in the ' Quarterly' and ' Blackwood '—then [*thus* ?] to drag his memory through the mire that had poisoned his living existence.* As if the fact that an edition of his works were called for a quarter of a century after he had been laid in his grave, was not vindication enough. As if the monument

* This does not seem as though Dilke knew more than all the Keats circle. Brown, no more than Keats himself, would have fallen into the mistake of supposing that the ' Quarterly' and ' Blackwood ' " poisoned the poet's existence."

to his fame would be more genial in its influences if built up with the
stones that had been hurled at his living head. As to George I have no
doubt that he would, on proper representation, forward Mr. Milnes's
views, and hold himself obliged. Years since I had full power from him
to treat for the copyright of his brother's works, and he was most anxious
to bring out a handsome edition and sacrifice the cost if necessary. I fear
indeed that I alone am responsible that no such edition was published. I
however had but little leisure at the time to attend to anything, and there
were objections which do not perhaps now exist. These facts I state in
justice to George Keats, for such has of late years been the disarrangement
in all American affairs, that he may not now have it in his power to do
what he was then most anxious for. He must, however, be written to by
some one in whom he has confidence, for he does feel that he has been
strangely treated. While called on, and very properly, to pay every
shilling of his brother's debts, which indeed he entered into legal engage-
ments to do at a time when he never hoped to receive a shilling from his
brother's estate, he never received book, letter, paper—no, not so much
as an old volume or a refuse sheet that had belonged to his brother. I
mention these facts because Louisville is not beyond the twopenny post,
and too far for explanation and rejoinders. If you mean to write yourself
I have no doubt he would be happy to hear from you, because I know that
he is grateful for your kindness to his brother—but I doubt if he would be
very communicative to strangers.

"I should be happy to enter more freely into this subject could you
favour me with a call—or I would visit Burlington Gardens if I thought
it likely that I should find you disengaged.

"I am, my dear sir,

- "Yours truly,

"C. W. Dilke."

One of the last acts of Severn before he left Rome was to
pay a farewell visit to the grave of Keats. He expected to
find no one at that solitary spot, and at that unusual hour,
but to his surprise he saw two young people, evidently
lovers and as evidently English, kneeling (hand in hand)
and kissing the earth where lay the dust of the poet they
loved so well, and for whom they sorrowed so reverentially.
He did not disturb them, or advance : but, from his vantage,
made a rapid sketch of the scene.

The painting from this sketch was the first picture—
apart from commissioned canvases on hand — which he
made after he had settled down to his new English life.
'At the Grave of Keats' received as chief title the simple
but significant word : *Fame.*

CHAPTER IX.

FOR nearly twenty years there is little to chronicle of Severn's life. From 1841 to the end of 1860 he enjoyed an uneventful and industrious art-life in London, occupying himself otherwise almost solely with domestic and social interests, and, ever and again, with various literary undertakings. At no time a good correspondent, though so often the recipient of letters, he seems to have had little intercourse with his friends in Italy, except by short notes and casual messages; nor do they appear to have been much more communicative during his long stay in London. The death of Charles Brown was a shock to him, though he had been so far prepared for it by his friend's several serious illnesses. Since Keats, he had intimately known and loved no one so much. In a note to Charles Eastlake he says that he feels as though his sense of youth had gone for ever, with the death of that dear friend and comrade.

But, of course, he had many interests in London, apart from those all-absorbing ones which he formed in his studio. He was delighted to see his own people again; to meet some of the friends whom he had known in those days when the young poet had fraternised with the young painter, and had gone together to look at the Elgin Marbles, or for

long walks into "the greening" (as Keats once exclaimed
the country in spring should be called), or had sat in the
low sitting-room at Hampstead and discussed Spenser,
Shakespere, and Milton; and glad also to resume acquaintanceships made in Rome and elsewhere in Italy. He
had already won, in Rome, the friendship of Mr. Ruskin.
Every reader of 'Praeterita' will remember the author's
account of how he first came upon Severn and George
Richmond, at the former's house in the Via Rasella, when
he visited Rome in 1840; and his delightful reminiscences
of Severn at that period. And now, in London, the latter
always found a hearty welcome at the house of Mr. Ruskin,
senior, at Denmark Hill. He saw much of Eastlake, Uwins
and other fellow-artists, and, as he remarks later in a
journal, was continually being surprised at meeting with,
or being called upon by, persons who sought or were glad
to encounter the man who had been the intimate friend
of Keats, and in whose arms the poet had died. There was
literally not a year of his life, in the close on sixty years
which followed the death of Keats, wherein he had not
cause to congratulate himself on having accompanied the
dying poet to Italy, and to feel half perplexedly grateful
to the abiding influence of his dead friend.

"'It seems to me that his love and gratitude have never ceased to
quicken with cool dews the springs of my life,' he wrote to William
Haslam: 'I owe almost everything to him, my best friends as well
as my artistic prosperity, my general happiness as well as my best
inspirations. . . . . . . He turned to me suddenly on one occasion,
and, looking fixedly at me a long while with a fiery life in his eyes,
painfully large and glowing out of his hollow woe-wrought face, said,
'Severn, I bequeath to you all the joy and prosperity I have never had.'
I thought our poor friend was wandering again; and soothed him
gently. 'This is the last Christmas I shall ever see—that I ever want
to see,' he said vehemently, an hour later, and as though no interval
had elapsed; 'but you will see many, and be happy. It would be a
second death for me if I knew that your goodness now was your loss
hereafter.' . . . I have often remembered these words, and others he
often said to me, and I do believe that the dear fellow *has never ceased to
help me.* I thank God I am so happy as to live to see his growing fame.
It will be to my lasting honour to be bound up with him. I send you
an MS. with this, and Brown's letter. You may not have heard that

young B. [rown] is not coming back; so you can write to him at New
Plymouth, Taranaky, as you suggest." . . .

In the first part of this letter, dated the 24th, Severn
speaks of his ardent hope of success in the Westminster
Cartoons competition; and added incidentally that he was
fortunate in having the friendship of Mr. Gladstone:

"I am honoured in having won the friendly regard of this eminent
statesman, a man who is as great and worthy in himself as he ever can
be in politics. He is the latest, though probably not the last of the
men of eminence who have in the first instance been attracted to me on
account of their interest in Keats." At the end of the letter he adds:
"I am rejoiced to be able to tell you that I have just received a letter
from Mr. Gladstone, assuring me of the success of my cartoon. This
elates me greatly, and I am encouraged to hope that there is a future
for historical art in this country after all—besides being relieved at my
necessarily improved prospects, a change of vital importance to me now
with my growing family and heavy responsibilities." *

This competition for one of the commissions to paint
the Westminster frescoes was one of the most exciting
episodes in Severn's life after his return to England from
Rome.

But here, for the sake of chronological sequence, room
may be found for the following letter from Mary Shelley.
It affords further evidence of the artistic side of that
remarkable woman's nature:

* Severn preserved this and several other letters from Mr. Gladstone.

"13, C[arlton] H[ouse] Terrace,
" June 24th, '43 (Night).

"My dear Sir,

"Mr. Rogers dined with me this evening, and hearing that the judges
had to-day been engaged in passing sentence on the cartoons, I ventured
to ask how one, which had for its subject the Princess Eleanor drawing
the poison from the wound of Edward in the Holy Land, had been considered to stand. He told me that I had better not tell him whose it
was, but that I might mention to the artist who drew it, that according
to the sentence of all the judges—except Lord Lansdowne, who had not
yet seen the cartoons—it was in the number of the successful and selected.
It gave me very great pleasure indeed to learn this, and I am anxious, in
case it should not have already reached you, to lose no time in making it
known.

" I remain, my dear Sir,
" Most faithfully yours,
" W. E. GLADSTONE."

Rue Neuve Clichy. No. 3 Rue de Clichy, à Paris,
15th Dec., 1843.

."Dear Mr. Severn,

"It is some months now since, with the deepest regret, I left Italy. I have been in England since, and continually intended seeing you; but, not remaining in London, I have not been able. I am now come over here for a few weeks. When I return I shall hasten to see you and Mrs. Severn. I can never express how much obliged I was to you both for the letters you sent to me for your acquaintances at Rome, who showed their respect to you and their own goodness by the very great attentions they paid me. I had hoped to spend this very winter in the Eternal City, but I must wait for other days before I revisit it. I now write to you on a subject in which I am much interested. I shall be truly obliged to you if you will consider it and give me counsel and information. Do you know the picture of Titian—the 'Woman taken in Adultery'—did you ever see it? It was in the Galleria Calderara at Milan: the print at least you know, made from it by Anderloni (Colnaghi, the printseller, has an impression). Is it not the second best of that admirable master? The 'Assumption' being the best? Is it not worth a very large price? Would it not be an excellent thing that our National Gallery should possess it? A Milanese nobleman possesses it, who does not consider himself rich enough to retain a *capo d'opera* of such great value, and wishes to sell it. He expects to receive, of course, several thousand pounds. It is established genuine by incontestable evidence, and is in excellent preservation. In size it is eleven feet by five. How could it be brought before the consideration of those who might propose it to Government for the National Gallery? Or indeed what is the right way to bring it before the consideration of Government? The difficulty seems to be that the picture is at Milan. To bring it away will cost some hundred pounds, and its possessor wishes, before he spends these, to have knowledge of how far it is probable that it can be sold in England. As far as I can judge by the print, and as far as I know the value of so great a work of Titian, it seems to me that we English ought to possess it, and that our National Gallery, not over rich in first-rate paintings, would acquire great glory from possessing this one. Its originality is, I am told, incontestable. Let me have a line of advice, and telling me your ideas on the subject, as soon as you can.

"Ever yours,
"Mary Shelley."

Between 1848 and 1850, Severn painted, among others, portraits of Mr. Gladstone and Mr. Monckton Milnes. In a brief (undated) note from Thomas Collins, it is stated that Mr. Mote would be entrusted with the engraving of the portrait of Mr. Gladstone.

Early in 1851 he heard with great regret of the death of William Haslam, the friend who had introduced him to

Keats some six and thirty years before, and for whom the poet had always expressed a great regard. In a letter written 9th February, 1852, by Mary Haslam, his wife, it is stated that he broke down under the heavy pressure of business and financial embarrassments, but that "his end was peace." He died on the 28th of March, 1851. His sister, whom Keats seems to have known also, was living in Paris in 1876.

Most of Severn's correspondence for the next fifteen years is of a merely casual and uninteresting kind. Far and away the most interesting and remarkable letter which he received was from Mr. Ruskin, shortly after the author of ' Modern Painters ' had gone to Venice in 1843. Students of Mr. Ruskin's work will note the suggestive fact that so early as 1843 he wrote exactly as one might anticipate his writing in any of his latter years. The letter was in answer to one from Severn (whom he had come to know through George Richmond; in the first instance, in common with Mr. Erskine of Linlathen, the Duke of Bedford, Mr. Gladstone, and others, because of the interest of Severn's association with Keats) telling him of the writer's success in the Cartoon competition for the Westminster frescoes:

" *Venice,*
" Sept. 21st (1845 ?), 1843.

"My dear Sir,

"I am sure you will excuse my not having answered your kind letter before, when I tell you that I have been altogether unhinged by the condition in which I have found Venice, and that every time I stir out of doors I return too insensible to write or almost to speak to any one. But I cannot longer defer expressing my sincere gladness at your well deserved success, and my sympathy in all the enthusiasm of your hopes, so far as regards your own aims and prospects, and I am also glad for the sake of our national honour, that you are to be one of its supporters. But with your hopes for the elevation of English art by means of fresco, I cannot sympathise. I have not the remotest hope of anything of the kind. It is not the material nor the space that can give us thoughts, passions, or powers. I see on our Academy walls nothing but what is ignoble in small pictures, and would be disgusting in large ones. I never hear one word of genuine feeling issue from any one's mouth but yours, and the two Richmonds', and if it did, I don't believe the public of the present day would understand it. It is not the love of *fresco* that we want : it is the love of God and his creatures; it is humility, and charity, and self-denial, and fasting, and prayer, it is a total change of character. We want more faith and less reasoning, less strength and more trust. You neither want walls, nor plaster nor colours—*ça ne fait rien à l'affaire* —it is Giotto and Ghirlandajo and Angelico that you want, and that you will and must want, until this disgusting nineteenth century has, I can't say breathed, but steamed, its last. You want a serious love of art in the people, and a faithful love of art in the artist, not a desire to be a R.A., and to dine with the Queen: and you want something like decent teaching in the Academy itself, good training of the thoughts, not of the fingers, and good inpouring of knowledge, not of knocks. Never tell, or think to tell, your lank-cockney, leaden-headed pupil what great art is, but make a great man of him, and he'll find out. And a pretty way, by the by, Mr. Eastlake takes to teach our British public a love of the right thing, going and buying a disgusting, rubbishy, good-for-nothing, bad-for-everything Rubens, and two brutal Guidos, when we haven't got a Perugino to bless ourselves with. But it don't matter, not a straw's balance. I see what the world is coming to. We shall put it into a chain-armour of railroad, and then everybody will go everywhere every day, until every place is like every other place, and then when they are tired of changing stations and police, they will congregate in knots in great cities, which will consist of club-houses, coffee-houses, and newspaper offices; the churches will be turned into assembly rooms; and people will eat, sleep, and gamble to their graves.

"It isn't of any use to try and do anything for such an age as this. We are a different race altogether from the men of old time; we live in drawing-rooms instead of deserts; and work by the light of chandeliers instead of volcanoes. I have been perfectly prostrated these two or three days back by my first acquaintance with Tintoret; but then I feel as if I had got introduced to a being from a planet a million of miles nearer the sun, not to a mere earthly painter. As for our little bits of R.A.'s calling themselves painters, it ought to be stopped directly. One might make a mosaic of R.A.'s, perhaps; with a good magnifying glass, big enough for Tintoret to stand with one leg upon. . . . (Sept. 29th), if he balanced himself like a gondolier.

"I thought the mischief was chiefly confined to the architecture here, but Tintoret is going quite as fast. The Emperor of Austria is his George Robins. I went to the Scuola di San Rocco the other day, in heavy rain, and found the floor half under water, from large pools from droppings *through* the *pictures* on the ceiling, not through the sides or mouldings, but the pictures themselves. They won't take care of them, nor sell them, nor let anybody take care of them.

"I am glad to hear that the subjects of our frescoes are to be selected from poets instead of historians; but I don't like the selection of poets. I think in a national work one ought not to allow any appearance of acknowledgment of irreligious principle, and we ought to select those poets chiefly who have best illustrated English character or have contributed to form the prevailing tones of the English mind. Byron and

Shelley I think inadmissible.   I should substitute Wordsworth, and Keats or Coleridge, and put Scott instead of Pope, whom one doesn't want with Dryden.   I think the 'Ancient Mariner' would afford the highest and most imaginative method of touching on England's sea character. From Wordsworth you get her pastoral and patriarchal character, from Scott her chivalresque ; I don't know what you would get from either Dryden or Pope, but I suppose you must have *one* of them.   However, anything is better than history, the most insipid of subjects.   One often talks of *historical* painting, but I mean *religious* always, for how often does one see a picture of history worth a straw ?   I declare I cannot at this instant think of any one historical work that ever interested me.

"I beg your pardon very much for this hurried sulky scrawl, but conceive how little one is fit for when one finds them covering the marble palaces with stucco and painting them in *stripes !*

"Allow me again to thank you exceedingly for your kind letter, and to express my delight at the good news it contains, and believe me, with compliments to Mrs. Severn,

"Ever most truly yours,

"J. Ruskin."

Although the following letter from an unknown correspondent is of considerably later date than that of Mr. Ruskin just quoted, it may for convenience' sake be given at this place.   Its date is somewhat uncertain.   At first sight the year seems plainly to be 1826; but as Byron was born in 1788, it is obvious that he could not have had a son old enough to act as his biographer two years after his death in 1824.   Though it is difficult to see in the formation of the third figure any resemblance to 4, the letter probably was written in 1846, if for no other reason than that it is addressed to Severn in London, when he was living at 21, St. James Street, Buckingham Gate, whereas in 1826 and 1836 he was in Rome.   It is possible, but unlikely, that it may have been written in 1856.   It caused the recipient no slight astonishment.*

"2, King Street, Greenwich,

"June 22nd [1846 ?].

"Sir,

"I will not venture to offer an apology for the liberty of addressing you, permit me to hope that the motive will serve as an excuse.   I am engaged at present in writing a life of the late Lord Byron, in a chapter of

---

* The 'Life of Byron' is by no means apocryphal, I understand ; though the MS. has not yet come to light, and perhaps never will.

which I speak of poor Keats; and to you as the friend and companion of the poet I would now appeal for such information and facts as you may have treasured up in your memory. I am a great admirer of Keats as a poet and as a man, and I shall with great pleasure receive the new editions of his writings, which Mr. Monckton Milnes, if I am not misinformed, is at present preparing. During my stay at Rome I frequently bent my steps to the tombs of Keats and P. B. Shelley—those twin-brothers of misfortune and disappointment—and well might a poet wish to find such a last resting-place. I have longed to possess a memorial of Keats—may I hope I shall not appear too presuming or selfish, if, in the ardour of acquisition, I even make bold to say that I shall value highly any *record* however trivial of your friend? The memory of Keats is almost as dear to me as that of Byron, and how dear *that* is to my heart you will conceive when I tell you (*this in confidence*) I am the son of the author of 'Childe Harold.' Anticipating your pardon for this intrusion, I remain with great respect, Sir,

" Your obedient and humble servant,
"GEO. GORDON BYRON."

The following letter is interesting, though the second sheet is missing and the writer is still unknown. All enquiries at the British Museum Library and elsewhere have failed to discover the "art-novel Titian" or its authorship. When the Severn MSS. came into the present writer's hands, this letter was one of a packet of notes from Mr. Gladstone, to whose penmanship, moreover, it might readily be attributed. No doubt "Titian" will come to light some day: or, at any rate, the writer of this note be discovered. I do not think that the resemblance of Keats's features to those of Cobden have been noticed by any one else.

" *Oxford*,
"April 15th, 1844.

" DEAR SIR,

"I have been so much occupied since I had the pleasure of receiving your note, that I could not earlier acknowledge it. I now must thank you for so promptly and kindly writing to me. I am gratified at finding that my conjecture was correct, and that *you* were the Mr. Severn whose kindness soothed the dying moments of poor Keats. I was a lad when he died, but recollect being struck then with a sense of the injustice done him. The first poem of his I ever read was the sonnet on first reading Chapman's 'Homer,' and that made me eager to read more. Next I fell in with the 'Ode to a Grecian Urn,' and some time elapsed before I met that glorious 'Ode to a Nightingale,' which I thought then, as now, one of the finest things in the language. After this, and when I could fully understand them, I read 'Endymion,' 'Lamia,' 'Isabella,' 'The Eve of St. Agnes,' and 'The Hyperion.' The two last, I fancy more than all the rest.

"Mr. Taylor, who was his publisher (32, Upper Gower Street), shewed me his bust and several portraits. You will be surprised at the likeness between these and that most poetical matter-of-fact man, Mr. Cobden.

"Perhaps you have seen Mr. Cobden, if so, the feature-resemblance and the expression-likeness must have struck you.

"If I had not felt deep interest in the personal history of John Keats, perhaps I should not have written my art-novel, 'Titian.' That book exhibits the struggles of a gifted mind—almost crushed by wrong, neglect, and evil fortune. One part of the preface to 'Endymion' I quoted ('there is not a fiercer hell than the failure in a great object'), and I preferred making a painter my hero, because it would have been difficult to exhibit the struggles of a man of letters,—because in Titian's case I could wind up with ultimate success,—and because the time, scene, and personages were more susceptible of being picturesquely treated than if I had a modern scene and person.

"But I need not take up this sheet with the intention of writing about my own doings. You may see, however, ——"

Severn, however, with all his regard for Mr. Ruskin's judgment, was not to be dissuaded from the desire to paint frescoes. Naturally, he was the more eager to undertake remunerative work of this kind on account of his waning prosperity. He found that he could not sell pictures so readily as before; to some extent, no doubt, from the greater supply and relatively less demand in London beyond what he had experienced in Rome. He was glad when he had one or two, even one commissioned picture on hand. He even thought of resuming his old stand-by, miniature painting; but he soon ascertained that miniature portraits were no longer the vogue. It was with eager goodwill, therefore, that he availed himself of every opportunity for decorative painting. His most important undertaking of the kind was under the patronage of the Countess of Warwick.

On the 24th of September he wrote to his mother:

"I am engaged in painting two large fresco-pictures, in many respects the most important works I have ever done, as they are the first examples in England of architecture being decorated with pictures in this style, and also in that it is the first real opportunity I have ever had of producing such things. The Countess of Warwick is my liberal patroness, and

lives here five months in the year. She received the place, a gift from
her son, the late Lord Monson, who died at the early age of twenty-five,
in the year 1841. He had partly built this magnificent hall in imitation of
a fine building at Rome, and the building has remained unfinished ever
since. Cornelius, the great German painter, was to have done what I am
now doing, but Lord Monson's death changed the plan, and so it has
remained until Providence has placed it in my hands that I may distinguish myself and get ample employment in this my favourite way.
Lord and Lady Warwick are very kind to me, and although I was a
stranger to them till a month ago, yet I am treated as a friend. There
are no bounds to the praises they bestow on my progressing work, even
from the first outlines."

Among the more important pictures in oils painted by
Severn during this period, mention should be made of
'The Campagna of Rome' (bought by Mr. Gladstone);
two Roman-life pieces, for Sir Charles Lamb; 'The Last
Days of Pompeii' (Baroness Braye); 'Endymion asleep
on Latmos,' the features resembling those of Keats (Mr.
Elliott); 'The Villa d'Este at Tivoli,' and 'The Lake of
Albano' (Major Richard Sykes—who purchased at least
four pictures from Severn); 'The Lake of Nemi, from
Nemi' (Sir E. Vaughan); 'The Lake of Nemi, from
Genzano' (?); 'Rinaldo Reposing' (Sir Thomas D.
Acland); a larger and slightly enhanced rendering of
'The Praying Girl,' called 'The Praying Woman and
Child' (Louisa, Lady Ashburton); and 'The Talisman'
(Her Majesty Queen Victoria).

Subsequently he undertook some book and magazine
illustrating work, though he did nothing of any mark
in this *genre*. In 1853 he was invited to contribute one
or two drawings on wood to the first illustrated edition
of the 'Proverbial Philosophy.'

The example of his friend, Sir Charles Eastlake, and
the more immediate influence of two books, Mr. Ruskin's
'Modern Painters' (Vol. II.) and Lord Lindsay's 'Sketches
of the History of Christian Art,' led Severn in 1847 and
the ensuing years to devote much of his spare time to
literary composition. In connection with Lord Lindsay's
book the following words by Mr. Ruskin will be read with
the greatest interest. They occur in a letter written by

EARLIEST STUDY FOR PICTURE OF "ARIEL."

To face page 210.

him to Severn early in 1847, in reply to one concerning the state of religious art in England.*

"What you say of the want of feeling for Religious Art in England is too true, but happily it exists more among the Artists than the Public. There is a violent current of feeling turned that way at present, and I anticipate much from Lord Lindsay's forthcoming book. Produce anything we shall not, at present, but I fully anticipate seeing the Carraccis and Murillos and Carlo Dolcis, and coarse copies of Titian and Rubens, and all the tribe of the potsherd painters, and drunkard painters, cleared out one by one from our Galleries; their places supplied by Angelico, Francia, and Perugino—so far as the works of these great men are rescuable from the grasping apathy of the Italians, who hold them fast as a dead man holds what was once near his heart, though it is no use to him now. You may regret the state of things in England, but in Italy it is something frightful. With us it is ignorance and bad teaching: with them a mortal corruption of the whole mind. But there is one element in the English mind, which will, I fear, keep it from doing anything very pure in art—its consciousness of the ridiculous. So long as a painter dreads giving a ludicrous idea—so long as he feels *himself* in danger of laughing, or *mocking* at anything—so long he is always tumbling on the other side, and losing sight of Truth in the effort to be sublime—losing sight of that genuine, heartfelt, faithful, loving realization, which is the soul of Religious Art. Now the state of Italy at the time of her greatest art, was something to put *laughing* nearly out of the question. Battles like Montaperto or Meloria—governors like Eccelino—kings like Charles of Anjou—keep the corners of people's mouths down wonderfully: and at the time of the great burst of Florentine intellect—at the time of Dante—the great representation of all the brightest qualities of the Italian mind—the public and private suffering and *exertion* was so great, that I should hardly think a man in Florence ever smiled. The portrait of Dante, which has been drawn with extreme love and faithfulness by Giotto, and which is beyond all comparison the finest example of that master I have ever seen, is in its quiet, earnest, determined, gentle sadness, the very type of the spirit of the good men of his time (and in his time men were either very good, or very bad); it is, the 'sad-wise valour, the brave complexion, which leads the van and swallows up the cities.' But you cannot conceive a smile on such a face (and the Italians, even in their degradation, retain this peculiar incapacity, they seem insensible to the ridiculous). Hence you will find, in all the works of the time, a fervent desire to put pure truth before you, by whatever means, or image it can be suggested. When Dante tells you that the Head of Ugolino was in Hell so above that of the Archbishop

---

* For Mr. Ruskin's estimate of Lord Lindsay's work, *vide* 'The Quarterly Review' for June, 1847: "The Eagle's Nest," p. 49: and "Val d'Arno," p. 199, where he writes of Lord Lindsay as 'his first master in Italian art.'

Ruggieri that the one seemed to be hat to the other, he has evidently not the slightest idea or fear of making you smile. His own feelings are too intense and serious to admit of any the slightest degradation by the image, and he says just what will make you understand the position of the heads thoroughly. And so always: the souls meet and kiss in Purgatory, [come] *S' ammusa l' una con l' altra formica—Forse a spiar lor via—e lor fortuna.* Guido Guinicelli plunges into the fire, *come per l' acqua il pesce undando al fondo.* To anybody who has ever seen an ant or a fish, these images explain the whole thing in a moment; but a modern poet would be mighty shy of such. Now the moment you can sweep away all conventionalities, and manners, and fears, and give to an Artist this fervent desire to tell the pure truth—and such intensity of feeling as dreads no mockery—that moment you lay the foundation of a great Art: and so long as you have artists who think of what will be said, or who struggle to get something higher and better than God's great truth, so long all you bring will be foam. It is inconceivable how much this single defect in the English character prevents us and pulls us back. A defect I call it: for I conceive there is nothing ridiculous in the World. There is too much of the pitiable and the melancholy ever to leave room for the ridiculous, and the tendency to turn serious things into jests is a plague spot in us, which hardens us and degrades us. George Herbert has it 'the witty man laughs least—for wit is news only to ignorance.' Give a man a quick sense of all that pollutes, of all that is 'earthy, sensual, devilish,' and *no* sense of that which is to the vulgar laughable, and you will have a pure art. Till you can do this there will be little done in England."

Severn projected a series of lectures upon the great Italian artists, though he does not seem to have actually written any, with the exception of a fragmentary paper upon Raphael. He set himself to the task of continuing a romance of the time of Titian's residence in Rome, in which the great artist plays a background part, begun in Rome in 1839 under the title 'The Dead Hand,' but ultimately intended for publication as 'Love's Triumvirate.' Besides this ambitious undertaking, he wrote one or two short stories; a series of 'Imaginary Letters of the Great Painters and their Contemporaries: Intended to illustrate the theory of the application of Art to other things, and of the Extraneous Influences that affect Great Art' (1848); one or two short essays on fresco painting; and miscellaneous papers upon art-subjects.

In the main, however, Severn's literary work was done

within the fifteen years following his return to Rome in 1861,
as British Consul. The only published writing of his that
is widely known—indeed, with the exception of a short
story called 'The Pale Bride,' his sole publication—is the
article in the 'Atlantic Monthly' for 1863, so familiar to
all Keats students under its title 'On the Vicissitudes
of Keats's Fame.' The great wish of his latter years was
to see the publication of what he called his 'Adonais'
volume, which was a folio edition of the 'Adonais,' with
annotations and notes, to be illustrated after specially
made designs by himself and his two artist-sons Walter and
Arthur. The lines selected by Severn for his commentary,
or as his texts for occasionally lengthy notes, are these:

> "Till the future dares
> Forget the past."

> "The third among the sons of light."

> "Most musical of mourners, weep anew."

> "But now thy youngest, dearest one, has perished,
> The nursling of thy widowhood, who grew
> Like a pale flower by some sad maiden cherished
> And fed with true love's tears, instead of dew."

> "To that high Capital where Kingly Death
> Keeps his pale court in beauty and decay
> He came and bought with price of purest breath
> A grave among the Eternal. . . ."

> "Why linger, why turn back, why shrink, my heart?—
> Thy hopes are gone before: from all things here
> They have departed; thou shouldst now depart."

and, finally, the last stanza, ending—

> "The soul of Adonais, like a star,
> Beacons from the abode where the Eternal are!"

The publication was never undertaken: perhaps because
Severn's notes as they stood were insufficient (though he
intended to add many more, indeed to comprise in the
volume all his reminiscences of Keats), and partly, no
doubt, because none of the illustrations were done.

But all literary work was given up or postponed when

the, to him all-important, chance of his obtaining the post
of British Consul at Rome arrived.*

' He was eager to get the office.   The pleasure of being in

---

* To this end he chiefly trusted to the influence of Mr. Gladstone and
to the recommendations of eminent men who had known him in Rome,
particularly Baron Bunsen, and Mr. Odo Russell (afterwards Lord
Ampthill).   Having secured aid from these, he wrote to Mr. Monckton
Milnes, among others.   This letter may be given first, as it indicates the
reason for the occurrence of a vacancy in the Roman Consulship.

"83a, *Eccleston Square,*
"Monday, October 22.

"My dear Milnes,

   "I trust you will be glad to hear that I am a candidate for the consulship at Rome about to be vacant by Mr. Charles *Mausoleum* Newton (who
is about to become my son-in-law) preferring the British Museum.

   "Mr. Gladstone has given me a very warm friendly introduction to
Lord John Russell, explaining my real fitness for the place and even some
of the advantages of my having it.   Also the good Baron Bunsen, with the
like friendship, has written to Lord John more particularly on my
capacity for the peculiar work, as at Rome I often had to act with him in
the numerous services I was accustomed to render to my country-people.
Then my twenty years' Roman sojourn and my familiar acquaintance with
the Italian language and the historical literature, and the friendship and
patronage of Cardinal Weld (although I am a Protestant), gave me a fair
standing which has never been impaired, and my large altar-piece at the
Cathedral of S. Paolo is the only public work in Italy by an Englishman.
But one singular service I could render : *in finding rare works of art for
our galleries and museums*, and looking after them in these sad times.

   "But you'll say 'what have I to do with all this rigmarole?'   It is
this—I see that you are to be honoured with Lord Palmerston's visit, and
as you are famed for your attachment to your old friends, I think it just
possible that you may have a *pretty moment* wherein you can advocate my
claim with your usual *nailing* eloquence—for you see I am most anxious
to return to dear old Rome.   My six children (for whose education we
returned to England) being all well settled, my wife and I incline to a
'Darby and Joan' life and to resume 'da capo' in Italy.

   "My health and strength are first rate and I am equal to any amount
of business, indeed beyond that of my first visit to Rome.

   "So I will e'en hope that you yourself may remember some incidents of
my useful life at Rome, and be able to clench the nail already so well
driven in by Bunsen and Gladstone.   I often had occasion to hear of Lord
Palmerston during the famed trial of mine of three years' Roman durance
and iniquity, which so annoyed Sir Brook Taylor and for which the former
Pope offered me a compensation through Chev. Bunsen.

   "Please to understand that I do not now pretend to the Consulship for
the salary but for a solid return to the very useful life at Rome.   My
painting flourishes and I have noble patronage—the Duke of Devonshire
(as I had the last), and my present works are thought to surpass all I
have done.   You are almost the only friend never seeing them, but you
sent me charming excuses which was better.

"And I remain,
"Your anxious friend,
"Joseph Severn."

London had waned, particularly as he realised with deep regret that a new movement of the tides of art was leaving his "life's barque" stranded. No doubt a man of so much resource, of so winsome a personality, and with such genuine if too often mediocre powers in art, would have found enough employment to enable him to live in comfort. His three eldest children were no longer dependent upon him: and the three younger were likely soon to support themselves. Still, the struggle of life would have been a hard one; indeed, so it had already become. The emoluments of the Consular post at Rome were certainly not great, but they ensured a competency. Moreover, a great desire came upon him to return to Rome, where the happiest as well as the most prosperous years of his life had been spent. He thought longingly of the place, of the life, of the artistic atmosphere, and of the friends who still lived in that city.

Before midsummer he had obtained all the needful letters of recommendation. Early in June he wrote to his old acquaintance, Dr. Quin:

"*83a, Eccleston Square,*
"4th June, 1860.

"MY DEAR DR. QUIN,

"I was distressed to find you so ill that you could not see me, for you have ever been a most kind and faithful friend through a long course of years, unchanged amidst the change of everything about us. I told you of my being a candidate for the Consulship at Rome. It prospers, as every friend has given me a warm testimony; and even the Queen, to whom my daughter wrote, gave a favourable and gracious answer. The only obstacle is a rule in the Foreign Office that each Consul on his first appointment should not be more than fifty years of age. Now I am just on the wrong side of it,* but my health, strength, and even sight place me comparatively on the right side of it; and it now occurs to me that a

---

* A record of seventeen years on the wrong side is a goodly burden for "just" to carry. An extract from his Journals in 1863 proves not only that his disguise of his actual age was systematic, and for obvious reasons, but that all accounts of his rare youthfulness and alertness of mind and body must be unexaggerated. "To-day I attain the age of 70 . . . . and 'tis singular that I am obliged to conceal my age most studiously, for my office has to do with it and my enemies would triumph over me did they know that I am now 70 years old, for I am considered as between 50 and 60, but rather to the 50, so that 'favourable looks' are my good fortune."

testimonial from *you*, as a distinguished physician, would greatly help me, for you have known me so long through all kinds of changes. Perhaps my twenty years' sojourn at Rome gives a positive claim as to knowledge of the language and people, and I trust that the happy success of my six children may be some little addition to that claim. My artistic power would enable me to look for rare works of Art, and attend the wants of our English people. I propose to go to Rome in about a fortnight to resume my Italian Art, *independently of the Consulship,* which may or may not come to me, and if I do not ask too much in your present state (though I beg you not to think of it, if it is the least inconvenience), it is to write me a letter as a testimony (rather of my health and strength than of my talent and character), or to Lord John Russell if you like, but 'twill be the same to me, as I have to enclose several. I should tell you that the Chancellor of the Exchequer supports me warmly, as did the late Baron Bunsen, and indeed I have reason to be pleased at the manifestation in my favour and the joy expressed at the prospect of my being placed at Rome. Good-bye, my dear Dr. Quin. I will hope that before I go I may have the pleasure of seeing you and finding you recovered.

" Yours truly and obliged,

" JOSEPH SEVERN."

The letter from the Baron Bunsen, just referred to, may be quoted here. It is addressed to Lord John Russell, and marked "*private*": and has additional interest from the political sagacity and foresight which it displays. It was, moreover, one of the last letters despatched by its distinguished writer, who dictated it from his death-bed.

" *Bonn,*
"12th October, 1860.

"MY DEAR LORD JOHN,

"I have no hesitation in recommending to your kind notice *Mr. Joseph Severn,* who I understand is anxious to obtain the British Consulship, now vacant, at Rome. I believe Mr. Gladstone has already given him a warm testimonial, but having known Mr. Severn for many years at Rome I can testify to his peculiar fitness as a Consul there, for during the years he spent at Rome he made himself universally useful and popular among the English residents. I may also add that in an intrigue got up against him by jealous Italian artists and the clerical party on account of an order given him by Cardinal Weld for an altar piece in St. Paul's, Mr. Severn had the whole of the more enlightened and liberal Italian public on his side. From his intimate knowledge of Italian affairs and his social relations with Romans of all classes, I should also consider him as very likely to be useful to your diplomatic agents. I will conclude by saying that I never knew an artist possessing so much *practical* knowledge and ability as Mr. Severn. I am so suffering at present that I am not even able to receive visits, much less to pay any, otherwise I could not have denied myself the pleasure of waiting upon you while in this neighbourhood, but I cannot let this opportunity pass without expressing my sense of gratitude as a statesman, a Christian, and a man, to you and Lord Palmerston for having not only proclaimed but also enforced the principle of non-intervention in Italy. I am sure you agree with me that Venetia cannot in the long run be withheld from Italy, but at the same time, that it would be a disgrace to Europe if the question could not be solved without the aid of arms and the danger of a general European conflagration. I believe that not only the enlightened public all over Europe but also a large proportion of public opinion in Austria, which is even represented in the council of the Emperor, would hail such a solution with the greatest satisfaction, supposing the financial interests of Austria and the honour of the Imperial house were ensured.

        " Pray believe me, ever yours faithfully,

                " BUNSEN." *

Severn, however, on the advice of Mr. Gladstone and other friends, postponed his departure to Rome till after the end of the year, or till he should hear definite news as to the vacant post. His patience was rewarded by a welcome note at the end of January, communicating to him his election to the coveted office.

A few days before the good news, he received the following cordially complimentary note from Mr. Ruskin; naturally, then and later, among the most valued of all the letters sent to him or on his behalf at this time—for all his disagreement from the writer in "minding the Raphael cartoons or frescoes profoundly."

             " *Denmark Hill*,

               " 23rd January, 1861.

" DEAR MR. SEVERN,

    " Indeed it gives me great and unqualified pleasure to hear that you wish to obtain the Roman Consulate. What testimonial can I offer to

---

    * On the day after his appointment Severn wrote to the Baroness Bunsen, and attributes his success to her late husband's generously worded letter. " I ventured to ask from the Foreign Minister that precious memorial, the beautiful letter on my behalf dictated from the death-bed of that great and good man. It was kindly sent me, and the appointment with it. When I read the letter I at once understood how my success had been brought about, and how that Ld. J. R. made up his mind. . . . . It is my earnest hope that I may be able to come up to the fair promise therein made of me, made on the remembrance of thirty-five years of unbroken friendship with which I was honoured and blessed, and which during that long period never changed, except to increase till it came to that climax, that most Christian act of love, that ensured my success."

you, that will not be a thousand-fold out-testified by the consent of all who know you, and who knew, in those old times of happy dwelling in the ruinous Immortality of Rome: where English and Italians alike used always to think of Mr. Severn as of a gleam of living sunshine—in which there was no malaria of mind—and which set at one, and melted into golden fellowship, all comfortless shadows and separations of society or of heart. Consul! Truly and with most prosperous approbation it must be.* I shall say with Menenius—'Take my cap, Jupiter, and I thank thee.' As for Raphael Cartoons or frescoes—you know I mind them not profoundly, but all that I do mind profoundly I know that you have eye for also, and as I cannot fancy anything pleasanter for English people at Rome than to have you for Consul, so I can fancy nothing more profitable for English people at home than that your zeal and judgment should be on the watch for straying treasures as in these changeful times may be obtainable of otherwise unhoped for Italian art. I would say much more, but in the hearing of your many and dear friends I feel all that I can say would be but impertinence, and so pray you only to believe in my most earnest wishes for your success, on all conceivable grounds: and to believe me here and at Rome and everywhere,

" Affectionately yours,

"J. Ruskin.

"Sincerest regards to Miss Severn. I rejoice to hear Mr. Newton's † coming to Rome."

Shortly afterwards Severn wrote again to Mr. Ruskin, remarking how difficult it was to arrive at *safe* rules in the study and practice of art: and how even the author of *Modern Painters* could not always be taken literally. Mr. Ruskin's reply does not seem to have been kept by Severn: at any rate, it has not come before the present writer. As, however, it is known to have been in substance similar to one written from Oxford at a later date to Severn's eldest son Walter, then a young artist of singular promise, the latter note may appropriately be quoted here:

---

* There are no inverted commas here, though the mention of M enenin in the next sentence gives the clue to their source.

VOLUMNIA: " Honourable Menenius, my boy Marcius approach es ; for the love of Juno, let's go."

MENENIUS: " Ha ! Marcius coming home?"

VOL.: " Ay, worthy Menenius ; and with most prosperous approbation."

MEN. : " Take my cap, Jupiter, and I thank thee:"

—*Coriolanus*, Act II., Sc. 1.

† Miss Mary Severn married Mr. [afterwards Sir] Charles Newto n. Her elder sister, Claudia, was at this time married to Mr. Fredk. Ga le, the well-known amateur cricketer.

> " *Corpus Christi College,*
> " *Oxford.*

"My dear Walter,

"I am very glad you like to talk, or write to me, and very much more glad that you are in good spirits and have sold your pictures. They deserved to sell, and you need not vex yourself at being out of the ' *Running.*' To be *in* the *Walking* is far pleasanter. You do not need to study from nature in the way you have planned, you may make good sketches that way, as you do now,—but not so good as the hurried ones. What you do want is to draw any one thing, for once in your life, thoroughly, as far as you can, and to get the roundings of it by real drawing. To do this once would open your eyes to an entirely new order of effects in nature, which are at present as invisible to you as if they were of another world. Yes;—myriads of people have been wrong by reading *Modern Painters*. But that is because they pick out the bits they like—as for the rest—' Ruskin's all wrong;—we know better than that.' But I have never yet known any one go wrong, who would do *all* I bid him. Not that I know many such! Of course there are many weak persons, who have really no invention. And these will draw still life badly;—but their invention would have been worse.

"Ever most truly and affectionately yours,

"J. Ruskin." *

One of the last things Severn amused himself with doing, after all arrangements were made but before he had

* In this connection, room may be found here for two other letters from Mr. Ruskin, both addressed to Mr. Walter Severn: the longer, personal; the shorter, a brief reply to an enquiry as to the meaning to be conveyed in the titular words *Fors Clavigera*. Both notes were written in March, 1875 :

(1) " The Fors is fortune, who is to the Life of Men what Atropos is to their death, Unrepentant,—first represented, I believe, by the Etruscans as fastening a nail into a beam with a hammer. (Jael to the Sisera of lost opportunity.) My purpose is to show, in the lives of men, how their Fortune appoints things irreversibly, while yet they are accurately rewarded for effort and punished for cowardice and folly.

"J. Ruskin."

*   *   *   *   *

(2)   " *Brantwood, Coniston,*
> "March 26th, 1875.

"My dear Walter,

" I had better not put off, though I am hurried to-day, telling you how glad I am to hear of any likelihood of your putting your power of sketching to real service. I have never myself seen anything so wonderful, in its way, as your power of obtaining true and complete effects in limited time. And if I were travelling myself in a country of which I wished to convey knowledge to others, I would rather have you for my aide-de-camp than any other artist I know, without exception. I never saw so steady truth united with so dashing rapidity, and I am even in some doubt of the expediency of the advice I ventured to give you as to actually left for Rome, was to write the following humorous parody of Hamlet's famous speech beginning, "To be, or not to be." The occasion was the production of Mr. Walter Severn's first etching :

> " To bite, or not to bite, that is the question—
> Whether 'tis nobler in the artist to suffer
> The paleness, woolliness, and fog of dry-point
> Or to take arms against a sea of troubles
> And, by opposing, end them ? To scratch, to bite
> No more : and, by a bite, to say we end
> The etching, and the thousand pallid things
> The plate is heir to—'Tis a consummation
> Devoutly to be wish'd ! To scratch, to bite—
> To bite, perchance to fail, aye there's the rub :
> For in that failure what dire holes may come
> When we have shuffled off upon the printer
> What must us ease—There's the respect
> That makes this etching seem so long a bore.
> For who would bear the whips and scorns of fame,
> The printers' cheat, the scorn of publishers,
> The pangs of déspised art, the plate condemn'd—.
> That patient etcher of the unworthy takes,
> When he himself might his quietus make
> With a bare Photograph. Who would etchings etch,
> To grunt and sweat over a greasy plate—
> But that the dread of something after ' Bite,'
> That undiscover'd process, from whose toils
> No etcher e'er returns—puzzles the will
> And makes us rather bear those ills we have
> Than fly to others that we know not of ?
> Thus ' biting ' doth make cowards of us all ;
> And thus the native hue of resolution
> Is sicklied o'er with the pale cast of thought ;
> And etchings of no strength at all or moment
> With this regard, in bitings pass away
> And lose the name of action—Soft you, now !
> Be all my pangs forgotten ! "

----

methods of more detailed study. As a traveller your method is the best possible. If, indeed, you were to stay at home, and wished bringing out all your higher gifts, you would need other kinds of practice, but they would diminish your rapidity and courage, and scarcely add, for *public* service, to your skill.

" Ever affectionately yours,
" J. RUSKIN."

CHAPTER X.

Mr. Ruskin on the East wind—' Imaginary Letters '—' Michael Angelo to Vittoria Colonna '—' Fra Savonarola to Fra Bartolomeo '—' Galileo to Milton '—Light and Sound: A New Theory '—' Divine origin of the octave '—Severn's story: ' The Pale Bride '—Severn's novel: ' The Dead Hand '—Projected novel: ' The lost Throne.'

OF the several literary undertakings of Joseph Severn, the earliest of any note is the series of imaginary letters from the great painters and their correspondents, written in 1848. The drift of the series is " to illustrate the theory of the application of the principles of Art to life, and *vice versâ*." " We are at last emerging," writes Severn, after some remarks on the spirit of sectarianism having been the great blight of art in England, " from these ugly, whitewashed puritanical blights, which have pressed down upon us as a nation; just as London is commonly in gloom from a vast rolling billow of fog or smoke, worse always when blowing from the east,* but at all times causing heaviness of spirit, and innumerable moral and physical evils, a similar murky cloud of Puritanism and Sectarianism, or by whatever name the thing be best called, is always striving to manufacture a besom wherewith to sweep away all the rainbow-glories of the imagination, all that innocent sunshine of life, wherein we love to recreate new brightened ways for our tired wandering feet, such as we see so

---

* " I am so glad Mrs. Severn likes my fresh strawberries. I should have had pretty ones by this time, but for this fiendish east wind, which gives me a deep and true horror, and is, rightly thought of, a plague such as centuries have not witnessed." (*From a Letter from Mr. Ruskin.*)

readily as children when we do not place tyrannic bonds
upon our imagination."

. It was an undertaking, however, for which Severn was
quite unfit. He was no critic, nor was he a scholarly
student of his own or any other literature; while even of
the history of Italian painting he had but an unsystematised
knowledge. With all his familiarity with Raphael or
Michael Angelo he could at no time have written anything
of importance upon either, for not only was he by nature of
an uncritical mind, to which comparative estimates were as
alien as purely æsthetical appreciations, but he had never,
pen in hand, that concentrative faculty which, brush in hand,
was his safeguard and strength.   Moreover, by 1848 his
literary experiments had been too few and unimportant to
enable him to write with any ease or even correctness.
Possibly, he might have succeeded with a simpler subject
or less ambitious scheme; though even when, some fifteen
years later, he wrote his article on the "Vicissitudes of
Keats' Fame," it had to undergo much necessary revision
from the editor of the *Atlantic Monthly*. His Reminiscences,
whether written in the "fifties," "sixties," or "seventies,"
could not possibly be printed as they are; though, it may
be added, only small technical corrections are needed
wherever he writes as it were straight from his heart, as
in his loving recollections of Keats.   His foremost literary
achievement of a non-reminiscent nature is in his novel, and
thereafter one or two art-essays written in the "seventies."
He was so excellent a *raconteur* that he might have been
able to train himself to become a successful novelist;
and no doubt he was much better qualified to write a
romance than to enter into rivalry with Walter Savage
Landor in a field which that master of literary form had
made his own. His novel was admired by Odo Russell
and other good judges; an Italian lady, his friend the
Countess Lovatti, wished to translate it into her own
language; and Heine's friend, the eccentric Countess de la
Rocca, wished to render it into German, and even did go
some length with it. But by 1848 his radical literary

faults of slovenliness of expression, inconsequence, and indifference to essential particulars, were not to be overcome. It would, therefore, serve no good end to place the series of these " Imaginary Letters " before the reader, particularly as few of them have any " fundamental brainwork " to justify the labour of much revision. But as Severn thought well of his unfinished book, and as they afford hints of the man himself, they should not wholly be put aside. Three of the shortest may be given: as it happens, they call for comparatively slight revision.

" MICHEL ANGELO TO DONNA VITTORIA COLONNA.

" *Rome,*
"April, 1520.

" FAIR AND ACCOMPLISHED LADY,

"When I wrote you the description of the Transfiguration of Raffaello d' Urbino I had just had the gratification of finding the gifted painter at work on the head of Christ. At that time it seemed to me perfect, and yet I am assured he went on finishing it as if it were to be the last of his works—and the last it is, for he has been suddenly cut off by a fever at the untimely age of thirty-seven. All Rome weeps for him, from Pope Clement down to the commonest lovers of the Arts. To me this sudden news has been doubly painful, as only a few days since I saw him alive in all the brightness of his genius and manhood, engaged on an immortal work, which he seemed to execute with ease and even gaiety. When I looked upon the work and upon the painter, the one containing such depths of art, such powers of originality; and the other with such gentleness of nature, in person and in mind; I then thought him the happiest of mortals. Now I have seen him pale in death, stretched on his untimely bier. The undying work of the Transfiguration on which he was occupied, and which his sorrowing disciples had placed at his head, seemed like his soul still hovering amongst us. He is gone, but in this sublime work he painted the way he had to go and which we have to follow. Still in death the same calm smile as in life lay on his beautiful countenance. When I looked on the picture and the painter's lifeless form together, the work increased in my estimation. How noble a trait is it, in this immoral age, that his latest work is proper to be placed over the artist on his deathbed. Ah! how great a change, what a test! How few show such real power in their works that any is at death thought worthy to be placed about them. Here is a proof that painting ought and must carry with it a moral purpose to be really effective and great. Here am I, an old man in comparison, receiving a lesson in Art and Religion from one so much younger. The direct cause of his death is differently related; the physician tries to defend himself from the universal condemnation.

Raffaello had been suddenly called by the Cardinal Riario about the Vatican frescoes, and hurrying to and fro on this important business in the first great heat, he took a fever, and the Doctor imprudently bled him, when he was too weak and delicate to bear it. I give you the account as I received it from Giulio Romano, who now takes the artist's place, and is his executor. Perhaps the most extraordinary thing about this extraordinary being is that the talents which in other men excite envy and jealousy and all bad feelings, in him inspired the most ardent friendship in the various professors of Art who were so fortunate as to know him. He won them to his purposes of carrying out divers works, by the fascination of his manners, and the splendour that attended his footsteps. Hundreds of artists were employed by him. From every part of Italy he employed them to copy from the early works in all three arts, and he even sent into Greece two young men, a painter and a sculptor, to model the works of Phidias at Athens. How truly does he seem to have been born for the advancement of the art! To him it was immaterial what he took from other men's works, as he always added more of his own. In some cases he has introduced whole figures from the works of others, which stand with more propriety and effect in his, than even in the originals. He was destined to improve everything he touched. The figure of Christ in the Transfiguration I remember on an old fresco near Florence, but how he has ennobled it ; who ever cared for it until he condescended to copy and improve it! He has left a glorious example in his Vatican labour. No doubt he was able to produce so many works (an unrivalled number when we consider his age) by the judicious selection of his helpers ; as well as that his style was one that enchanted his scholars. May one dare to suppose that he was so suddenly taken from the world as he had given the highest perfection to the Art that humanity is capable of ?

"Addio, my beloved and accomplished friend,

"Your faithful but antique St.,

"M. A. BUONAROTTI."

"FRA SAVONAROLA TO FRA BARTOLOMMEO.

"*Florence.*

"ESTEEMED BROTHER IN GOD,—

"There are so many misstatements and falsehoods chattered about in malice as regards those parts of the doctrines which I preach concerning the fine arts, that I am induced to take up the pen to write to you, my believing friend, who, in the midst of the scandals of Rome, I know will stand up, vindicate, and even paint for the cause I am sinking under. You will perhaps even return to your persecuted friend when you learn all the disasters that surround and hem me in. You have shown to the world what the purity of art can effect. You have shown the loveliness and charm of painting in raising our passion for the arts above the grovelling degradations of humanity, and therefore can well understand why I am so unjustly called the persecutor of the Fine Arts, when I have merely attacked the vicious tendency and irreligious nature of our great

Florentine works. I confess to you that I have with my own soul denounced these wickednesses in every way that seemed to me effective; that I have prayed whole nights to our blessed Redeemer that He would make me the instrument to dash to the ground these pagan works, which, fostered and caressed at Rome in the very nostrils of the Pope, are yet the sinful cause of gross idolatry and profligacy—aye, and even paganism in all shapes and tendencies. For this I have laboured to raise painting to be the handmaid of devotion, for there is nothing so simple and touching wherewith to impress the vulgar with the blessed truths of our Holy Religion. And Christ in His benign goodness looked down and blessed my humble efforts, even to the destruction of all the works of Art in Florence, and now when I am looking about to reap the fruits of my preaching, these fickle Florentines have turned about, neither rejoicing in the loss of their works of Art, nor finding a purer life in accord with their inclination. The Pope's spies are amongst them, instigating their minds to destroy me. Oh, my dear brother and friend, fly to my aid; for I am sinking, and long for those days to return when you and I, in the Monastery of Santa Maria di Fiori, devoted our minds to these divine objects for the restoration of pure religion. Now that so much has been effected, come back to my aid, I implore you; for our task is only half done, and, alone, I am sure to sink under the weight of malice and treachery that is bristling up about me. But you may like to know from me the history of the late great bonfire, when I revelled in the destruction of all these profane works.

"You must know in the first place that I had long perceived a desire in the Florentines to give up all these wicked things, and I proposed that a large pile of wood should be kindled in the square of Santa Maria, and that every good Christian should fling into the fire every work of Art, be it picture, engraving, or even statue, that dishonoured the cause of religion and decency. Thousands at my bidding brought their various works of Art, and with their own hands threw them into the flames. This continued a whole morning, and I did all in my power to encourage the cleansing the city of such pestiferous wealth. The memory of that day begins to pass away, and the Pope's spies accuse me of heresy, and so I have now to prove that my faith is orthodox; and that it is solely against the luxury of the church, its pagan practices and mundane discipline, that I have contended. I yet fear that I may not prevail, and that the wicked power of the abused church may crush me.

" (Unsigned.)"

"GALILEO TO MILTON.

"MY REVERED FRIEND,—

"When I first had the singular happiness to be visited by you in the Inquisition prison, we discoursed on the light and truth of those immortal subjects for which I was suffering in darkness for having proclaimed and for having persisted in. Then it was that we swore in

Q

the silence of our hearts, to live and die for these things. As we were not
allowed to speak on them, no doubt we felt them the more. What
.changes your dear country is undergoing for the cause of truth ; really it
would seem that mortals were destined never to arrive at it, but blunder-
ingly—that the light of truth so dazzled them that they never could see
their way, but with a blaze before them indistinct in its nature, and with
darkened perils under their feet. I received your noble sonnet on the
massacre of the Italian Protestants in the Alpine Valleys of Piedmont,
and shed many tears over it in secret, as every true Christian must.
From it I conclude that all your works are necessarily of a pathetic nature,
like the conflict of the times you live in. Yet here in Italy we are in a
little outward sunshine, both in Religion and Politics, and there may be
fine things going on, which, not being allowed by the Inquisition to tell
the truth, yet hold up an agreeable aspect of beauty and nature. No
soul-stirring truth is told, but yet no falsehood is disseminated. Of this
description just now there is a new fresco picture, by Guido, at the
Rospigliosi Palace, which seems to me, as it seems to everybody, the
most lovely work ever done. It represents Aurora flying onward, dis-
pelling the night and its vapours of gloom. She gaily throws about her
numerous flowers, which seem to collect the dew as they fall towards the
grateful earth. She is a beautiful and graceful figure in ample flying
folds of saffron windings, which do not conceal her feet, with which the
earth is to be blessed.

"She looks round on the ample light and radiant power of Apollo,
who in his never-resting car guides his bounding Steeds, who seem to
splash about the light he breathes on all sides; but more particularly he
seems to inspire the gentle hand-in-handed Hours who so gratefully encircle
his car, that he seems almost upheld by them. There is no end of their
varied attitudes: some are turned from you like the hours you lose, some
look cheerfully and catch your eye like the moments you profit by and
enjoy, but they all go tripping on to show you the moral that Time never
stops. All this golden light would be overpowering were it not that
Guido has given one little touch of contrast, for down below on the right-
hand side, deep under Aurora, you see the fresh blue mysterious sea, dark
and lovely in its nature, yet about to be impressed with the moving light
which has already begun to tinge its shore.

"This singularly fine work is on the ceiling. Carlo Maratti pointed
out to me that Guido, in the happy composition of the Hours, had availed
himself of an antique bas-relief at the Villa Borghese, which may also
have given to him the idea of the picture; but if so, like a great genius,
he has made the adaptation beautiful to our eyes by the marvellous way he
has set it. In the marble I should not have been struck so much with
the three figures hand in hand, but when they are made to represent the
hours about the car of Apollo, then it is that the beauty comes out.
Really it would seem that the application of a fine thing were superior to
the invention of it, and this would account for so many great things
having remained dormant for ages until some masterhand found the way

to apply and make the thing useful. This work is done for Cardinal Barbarini, and is thought to be the *chef-d'œuvre* of the fascinating Artist.

"(Unsigned.)"

If the shortcomings of Severn's essay on 'Nature's Law of Harmony in Colours,' and that 'On the Superstition of the Etruscans' were merely literary, these articles might be revised and published. Unfortunately they have the radical drawback that they were written in ignorance of the works of specialists, and even, it must be admitted, in ignorance of the subjects treated. The reason for writing his Etruscan essay, as given by Severn, is his astonishment at Mr. Dennis, in his great work on Etrurian remains, having omitted to describe or even perceive, what from the outset Mr. Dennis had known, and had continuously demonstrated : namely, that the ancient Etrurians were a distinct people from the Latins, with different ethical conceptions, and, in a word, with a wholly peculiar method and manner in the conduct of their ceremonials of death.

The essay on 'Light and Sound: A New Theory,' is merely a longer, more intelligible, though not more scientific, version of 'Nature's Law of Harmony in Colours.' The only really original things in this "new theory" are the few evidences of close observance of colour-effects —and, pre-eminently, the extraordinary theory as to the divine origin and nature of the octave in Music. It may, however, be given *in extenso*, if for nothing else than as an example of Severn's method and manner in an art wherein he was in every way unfitted to excel. Severn himself thought highly of this essay, which is a further reason for its inclusion. In the Diary entry (July, 1873) relating to it, he states that it was written that day in four hours, after he had "tried to give it form and place for five years."

ON LIGHT AND SOUND.

A NEW THEORY BY JOSEPH SEVERN.

IN that magic beauty of sunset, which is felt universally, in the splendid colouring of every object down to the smallest leaf, the eye is so gratified as to seek and prefer that moment to every other wherein to behold the aspect of nature. The cause of this charm is, that every object at sunset is illuminated with the prismatic colours. The moment the sun goes down below the horizon, the rays are reflected on the atmosphere round the earth, and thus the exquisite colours seen in the prism are thrown on every object.

This may be observed when the sun's rays show the colours, particularly under the roofs on the walls when the orange, yellow, and red rays form a beautiful band; while on objects that are shaded from the sky, the most intense blue, like ultramarine, may be seen. At this moment the sky overhead actually throws a stronger light than the sun itself, which, although it is below the horizon, yet illuminates the sky, though not with prismatic light.

The prism, discovered by Sir Isaac Newton, gives the colours which compose the light distinctly, and thus when passing through the glass triangle the rays are broken, as in the sun at sunset.

It is this sublime moment which the great Titian generally represents in his works, and more particularly in the picture at Rome, called the ' Sacred and Profane Love.' The two figures are sitting on a sarcophagus, one in a white dress, the other naked, but with a red mantle falling from the shoulder, and a white girdle round the waist. The very fine landscape gives the effect of the sun when just below the horizon, so that every object has the golden outlines. But the ample cool light from the sky falls on the two figures, giving little or no shade. This fine work forms the most remarkable contrast to the shade-hunting pictures of the Bologna school.

The most striking example of reflected sun's rays I remember, was at Tivoli, in the Grotto of Neptune. Before the course of the river was changed, a large portion of the water dashed through the grotto, and at a certain hour in the morning the sun's rays entered this dark grotto, and were reflected or broken on the spray. The effect was sublime, for in the dark cavern the colours, red, yellow, blue, green, and orange, were seen in all their purity, a lovely Iris which danced about on the spray, and in its brilliancy seemed like a divine spirit.

It was this sublime sight which first suggested my enquiry into the real nature of Light.

Being in Italy, where the clearness of the atmosphere reveals more readily the colours composing Light, I was enabled to carry out my enquiries. One evening I observed the orange and red tints under the hat of a friend, extending two or three inches down from his forehead, and on his gently lifting his hat at my request I saw the colours go with it, leaving the clear sky-light on his face. Experimenting in this fashion I plainly apprehended the principle by which Titian painted.

In the composition of light (of the five colours, with black and white) the first thing to observe is its unchangeableness, for the colours remain the same under every remove of the prism—in their positions and in their proportions—and this Law of Nature extends to the harmony of colours in a most beautiful and mysterious way.

If any one of the colours is examined in the sun. the eye instantly of itself forms the contrasting or complementary colour—viz., if a red wafer be placed on a sheet of white paper, and be looked at in the sun, in a short time a green wafer will be seen by the side of it. If a yellow wafer be placed in the same way, and looked at in the sun, in a short time a purple wafer will be seen by the side of it—and if a blue wafer be placed, an orange wafer will be the result.

This remarkable property in the eye is a subtle law of nature as regards harmony of colours. So that whatever we look at as regards colour, the eye involuntarily forms the complementary colour. Thus to red, green is formed by the eye, which being composed by yellow and blue, completes the diagram as formed by nature. As it is the same of the other colours, not only the blue and yellow, but also all the various tints may be compounded of the three primitive colours, so nature has given to the human eye (visibly) to form the contrast which contributes the actual harmony.

Even to the black and white the same rule invariably applies—viz., if a black wafer be placed on the white paper, and looked at in the sun, a white wafer will immediately be seen by the side of it—and *vice versâ*, if a white wafer, though on a grey ground, a black one will be seen.

In attempting to explain this marvellous property in the eye I am not aware but that I may be attempting it for the first time, or that it may be more clearly done by some one else, of whom I am not aware.

If the eye be somewhat constrained by the finger in the inner corner towards the nose, a brilliant Iris will be seen within on the other side of the eye, and only by " the mind's eye." This I take it is the wonderful way nature forms the harmony, and forms it continually. This external Iris is an invisible part of the Brain, for in the description of the Brain I have never met with any notice of it, and I am now laying greater stress upon it to demonstrate how kindly nature instructs us in the law or harmony without any intuition but nature's impulse. This law of harmony extends to sound in music quite on the same principle as in colours, and the human ear has the same property of forming harmonies.

And I have often heard that in one instance of very fine ears, if a note were struck, the ear immediately formed the third, fifth and octave to it.

The scale of colours and that of sounds seem to me almost the same— viz., the red, yellow, and blue form the treble, tenor and bass. The green, orange, and purple form the contralto, the high tenor, and the baritone.

Then the octave, which we receive from nature, and is not only born with us, but must have existed in all times, and in the same proportions; this octave must have been the same to the ancient Greeks as to other nations. It is perhaps one of the most mysterious links with the invisible world, that this property of sound always exists, though we cannot tell how we got it, or how we exercise it, for in an instant we perceive a note out of tune: how is this?

The octave in music is the most charming mystery in nature, and its form is so positive that we may fairly conclude that it exists in the unseen world invariably the same.

Light is more apparent to us, but none the less coming to us from another world unchangeable in its nature like the sounds.

The octave in music is composed thus :—

> From the 1st to the 2nd is a whole tone.
> From the 2nd to the 3rd is a whole tone.
> From the 3rd to the 4th is a whole tone.
> But from 4th to the 5th *is only half a tone.*
> From the 5th to the 6th is a whole tone.
> From the 6th to the 7th is a whole tone.
> From the 7th to the 8th *is only half a tone.*

In this seeming inequality of the two half tone intervals, all the beauty, all the infinite variety of modulation exists, for on whatever note the dominant is fixed, the same proportion is kept up, the same half tones are found by all the whole tones being divided by the flats and sharps.

Perhaps nature's indulgence has been greater in allowing us this octave than in anything else, for we know, for we are sure, that the octave is a divine privilege, that it exists in the upper world, and that we are allowed to participate in it. It shows that we are immortal beings, and that another world exists to which we are to be united.

The same rule applies to colours, for they are inexhaustible, and we know at every instant in the light they come to us from the happier world where such abstractions exist. We are sure that it must be a positive world, as the law of harmony is positive, and indeed we may state with comparative assurance that the Divine Author has bestowed on us unchangeable and eternal links in colours and sounds.

Of the two or three short tales which Severn wrote, the only one among the Severn MSS. is the short ghost-story entitled 'The Pale Bride.' After he had written it, the subject took great hold of his imagination, and mentally haunted him for a long space of time. He projected several pictures in illustration of the more striking episodes : for example, the first time that the eyes of the mysterious stranger looked on her lover with the glassy stare of death— when he saw her, when he had gone abroad for his homeward voyage, looking at the sea from the spot where he had first seen her, in the same dress, with the same averted face, in the same attitude—and when, the lover's dead body having been thrown from the raft by the few survivors of the shipwreck, " the silent woman " leaps overboard to the place where it disappeared, and rises no more. Readers who remember the incidents of Severn's first voyage to Italy, will note that the ship in ' The Pale Bride ' has the same name as the schooner in which he and Keats sailed.

THE PALE BRIDE.

[In the possession of a Devonshire family at Plymouth there is the following journal of Mr. Woolley's voyage to Barbadoes, in search of a property which was nearly lost to him, and which he finally recovered, though not to enjoy. We are now allowed to print it.]

December 1st, 1793.—I have to-day begun to prepare for my long and doubtful voyage in search of the Barbadoes estate of my uncle Woolley, and have just heard that he did leave some kind of will; at all events there cannot be a doubt that I am his only heir. I have enquired and settled the price of the voyage, which is £75 ; and I have been twice with my solicitor, Mr. James Price, who assured me I can never succeed to the estate or possess it unless I go at once to Barbadoes. This is a hard task at present, as I have had to give up my little shop and my carpenter-trade and sink down to an idler's, but God's will be done. My father and mother implore me to do it, my friends wish it, and the lawyers insist on it, so what can I do but prepare, yet I do it with a drag.

December 2nd.—Yesterday as I could not go to see my poor Mary once, I have determined to see her twice to-day. I found her pale and ill, and for her I would waive all going, save that she insists on my going, and secretly in my ear to-day whispered that *she would go with me*—that we could be married at once, but that her father, she is sure, would not consent on account of her health. I was so struck with this charming appeal, that it seemed to make my voyage shorter and my success certain, and I lost not a moment in finding Dr. Magnus, and making sure of his consent to let his daughter go. I found him returning home to dinner, and made my earnest request to him, at which he turned pale and was dumb. I represented to him our long and faithful acquaintanceship, his liking for me, and Mary's unfeigned attachment; still, he shook his head. I implored him to consent, when he sighed bitterly, and, grasping my hand convulsively, said that his daughter's health would not bear it, that she would die on the voyage, and, he added, "She is my only child, and I live on the preservation of her life; she grows into the dear, dear resemblance of her mother, and I live upon that resemblance, being my dearest and only tie in this world. Forgive, forgive my weakness of heart, but attend, and believe in my professional skill. As I felt that I should be seemingly harsh in this sad opinion of Mary's health, I yesterday called in Dr. Yeats and Dr. Upton, who, I am grieved to tell, more than confirmed my sad prognostic that the voyage would kill Mary, and that here she has at least the chance of recovery." Of course, I was now struck dumb in my turn, for all the doings of my life turned upon Mary being my wife; but here was a long voyage, and an affair of a year, and yet doubt in the separation: yet what could I say to this excellent doctor and good father. I had not a word. We remained in silent tears leaning on each other's shoulders, without words, yet figuring all the worst disasters as we watched each other's tears dropping to the ground. O! each tear told me a history. Might I ever meet her again?

December 3rd.—All my property being sold for this voyage, my carpenter's shop let, there was no alternative, go I must and leave Mary behind, all our planning upset, her health declining, and who knows but through this—but I must proceed.

Just returned from seeing the ship *Maria Crowther*, Captain Walston, who is to sail to-morrow night: all my luggage is just now going.

December 4th.—I must go and hear again what dear Mary has to propose, and if her father has made any show of consent, or even told her of his decision.

10 o'clock.—Found my dearest sunk in grief, much changed, and unable to speak. Her father had told her of the bad opinion of Dr. Yeats and Dr. Upton as regards her strength and health for the voyage, and that she would be sure to die, and that then he would die too. She told me also, in floods of tears, of her father describing again and again my attempt to save her mother from drowning, how near I was to it, and that he had ever since regarded me as his son.

My Mary fainted with anguish. She looked so beautiful even in her paleness, and I longed to open with kisses those dear eyes that were covered with the long eyelashes heavy with tears. Dr. Magnus came in at the moment and helped to restore her to herself, but it was only to greater grief. Yet he reasoned so well, he tried to shorten the voyage by so many incidents of good fortune; then he represented the Barbadoes property as giving her a carriage, with a crest with his three boars' heads and my saw upon it, till trembling Mary looked up and smiled. He assured her of her quick recovery if she would remain quiet and go to Mount Edgcumbe, where her uncle was village schoolmaster, and so she would have a complete change, and Lady Mount Edgcumbe would look kindly after her.

All this time the slenderness of all our means convinced me that there was no putting off my voyage, for ruin stared me in the face if I remained long idle. We had not at first looked at this event all round and round, and did not see anything but our fond attachment, she seventeen, and I only twenty-one. But now the whole weight of woe came plump upon us. "Coming events cast their shadows before," and the reverse of the sunny picture now turned our eyes inward: but there was no alternative. I went home at two o'clock to prepare for my departure.

December 5th.—My father and mother are in joy that I am really going, for they seemed to sink at the thought even of delay, much less staying. They have put me on my duty as a son, for by the acquisition of this property they hope to live after all their cares in tranquil decline, with no thoughts of money troubles such as are now shortening their lives. Ah! how I feel the painful truth of this; how well I know that they had expended their last pound to provide for me; and that Dr. Magnus could but barely afford them a meal if they should chance to want.

5 o'clock.—Dragged my steps to have a last glimpse of Mary, and was astonished to see how she had picked up, and how cheerfully she received me. But as her tears dropt on my hand I felt them scalding hot, and trembled to think how much they differed from her smile, and how much suffering she must be in—yet she continued cheerful and said "Goodbye, Jamie," with even an earnest voice. And so I have left her for ever. For ever, do I say? and why? I cannot tell, but the weight of her fate hangs on me so heavily that I cannot think of it. I seem to have killed her by going.

7 o'clock at night.—On board, in a gloomy, threatening night. The Captain very kind, and indeed all the passengers, of whom there are seventeen. How miserable and forlornly I hear the sea beat against the ship's side where I am preparing to sleep. O! that I could open this port-hole and let in my Mary like a spirit to cheer me again with that last dear smile. To bed, but not to sleep.

All the dreary, never-ending night I was listening to dreary waves that were taking me from my dearest. I arose, and by the dim lamp write this, but sea-sickness begins to torment me.

December 6th.—The dawning light, for which I so longed, brings me no consolation. My sickness, though abating, leaves me no comfort, for I see my dear Mary at every turn of my head, whether I look up or down, right or left, there she is and always in tearful suffering.

10 o'clock.—I crawled up on deck, where I found many persons assembled, and they all looked towards me except one lady, whose dress and whose figure seemed to me like Mary. Surely that is her bonnet which I gave her last year? That gown with the violet pattern is like hers, and that gloved hand, whose can it be to be so like hers? I sank down with the bewilderment, and prayed for the well-being of Mary.

Again I raised my head, and there was her exact image, except that I could not see her face. I tried, but her position prevented me. Yet as she leaned her head upon her hand, the attitude was so like Mary's that I became frantic. I jumped up and strode over to the ship's side, where I should have fallen into the sea had not a sailor caught hold of me, but in the effort, although it was but a momentary glance, I caught the lady's eye. *It was hers, but it was Death's.* I sank again into the sailor's arms. I am now somewhat recovered, and those dear eyes bend over me. At times she has me by the hand, but how came she here? *Is* it she? Where is her father?—all which I would have asked, but I seemed choked with agitation. Can it be her? but can I doubt it? Who else could be so like herself. My breath still fails me. I have not words to ask how she came, but inwardly I look at her and think that she must have stolen away to the ship in the last extremity, and then waited concealed until

we actually sailed. Now we are passing "Land's End," of which I can
believe in the identity, but I cannot believe in my dear Mary's. There is
some inexpressible thing which makes us unlike each other, yet I am
unchanged, these hands and this pen are mine, there is my trunk with my
name on it, and here is my journal up to December 6th. I tremble to
behold her again, and why? My knees tremble as I rise to go on deck,
but I must see that dear object.

12 o'clock.—I found her looking on the sea in the same attitude as when
I saw her at first; with the same bonnet and same dress; and in the
same place. Will she look at me? Her gloved hand hanging down, I
made an effort to touch it, and I think I caught her glance, but of this I
am in doubt. I said, "Are you not my dear Mary?" and I listened
for her soft voice, but there was no reply. Yet I felt one finger touch my
hand; it was her little finger. Again I asked how she was thus by my
side, she pointed the other hand (which was resting on the ship's side) to
the last sight of land, and groaned. Ah! what a groan was that, and how
removed from the last cheerful smile I got in her father's house. We
remained unable to speak. Such was the strain of our suspended breath,
that the waves seemed to answer to my palpitation. I was roused at last
by the bell sounding for dinner. Everybody about rose hurriedly, and the
vision of my Molly gently too, and so she followed them and I her. She
glided down the cabin stairs, and I fell in following her; the cabin boy
helped me up, and when I got to the table I found her by my side. I
watched her eating, for I was more and more afraid, and had not power to
offer her anything. The steward put some roast beef before her, but she
only took one morsel of bread and sipped some water. She did not answer
the steward except with a movement of her head. In my wonderment I
did not touch a bit of dinner, my appetite was gone as though I never had
it. She glided away with the company, and after awhile I called up
courage to follow her. On the deck I found her sitting in the same place,
in the same attitude, looking at the waves. The sea increased, the wind
was high, and I head the distant thunder. I shrank from my watching
position, on the approach of sea-sickness again. The cabin boy came to
help me, for I was very ill, and they had to carry me to my berth. For
hours and hours I was sick to death, and wished to die. At midnight,
when the storm was a little hushed, and I was about to sink into restless
sleep, I turned suddenly round, and who should be before me but my dear
Mary. In the dim light the figure was uncertain, though I could see the
eyes glisten. I strove to move nearer to her, and was surprised to find she
was less visible. She waved her hand gently over me. I felt an involun-
tary inclination to sleep. I slept till the broad daylight, and then I awoke
and perceived her still watching me like the polar star. I spoke, but there
was no reply. She put her fingers to her lips, and I felt my tongue as it
were paralyzed in my mouth. What can this be? am I ill or mad? or
can this be a reality?—but 'tis so wonderful I'll write it down that at a
future time I may believe it myself. So I turned over to get my journal,
and in the instant she had vanished. Certainly I was not looking towards

the door, so I cannot say if she went out of it. I reflected on all this strange fact, if fact it was, and could not understand it. I found myself unable to rise and my pulse was fevered. I saw the Captain come to me and ask me questions, which I was unable to answer, and then the doctor, and then I saw him take out his lancet, and after this I swooned.

December 14th.—A week, I find, has passed, and I have been insensible during the whole time from lightheadedness and fever of mind as well as body. They lifted me up, but I was unable to stand, and so I was lifted back again, and to give me air they opened the port-hole, through which on the first night I longed to receive the spirit of Mary. But the light was too great for my weakened sight, so I turned away from it, and I soon perceived that it became dim and I was afraid to look, but after many attempts I did and beheld—what! the spirit of my love. She reclined partly within and partly without the doorway. Her eyes were bare, and showed me death in so mysterious a form that I know not how to write it. The dusk had hid this most unearthly look. They seemed like eyes that had never been closed in death, though they were ghastly with a death-like vacancy. I saw them but an instant, and when I looked again it was only on the violet gown, which I could perceive was blowing in the wind. I felt its undulations pass over me, and I could see the last violet on the stairs, when I sunk again in my weakness and amazement, and could not reason on the reality or the dream, or if I was really on the sea.

December 15th.—The Captain and a sailor very kindly got me up on deck, and I was placed on a bed and begun to revive and be like myself; yet I hadn't strength to raise myself or turn round, but the happy feeling of returning health and consciousness was delightful. The sea breeze was fanning me and playing on my wan cheek, when, in my enjoyment, I perceived a hand advancing on my pillow, but I had not strength to look up and back to see the face, yet the hand touched my cheek and was deadly cold. The touch gave me artificial life, and I forced my head up and saw the glistening eyes and the pale face of what I thought my own Mary, but oh! how changed, how pointed her chin, how sunken her cheeks, and how slim the finger on her lip, which trembled with weakness. She evidently made signs to me to be silent and secret, and what would I not do to have her beside me.

She leant on my pillow, and I could perceive that her elbow made no impression on it. Her gentle breath passed over me in the wintry air, and I tried to stop it with mine. The sun shone, and I could see the pretty meeting of our breaths, but hers was clearer and whiter than the sun-beams. To-day they gave me food, and I had some appetite, though not of the craving kind, and I gained strength by little and little.

December 17th.—The Captain helps me to walk, and the Silent Lady (as he calls my Mary) walks on my other side. He asked me if she was dumb, as he believed no one had heard her speak, and if I was related to her. I was afraid to answer these questions as the finger on the lip was before my eyes, yet from day to day my uneasiness has abated, and whatever my fate I felt the more reconciled to it.   I think my Mary may possibly be even my guardian angel.

At all events, I feel prohibited from talking about her, she has inspired me with a silent reverence.   I whisper to myself that she may be Mary's ghost, but I have nothing to decide me one way or the other.   We walk up and down and spiritually understand each other.   Her eyes converse with mine; but, O! if they should ever shine without that mysterious veil as of shadow—but let me not try to write it, or I shall die.

December 22nd.—   *   *   *   *   *

(There are many entries omitted intentionally, as they are much the same.)

January 1st.—Here is New Year's Day, and nothing new to write down.   My unearthly companion is still with me, but I have got to be no longer afraid of watching her.   What all this will end in I cannot tell.   Will she meet me in Barbadoes like herself, will she be really my Mary—am I in a dream? and shall I wake up to find her a substance?   It may be that the sea air has spiritualized her dear body, and that the mortality will come to her again when her feet touch the 'terra firma,' and she breathes the air of land.   This fatal dream seems to have no end, and yet it must, and I'll believe that providence intends my happiness, but now puts me to the test of patience, prudence and forbearance.   I must bide my time.

January 14th.—A little incident has made me fall back into my first fears.   Last night, as we were walking on deck in the light of the rising full moon, my mournful companion happened to be before me, and had actually turned round to look at me, and see, as I supposed, if I were following her.   The large full moon was behind her, when to my horror I could see its *form through her*, and it illuminated the back of her head, and showed me once again *those death-like eyes*.   I sunk down at the sight, and although I closed my eyes that I might not see hers again and die, yet even then I could see the eyes faintly, and dared not open mine—not even when I felt her cold dead hand pass over them.   How should I ever get up and recover myself, and what was to follow?   Suddenly a dozen voices cried out, " Land, land," and every one rushed on deck.   In my amazement I looked round, and found my visionary companion leaning on my shoulder.

We soon neared land, and all was bustle.   The confusion of boats, voices, waves, and distant hubbub turned my head.   I looked about and found that my companion was nowhere visible.   I sought through the ship, waited until every one had left, and then alone, with my baggage following, I proceeded to the Barbadoes Custom House.

January 25th.—Here I am, with everything settled.   My law business was easy, and although it required my presence, yet it was soon done, and I had the happiness to be the possessor of ninety thousand pounds in money, and more than half that sum in local property.

This increased my anxiety to return to my anxious parents and my dear Mary.   Three weeks had I passed, and no sign of her or her spirit on land.   My eye looked everywhere for her, but looked in vain.

February 14th.—My property all arranged, I proceeded to embark again in the *Maria Crowther*, and felt a more substantial man, aye, and equal to meeting ghosts. The passengers were arriving on board, when a veiled lady passed me, and it at once struck me that she was my former mysterious companion. This time the Captain was impressed, and demanded of her if she was a regularly passed passenger, and her fare paid. She answered not, but produced a paper signed, which satisfied him, and I saw him bow to her, his eyes downcast, yet following as much as they dared.

February 15th.—In the morning I saw her sitting on the deck, and looking on the sea in the same gown, the same attitude, and the same place. We resumed our acquaintanceship silently. But at last I began to weary of, as well as dread, this apparition of my love, yet without one charm of my dear Mary, for the face had death in its silent horror, and the eyes something more. Yet, as I say, we resumed our companionship and our silent conversation, though I confess I had less and less inclination to speak. My days are passing in perpetual gloom——" Here the journal breaks off, and the reader must follow the account of Dr. Magnus. His daughter died on the 2nd of December, suddenly, of paroxysm of the heart, and was buried at Plymouth.

The ship in which James Woolley was returning was wrecked off the Bahama Islands. The Captain, three sailors, and two of the passengers were saved. He was one of the two, the silent lady the other. But ere long he died of hunger and thirst, and when the castaways proceeded to throw the body into the sea, the silent lady jumped from the raft after it, and sank, never to rise. All the property was made over to old Mr. and Mrs. Woolley, and they lived to a great age. They often referred to this very journal which we now print, and which was singularly preserved by the Captain's supposing it of value as appertaining to the Woolley estate.

The historical romance, called at first 'The Dead Hand' and afterwards 'Love's Triumvirate,' was begun, as has already been noted, at an early date, and long before its author's departure from Italy, though it was not finished till the summer of 1863, two years after his return to Rome. It is the only literary composition by Severn—apart from his autobiographical reminiscences—which has any claim to serious consideration. In length it fully equals the ordinary three-volume novel. The plot is a sufficiently good, if not a strikingly original one, and the incidents are fairly well evolved and of continuous interest. No part of the romance lends itself to excerption, so it would be useless to quote a chapter, or even portions of chapters.

The story opens at the time of the Inquisition in Rome,

and when the severest search was made for heretical books.
One day, at the customs-office, a box is opened, which
apparently contains nothing save a human hand. A certain
Padre Ambrosio orders the box to be nailed up again, and
then takes it away with him; in the privacy of his own
apartment he reopens it, and finds a long narrative in MS.
He reads this carefully, and ultimately, instead of making
the matter known to the higher authorities of the Inquisition,
replaces the MS. in the box beside the shrivelled hand, and
sends the package to the address in Saxony which he had
found duly indicated.

So much for the prologue. The story, as set forth in the
MS. discovered by Padre Ambrosio, follows in Chapter II.
In this chapter the reader is introduced to two young
officers, Herman and Gabriel, in the army of Charles the
Fifth, who are discussing the absorbing topic of the time,
the Reformation, and incidentally their own prospects.
Gabriel is indifferent to the great cause so long as all goes
well with his own fortunes: Herman is a determined
enthusiast. The scene is changed in the following chapter
to the interior of a convent in the Campo Vaccino at Rome.
There the Abbess, Donna Chiara, a bigot, rigorously rules
twelve nuns, one or two of whom, nevertheless, are aware of
the great changes which are taking place in that outer
world of whose sinful doings they are supposed to know
so little. These would-be rebels determine to escape from
Donna Chiara's tyranny. By a daring, and what would be
now-a-days an impossible ruse, they attract the attention of
two young German officers, who chance to be in Rome on
a mission, and to be passing by the convent; almost needless
to say, the young officers are Herman and Gabriel. But
the reader does not reach the end of this episode in
Chapter IV., where, instead, he is conducted to the house
of the great painter, Titian, then with his daughter
residing in Rome. Some of Titian's pictures are described,
particularly his 'Danæ,' so much admired by Michel
Angelo. It happens that the famous artist's daughter
(whom Severn throughout calls " Signora Titian," strange

as the mistake may seem for an Anglo-Italian) has a friend
in the convent of the Abbess Donna Chiara ; and one day,
after a visit to her, she returns to find that the two young
German officers have come to her father's studio to see his
portrait of the Emperor Charles. Titian asks her about
her friend, and Herman overhears and is deeply interested
in her reply. Finding her visitors sympathetic, she speaks
strongly against the imprisonment of Sister Teresa, contrary
to the promise made when she entered the convent ; and,
in her narrative, includes Sister Teresa's great friend, Sister
Clara Colonna. She has no portrait of the former, but
shows a miniature of Sister Clara to Herman, who is startled
to recognise the features of one whom he had met a year
ago, and had straightway fallen in love with.

Next day " Signora Titian " visits Teresa again, and
learns that, in her efforts to attract the attention of the
German officers whom she had seen passing, she had
recognised a young noble who had admired her before her
seclusion, though she had had no intercourse with him. This,
of course, is Gabriel. It is ultimately arranged that Teresa
and Clara attempt to escape by one of the windows in the
garden of the convent, one which Teresa knows to be
insecure. When the time is at hand, the two young men
take up their position under the Arch of Titus and wait ;
but, suspecting that they are watched, they feign intoxica-
tion. As a matter of fact the Padre Ambrosio and the
Abbess have had their suspicions aroused, though the latter
is too much occupied with Lady Vittoria Colonna, who is
a guest at the convent, pending her departure for Viterbo,
to pay much extra heed to her nuns. Herman and Gabriel
have reluctantly to leave with their object unfulfilled.
Meanwhile Herman has fraternised with an Italian novelist.
an unconventional scribe, who writes his *novelle* only from
actual incidents witnessed by himself, and, when subjects fail
him, does not hesitate " to provoke people to an episode "
as he euphemistically puts it. From this individual
Herman learns much that confirms him in his devotion to
the cause of the Reformation.

In the tenth chapter there is a description of a grand tournament in the Colosseum. Herman at last enters the lists, and challenges a Roman noble, whom he vanquishes only to discover that he is the brother of Sister Teresa. They fraternise forthwith, and Count Orsini is obligingly communicative. He explains why his sister was punished by immurement in the convent; warns his companion about the espionage that everywhere prevails; and incidentally mentions that two implicated individuals (how or why implicated is not very clear) are to be burned next day in the Piazza di San Claudio. Thither (in Chapter XI.) Herman goes on the morrow. Of the two condemned unfortunates one is an Italian and the other a German; and in the latter he recognises his cousin, who had been for five years studying at the Roman College. Herman is in time to save his cousin's life, by an appeal to one of the Emperor's high officials who is present, though he is unable to get a reprieve for the Italian, who suffers death at the stake. The reprieved cousin is left in prison, while in Chapter XII. Herman and Gabriel plan anew the rescue of the fair nuns. When all is ready they go the Colosseum at sundown and wait in the dusk till the moon has risen, when they move further into the darkness near the walls of the convent garden. They descry the nuns, but Donnas Teresa and Clara indicate their inability to help themselves, though they can do so only by gestures. The rescue has again to be postponed. Meanwhile the cousin has, owing to the Emperor's request, been set at liberty. He joins Herman and Gabriel, and offers to assist them in carrying off the imprisoned ladies by force. This, however, is too great a risk for them. There the three companions go to the catacombs—mainly so as to give the author an opportunity to describe these subterranean haunts of the refugees and conspirators and suspicious characters of Rome, as, at the period in question, the catacombs were. Ultimately it is arranged that the cousin, who is a young priest of noble family, and Count Orsini, are to deceive the abbess during a nocturnal ceremony in

the Church of the Via Crucis. It is a special occasion, and
the abbess and nuns are preoccupied with the picturesque
and strange procession by candlelight which moves before
them. Count Orsini tries to see his sister, but she is not
visible. It is clear to him that a closer watch than
ever is kept upon Teresa, and he determines to give
Herman and Gabriel all the assistance he can for her
rescue. Even Don Gregorio, the priestly cousin, with an
engaging gallantry at variance with his vows and profession, offers to become a practical partner in the escapade.
Indeed it is he who, in company with the two officers,
make the new attempt. They have rope-ladders, duly concealed, and hope for success; but when they draw near,
they perceive three stalwart young priests forming a night-
watch just outside the convent. Don Gregorio advances
alone, gets into pious conversation with the priests, and
manages to allure them inside the chapel of the convent.
Herman and Gabriel make the most of their opportunity.
Having mounted the ancient wall and descended into the
garden, they succeed in gaining the window of the room
where Teresa is kept. When they have wrenched away
the feeble iron bars, they discover that Clara is there also.
The two nuns are hurriedly helped to descend, and are then
clad in the disguising robes which their rescuers brought
with them; whereafter, the outward wall having been
cleared, all four at last safely reach the deserted Forum.
Here, however, Clara's excitement overcomes her, and
she faints. The ensuing chapter abruptly leaves the
fortunes of the lovers. The author describes Titian in his
studio at the Vatican, before his portrait of Pope Paul III.
The painting is put out to dry in the sunshine, and the
passers by all kneel reverentially before it, notwithstanding
its "ferocious look." Then follow some reflections and
moralisings. In the seventeenth chapter we meet again
the peripatetic Roman novelist, who, delighted with having
got so many "bits" for his next story from Herman, tries
to provoke him into "odd courses; among others, to set
fire to the convent, so as to give him (this gay mannerist)

an opportunity to describe from the life the picturesque destruction of a convent by Greek Fire." He, however, assures Herman that he has the power to extinguish the flames readily—"at least sufficiently to save the younger nuns." This, it must be explained, occurs before the incident of the escape of the nuns.

There is now a return to this event. The novelist is in the Church by the Via Sacra, when he hears a tumult without, followed by cries indicating that nuns are being carried away. There is a wild commotion, and there would be a stampede, did not the abbess enter with her nuns (less two), and at the same time order the guards to surround the exits and let no one pass. But all precautions are too late. Gabriel has helped Teresa to the spot where the horses had been left, and in a few seconds he and she are well away on the lonely road leading from the western walls of Rome to Ostia. But Herman, in endeavouring to follow with the unconscious Clara, stumbles over a recently excavated antique group and falls into the gaping hole in the ground, with the result that he is stunned, and poor Clara's leg is broken. Before he can resume his effort to escape, the guards have found that their birds had flown; and in a few minutes the whole mob of soldiers, priests, and excited people bears down upon the unfortunates, who are soon visible in the torchlight. Herman attempts to defend himself but is soon overpowered, while Clara is carried back to the convent in a half-dying condition, notwithstanding the singularly æsthetic pleasure of the convent-doctor, who happens to be on the spot, and does not wish the fair nun to be removed, "as she is in such a fine attitude."

In the next chapter Clara is described as being in agony, and almost near death. "Signora Titian" has visited her, and has obtained permission for the Emperor's surgeon to attend and do what he can for the broken limb; yet she is not at ease, for she notices a peculiar and stern expression on the face of the bigoted abbess. When the bone has been set, and all are gone, the nuns tenderly carry Clara back to her cell, though the oldest sister horrifies her by whisperingly warning her that she had better die at once, as it is the abbess's intention to follow the old-time punishment, and to have her bricked up, to die in starvation and misery. Finally this awful news comes to the ears of " Signora Titian," who, unable to credit it, confides in her father, who, however, confirms the rumour and adds that nothing can be done. The unfortunate girl is not even to be allowed to take farewell of her brother. Everything is done to save her, but without avail; and the several plots for rescue all fall through. Even the motive-hunting Roman novelist haunts the neighbourhood, and tries to persuade the priests of the convent to " some romantic extremity." Poor Clara is in horror and despair, though a faint gleam of hope comes to her after a visit from the Padre Ambrosio. With outward severity he denounces her as a heretic and evil-doer, but she imagines she sees a pitying and even meaning look in his eyes as, unseen, he slips a sealed paper into her hand.

The narrative of Gabriel and Teresa is now taken up. They reached Ostia, and hoped to find a vessel about to sail from Fiumicino; but were disappointed. Gabriel bribes a peasant woman to sell her festal dress, and with this Teresa disguises herself in the semblance of a charming contadina. He too disguises himself as a peasant, and keeps away from Teresa, while, to still further avert suspicion from the guards at Ostia, he chops wood all day in the neighbouring pine forest of Fusano, whither Teresa carries him his dinner at noon. But ere long she succumbs to the malarious air that ever broods around Ostia, and, in order to save her life, Gabriel goes to Rome, disguised as a peasant, so as to procure the services of a doctor. He seeks " Signora Titian," who refuses to apply to the Court Doctor, and at the same time tells him of the sad fate hanging over Donna Clara. But at last he finds a doctor willing to accompany him. The physician, however, is suspicious that Teresa is no contadina, though he does not seem to have detected Gabriel for all his German accent

and ignorance of the vernacular; at any rate he confides
to him that he believes the invalid is none other than the
'escaped nun, for whose capture a large reward has been
offered. It is now Gabriel's turn to be suspicious. He
follows the doctor, and sees him speak to the Papal police
at Ostia. He resumes his former disguise as a woodcutter,
and he manages to mislead the doctor a little way into
the forest. The man is jubilant at his discovery and in-
cautiously betrays himself, so without more ado Gabriel
raises his axe and cuts him down. In great fear that all
is lost, he is returning to the cottage for what may be a
last glimpse of Teresa, when, in the far roadstead, he
descries a vessel, and one evidently getting ready to depart.
With all haste he gains the cottage, takes Teresa in his
arms, and places her on the cottager's donkey. By a short
cut across the great swamp the refugees gain the shore
while the police are still searching in an opposite direction,
and succeed in getting safely aboard the vessel, whose
sails are already set and anchor up.

The next chapter is mainly devoted to the ecclesiastical
trial of Donna Clara. Ultimately she is condemned to be
bricked up alive, with a small supply of bread and water,
and a single wick-light. Her one hope now is in the
Emperor's doctor, of whom she has begged a last favour,
to which he has assented. The chapter that follows is
somewhat wearisomely occupied with the sayings and
doings of the irrepressible Roman novelist; and it is a
relief in the next again to follow the fortunes of Gabriel
and Teresa. Just as the captain was about to lay-to for
some late cargo which he saw arriving, Gabriel noticed a
commotion at the spot where he had slain the treacherous
doctor, and soon after caught sight of his and the nun's
pursuers making for the shore. He at once told the
captain a different version of his story, and offered him a
heavy bribe to sail away at once; an offer which the mariner
readily accepts, and gives prompt orders accordingly.

Back again, in another chapter, to the unfortunate Clara,
who is now calmly preparing to undergo her doom. The

Emperor's doctor, in saying farewell, admits that he has told her story to the vagrant novelist; whereat she begs him to secure the MS. at any price, and then secretly whispers some words in his ear. She then says good-bye to Titian's daughter, and sends a "dying message" to her brother. It now appears that "Signora Titian" was interested in Donna Clara only because the nun was her *protégée*; once sentenced to be immured, Clara ceased to be interesting! The lady therefore looks about for some one else, and ends by "adopting" the novelist, with whose story of 'The Unfortunate Nun' she is so delighted that she promises to show it to the great Aretino, then on his way to Rome.

There is an abrupt departure from the main stream of narrative in the next chapter, which describes the persecution of the Reformers in the north of Italy, their protection by the intrepid Duchess of Ferrara, and the departure for Ferrara of Titian and his daughter. But after this unnecessary interlude we are taken back to the convent, and to the horrible ceremony of the walling up of the doomed nun. When the bricklayer has almost finished his work, Clara's sister-nuns take farewell of her, and then the last sacraments are administered, while from the organ in the church is heard the solemn strain of the *De Profundis.* The bread, water, and small lamp having next been placed in the aperture, Donna Clara is then lose to sight.

In the following chapter is set forth the attempt of three pitying nuns to liberate their wretched sister. They have to wait till near dawn, but at last they reach her cell. In a short time they have removed some of the freshly-mortared bricks, but they find Donna Clara already dead. In their despair they do not hear the approach of the vigilant abbess, who finds them *in flagrante delicto,* and tells each that she is arrested. At the same time, Clara being dead, she allows the body to be taken out and laid upon the bed in the cell. The doctor is summoned, and after his inspection he entreats the abbess to permit him to perform a solemn promise, namely to cut off Clara's left hand. The abbess refuses, but has to yield when he shows her the official authorisation.

The doctor next obtains the history of Clara as written by the novelist, and this he encloses along with the severed hand in an oaken box which he has prepared. Finally, he places in it the last will and testament of the unfortunate nun, and then, having made all secure, addresses it to Herman in Saxony, whither that unlucky warrior had gone when, at the instance of the Emperor, he was liberated from prison. This was the box which Padre Ambrosio, as an officer of the Inquisition, chanced to open; and which, after full consideration, he allowed to go to its destination.

Meanwhile Gabriel and Teresa have safely arrived in Saxony, and it is they who, shortly before their marriage-feast, receive the box intended for Herman, who has not yet reached his home. When he does arrive, and in time for the festival, he is amazed at the contents of the box, but at last sees a meaning in the hand having been sent to him. He becomes a godly dreamer, and ultimately a devout Catholic. Faithful all his life to the memory of Donna Clara, he spends his latter years among the noble brotherhood of the monks of Monte Carona.

Thus ends the romance of 'The Dead Hand.' As will readily be realised, it has enough matter to make a successful novel. Unfortunately, the execution sadly lags behind the conception, save in the purely descriptive and incidental passages. For one thing, the author is maddeningly indifferent in his use of his personages' names. " Herman " is constantly made to do duty for " Gabriel," and *vice versâ ;* and equally indiscriminate is his use of " Teresa " and " Clara," not to speak of occasional change to " Candida " for either " Clara " or " Teresa " or both. " Signora Titian " is the old friend of Clara, whom she never saw till in the convent, as often as of Teresa. At the very time when Herman is in the convent garden endeavouring to escape with Teresa—no, Clara—he is also forgetfully represented as engaged in conversation with the Roman novelist *before* his attempt at rescue; while the muddle is further enhanced by the fact that this conversation takes place in the church at the moment the worshippers are disturbed by the shouting of the persons who had witnessed the escape of the nuns with Herman and Gabriel. As if to make confusion worse confounded, the hours of the vesper-service and the escape do not correspond.

Yet, withal, there is enough in the novel to have made success fairly sure, if some judicious friend had revised the MS. for Severn. To the last he expected to make "a hit" with it, though it is doubtful if it ever was submitted to any English publisher.

In his Diaries he gives a summary of a new novel, to be called 'The Lost Throne,' which he projected in the summer of 1864. It was to be "founded on the incidents of the life of the ex-King of Naples, particularly on the facts within my own knowledge;" and the plot was "to turn mainly on the dark designs of the Jesuits." If the romance had been written as projected, its incongruities and improbabilities would have handicapped it too heavily to make any success possible.

CHAPTER XI.

It was, says Severn, one of the most thrilling moments in
his life when, after close on twenty years' absence from
Italy, he again saw Rome across the Campagna, a hazy
purple splatch in the distance. Formerly, he had slowly
approached it from Naples, in that long first drive in Italy
which he and Keats took together, one of them at least
looking to Rome as the Mecca where salvation was to be
found. Then, too, he was as poor in means as in reputation,
and only his buoyant temperament enabled him to face
confidently whatever hazards lay before him. *Now* he was
returning to the city where his true home was, which he
loved and knew better than that grimy London which was
his birthplace though not his real *alma mater*: going back
after a long and successful career, and to a post of honour
and influence.

"Imagine *me*, Joseph Severn, the lad who was so accustomed to ill
health and poverty: without social advantages, or even adequate training:
who left home one wretched unforgettable night, and more as an outcast
than as one going on an honourable venture: imagine *me*, now, in my
sixties, a successful artist who has his works in all the great collections in
England, and in no less than three Royal Private Galleries, going back to
the Rome where name and fortune first came to me, as the chosen
representative of the British Empire! I am proud as well as grateful to
be British Consul at Rome: but I think I would gladly slip back forty
years, to be once again travelling to Italy with my beloved Keats, and

AUTOGRAPH PORTRAIT OF SEVERN (*ætat circa* 27).

To face page 248.

even to be in Rome tending him again, for all the suffering and anxiety of that bitter time. But the more I think of it the more thankful I am for the eventful course of my life. What would our poor father have said had he known that his 'little Joe' would one day be British Consul to the Papal Dominion?"

Elsewhere Severn records how, though he visited the grave of Keats soon after his return and did so not only "without pain but with a proud exultation," he never, from the first days of his Consulship—or, indeed, from the time of Keats's death—was able to pass, "without the throb as of a wound at his heart," across the Piazza di Spagna from the Via Due Macelli eastward, or down to it by the western side of the Spanish Stairs.

"Here in Rome, as I write, I look back through forty years of worldly changes to behold Keats's dear image again in memory. It seems as if he should be living with me now, insomuch as I never could understand his strange and contradictory death, his falling away so suddenly from health and strength."

In the 'Adonais' folio, again, he writes:

> "Till the future dares
> Forget the past."

"It *has* forgot the past, and half a century confirms the change. Here in Rome, after this long interval, I am bewildered in trying to reconcile the glowing fame of Keats with his cruel death and extinction, for they belong to each other. To me it seemed at one time as though it were swept away for ever. His own touching line which he wished to be inscribed on his tomb, '*Here lies one whose name was writ in water*,' gives the history of his sad fate but does not intimate the marvellous changes that fifty years have brought about, or that the name 'writ in water' should now be written in the hearts and minds of all the lovers of poetry and humanity. This was a 'consummation devoutly to be wished,' but who ever thought it was to be accomplished, who ever saw this bright spot on the trembling horizon, who ever thought that even the party-organs which endeavoured to destroy him would at last cherish his ashes, and make of his high achievement a jewel in the crown of Poesy?

"But this marvellous metamorphosis was not so much the influence of the Poet's immortal works as of the changes in the changing world, sometimes for the worse, sometimes for the better, but always an intellectual lottery in which the world delights. In this strange interval, I seem to have passed some five hundred years, so varied are the events and changes I have gone through, instead of having lived merely my present eighty years.

"Dwelling in the remembrance of my illustrious friend, I now sit down in the enjoyment of a great victory for which I seem to have been living, and which was in store for the few personal friends of the Poet.

"'Twas in the year of the Reform Bill, 1830, that I first perceived a rustle of opinions, but not conjecturing for a moment that it would or could call up the spirits of Shelley and Keats I did not venture to open my eyes, as ten years had passed away in the darkness and oblivion of an ungrateful world, when I was suddenly amazed at the announcement that Galignani in Paris was actually publishing the works of these *obscure poets.*

"Shortly thereafter I received the edition with the portrait of Keats engraved from my drawing. I was unprepared for this delight, and prepared myself against disillusion by striving to disbelieve it, when shortly after I was sought out at Rome by many of our younger aristocracy, who then formed what was called 'young England' and was composed of young men of varied intellectual accomplishments, particularly in poetry. As they were amongst the most distinguished individuals of the day I felt honoured by the compliment to the dead poets, but it was to me a riddle, as the former persecution of the two poets was almost confined to the aristocratical party of the Conservatives. Then politics ruled the world even of literature; for all was judged by the political bias. I was a great sufferer, after the death of Keats, from the scorn and sneers passed upon his memory, as he had been a Liberal. Even the pathetic line on his tomb, 'Here lies one whose name was writ in water,' was particularly made the object of ridicule. It was often repeated to me like a Pasquinade 'Here lies one whose name was writ in water *and his works in milk and water.*' But I will not go back any longer in calling up these scornful incidents, but rather try to account for this great mental revolution. Perhaps the most striking part of this new drama was the mysticism in religious opinions which now became associated with Shelley's poetry, and I then for the first time heard him named *as the only religious poet of the age:* whereas in his lifetime, particularly when he mentioned me in his beautiful elegy on Keats, he was denounced as a vile infidel; and my friends, when they saw my name in the 'Adonais,' wrote to me imploring me to give up all acquaintance with this wicked man as it might ruin my career as an artist. Meantime, this compliment which Shelley paid me has procured me the enduring friendship of many distinguished men, and I may here particularise Lord Houghton, who has written the admirable Life of Keats, a work greater as it is the devotion of one poet to another, like that of Shelley to Keats."

Following the quotation, in the 'Adonais' folio,

> "To that high Capital where Kingly Death
> Keeps his pale Court in beauty and decay
> He came and bought with price of purest breath
> A grave among the Eternal," * * *

Severn has a note substantially the same as a passage
which appeared in his article in the *Atlantic Monthly*.

"It only remains for me to speak of my return to Rome in 1861, after
an absence of twenty years, and of the favourable change and the enlarge-
ment during the time of Keats's fame,—not as manifested by new editions
of his works, or by the contests of publishers about him, or by the way in
which most new works are illustrated with quotations from him, or by
the fact that some favourite lines of his have passed into proverbs, but by
the touching evidence of his *silent grave.* That grave which I can
remember as once the object of ridicule, has now become the poetic shrine
of the world's pilgrims who care and strive to live in the happy and
imaginative region of poetry. The head-stone, having twice sunk, owing
to its faulty foundation, has been twice renewed by loving strangers, and
each time, as I am informed, these strangers were Americans. Here they
do not strew flowers, as was the wont of olden times, but they pluck
everything that is green and living on the grave of the poet. The
custodian tells me, that notwithstanding all his pains in sowing and
planting he cannot 'meet the great consumption.' Latterly an English
lady, alarmed at the rapid disappearance of the verdure on and around the
grave, actually left an annual sum to renew it. When the *Custode*
complained to me of the continued thefts, and asked what he was to do, I
replied, 'Sow and plant twice as much; extend the poet's domain; for,
as it was so scanty during his short life, surely it ought to be yielded to
him two-fold in his grave.'"

In his Diary for 1861, also, Severn records his pleasure at
meeting Señora de Llanos with her husband, son, and two
daughters.* Her married daughter, too, was in Rome at
this time—her husband, Mr. Leopold Brockman, having an
appointment as chief engineer of the Roman railways. Mr.
Brockman was shortly afterwards created a Count."†

For reasons which will become apparent later on, I have
decided to give here some letters of a much later period in
Severn's life. Even among these there is no particular
need of chronological sequence: so I will print first three
or four dated in 1877, each of the first three having direct
connection with Keats's sister, Señora de Llanos—who, it
may be added, visited Rome and saw Severn on more than

* Señora de Llanos' only son was named after her illustrious brother.
Señor John Keats de Llanos is still living in Spain.
† Señora de Llanos' eldest daughter was, as Contessa Brockman, one of
the models for Severn's picture of 'The Marriage of Cana,' painted in
1863.

the one occasion just referred to.* Those who realise the pathos underlying the dignity of this letter, and are ignorant of the circumstances of Frances Keats's latter days, will be glad to know that relief, though late, did come to her in her need. It may be added that she survived her eldest brother nearly seventy years. Her death happened at Madrid, in 1889.

"5, *Calle de Lista,*
" *Barria di Salamanca,*
" *Madrid,* July 27th [1877].

"My dear Mr. Severn,

"Being anxious to hear of your well-being, I commissioned a Spanish friend of ours, who is now in Rome, to pay you a visit on my part. He tells me that he called upon you; but had not the pleasure of seeing you, as you were at the time taking your siesta.

"A short time since I received a letter from Mr. Buxton Forman, informing me that he is now occupied in a work which has connection with the life and poetry of my dear brother; and he is anxious to identify the people mentioned in Lord Houghton's 'Life and Letters,' vol. I., page 228, whose names are not given. Of course I can give him no information on the subject, nor does it appear to me at all necessary. There is no doubt that the lady therein mentioned was not Miss Brawne, as she was not an East Indian, nor had she a grandfather living at the time.

"Do you still continue living with your English friends, in peace and tranquillity, your children well married, and prosperous, so that you have only to care for your health, and maintain your old cheerfulness which is more valuable than gold, and all the vanities it may procure? Do you still amuse yourself with your painting?

"For ourselves we have unfortunately gone down in the world, and up to a fourth floor.

"Unfortunately we lent our capital to Leopold, and all has disappeared. He has been unoccupied for some time, and consequently much embarrassed. He is now, however, Director of the Railroad of Jerez and Sanlucar, but as he has six children, and many debts to pay, he can give us but very little assistance. Do you think you could obtain a pension for me through Mr. Gladstone? If it is not unpleasant to you, you might make the request to him; but on no account if you feel the least dislike to ask him a favour.

"In one of the English papers a short time since I saw that the Queen had granted a pension of £100 to each of the three *great* grandchildren of De Foe.

---

* When on her first visit to Rome, Señora F. Keats de Llanos planted two bay-trees beside her brother's grave.

THE GRAVES OF SEVERN AND KEATS.

To face page 252.

" How are Eleanor and Arthur? When you write remember us kindly to them.

" Mr. Llanos and family join me in warmest wishes for your health and happiness, and believe me to remain,

" Yours most sincerely,
" F. KEATS DE LLANOS."

Before she wrote to Severn again, in the early autumn of the same year, she received the following letter from an unknown grand-nephew, Mr. John Gilmer Speed, the grandson of George Keats:

" *No. 35, Park Row, New York City,*
" July 29th, 1877.

" DEAR MADAM,

" When I say that I am a grandson of George Keats, I feel sure that I forestall the necessity for an apology for addressing you.

" On account of recent publications in regard to John Keats, including Haydon's Autobiography, and several newspaper articles, one of which I send you by this mail—an unusual interest is excited regarding your brother's history. Several of these articles have revived stories that it would have been better never to have touched; but having been written about, I deem it were well that they should be truthfully told. In Haydon's Autobiography he says that during Keats's last year he was nearly always under the influence of strong drink, and that his spirits rose and sank according to his potations. You will notice in one of the letters, in the newspaper I send you, that John Keats wrote his brother George, that he, on account of Haydon's disregard for his moneyed obligations, could never be friends with him again. It occurs to me, that in denying this story—if it could be done on good authority—this remark about Haydon could be used with effect, as showing that two years previous to Keats's death the intimate relations of which Haydon speaks and through which he gained the knowledge imparted, did not exist. The papers are making much of Keats's ' Charmian,' and, on what they say is Mr. Dilke's authority, assert that she was not only cold to him living, but indifferent to his memory after he was dead. This does not accord with what Lord Houghton has said on the same subject. Another story is that my grandfather was so sensitive on the subject of the family origin, that it has never been correctly chronicled; others boldly assert that, like Jesus of Nazareth, the poet was born in a manger. My excuse for calling your attention to these matters is that I intend writing a biography of John Keats; and would be glad to get your testimony in regard to the subjects herein mentioned, and also any other information you might kindly suggest. If to this you will give your earliest convenience I will feel that a very great kindness has been conferred. Please understand that under ordinary circumstances I regard the discussion of such subjects as these very indelicate, but inasmuch as they have already arisen, I think they had as well be disposed of. If my mother was here she would send her love to you, as it is I do it for her. Believe me to be with feelings of great respect, dear Madam, your faithful and obedient servant,

"JNO. GILMER SPEED."

It is naturally not surprising to learn that this communication was "anything but pleasant" to the sister of Keats. Her letter to Severn is sufficient, even if other overwhelming testimony did not exist, to prove the gross untruth of Haydon's allegations.

"5, *Calle de Lista, Madrid,*
"Sept. 3, 1877.

"MY DEAR MR. SEVERN,

"I enclose to you a letter which I have received from the grandson of my brother George, which is anything but pleasant to me. I have not seen the Autobiography of Haydon; but from what my nephew says it contains a shameful calumny against my dear brother. Though perfectly persuaded of its falsity I have not the means of answering it in such a manner as to prove it a falsehood. Tell me, can an answer be given strong enough to remove the only stain upon a character so pure and noble, or must we bear it with patience?

"It seems my nephew intends writing another biography. I am sorry for it, as I don't think he will improve upon Lord Houghton's or rather yours, where all has been said, and said well.

"How sorry I am that John is not in Rome to copy for me your 'Marriage of Cana'—and the 'Pot of Basil.' As you suppose, he is doing very little, he is so shy and serious that he does not manage to introduce himself among people who might be of service to him.* Rosa has made great progress in music, and is quite a professor.

"I can't understand how you could ever have had enemies, you who are so kind and desirous of serving everybody. After all you are a most fortunate fellow to have obtained two pensions, when you could only have expected one. I cannot express to you my regret at not being able to send my subscription for the tomb of my dear brother. It seems the original stone has not been removed, but repaired and raised, and a low wall of stone has been placed around the grave. Do you know whether the two bay trees I planted still remain?

"I return you my warmest thanks for your sincere interest in my welfare. I mentioned Mr. Gladstone as likely to serve me, from the great admiration he feels for the genius of my illustrious brother. Though he is not in office, he must have many acquaintances of influence. You will

---

* Keats's nephew, John Keats de Llanos, in addition to a certain artistic faculty, inherited that literary bias which in some degree characterised each of the Keats family.

do well to apply also to Lord Houghton, he may perhaps feel inclined to serve me.

"Our kindest remembrances to Eleanor and Arthur.* Believe me,
"Very sincerely yours,
"F. KEATS DE LLANOS."

On the occasion of her second visit to Rome, in the late autumn of 1863, Severn saw her and her family frequently. In his Journal-entry for 29th October he writes: "Last night . . . . . she and I talked over all our cares and felicities like brother and sister;" and from several other entries during the next three or four months it is clear that Keats's sister was again and again a useful adviser and mediator in certain difficulties in which Severn was then involved. He wrote an enthusiastic account of their friendly intercourse to Chas. Cowden Clarke, who, early in February, wrote the following pleasant note:

"*Villa Novello,*
"*Crosa, L. Giacomo,*
"Genoa, Feb. 11, 1864.

"MY DEAR SEVERN,

"For many, and many a day I have not been so charmed and interested with a letter, as by the one you sent me [us] the other day,—and, like a *thorough man of business—with no date to it.*

"That meeting with Mrs. Llanos was equal—and with your description of it—to a pure romance. Lord! how palpably does the event represent itself to me, my seeing her,—a very young child, walking round the grass-plot in our garden at Enfield, with her brothers: and my mother saying, 'That is a very sweetly behaved child!' If I recollect correctly—she most resembled her brother George, who was very like his mother. John was the only one in face and figure like the father. Mr. Llanos I think I saw but once, and then casually. I believe he was a very fine fellow; by which (of course) I mean that he was a Liberty man. I suppose she is alone in the world with her daughters. Remember me *most* kindly to her, accompanied by every cordial wish for her happiness. It was, indeed, worth while to have written that little memento of her noble-hearted, as well as noble-minded brother—to have the reward—the last in the world I should have expected,—the approbation and thanks of his sister, thinking all were gone. With regard to what you propose in your letter respecting an

---

* Twin children of Mr. and Mrs. Severn: born in London in 1841. When, in 1861, Severn went to Rome as Consul, his wife was too great an invalid to go with him. She died at Marseilles in April, 1862. Her husband arrived just too late to see her again in life.

amended life of him—'a consummation, &c., &c.,' I could not *now* do so important a work, if at any time I were worthy, for, if you see the English papers at all, you will know that Mary and I are in the thick of an engagement to edit an edition of Shakespeare for Cassell, Petter, and Galpin, in penny numbers with notes; each No. containing two illustrations by Selous —and beautifully executed. The third No. will be out on Saturday next. This undertaking will occupy us for many months; but I'll tell you what I will do; if you will clap your shoulder to the wheel, and add all you know; and induce Mr. John Taylor (by the way, who is he?) to help you; and if you will incorporate my reminiscences, I will see the book through the press for you. There ought to be a better life of him. *Between ourselves,* Holmes told me that Coventry Patmore was the writer of the so-called 'Life of Keats.' If we should meet (which I trust we may; and, perhaps, ere long) I could talk much more of this matter to you. In the meantime, think over this proposal of mine. And, my dear Severn! with a multitude of sweet thoughts of past happy times coming over me— Well-walk, and other scenes;—With Mary's and my kindest regards, believe me, yours in perfect sincerity,

" C. COWDEN CLARKE."

Room may be found for the following excerpts from Chas. Cowden Clarke's letters of a later date. The first, dated 1864, is in acknowledgment of Severn's Keats-article in the 'Atlantic Monthly' for 1863. The second is addressed to Clara Novello, then staying with the Severns. The others will be noted by all interested in the subject of Keats's portraits. Many of these, which pass as the work of Severn, are certainly not by him. Chas. Brown, Seymour Kirkup, and others, known and unknown, made copies: some good, some bad. Among Severn's own authentic replicas there are one or two of markedly inferior quality. The reader should consult Mr. Buxton Forman's excellent paper on the subject in the first volume of his monumental edition of Keats's writings.

" *Villa Novello, Via San Giacoma, Genoa.*
"September 13th, 1864.

" MY DEAR SEVERN,

" I have indeed much to thank you and your amiable daughter for in the rich packet that reached me two or three days ago; assure her that I feel her kindness in undertaking such a task, very sensibly. 'Tis true the 'labour was one of love,' both for the matter copied and for the honoured and cherished Author of the work.

"And as regards the composition itself, I have been exceedingly interested, both in the variety of incident and in the easy and unhackneyed character of your diction.

"Your account of Rogers, I confess, both astonished and shocked me; I had conceived so different an opinion of the man. Of Walter Scott—no! I was *not* 'astonished.' Never can I forget that he was a promoter, if not a proprietor, of the 'Beacon,' one object in the starting of which infamous publication was, to extinguish Hunt and Keats.

"Hunt could complain of no *just* warfare; but what offence had the Boy-poet committed, except that of having been praised by a Radical. Scott was a brilliant genius, but wonderfully remote from being a 'Great Man.'

"One point in your article (since you handsomely require my honest opinion) I must regret the publishing, and that is, the last moments of our beloved Keats. By the tone and character of your narration you have led the world to believe that he was an unbeliever in Christianity, a circumstance totally unknown to any person beyond his own circle: for there is no trace of such a fact before the public from his own writings.

"Now if you suppose that any reader of the 'Churchman,' the 'Guardian,' the 'Watchman,' or the 'Record' (the bulk of the so-called Religious World) will be moved one hair's breadth in their opinion of his reformation from your description, I think you are of an easy faith—for a man of the world.

"With respect to your proposed plan for illustrating the 'Adonais,' &c., &c., of this I cannot but think with glowing anticipation. Mary echoes me; and Alfred—who is worth his whole race for a publishing opinion—said instantly, 'What a charming book it would make!' I therefore strenuously advise your instantly making your arrangements with a publisher (why not Moxon?) and setting tooth-and-nail to work, so as to be out, if possible, neck-and-neck with Houghton's life.

"All that we can say about Emma's movements is naught; of her *thoughts*, that they are constantly upon 'Dear Rome!' 'Rome first, Rome last, Rome midst, and without end.'

"Hoping to hear early news of your being hard at work; and with kindest regard from my Mary and all, believe ever, my dear Severn, that I am yours most truly,

"C. COWDEN CLARKE.

"Give my kindest regards to Madame Llanos, and tell her that I have her little figure now before me walking with her brothers round the grass-plot."

"May 3, 1875.

"How you will stare to see a letter (even of two lines) from me! But the fact is, I long to have what I have been led to expect from my *honoured* and valued old friend, Severn. Will you then do me the kindness to say that I hope he will fulfil his promise and send me his sketch for the tomb of Keats? Whether it be altogether what he himself may approve, it will infallibly tend to, and even *ensure* the result of its future establishment. I have completed what I intended to add to the

s

future edition of my 'Recollections,' in which I have included the last
sonnet, with his noble and perfect friend's *first* sketch profile; and the
last profoundly affecting one. If he have any other Art record of our
beloved, and my school-boy companion, and teacher, I should gratefully
include it with the precious catalogue already promised to me."

" *Genoa*,
" June 2, 1875.

" DEAR SEVERN,

        " Accept my cordial thanks for the truly kind message you sent me
through Sir Vincent Eyre in the letter you addressed to him here awaiting
his arrival in Genoa. He called upon us a few days ago, having been
delayed on his way by visiting Pisa, &c., &c., and when he came he told
us that you had obligingly commissioned him to say that you have
various memorials of our beloved Keats which you would place at our
disposal when you know the nature of the book I propose bringing out
relative to him. The book will consist of a reprint (with some additions)
of my 'Recollections of John Keats' in the form of an elegant illustrated
drawing-room book, and the illustrations would include your beautiful
profile-portrait of the young poet's head (of which I possess an excellent
copy made by my lost brother-in-law, Edward Novello); a fac-simile of
his autograph presentation of his first volume of poems to myself; a
fac-simile of the manuscript sonnet he wrote into my copy of Chaucer's
'Flower and the Leaf,' &c. To these would be added that exquisite and
most touching sketch of Keats asleep during his last illness, by yourself;
and (in consequence of your now expressed generous intention of furnishing
me with them) the 'Memorials' mentioned by Sir Vincent Eyre.
    "In case the publishers resolve upon producing the work in question, I
shall not fail to let you know, that I may request the fulfilment of your
very friendly promise, and meantime believe me to be, with affectionate
regard from my wife and myself,

" Your obliged and attached old Friend,
" CHARLES COWDEN CLARKE."

" *Genoa*.
" June 3, 1875.

" Curiously enough I wrote to you yesterday, and now, this morning, I
receive your most kind and delightful letter of the 28th of May, enclosing
me the exquisite sketch of your 'first idea of the Keats's Statue.'
    " I can hardly sufficiently express my sense of your kindness in sending
it to me, or of my admiration at its beauty. Even this slight sketch so
wonderfully well indicates his features and look as well as his favourite
attitude. The suggestive touch of sentiment, too, conveyed by the lyre
having only a portion of its strings, is a lovely thought, as denoting the
interruption by early death of his poetical career.
    " You rejoice me by what you tell me in your letter of the interesting
'memorials,' as well as of your being 'now on a work of Isabella and the
pot of Basil,' and of your 'cogitating a portrait of Keats in a rural scene
with the full moon.'

"It does my heart good to see the evidences of your wonderfully preserved *youth in age*, my dear old friend. Your '81' years and my '87' may interchange a hearty grasp of the hand and congratulate each other on being permitted still to enjoy life so energetically.

"God bless you! With love from my wife and myself, and warmest thanks for your dearly welcome letter, I am, dear Severn,

"Yours faithfully and gratefully,

"CHARLES COWDEN CLARKE."

" *Villa Novello, Genoa,*
"27th November, 1877.

"MY DEAR MR. SEVERN,

"Many thanks for your kind letter of 23rd Inst.

"I will not fail to continue the search you enjoin and which has already been prosecuted, for the copy supposed to have been made by my brother Edward; but if it be in existence it would hardly serve your purpose, inasmuch as that as well as others made in our family were all drawn from H. Meyer's engraving in Leigh Hunt's 'Lord Byron and His Contemporaries,' so that these copies are *one remove more* from your original beautiful pencil-sketch of dear John Keats.

"Thanking you cordially for your kind promise to send me a photograph when this most precious original is discovered,

"I am always, My dear Mr. Severn,

"Yours faithfully,

" MARY COWDEN CLARKE."

" *Villa Novello, Genoa,*
"20th November, 1877.

"MY DEAR MR. SEVERN,

"It was with true pleasure that I yesterday received your most friendly letter of the 17th Inst. containing the welcome tidings of your now feeling in better health and having 'resumed' your 'painting.' You mention a copy having been made by my younger brother Edward of the portrait you drew of Keats, which he gave to Leigh Hunt; but we possess no copy by Edward, alas! and I the more regret this since you request its loan from me for engraving in a proposed Library Edition of the poet's works, and to have to leave a request of yours uncomplied with is a pain to me. Several copies were made for us of your sketch (as engraved and printed in Leigh Hunt's book, 'Lord Byron and Some of His Contemporaries,') from Henry Meyer's facsimile of your drawing, but it was by mistake we told you one of these copies was made by my lost brother Edward. Do you remember the letter my beloved husband wrote to you in June, 1875, wherein he (replying to your question as to the nature of the book on Keats which he always hoped to bring out) told you that it would consist of a reprint (with some additions) of his 'Recollections of John Keats' in book form, and that the illustrations would include your beautiful profile portrait of Keats (the one facsimilied by H. Meyer), your exquisite and most touching sketch of Keats asleep during his last illness, and your graceful pencil-sketch of a design for Keats's monument?

S 2

"I still (and even now more earnestly than ever) hope to see this intended book of my dear Charles's published according to his long-cherished strong desire; and, as I learn that your *written permission* to print these several drawings would be requisite ere I could fulfil my hope, I trust you will kindly send me the needful few lines authorizing me to publish your lovely three sketches.

"I lately received a very agreeable letter from Mr. H. Buxton Forman (who generously sent us a copy of his handsome edition of 'Shelley's Works') mentioning that he is in pleasant correspondence with you, and that he is about to issue 'a little volume of Keats's letters.'

"Wishing you a happy continuance of good health, I am, my dear Mr. Severn,

"Yours faithfully,
"MARY COWDEN CLARKE."

There is hardly need to explain at this late date that the poet-traveller and colonist, Mr. Alfred Domett, is identical with "Waring" in Browning's well-known poem. All who have wondered "what's become of Waring," as well as those who know the literary work of Mr. Domett, will read with pleasure one of his few published letters. With Mr. Domett, with the exception of Mr. J. G. Cooke, has probably passed away the last person who knew Charles Armitage Brown. The reader will of course be able to see wherein Severn's correspondent was at fault. Of the two copies of the full-face miniature portrait of Keats made by Brown after Severn's original, I am of opinion, though not certain, that the portrait of Keats, attributed in the catalogue of the National Portrait Gallery in Edinburgh to Joseph Severn, is one. It is almost certainly not Severn's handiwork, unless done very late in life; but it is possible it may be by Seymour Kirkup, though without his characteristic delicacy of touch and tone.* In reference to Mr. Domett's closing paragraph, it is

* In connection with the mention of Seymour Kirkup at this period may be given another of the many characteristic letters written by him in his old age, when he had become what he called "a philosophical spiritualist."

"*Florence: Ponte Vecchio*, June 23rd, 1864.

"MY DEAR SEVERN,

"Your last letter was answered so long ago that I don't remember what it contained. I should have written again, but supposed that you were so engaged in diplomacy that you would find me troublesome. I wanted to recommend to you my friend Daniel Home, but I was sure if he

a welcome surprise to learn that there was sufficient likelihood of sale to justify an American bookseller, in the then

wanted protection he would be sure to find it in you, who have done so
much good to your countrymen and others; and I foresaw he would need
it to defend him against the Jesuits and priests, who are, of course, omni-
potent in Rome; and so it turned out, and I saw from the newspapers
that you had done all you could for him. I can answer for his being
neither an impostor nor a sorcerer (which is absurd), and I have found
him a man of honour, by actions, not by words of his or hearsay of others;
and I know him to be very generous, though poor, and goodhearted, all
which is in his favour, and so likewise are the phenomena that spontaneously accompany him, and of which I have had sufficient experience
in my own house, watched and guarded with the most suspicious incredulity, which is stronger with me than with most people, as, perhaps,
you may remember, for I was always so.

"My own proofs of our existence after death are entirely independent
of Home, and began before I knew him, or the works of Judge Edmonds,
which confirmed them; and they settled my creed, very far from
canonical, either Roman or Calvinistic, which, *entre nous*, are about
equally blasphemous and Jewish. But I will not write all I could, for
fear this should never reach you. I doubt if all your letters have come to
me, and the one I have just received was left for me—I was out—by a
priest! I know the Frescobaldis and Mr. Hart.

"Do you ever see Miss Ironsides? A friend of hers (Mrs. Ramsay)
lately came to see me. Miss Ironsides was gifted as a medium, but her
weak, vulgar mother extinguished her, and encouraged her in commonplace studies under the direction of snobs, when she might have been a
painter of the imagination, like my old friend William Blake, who, I
thought, was mad, but I don't think so now. Flaxman, Stothard, and
Fuseli were all suspected, and so were Danby, Varley, and even Martin;
anyhow, they were original and showed mind, and even old West was
sometimes a mystic, and Barry and Loutherburg. After I proved the
truth of Spiritualism, which I scouted for a long time, I was induced to
follow up my experiments in hopes of some day seeing something worthy
to paint. I longed for a good vision, and do still, but I am not enough of
a medium. I have only seen, heard, and felt enough to be sure of the
existence of spirits; neither books nor men were enough for me, and I
sought witnesses of my experience, and would not rely on my own
impressions alone, which might have been effects of imagination, waking
dreams! But when half-a-dozen people were present, they could not all
be dreaming of the same thing. A lady wrote to me the other day that
Home had been raised in the air a hundred times since he came to London,
and had been seen by 1000 people.

"Basta! you have doubtless heard enough about it, and I have seen
enough in my own house.

"What are you doing in painting? Bible subjects are worn out, and
were never interesting to me. I have an Italian book that says the
Madonna ought to be painted ugly, as she was sixty when she died.
Young John lived to a hundred and was buried, but never died,—his grave
moves. He is waiting for the last day to fulfil the prophecies. Read Sir
John Mandeville's travels in the East in 1345,—an orthodox Englishman!

"I have been long an admirer of Dante, but I think Shakespeare a
greater poet. Dante has been much with me in this room. His poem is
not true, and Beatrice was not a *portinari*, as it has proved.

(1834) small town of Buffalo, in the issue of an edition of the poetical writings of Shelley, Coleridge, and Keats. This purchase by Mr. Domett occurred in the same period as that wherein Robert Browning, then a youth, vainly sought in the part of London where he lived for a volume of Shelley's poetry—and when his mother was told by the more catholic bookseller of Oxford Street, who brought her the chief writings of Shelley, that "here were also the three volumes of the poetical works of a Mr. John Keats," &c.—in other words, that the rarely asked for writings of one poet should be companioned in sale by the still more rarely sought verses of one even less known to fame.

"32, St. Charles Square, North Kensington,
"London, W.

" Sir,

"You will be surprised at receiving a letter from a perfect stranger ; but I trust that the circumstances I am about to mention will prove an excuse for the intrusion.

"Among my friends in New Zealand (where I passed thirty years of my life) was, and *is*, a Mr. Charles Brown—son of Charles Armitage Brown, who emigrated with his only son to that colony about the year 1839 or 1840, and died at New Plymouth there a few years afterwards. Charles Brown, the son,—since Superintendent of the Province of New Plymouth,—ten or fifteen years ago, gave me a sketch in Indian ink—being a portrait of poor Keats, the poet, on his death-bed ; at the foot of which is written : 'Copied from a drawing by Joseph Severn, 28th January, 1821, 3 o'clock morning, drawn to keep me awake.' This, as Charles Brown told me, was done by his father, the intimate friend, as you know, of Keats.

"The copy, I think, bears evident marks of being most truthfully and carefully executed ; and seems to prove that the original must also have been a most truthful and striking likeness of the ' poor glorious' being it represented. For besides its obvious resemblance to the published portraits of Keats, it shows all the affecting changes in the lineaments of

"The Pope has forbid the title of 'La Divina Comedia.' Here is too long a yarn for a busy man like you. I wonder if you could get for me the report of a trial in Rome, printed about fifteen years ago, of a Count Alberti for forging and selling some MSS. of Tasso? If you could secure me a copy I will take care to repay you, and let you have the reading of it before you send it me, either by the post or private hand. It is very curious, and would amuse you. Tasso was in favour with good spirits, like Socrates. Adieu, dear Severn.

"Yours affectionately,
"Kirkup."

the countenance which the disease of which he died must have produced. The face is wasted and thin ; the tangled hair thrown about the brow in locks which look damp and straightened a little out of their natural curl by midnight perspirations. The expression, as he his asleep, is resigned and tranquil ; and but for this, the portrait would be intensely painful to contemplate. Indeed, it *is* almost so, in spite of this ; and, with the words at the foot of it, makes the most pathetic piece of drawing I have ever seen either on canvas or paper.

"The words just alluded to, which I have copied exactly as they stand, seem to render necessary the inference that Mr. Brown *made the copy* at 3 o'clock in the morning to keep *himself* awake. Charles Brown (Jun.) could not tell me much about it ; but, as far as I remember now, seemed to think that the last words were written by yourself on the original portrait. But as they are all in precisely the same hand, and as there are no inverted commas or other mark to distinguish the first words (' Copied from a drawing by Jos^h. Severn ') from those which follow, 1 cannot but conclude that Mr. Brown (Chas. A.) was himself watching by Keats's bedside when he made this copy, and perhaps had relieved yourself, for a short time, in the performance of that last painful act of friendship.

" As the fact (if it be one) of Chas. A. Brown's having attended Keats at all during his last illness, is not mentioned in any life 1 have seen of the Poet—and especially is not alluded to by Lord Houghton in his Memoir, it occurred to me that the best way would be to apply for this information *directly* to the source from which it could most certainly and conclusively be obtained. And therefore it is that I am taking the liberty to address you on the subject.

" Perhaps you could also enlighten me on another subject connected with the portraits of the great poet. Charles Brown also gave me in New Zealand a life-size medallion profile-portrait of Keats, which had belonged to his father. It is in plaister of Paris, oval in shape, in a square frame of dark oak. It is evidently the same portrait which is given in outline at the head of Monckton Milnes's Memoir in his Illustrated edition of Keats's poems ; and which, in the list of illustrations prefixed, is described as the ' Head of Keats—from a medallion by Giuseppe Girometti of Rome.' The engraving shows in every line that it is an exact copy either of mine or of some original of which mine is also a copy. 1 have no idea where the original is, or whether this of mine (formerly Chas. A. Brown's) is a replica of an original also in plaister—by the same artist ; or merely a copy by some other person. If you could give me any information on this point, I should take it as a great favour.

" I hope you will not think it out of place, or *not pertinent* if I add that I should have much pleasure (in addition to that of obtaining the information I ask for) in receiving any communication from one, in whom 1 have all my life taken an interest, and for whom in common with numbers in all parts of the world where the English language is read or spoken, I have entertained all the respect and esteem which Shelley's beautiful eulogium in the Preface to ' Adonais ' could not but create—a heartfelt eulogy which has given such an enviable immortality to your name and your noble friendship. That preface is before me as I write—in a copy of an edition of Shelley, Coleridge, and Keats, which I bought so long ago as 1834 at 'Buffalo,' now a great town on the American side of the Falls of Niagara. So far famed was your friendship for 'Adonais —even at a period so long since passed away!

" With renewed apologies for giving you this trouble,

" Believe me, Sir,

" Faithfully yours,

" ALFRED DOMETT."

The following remarkable letter by Mr. John George Cooke, the friend of Edward Trelawny, will be read with close attention by all interested in that latter-day Viking, and in what Mr. Cooke alludes to as the Byron and Shelley period: as well as by all who bear Charles Brown in kindly remembrance. It is printed here, though nominally addressed to his friend's son, and his own friend, Mr. Walter Severn :*

" June 29th, 1878.

" As touching your request to write any news of Trelawny, 'Pirate' Trelawny, or others connected with the Byronic, Shelley or Keats period, I fear I can give you nothing very interesting. J. E. Trelawny—if he were fourteen at the battle of Trafalgar, which he missed seeing owing to the supineness, as it has been stated, of his Admiral, Duckworth, in getting to sea and joining the Fleet under Lord Nelson and Collingwood—must now be eighty-seven years old, is, I believe, very hale and strong. Some four years have elapsed since I used to see him at the Turkish Baths at Brompton, and a finer specimen of a man of his age, it would be hard to see; he peeled as clean and muscular as a man of fifty. Your father will have two years ago read the remarkable testimony of an Italian boatman, at Spezzia, I think, who related to his, Trelawny's, daughter Letitia, the story current in that part of Italy that Shelley's yacht had been run down by a fishing-boat, no doubt with villainous intent, as they had heard and believed Lord Byron with money was on board the yacht with Mr. Shelley and Captain Williams. It sounded *vero*, if not *ben trovato*. Trelawny must have had a rude shock, if he, the old pirate, could be shocked, at the Goring Divorce Case lately. . . . Did I ever tell you of the unlucky end of the brother, Edgar Trelawny, the only other child of that ill-fated match of Trelawny and Mrs. Goring (*divorcée*)? He married some woman of quality and made himself rather conspicuous in England, representing himself as a convert to Romanism; that was

---

* Edward Trelawny died in 1881. It was his wont to say that the only authentic likeness of him is the old Captain in Sir John Millais's picture 'The North-West Passage.'

true, but added that he was the son of Sir John Salisbury Trelawny, the Pirate's cousin, which he certainly was not. He imposed himself upon Lord Denbigh and some other illustrious perverts; in the end he died rather suddenly. . . . Did I ever tell you a wonderful story—no doubt there were hundreds extant some forty years ago—which I heard when a midshipman in the Mediterranean in 1835, not so very long after the Greek War of Independence, when Trelawny distinguished himself? It is a curious and rather a ghastly story. Your father will well remember that when Trelawny was in Greece he lived *maritalement* with a daughter of the great Greek Chief Odysseus in the Morea, and she had a child by him. When Trelawny left Greece for Italy he took this child with him. Months afterwards the Odysseus family was made aware of the certainty of not seeing their respected son-in-law again, and wrote to him begging that the child might be sent back. A long time passed, and at last comes a letter to say if the Chief Odysseus or his representative would come across on a certain day to the Custom House at Zante, the child should be forthcoming. A *scampavia* was dispatched and away went some of the Odysseus family to Zante. The Custom House authorities could give no account of any child, but they stated that a box had arrived *viâ* Corfu, which it was much wished should be removed by the Greeks, as it smelt offensively. Whereupon the box was delivered and opened, and a child's body, dead some weeks, appeared; whether any invoice or remarks by Trelawny accompanied it I never heard. The child had died, and he took this grim and savage way of ridding himself of all connection with the Odysseus circle. I wonder I never thought, when in New Zealand some thirty-five years ago, and in constant communication with Mr. C. A. Brown, of asking him if he had heard this story. My sister, who has been dead some fourteen years, was wife to the British Resident, Major John Longley, a brother of the late Archbishop of Canterbury, and she had heard it from Zanteotes, although it must have happened before John Longley became Resident.

"I saw a great deal of Mr. Brown when in New Zealand; poor gentleman, he made a great mistake in coming out to a then wild and savage country, and where he was miserable. His son had gone before him, and this was the inducement. He amused me by long stories of Keats, Shelley, Byron, and Trelawny, and your good father, and the Hunts, &c. &c. He died a sturdy Deist, and was very indignant at the attempt of some Baptist or Independent persons to give *him* comfort. He used to quote to them the reply of Voltaire when questioned as to his belief in our Saviour. 'For the love of God, Sir, speak to me no more about that *Man.*' He was buried outside the churchyard at Taranaki (New Plymouth). His son and myself were his mourners, and there, under the beautiful shadow of our glorious mountain Taranaki, after life's fitful fever, let us hope he sleeps well. Now I have bothered you enough. What evening shall I come and smoke the calumet?

"Yours ever,

"JOHN GEORGE COOKE."

The following letter from Seymour Kirkup may be read as representative of his frequent correspondence with Severn at this period.

"August 18th, 1861.

"My dear Severn,

"I never thought Overbeck a *fine intellectual creature*, but an ignorant humbug. Gibson described his great picture to me with admiration and equal ignorance. The subject was a bad one, a collection of portraits of old painters, taken, as you say, from prints; all the schools, the English represented by an infant. This dauber of brickdust and pewter, without drawing, presumed in his ignorance to despise such giants compared to him as Reynolds, Opie, Stothard, West, Lawrence, Fuseli, Turner, Flaxman, &c., &c. Ignorance and vanity. As for his imitation of the ancients he should have looked at the works of Giotto here for colour, and he would not have abounded in such detestable lead colour as I have seen. In fact he has copied only the defects of the old time, viz., hardness, meagreness, and sameness. Nay, he may look at the Florentine M. Angelo in the Sistine, and he will see effects of colour worthy of Venice —the Jerome, Daniel, Zachariah, Sibyls, &c. You say he is devout to the political church. So is many a solemn ass and many a Jesuitic knave. What is your Gothic or Christian treatment of the [your] Marriage [of Cana]? What would you call that of P. Veronese? Neither; but the princely magnificence and worldly splendour of Venice, eclipsing even the story itself. Wealth, luxury, palaces, concerts, and a blaze of colour, so fine in its way as to make the subject commonplace and leave it beyond the reach of any follower. You have no chance, nor Miss Ironsides, who is all wrong, and has mistaken her vocation. Scripture subjects are worn out. They make no impression, like old-fashion music or sermons. The public sleep over them; like the bedstead of Baucis that was turned into pease,

> " 'Which still their old employment keep
> Of lodging folks disposed to sleep.'

"The Venetians sacrificed their Christianity, if they had any, to worldly magnificence. That fine picture of Bonifazio, 'Dives and Lazarus,' is another example of it. Lazarus is disgusting and therefore eclipsed by the prevailing wealth of Dives pervading all the scene, but the marriage was one contradiction beyond this.

"There is a wedding dinner of poor country people, so poor that even the wine falls short. Then think of the scene of P. Veronese! An absurdity, but such execution conquers all. Who can hope to surpass that? I do not like sacred subjects in general, nor costume pictures. David was a failure, but the classic is not exhausted by him. There is still a field open: Drawing from nature with the help of the antique and colour like Titian. Our 'Bacchus and Ariadne' and the Spanish sleeping 'Ariadne' are the models of a new school, which somebody will find out. We are too old. There are other specimens and hints even in Rome (the

Borghese). Etty might have done much if he had hit on it, or Haydon.
A combination of great talents in those two elements, and then a genius
of imagination worthy of the rest. Who can bear to think of the poor
child's-play of the solemn Mr. Overbeck—and you, coming from England,
and I suppose Paris! But I am in the dark about them in the present
day. I fear they are wofully gone down. Eastlake had better have
stuck to his palette than the study of after-dinner speechifying. Detestable! By the bye they said that you had been *favoured* by *him* at the
expense of Haydon in the affair of the cartoons. You accuse him now,
his pride. As for his wife she cannot hinder his painting. She complains
of his tyranny, and told a lady of my acquaintance that he would not even
let her know where he was going, and he set off to Italy.

"You say people are fascinated and never recover their sober reason.
They must be crazy, I suppose. Take care of yourself. You talk of a
new Jerusalem of Art and breathing in company of its *immortal spirits !*
Now real Spiritualism is a science that requires the greatest exercise of
reason. You are afraid of being *carried off your feet.* I could tell you a
strange story. There is no fear, and I don't meddle with everybody's
opinions. Miss Ironsides has some favourable dispositions, but her stupid
mother cramped them, and she has gone wrong ever since she went to
Rome amongst ignorant people, until she has fallen into the vulgar and
commonplace, by all accounts. I only judge from hearsay. I hate the
cant about *Art* and *artists,* her art and my art, artistic gossip of art and
artists and early art and primitive art, love of art, &c., &c. I never called
myself an artist; I said painter at once; I had rather have added glazier
than artist. All the tea-drinking old maids were full of their pretty
artists and all the little drawing-masters, daubers, and parasites of art
were full of the name, whilst the great were always sneering at it. One
told me he had a clever artist travelling with him. It was his cook. A
lady bestowed the title on her hairdresser. It is not that I care for such
classification, for I am very democratic, but I am sick of the vulgar cant,
and find that others are so too, so if you publish anything avoid it. The
word is prostituted and blackballed.

"Your pergola is better than columns, and your idea of the water in the
act of changing is new, but I fear it is not enough to be the making of it,
even if it can be done, which is difficult.

"I have a drawing by Miss Ironsides of an angel and a child which
she saw in a crystal of mine. It is not much, but it is *enough* to prove
that she has the faculty, a rare one, and more valuable than worn-out
Bible pictures, thanks to her mother and Roman advisers. I have some
wonderful and curious drawings of visions. I have only wished to
succeed myself, as has been done in America, but I have not the power.
I only have that of bringing it out in others. I know no one to carry
books to Rome. They won't do it, they are afraid, and I have lost so many
books that I have lent, or commissions sent, that I have long refused,
and have a paper, pasted in my library many years ago, to say so. I am a
collector, and have many thousand. I have a hundred and more of Dante,

and seven MSS. of him, many on our English Round Table in all languages, a great many on occult sciences, literature, antiquities, painting, &c. . . .

" Yours sincerely,
" S. Kirkup." *

In a letter dated April, 1868, he communicated a fact which, I believe, is little known:

" You have heard that the King has made me a knight and a baron : for some discoveries I made in Florence respecting Dante, so I suppose. All that is said in my diploma and other papers is,

' In considerazione di particolari benemerenze.'

I never knew more, and the minister who recommended me to him died of the cholera in Sicily. He was a Sicilian, and I had never heard his name till then (Natoli) or knew any of his friends. It was a perfect surprise to me, always the same poor devil of a painter, on which account I only call myself chevalier."

Either in the second or third year of his Consulship, Severn heard rumours that the Pope was about to issue a Schedule of Special Instructions to his Voluntary and Official Guard during Holy Week, with particular stress on their line of conduct towards heretical foreigners who might be present at the ceremonies in St. Peter's : and, it was said, His Holiness was emphatic in his determination neither

---

* The following excerpt, from Seymour Kirkup's last letter to Severn, written in 1870, will interest musicians :

" You ask about my scale of chords ; I enclose it. You will see all the possible combinations by thorough-bass reduced to *one line* of music paper ! It is written for one key only, that of *Do ;* of course all the other eleven tones contained in the octave are subject to the same limitations. I have given it to several musicians and composers, asking them to bring me any chord that is not contained in this table, if they can find one. Two or three have brought what they thought they had found, either in their own works or the works of the great masters ; but they were mistaken, and I showed them where the discords were marked in my list. To make them more easily found I have marked them with the letters of the alphabet, and I have given them the old numerical signatures which were used by the old masters. The laws of modulation you of course know, and the usual preparation and resolution of discords. I have written upon all these subjects, and at the beginning I analysed four of the grandest and most chromatic symphonies, to see if I could find any chord not put down in my list, were enclosed. They were *Roberto il Diavolo, William Tell, Don Giovanni,* and *The Creation,* which last was the only one that had a crash that was intended for chaos no doubt, and is not to be considered as music. You will see it near the beginning, one chord only. It was too ugly to be dwelt on or repeated. It is followed by the rolling of the elements into harmony in sublime style."

himself any longer to endure, nor to permit the faithful to suffer from, the unseemly conduct of many Protestant ladies, British and American. Severn managed to procure a copy of these "Private Instructions." The following is a literal translation, which, alas, for all one's shame on account of those who gave cause for the deep resentment which undoubtedly prevailed, will hardly be read without amusement.

INSTRUCTIONS TO THE SECRET AND HONOURABLE GENTLEMEN CHAMBERLAINS WEARING THE SWORD AND CAP OF HIS HOLINESS, AND TO THE OFFICIALS OF THE PALATINE MILITARY CORPS, DURING HOLY WEEK.

" These Gentlemen Chamberlains will be responsible for the observance of that decency and respect due the holiness of the place and the ceremonies; and for the maintenance of order in all the partitioned sections separately entrusted to each Gentleman Chamberlain. The officials of the military corps have also a like responsibity in the various places assigned to their charge and watchfulness.

" The one will aid the other in the various objects of their respective offices.

" They must obtain obedience as regards order and decency by any means, however desperate; first beginning with the most insinuating supplications, and in the sweetest and the most imploring manner; but when this fails they must snatch away the offending lady without the hope of pardon, whoever she may be, and expel her from the holy place.

" It is to be particularly observed by the Chamberlains that they do not permit the ladies to stand bolt upright in the most solemn moments of the sacred functions, and most of all, at the elevation of the Mass. Whoever does not obey is (the solemn moment being over) to be dragged out of her place for disobedience. Also, this alternative is to be enforced for all acts of indecency which may be committed on other occasions by the ladies, such as feeding, guzzling, or laughing and screaming in an inconvenient manner. With the aid of the officials of the Swiss and Palatine guards (according to the place) there shall also be turned away from the Ladies' Sections all those gentlemen who are there chattering with these said ladies, and the guards are also to prevent any ladies from climbing up over the tops of the sections and then jumping down to get away quicker. Whoever attempts to transgress these orders is to be got rid of by any means, however ugly.

" At the close of every ceremony the sins of each offending lady will be reported to the Maggiordomo of His Holiness in order that the subsequent punishments shall be administered according to the circumstances.

(Signed)   " The Maggiordomo of His Holiness,

" M. BORROMAI ARESE."

Another example of unintentional humour is the following highly entertaining denunciatory epistle from Mr.
Morris Moore, the discoverer and possessor of the beautiful
little picture of ' Apollo and Marsyas,' finally purchased
for the Louvre as a genuine work of Raphael, though now
either attributed tentatively to that artist or indubitably
considered to be the handiwork of Perugino. The late
Mr. Morris Moore was not to be affronted with impunity
by any shadow of doubt as to the authenticity of his
" Raphael." The present writer well remembers visiting
him at his house in Rome one day in 1883, and the ordeal
he had to go through before and during inspection of the
unquestionably most beautiful and masterly ' Apollo and
Marsyas.' The slow approach, the skilful verbal incentives
to curiosity and excitement, the entrance as into a Holy
of Holies, and the withdrawal of a veil suddenly so as
to let the whole splendour of Raphael's genius flash forth
at once as convincingly or rather overwhelmingly, all this,
and the still more trying period to follow, are not things to
be forgotten. Fortunately for his peace of mind he never
received any such damnatory epistle as that addressed to
Severn, though that individual simply laughed at it as " a
very excellent farrago of nonsense."

"To Joseph Severn, Esq., English Consul at Rome.

"147, Via delle Quattro Fontane, Rome,
"April 12th, 1867.

" Sir,

"Your reply to my letter of the 7th provokes notice. To have
detected, in a plain request, a 'command,' argues either marvellous
subtlety of wit or ignorance of our vernacular.

" It is time you learned from Johnson, that 'to request' means 'to ask,
solicit.' You announce having ' sent my *letter* to Lord Derby.' As my
only letter was that addressed to yourself, and as you are silent upon the
packet of printed *Documents* and *Declarations* directed to Lord Derby, I
am left in doubt whether I am your debtor for an unsolicited favour, or
still your creditor for the execution of a legitimate request. But since
the remedy for what may be but confusion of language lies with myself,
I waive this point.

" In the face of the irrefragable evidence, printed and manuscript, with
which, notwithstanding your undeniable previous familiarity with the
case, I had been at the pains to furnish you, your constructive impeach-

ment of my veracity as to the authorities and witnesses whom I had quoted, is a specimen of knavish insolence too patent for comment. Indeed, your epistle is a nicely poised compound of meanness, duplicity, and silly inference, congenially served up in clumsy and vulgar diction. I at once submitted it to several competent persons, and was flattered to find them *unanimously* confirm my silent estimate of it. The superlative compliment which you think due to my 'tone' will certainly never be paid to yours. I agree that your smile could no wise advantage a '*universally* acknowledged first-rate specimen of the finest period of Italian Art'—'a work of Art of great national importance '—a painting 'acknowledged by all Europe to be the work of Raphael' (Lord Elcho, *Morning Post*, June 10, 1850: and Frederick Overbeck, *Illustration*, 7 Fevrier; and *Augsbourg Gazette*, 18 April, 1864), or indeed anything admirable, but I must demur to the fond illusion that your frown could blast it.

"Had you asked to see this masterpiece, I was bound to acquiesce; but, unwilling to wound, I should, to say nothing of the obvious slight to so many eminent authorities and unbought witnesses, have studiously shunned the bitter sarcasm of inviting the 'opinion' of one so utterly without status to sit in judgment upon Raphael, as Mr. Fine-Arts Consul Severn.

"Your prognostic, while possessing the first testimonies in the world to its genuineness, that *you* 'might not consider as a work of Raphael's,' a masterpiece which, to this hour, you have not even seen, suggests, apart from its arrogance, a graver consideration. It betrays *a foregone conclusion*, and so brings you within the scope of the distinguished Cornelius's highly endorsed denouncement, which for your further edification I retranscribe; namely, that 'only the grossest ignorance of Art coupled with equal effrontery, or malignity fed by lucre, could dare insinuate a doubt as to the authenticity of a work so eminently characteristic of Raphael, as the *Apollo and Marsyas*.

'But fools rush in, &c.'

"That one, foisted into place only to be pointed at as a sorry notoriety and to bring ridicule and contempt upon the name of 'Englishman' in a centre such as Rome, should play the hack to an unscrupulous faction, is a natural combination that has found in you consummate exemplification.

"MORRIS MOORE."

The succeeding note is given as an instance of how Severn, whenever he saw his way, made use of his official position to achieve some good for the people among whom he lived. The original, of course, is in Italian.

"To CARDINAL BERARDI.

"*Tolfa, Civita Vecchia,*
"6th July, 1870.

"MY LORD CARDINAL,

"I write from Tolfa to implore your Excellency to aid me in a good office for this most excellent people; for the supply of water. Last year, with the assistance of the illustrious Padre Secche, a fine spring was found in the mountains only one mile from the town, and the generous Padre calculated the work, the expense, and all the possibilities, which he pronounced to be met without difficulty. But on my return here this summer I am disappointed with the progress made; and it is all assigned to the want of money (or to the want of spirit?). The sufferings of the poor women in the winter going down in the frost and ice two miles for the water, as well as the excellent character of the people for industry, honesty, and religious faithfulness to their sovereign, induce me thus to trouble your Excellency and to implore you to intercede with His Holiness to grant them a small sum for carrying out this work. I beg to assure your Excellency that I join most sincerely in this supplication, naving now had four years' experience of this good and righteous people.

"Craving pardon for the liberty I take, and avowing that I would not take it, did I know any one else for this benevolent task, I have the honour to remain, my Lord Cardinal,

"Your Eminence's most humble and grateful servant,

"Joseph Severn."

In 1878 was issued the book to which he had looked forward with so much interest; the collection of Keats's letters to Miss Brawne. He could not but be gratified by the generously-worded dedicatory preface, and, as a friend has informed me, repeated in a voice broken by deep emotion the words " whithersoever the name of our ' Adonais ' travels there will yours also be found." But, as there has already been occasion to remark, his expressions of astonishment in his letter of acknowledgment to Mr. Forman cannot be taken too literally. Essentially a man of moods, he was ever swayed easily to this or that point of outlook; hence the innumerable self-contradictions one encounters in his statements, letters, and friends' reminiscences of his sayings and doings. He guessed, if he did not wholly understand, the causes of the secret grief of Keats, even before the last bitter days; and a few years later he heard every particular from Charles Brown. Severn, in fact, was always "understanding for the first time."

In the seventies Severn saw much of his eminent American friend, Mr. James T. Fields, when the latter was in Rome, and heard from him frequently when he was at his home in Boston. Two letters from this valued

FIRST STUDY FOR THE PICTURE OF "ARIEL," NOW IN THE SOUTH KENSINGTON MUSEUM.

To face page 272.

correspondent may be given: the first because of its allusion to the 'Ariel,' the study for which is reproduced here; and the second as of interest in connection with the matter touched upon above. It gives, moreover, an indication as to Severn's age at the time when he made the drawing of himself, which is reproduced in this volume. What is more important is, that it affords gratifying proof of Severn's regret—once he had really read from first to last the volume of Keats's letters to Fanny Brawne, and pondered the matter of their publication—proof rather of his "sense of outrage on the poet's memory," in the giving to the public letters so absolutely private.*

" Boston, U.S.A.,
"May 15, 1871.

"My dear Mr. Severn,

"It made me smile, when I began to read your letter this morning from Rome, as I opened upon the sentence in which you say you are afraid I may not remember you. When I cease to remember you, I shall ask to be quietly taken to the idiot asylum. Don't I mention your name at least twenty times a week, when I show those two charming pictures which I bore away from your studio in London so many years ago? The 'Ariel' hangs in my library, and the Gainsborough in the reception-room below, and they are both the delight of my eyes and those of my friends. The 'Ariel,' being on panel, has warped somewhat, and I am afraid to entrust it to any one in order to bring it back. How I wish you were here to-day, and were going to dine with me, and afterwards give me your advice touching the panel, and how to restore it!

"I will with very great pleasure have a photograph of that drawing of Keats, which you kindly made for me, taken and sent wherever you direct. You do not say in your note whether it shall be sent to you or Lord Houghton. Your daughter is right: the sketch is indeed admirable.

"I am charmed to hear you are still painting, and as I know you intend to live a good many years longer, I hope to see you and your works together some day in Rome. You and I, I am sure, would have many a long ramble together, and dear Keats would come in for a great share of our talk. Every spring I think of the early flowers in the Roman gardens, and wish I could gather them, as I have so many times in my life, during the first months of the year.

---

* Fairness to Severn demanded the insertion of the second of these notes; but it would be unwelcome as well as needless to print his letter to Mr. Fields, or to adduce further evidence of his pain at having his name associated with what he came to consider so regrettable a disloyalty to Keats.

T

"Do you ever hear nowadays from Mr. and Mrs. Charles Cowden Clarke, and where are they? Where is Mr. Newton, and are you altogether under the same Roman roof?

"Mrs. Fields joins me in kindest remembrances, and sincerely hopes with me that some day we three shall meet again.

"Most faithfully yours,
"James T. Fields."

"148, Charles Street, Boston,
"February 3, 1879.

"My dear Friend,

"If you could have looked in upon us when your letter arrived here a few days ago, you would have been amused with our enthusiasm over its advent. We had friends staying here who are just as familiar with your name as we are, and they too jumped for joy to hear the contents of that epistle, telling us of your renewed health. We had all heard of your illness, and longed to get word from Rome that you were recovering, so your letter made us happy to that extent, we could have rung our Boston bells for joy. Now please to go on increasing in health and happiness, and when you feel a little tired of the Scale Dante, come over here and let us have a good time over you.

"Yes, dear friend, I think with you that the publication of those Letters to Fanny Brawne is an outrage on the poet's memory, and I say so in my lecture every time I read it. To tear his heart out in this way, and exhibit it to the gaping crowd is pitiful indeed. You can have no idea of the interest there is in America touching everything that concerns Keats. When I show your portrait of him to the audience, every one rushes forward to look at it, feeling that now the true effigy can be seen. I always tell the story of your devotion to him, and now I shall show the beautiful photo of yourself at twenty-seven which you send me, and for which I return ten thousand thanks. My wife adds (with her love) ten thousand more.

"I shall tell Longfellow, when I see him next week, what you say of his Dante, and I know he will be pleased. We have lost Bryant during the past year, and to-day Richard Henry Dana (ninety-one years old) passed forward to take his place among the band of shining ones. Long-fellow will be seventy-three in a few days, but that is only boyhood compared to Dana and Bryant's term of years. After all, what is *age?* You and I are as young, under our waistcoats, as we were at twenty. Why not? You are in Rome, with your brush in hand, just as you were sixty years ago. Who talks of Age? Down with the caitiff, says

"Your affectionate friend,
"James T. Fields."

CHAPTER XII.

Severn's Consular years—Severn's latter days—Mr. Ruskin's encomia—
  Death of Joseph Severn—Suggestions for Severn's gravestone—Severn
  and his contemporaries—The 'Endymion' picture—Keats and Severn
  buried side by side.

It would be beyond the scheme of these memoirs to go
into as full detail in the chronicle of the consular years of
Joseph Severn as in that of the first five decades of his life.

It is true that these years were to him among the most
crowded with many interests, but others have given us
more exact and satisfying accounts of the drama of the last
days of the Temporal Dominion of the Popes, and of the
rise of that new Italy, which was so rapid when once, in
the saying of the Roman populace, the steam came from
the boiling water in the Sardinian kettle. As for the art-
work achieved by Severn between 1860 and 1879, there is
not much to be said. It is not equal to that of an earlier
and, artistically, more fortunate period, though the 'Marriage of Cana' and other ambitious undertakings prove
that, for all his advanced age and manifold avocations, his
real vocation afforded him occupation to the end. Among
his latest pictures was a portrait of himself at the age of
eighty-two, in his consular uniform, and with the decora-
tion of the Order of the Crown of Italy, which had been
presented to him by King Victor Emmanuel in recognition
of his many and valuable services to individual Italians
and to Italy and the Italian cause. Yet two years later
the veteran artist is still at his easel. He finishes his
'Isabella and the Pot of Basil,' and begins a small
portrait of Keats for General Sir Vincent Eyre. In these
latter days his thoughts and ideas are all animated by the

memory of his " dear and illustrious friend, so long while ago dead and yet so gloriously living." He is deeply touched and pleased when Mr. Buxton Forman sends him his volume of Keats's Letters to Miss Brawne, with its dedication to himself. The latest entry but two in the last of his long series of Diaries, is a record of his having just projected " a new Keats picture "; but it was never begun, for a few weeks later he was at rest from his labour in that sacred Roman dust where his heart already lay.

It was, from the first, an eventful period, and Severn was so busily occupied with matters of consular, urban, and national interest that weeks and sometimes months would pass without his putting brush to canvas. In his capacity as acting " Sardinian " consul also he had his hands full, and the early record of his official duties again and again sets forth his efforts on behalf of imprisoned or detained Italian workmen, and against all manner of high-handed and unscrupulous dealings on the part of the Papal Government. In the second year of his consulship he had become so accustomed to stirring times that he took everything that came much as he did sudden changes in the weather, and was equally ready to do anything or nothing as the circumstances might demand, whether it was the case of a fair countess who applied to him officially for funds to enable her to elope with an impecunious cavalier, rumour of collision between the French and Papal troops in the Forum during the Carnival, or reports of Garibaldi's " malignant activity " in the South, and of the corresponding ferment among the Roman populace. Nor was his position a pleasant one, for the Papal Government and party were incensed against Great Britain. All " liberal " officials were ordered to quit Rome. English residents became more and more uneasy, and when at last an English priest was attacked in the streets, many of them broke up their homes and left the city. Rome became a hotbed of evil passions. Just as Victor Emmanuel was said to be approaching from the North, and Garibaldi from the South, when the French troops were being moved backward and forward like chessmen, and British warships had anchored off Civita Vecchia, when in Rome itself there was a medley of crime, disorder, panic, defiant fury, sullenness, and general anticipation of vital change, when even a suburban train was attacked and pillaged by brigands, and when in the Holy City one hundred and seventeen murders or attempted murders were committed within three months, at this time the Pope elected to canonize twenty-one more saints. As Severn aptly remarks, if His Holiness had given orders for the construction of twenty-one more trains, or for the execution of twenty-one notorious assassins, or for the release of twenty-one unjustly imprisoned citizens, or even for the banishment of twenty-one mischief-pandering Princes of the Church, his action would have been more to the point and been infinitely more appreciated. Yet throughout the eventful years when the Papal Temporal Power tottered to or rather in its grave, and ere Victor Emmanuel entered Rome as King of United Italy, as well as in the troublous years that followed, Severn was a kind of Prince in the foreign society of Rome. He went to and fro, always serene, always affable, invariably quick to see the best side of every question, to mediate between bitter opponents and in bristling disputes. When, under his windows, a turbulent section of the populace was jeering at the Papal troops and crying out *Viva il Rè!* or *Viva Garibaldi!* he was sitting composedly at his easel painting his 'Marriage of Cana'; when the Romans were wild over the previous night's batch of murders, or the stoppage of a train by brigands just outside the walls, he was organizing parties to entertain Shelley's son and Lady Shelley, Madame Keats de Llanos, or other friends, or writing his reminiscences of his early days, or even venturing into the hill country to visit Frederick Overbeck at Rocca di Papa. Now and again even *his* equanimity was upset, as in the eventful year of 1870, which saw the burial of the Temporal Power, the advent of Italy among the Great Powers, the Declaration of War between France and Prussia, and, in July, the Promulgation of the Infallibility of the Pope.

Severn's concise comment is, "The world is going mad, and
all the dreams of civilisation are at an end." The fall of
the Temporal Power was a shock to him; he was astounded
by the Decree of Infallibility; but he was 'paralysed' by
the rumour that a lady had been appointed to the Chair
of Literature at Bologna.

His consulship came to an end in 1872, but he was
not left without permanent recognition of his services,
though the pension of £80 granted to him was a meagre
one. A few weeks later, however, he learned that he was
granted a further pension of £60 out of the Civil Fund.

In 1874 he hoped to gain recognition from the Italian
Government of his scheme for uniting the Mediterranean
and Adriatic by means of a canal from Ostia to Pescara, but
his project was looked upon askance, though commended
in theory. Four years later Victor Emmanuel died, and,
shortly after, Pope Pius IX. "Another tired old man will
follow them soon," wrote Severn.

There is a pathetic entry in the Diary wherein Severn
records the passing of his eighty-third birthday. The pathos
of the words is the more direct because of their simplicity
and isolation. His sole comment is, "I begin to feel the
loneliness of having lived too long."

He had lived a life singularly full of interest, and with
much of pleasure and charm. Perhaps his chief good-
fortune was his buoyant and happy temperament—a temperament which enabled him to declare again and again
throughout each decade in his long life, that such and such
a day, that this or that experience, was the happiest he had
ever known. He was one of those natures into whose
heart and mind a ray of sunshine entered at birth and never
vanished.

"But there is nothing," writes Mr. Ruskin, after his account of his visit
to Rome, and a tribute to the other friend, Mr. George Richmond, R.A., who

helped to make his stay so pleasant; "but there is nothing in any circle
that ever I saw or heard of, like what Mr. Joseph Severn then was in Rome.
He understood everybody, native and foreign, civil and ecclesiastic, in what
was nicest in them, and never saw anything else than the nicest; or saw
what other people got angry about as only a humorous part of the
nature of things. It was the nature of things that the Pope should be at
St. Peter's, and the beggars on the Pincian steps. He forgave the Pope
his papacy, reverenced the beggar's beard, and felt that alike the steps
of the Pincian, and the Araceli, and the Lateran, and the Capitol, led to
heaven, and everybody was going up somehow; and might be happy
where they were in the meantime. Lightly sagacious, lovingly humorous, daintily sentimental, he was in council with the Cardinals to-day,
and at picnic in the Campagna with the brightest English belles to-
morrow; and caught the hearts of all in the golden net of his good will
and good understanding, as if life were but for him the rippling chant of
his favourite song,—

' Gente, e qui l' uccellatore.'"

Severn enjoyed an exceptionally wide acquaintanceship;
and one of the best tests of his worth is the unanimity of
the high opinion of him held by all with whom he came in
contact. It is no small thing to have won so much friendship, such high esteem. Yet below all is his supreme claim
to remembrance. Neither the patronage of the great, the
friendship of the most potent statesman of modern times,
nor the panegyric of the most eloquent of all contemporary
writers, could do for the memory of Joseph Severn what has
been accomplished once and for all by his loving service
and unswerving loyalty to Keats. It is one of the most
beautiful episodes in literary history, and doubtless there
are some who have won the crown of laurel who would barter
their fame for such a consecration in the minds of men.

It was a long life, and well spent in the main. On his
death-bed Keats bequeathed to Severn all the joy and
prosperity which ought to have been his but never could be;
and it seems to one, looking over the record of these busy
and varied five-score years and more since the beloved
friend was laid below the violets he loved so well, that the
destinies which sometimes seem controllable by human will
had hearkened to the solemn bequest of the dying poet.

After the entry in the Diaries, quoted above—that telling
how, a few weeks before his death in his eighty-sixth year,

he projected a new Keats picture—there are but three other entries. One is under the date 15th May, and consists of a stanza from a religious poem. The others were written on the 1st and 7th of June, merely to say that the writer is weaker. " Fine weather at last " are the latest written words of one whose life's weather was fine throughout its long range from dawn to set.

He died quietly, and as if pleasantly tired, on Sunday, the 3rd of August, 1879. One of the latest words on his lips was " Keats," for to the last he was preoccupied with thoughts of the new picture he wished to paint, 'Keats lying calm in death, and a beautiful spirit bending over him.'

It was a pleasure to him to think, in what he knew to be his fatal weakness, that he would be buried near the two poets whose genius he so revered, and with whose graves, as he said once, he was more familiar than with any mortal habitation. Fortunately, he was unaware of, or had forgotten, a recent Roman law which necessitated the interment of Protestant foreigners elsewhere than in the *Cimeterio di Monte Testaccio.** But though buried in the newer cemetery, his body was removed thence two years later, and laid beside that of his friend. Lord Houghton, the Archbishop of Dublin, and other influential friends did their utmost to bring this about, and to raise a suitable commemorative stone over the new grave. The consent of the Roman Government was obtained for the first; for the second, there was no difficulty as to funds the moment the rumour of the project reached England and America: so little that there was no real need of the circulars which were issued.† Lord

---

* Commonly and mistakenly spoken of as the old Protestant cemetery, and, still more mistakenly, as the English cemetery. It is a cosmopolitan burial-ground, and the English dead are only a proportion among the American, German, Scandinavian, French, Dutch, Spanish, Russian, and even Asiatic. There are probably as many Germans buried here as there are English ; officially too, it is under the charge of the German embassy.

† It was well, however, to draw attention to the fact that Severn had other claims to remembrance:—" But Joseph Severn, besides being the ' friend of Keats,' has additional claims to be remembered with honour in

Houghton, who had already expressed a wish that Severn should be buried on one side of Keats, and he, in due time, on the other, so that the poet should lie "between his friend and biographer," was to come from Athens to conduct the ceremonial. Sudden illness prevented his arrival in time, and his place was taken by Mr. T. Adolphus Trollope, who, on the forenoon of a day early in March, spoke a few appropriate words to the large number of Severn's friends and Keats's admirers which had assembled, notwithstanding dull and threatening weather. There was none present who did not realise that poetic justice was fulfilled. Keats and Shelley lay but a brief space apart from each other; beside the elder poet, his friend Trelawny, beside the younger, Joseph Severn.

This beautiful graveyard near the ancient Ostian Gate was ever a spot wherein Severn loved to wander and meditate. Strangely enough, except at the last, he does not seem to have felt assured that in death as in life his fortune would be consistent, and that his dust would mingle with that of his friend.

"Sow and plant twice as much; extend the poet's domain; for, as it was so scanty during his short life, surely it ought to be yielded to him twofold in his grave." So he had said to the custodian of the cemetery of Monte Testaccio when, on his return from his long absence from Rome, he learned how constantly the violets were plucked from off Keats's grave. To Joseph Severn himself a fortunate destiny has yielded twofold.

It would be unnecessary to give all the proposals as to the inscription to be made on Severn's tomb, offered by eminent men and women of letters. It will suffice to select

---

the city which was his home during half a century. In his consular capacity (and till 1870 he was also deputy Sardinian Consul) he earned the lasting gratitude of many who benefited by his large-hearted and never-failing benevolence; including many Italian political prisoners and exiles whose restoration to the joys of liberty and of family life he was mainly instrumental in procuring during the late Pontificate; for which important services he received the well-earned distinction of 'Officer of the Order of the Crown of Italy' from King Victor Emmanuel."

one or two from the most distinguished. That from Lord Houghton may be given first, as the one finally adopted and now cut in the stone. "To the memory of Joseph Severn, Devoted Friend and Deathbed Companion of John Keats, whom he lived to see numbered among the Immortal Poets of England. An Artist eminent for his Representations of Italian Life and Nature. British Consul at Rome from 1861 to 1872: And Officer of the Crown of Italy, In recognition of his services to Freedom and Humanity." At first Lord Houghton thought the inscription should be in Latin. He wrote: "I have a notion that the inscription should be in Latin. If you think so too, I should get it composed by a competent hand; if you prefer English, I will try my own." In a note, dated 1st of November, 1881, the Poet-Laureate suggested "To the Memory of Joseph Severn, the Devoted Friend of John Keats, by whose deathbed he watched and whose name he lived to see inscribed among those of the Immortal Poets of England " (" and the rest as Lord Houghton's "). Dante Gabriel Rossetti thought that nothing could be more appropriate than Severn's own pathetic words telling of his ministration to Keats (beginning "Poor Keats has me ever by him "). In his letter he objects to the phrase in Mr. Walter Severn's suggestion, "In their death they were not divided." "Excuse my saying that the suggestion of the words ' In their death they were not divided,' must seem highly inappropriate to any one who recollects the original application of the phrase, viz., to Saul and Jonathan, who died on the same battlefield; whereas nearly sixty years elapsed between Keats's death and your father's." * Mr. Palgrave, not the least of whose several

* The following note from Archbishop Trench to Mr. Walter Severn indicates an omission—not " everything else "—in Gabriel Rossetti's proposal; but it is more worthy of quotation because of its protest against what so many must have felt the intolerable incongruity of the acrostical epitaph by General Sir Vincent Eyre which, with the accompanying and altogether unnecessary carved laurel wreath on the medallion let into the right side of the doorway to the cemetery, obtrusively affronts the visitor to the newer of the two old Aliens' cemeteries—for two they are. (That where Shelley lies was made in 1765: that where Keats, Severn, Augustus W. Hare, and others are buried, was opened in 1822. Henceforth there

claims to high consideration is his scholarly and in every way delightful edition of Keats's poetry, proposed simply "To the Memory of Joseph Severn, the Friend of John Keats, By whose death-bed he sate, comforting, and by whom, long since remembered high among the Poets of England, Friend by Friend, he is now laid in death."

It is strange that to no one seems to have occurred the memorable phrase in Shelley's dedicatory preface to the 'Adonais': "May the unextinguished Spirit of his illustrious friend . . . . plead against Oblivion for his name."

Finally, in this connection, may be quoted a letter from a relative of Mrs. Lindon ("Fanny Brawne"). Not only did Miss Brawne long outlive Keats, but she survived till late in the century; and, by a singular chance, this relative ministered to Joseph Severn in his old age. The following

---

will not be allowed any burials within a mile of inhabited dwellings; and the Roman municipality has decided that all interments will take place in the Campo Verano, a Roman graveyard over a hundred years old.)

"*Broomfield, Wicklow,*
"July 29, 1881.

"Dear Mr. Severn,—
"As you ask from me an opinion on the suggested epitaph, I will not refuse to give it, though I should certainly not have volunteered it unasked.

"Your father was himself a distinguished artist. He had too, in difficult times of Italy, played his part there so well as to receive honourable recognition of his work. No doubt he counted it a rare felicity of his life that he was able to minister to those last painful months of poor Keats's life. This will endear him much to those to whom Keats is dear—but this is very far from being the sole ground why he ought to be had in remembrance. My objection to Dante Rossetti's proposed epitaph is that it ignores everything else, and in this way is unjust to your father's memory.

"Sir Vincent Eyre's acrostic is so thoroughly artificial, and quâ acrostic so thoroughly out of its place, that I have, I must confess, a strong anticipatory misgiving as to any epitaph which should be the work of the same hand—but this observation is entirely for yourself. I am strong to believe that in the inscription which you have yourself prepared will be found what will best become the place and the occasion—and I would earnestly advise not to seek abroad what you will best find at home. I am ever,

"Very faithfully yours,
"R. C. Dublin."

letter explains itself: "I see by the *Italia* that you have arrived in Rome, with your father's old friend, Lord Houghton" (this was a premature announcement on the part of the *Italia*) "for the touching ceremony of placing your father's remains near the friend of his youth, as he, too, had always expressed the wish for, as well as being surrounded with violets, a flower and perfume he delighted in. They and the rose were his favourite flowers, and often and often I have taken them to him when he was no longer able to go out and see them blooming in the gardens. . . I have ordered my clerk, Signor Framminghi, to be the bearer of this note and to receive your wishes respecting the 'Souvenirs de Famille,' which Signorina Margherita, Dr. Valeriani's sister, begged to give up to the different members of my kind old friend's family. . . . One of my first thoughts on returning home will be to place a wreath of violets on your dear father's *new* resting-place."

When the news of Joseph Severn's death spread abroad there was a wide and earnest expression of the general sentiment with which he was regarded. To many it came as a startling surprise that the deceased artist and ex-Consul, who died so late in the century as 1879, had been the comrade of Keats. To the younger generation Keats seemed to have so long "dwelt in the abode where the Eternal are," that it was difficult at once to grasp the fact that his intimate friend had lived to a period when the personal tradition of 'Adonais,' and Shelley, and Coleridge, of Byron, and even Sir Walter Scott, had almost ceased to exist.

Soon after his return to Rome in 1861, forty years after Keats's death, he wrote: "I am now engaged on a picture of the poet's grave, and am treating it with all the picturesque advantages which the antique locality gives me, as well as the elevated associations which this poetic shrine inspires. The classic story of Endymion being the subject of Keats's principal poem, I have introduced a young Roman shepherd sleeping against the headstone, with his flock about him, whilst the moon from behind the pyramid illuminates his figure and serves to realise Keats's favourite theme in the presence of his grave.   This incident is not fanciful, but is what I actually saw on an autumn evening at Monte Testaccio the year following the poet's death."

There, sixty-one years after the death of the friend with whom his name is immortally associated, he, too, was laid to rest. Side by side they lie in that sunlit grassy spot, darkened but once daily by the moving shadow of the pyramid of Caius Cestius.

APPENDIX.

I.

Appendix to Chapter VII.

(*Vide p.* 159, *et seq.*)

"Within this first year of my marriage a most agitating and ferocious persecution was got up against me through the agency of a man who was husband to my servant Teresa. She had been with me six years, and as my house was the large upper story of a surpressed monastery (in the Vicolo dei Maroniti) I allowed her to live with her husband and baby in my house. Her services were good, as she had been cook in a convent; a matter of importance to me, as my health had long been so delicate that the ordinary Italian cookery did not suit me. But on my marriage I was guilty of sad want of foresight in keeping on this said Teresa and her husband, for in a short time their conduct became so bad and dishonest that I was obliged to turn them away. I had scarcely done so, when lo! a law document was sent to me from the man, Giovanni Bartolomei, demanding seven years' wages on the preposterous plea of his having been my servant during that period. This he never was at any time, unless occasionally helping his wife constituted service. I had recommended him to all my friends, and he was commonly employed as a porter. This false and ungrateful charge was sustained by a large company of witnesses! Some of these perjurers declared that when making a door for me they had heard me undertake to give this man six crowns a month, and they even presumed to verify this by affirming that this happened on the 1st October, 1823. On looking over my papers I found that at the time they deposed to my making this agreement in Rome, I was at Venice with Charles Brown, and deeply occupied, and uninterruptedly resident there during my sojourn! To substantiate this I produced my passport for the occasion, which I had preserved, and also to prove their testimony doubly false I was able to show the lease of the altogether different tenancy which at that time I held: that is, while according to their deposition, they overheard me at my house in Vicolo dei Maroniti, I was really the tenant of the house in the Via S. Isidoro, more than a mile from the house these false witnesses had supposed me occupying when they made their rash statement! Having thus by the production of these documents so completely established an alibi, and disproved the perjurers, the judge, Signor Manari, requested a private interview with me. He received me with assumed kindness and openness, shaking hands with me in what I thought a queer ambiguous manner. He addressed me in very bad English, upon which, perceiving

I did not understand a word, he went on with his explanation in Italian.
The burden of this was, 'that the whole affair of Bartolomei was nothing
less than a conspiracy against me, and that he should forthwith give the
sentence in my favour.' Of course I was not a little surprised at this
unexpected honour of being so markedly favoured by the judge, and on
his own solicitation. I then left, and though vaguely surprised at the
expression on the judge's face, I was about to conclude that I had been
grossly prejudiced against Roman justice, when lo! and behold, I shortly
received the astounding notice that the same judge, the moment I had
turned my back, *pronounced the sentence against me!* But the explanation is more astounding than the fact. It is as follows: Signor Manari
on shaking hands with me (which I thought odd both as to the act and
in the manner) *expected to find a bribe.* His hand was of course involuntarily shaped for the occasion, and not finding a bribe from me he
felt that in the nature and business of Roman justice he must have one
from *some one:* and so he recalled the other party, instructed them to
put forward an entire new evidence (dating it a year later, so as to
correct their former error in time and place!) and then obliged them to
swear to it. Then at once, without hearing my second defence, he gave
the verdict against me, and sentenced me to pay 428 crowns (about £100)
and all costs. I confess I was completely overcome for the moment at
this base way of the judge entrapping me; for much as I had been
surprised at his begging the interview, and never having even dreamed it
was to the end that I might bribe him, yet I did not suppose such a
corrupt tribunal existed in Europe or possibly could exist. I should
mention that all the evidence was written and all got up by the lawyers,
the witnesses having nothing to do but to swear to it, which on every
occasion they did without a demur. Finding myself in this dilemma and
in a foreign country, and rather than be robbed by such a judge and such
a set of vagabonds, I determined to make a stand, for I happened to have
the sum in question at liberty, and that gave me more nerve to hold out.
Having, moreover, along with ample leisure, plenty of patience and a
calm temperament, I got in order most formidable opposition, which, if
it did not defeat (nothing could ever defeat such infamy but annihila-
tion of the whole Papal government), certainly suspended the sentence,
and enabled me to appear not only as a martyr to Roman justice, but
also as the advocate of an entire new judicial system. To this end I
presented myself to the newly-made English Prince of the Church,
Cardinal Weld; of whose uprightness and goodness I had heard something from everyone. As I was indirectly known to His Eminence by
my intimacy with several Catholics at the English College, and more particularly with Lord and Lady of Wardour (*sic*), he received me very kindly
and even graciously. Without hesitation, though with evident pain, he
listened to my account of the unjust conspiracy and trial. He took up
my cause, supposing with me that his dignity and rank as a Roman
Prince would enable him to get me justice, for I did not want favour.
But this proved an unfounded surmise. Of such an inveterate nature

was the flood of Roman iniquity, and so completely had it grown up into 'a wrong right' that not even the English Cardinal could stem the degrading tide of universal corruption among the Papal officials.

"The first step taken in my favour through the Cardinal was the granting to me of the right of appeal, and to take the cause into a new court. The new judge, however, soon made it known that he would do nothing but confirm the sentence. Fortunately by this time the whole affair had been noised about, and the Roman people were enchanted that such a case had befallen an Englishman, as their vile tribunals would be thus shown up to the world, and possibly reform be brought about owing to pressure from without. Cardinal Weld was greatly puzzled and even afflicted at the sad iniquity of things, and perhaps at the consequent exposure, for by this time the matter was in every one's mouth, the subject at every conversazione and at every café. The Cardinal then introduced me and my cause to the powerful Cardinal Odeschalchi, and I was granted an interview in company with my Roman advocate. Some short time before, my countrymen had kindly offered to subscribe the whole sum and present it to me, as I had done a public good, and as they wished to have the case published in all the European papers. This offer I had declined, both because I could afford with so much entertainment to lose the money, and as I did not wish to place myself in personal danger; and also because I was most satisfied with the kindness and candour of Cardinal Weld. The result of the above interview was that the Cardinal Odeschalchi finished by advising me "*to accept the subscription money discreetly, and when they came upon me for permission to publish the case in the European newspapers, to pretend that I had never so understood it.*' He advised me, in a word, 'to fill my purse with money, to get it honestly if I could, but at all events to get it.' I thanked His Eminence, but shook my head: and when I told Cardinal Weld the result he simply said quietly, 'That would never do, for your countrymen would send you to Coventry.'

"At this time Chevalier Bunsen, the Prussian Minister, as *my* friend, and Acton as Cardinal Weld's friend, came forward warmly *to* assist me. The first spoke directly to the Pope, and made His Holiness quite aware of the scandal it was to the Roman government at this particular moment when reform was being talked of. The Pope thereupon offered to pay me back the whole sum, by that time amounting to more than £150. On refusal, through the Secretary of State, Monsignor Tosti, it was then arranged that I was to have a new and fair trial : and it was explained that the cause had been lost by my lawyer's mistake. *When Bartolomei's witnesses, I was told, swore that I owed the money, I should, instead of proving that the man was not my servant, have sworn that I had paid the money, and should have outnumbered the other side's witnesses in swearing to this.* The Pope's own Secretary of State actually wrote a letter to M. Kestner, Hanoverian Minister, expressing this most scandalous opinion ! It was at last arranged that my counsel was to prepare a new brief of the whole case, and that the judge was to wait

until a certain day, a Thursday evening, I remember. This engagement
was made with Chevalier Bunsen, M. Kestner, and also Sir Brook Taylor,
who had meanwhile arrived in Rome on a mission from the English
Government to endeavour to bring about some reform in the Roman
Courts of Justice. Sir Brook Taylor, on finding this case of mine so
applicable to the business on his hands, took it up with much energy.
These gentlemen thought they had arranged it all satisfactorily, and that
it would be well got through, when, to the astonishment of all, on the
Wednesday (one day before the day agreed on) the judge, contrary to
his engagement so seriously made, *pronounced the sentence against me and
ordered immediate execution for the money!* It was then I had recourse
to Monsignor Acton, who was Supreme Judge. He desired me to defer
paying the money, but to let the legal officials return and seize whatever
they liked—which they did, taking down my pictures and packing them
up for sale. There was one, ‘The Sicilian Mariner’s Hymn,’ that I had
just done for the Marquis of Northampton, and the colours being still
fresh I was fearful that it might receive some serious injury, and so I
pretended it belonged to Cardinal Weld. It was not a little amusing to
see how the fellows drew back in sacred horror from touching it, when
the Cardinal’s name was mentioned. These pictures of mine having been
taken away, Monsignor Acton requested I would nominally redeem them
with something not liable to injury, and I did so with the gold medallion
given by the Royal Academy of London. Having done this, Monsignor
Acton called before him all these false witnesses, with Bartolomei at
their head, *and he got them to confess that they knew quite well that I
did not owe the money and that their head man was not my servant*, and
more, that I was an excellent person, *but that they were all poor men and
so deserved to gain!* The Monsignor upon this asked them how much
they would take, and in the end the original sum was brought down to
half! So finished the illegal part of this affair, which, from first to last,
dragged on through nearly three years, and cost me £95. At the end of
all this turmoil I was glad to find myself, if a loser in some respects, in
many other respects a great gainer, for I had not only won for myself the
esteem and friendship of so many persons I looked up to, but also I had
many excellent commissions given me, the principal one being from
Cardinal Weld himself, who had seen my sketch of the ‘ Revelations ’
subject, and who ordered the large picture as he said, ‘ of the patient
artist.’

“ This scandalous affair was never thoroughly cleared up. No one
could tell from what source the money came for Bartolomei’s ability to
sustain his case, for money he had in plenty. Many of my friends suspected it came indirectly from my old enemy, and certainly I confess
that I could not guess who else could have cared to spend so much
money upon me, or who had it to spend in such a way. I think,
perhaps, that Cardinal Weld may have known the truth, but kindly
concealed it from me.”

II.

Appendix to Page 168.

"One of the pleasantest things I ever had said to me, and said in the simplest and most unaffected manner, was the reply of Cardinal Weld on hearing the iniquitous decision of the Judge in my law-suit. The whole sum that I was calculated to lose by this sentence of priestly injustice was about £150; and as I had for some time determined to execute a large altar-piece from my Apocalypse sketch (twelfth chapter of *Revelations*) and trust to my good fortune for the sale of it, this monstrous sentence cut me off from all hope of doing such a work by depriving me of all the means I had in reserve for such an expensive enterprise. The Cardinal had seen the sketch several times and greatly admired it, and he had known my intention of doing it on the large scale, indeed of having actually begun it.

"When I told him of the result of the trial and the sum that I should lose, and that the consequence would be that this altar-piece must fall to the ground, he said, 'O no, the world cannot afford to lose that—you must do it for me;' and, taking my hand most kindly, he turned away his face, unable to conceal his emotion. This generous feeling towards me continued unabated to the moment of his death, although there were so many painful circumstances militating against his friendship towards me—for of the patronage of this liberal Prelate the extreme Papist party, with Monsignor ―――― at its head, had become jealous and even malicious. The English Catholics, not having on their side any Roman Catholic artist at Rome to compete with me, and as I resisted all their attempts at conversion, the bitterness inspired was most singular and revolting. It extended so far that at times Lord Clifford thought it his duty to tell me, and in every way to put me on my guard. During the lifetime of Cardinal Weld this was not of so much consequence, for I had not so many opportunities of observing it.

"The Cardinal came frequently to see my progress in my work, and perhaps no picture was ever executed under more pleasant or even favourable circumstances. It was wholly my own invention and choice, and at the same time I had the delight of carrying out my conception with the added guidance of this generous and illustrious patron. I should here mention that His Eminence never once inquired what the price would be, or how long the work would take me to do. Once he told me not to hurry it or inconvenience myself, for he could sincerely assure me of the great pleasure it gave him to see me occupied on such a work. He always repeated to me the praises he heard from foreigners during the progress of my work. Personally he was very attentive to me, and frequently invited me to dine with him, and, having a fine taste in music, I often had the whole attention bestowed upon me—for he performed on the French horn with great delicacy and expression—and on every occasion after dinner he requested me to play an accompaniment to him on the piano. This music after a while was considered to be not quite in accordance with the dignity and gravity of his high position as a Dignitary of the Roman Church, and His Eminence was invited to leave off playing the French horn; which, with charming gentlemanlike simplicity, he confessed to me. Before I knew him, and when Lady Clifford, his daughter, was alive, he was guilty of the sad scandal of going about with her in his carriage. Such a thing had never been seen before in the streets of Rome, and was soon stopped. No doubt it pleased and tranquillised all the priestly party, up to the Pope himself, when it pleased Providence to take away this only dear child on whom the Cardinal's affection was too much placed. Even the least rigorous considered the circumstance as unseemly.

"My having such a patron and painting such a picture was the source of not only much happiness to me and my wife, but it also enabled me to do many essential acts of charity to, and otherwise help my countrymen, particularly young artists; and the good Cardinal on all such occasions was very encouraging to me, and assured me that I never gave him trouble. Although in itself so slight an incident, one of the most memorable instances for me was that of Sir Edward Lytton Bulwer, who, when at Rome in 1832, was composing and writing his novel of *Rienzi*. He expressed to me his great surprise that he could not get a 'Gibbon' in Rome, and I confessed to him that I had one, but could not lend it to him, as I had received it through the kindness of Cardinal Weld, and had promised that I would never lend it, as it was a prohibited book. I confided the circumstances to the Cardinal, and, on my undertaking for myself and Sir E. Lytton Bulwer the utmost discretion, he kindly gave me permission to lend the 'Gibbon' to Sir Edward.

"About this time an incident of a serious nature took place which I really conjectured would at once deprive me of all the esteem and patronage of the Cardinal. On all occasions when a convert was on the carpet the priests of the English College, particularly Monsignor ——— and Dr. B——, made it their object to call on me and tell me the fact, no doubt in the hope that I might be induced to follow the example set me, for at times there was a great dearth of respectable converts — indeed they were mostly of such ambiguous character that we were induced to call them 'convicts' instead of converts. But on the particular occasion I am leading up to, one of better sort as to his circumstances (for the others were mostly needy and did the thing for a certain pension) appeared. His name was D——, and he was a Yorkshireman with two thousand a year. I had as a married man, been frequently warned against him, on account of his having introduced drunken and dissolute customers amongst my artist friends, such as were in every way undesirable, and in some instances tended to undermine promising artistic careers and good standing. This had been going on for more than a year. One day Doctor B—— called to tell me that Mr. D—— was about to be baptised by Cardinal Weld, he having been for some weeks a convert. As I knew the man to be a great reprobate, I told the priestly Doctor that it gave me much pleasure, as Mr. D—— would now no doubt change his life in changing his religion, and that I had lamented the dissolute ways he had introduced amongst my artist friends. He replied that 'On the contrary, he was changing his religion that he might get rid of his dissolute artist friends.' I was surprised at this slander, for I am sure a better set of men never existed than the English artists at Rome until this Mr. D—— appeared; and I told Dr. B—— so, but he persisted in his false opinion, which he well knew was false, as he had been long personally acquainted with most of the artists and could judge for himself. But he was guilty of the sad and singular meanness of going straight to Mr. D—— and putting *his own* words as it were in *my* mouth, and told him that I had just said ' that he (Mr. D——) was changing his religion that he might be quit of his dissolute artist friends.' Mr. D——, who in the midst of all his vices, was manly in his bearing, flew into a violent rage at this, and by the aid of a new English convert, Count Hawkis Le Grice (*sic*), sent me a challenge. Of course I appealed to Dr. B——, who in the coolest manner persisted in his falsehood, and as there was no compelling testimony from, and no satisfaction to be demanded of, a priest, I was obliged to accept the challenge, which I did on the second day after seeing Dr. B——.

" All my friends knew and believed in my statement—indeed I was gratified at the way they all rallied round me and relied on me; but yet it was my duty to render satisfaction to Mr. D—— for the injurious expressions I had been charged with uttering against him, and which, as I was in the toils of a priest, I had no way of disproving. Nearly a week passed without action on my part, till Mr. D—— indirectly made known to me that he would waylay me unless I gave him satisfaction. I was in some danger, for he was a kind of bull of a man, and could easily have annihilated me; so there was nothing but to try and match him with what little wit I might chance to have. Dr. B—— had pointedly denied that he had ever said ' that Mr. D——'s motives were to get rid of his dissolute artist friends'; but on the fifth day I thought of something that would make me a match for the priest and the bull. I wrote the following note to Mr. D——:

" ' DEAR SIR,—

" ' I regret exceedingly that I should have been made the instrument of slandering you in assuming that your change of religion was to rid yourself of your dissolute artist friends, when I am now so thoroughly convinced that that is not the case, since Dr. B—— himself denies it and thus denies his own words—but I am willing to render you any and every satisfaction on my part, as I never believed the assertion.

and this you will find from every one of our mutual friends. I
remain,' etc.

"This gave the highest satisfaction to Mr. D——, who wrote me expressing his thanks for my 'magnanimous generosity.' Dr. B—— was
content to get out of the scrape, though at the expense of being called a
liar, which he could well afford as a priest. Every one of my friends
was delighted. After this I discovered that Cardinal—— had got
hold of Mr. D—— for the purpose of marrying him to his sister, Miss
——, and to this end he was baptised and was to be created Duke of
Viterbo! The above affair and Dr. B——'s duplicity opened the eyes of
Mr. D——, and he went straight away from all the objects of the Church.
Cardinal——, being aware that Mr. D—— had a kind of seraglio of
Roman ladies, thought it would be a little awkward as regards the
marriage of his sister, so he delicately and indirectly proceeded to get all
the 'ladies' arrested and put into San Michele for the time being! The
bull at this went forth raving to the house of Cardinal—— and accused
the Cardinal and priests of being like himself in everything except in
charity, and in fact behaved in such a way that Lord Clifford had to call
all the men-servants to take him out of the house, which with great
difficulty they did, and only with help of Cardinal Odeschalchi's servants
to assist, who had been attracted downstairs by the roaring of the bull.
This affair did not surprise me, for I had observed at the musical parties
of Cardinal——, where Mr. D—— and Miss—— were often seated
together, that he was not in any way a person for decent society, his
conduct being somewhat similar to what it must have been in the company
of his 'ladies.'

" At this blow-up all Rome was in amusement, for Cardinal ——, Lord
Clifford, the Pope, &c., insisted on the English Consul, Mr. Freeborn, at
once making out Mr. D——'s passport. For some very clever reasons
the Consul declined, and such were the facts of the law that the Roman
Catholic party could not legally send away Mr. D——. He remained five
weeks in Rome after this, and during his stay acted a mock mass and all
kind of impieties as well as immoralities. He then departed for Leghorn,
where he died of brandy, having made a Protestant will (*sic*). This sad
affair, which must have cost Cardinal Weld much pain, and Cardinal ——
intense chagrin, and in which I was a chief actor, threatened to cut me
off from His Eminence, or at least such was my fear. But after Mr. D——
had gone, and it had all died away, I received an invitation to dine with
Cardinal Weld. I was at first alarmed at all the company talking of my
'bull' (they talked Italian), but when on the mention of Mr. D——'s
name the Cardinal's eye caught mine and I saw him smile, I was convinced
by that smile he approved of my conduct. Still, as I had been all along
shown up as a persecutor of converts, I thought it likely he would have to
strike me off from the list of his friends. The conduct of Cardinal——
was very mean, for he sacrificed his sister's respectability, and made
himself and her the derision of all the Italians and English then in Rome.

This was one amongst many of the awkward scenes I had to encounter and appear in (though none so bad as this), which my position as the *protégé* of Cardinal Weld, placed me in. But I could well afford to laugh at these minor inconveniences, for the Cardinal's kindness remained unimpaired until the moment of his death, and then I had to bear up against a load of malice and persecution in so many shapes and disguises that I was at times off my guard. One of the first charges was that I was cheating Cardinal Weld in getting an enormous price for my picture, on the ground of my pretending to him that I should become a convert; but I was able to make the proud answer, 'that not only was the price of the altar-piece never asked, mentioned, or fixed, when the picture was commissioned; but also that the Cardinal had never on any occasion talked about conversion in any way.' In this I was borne out by Lord Clifford. Then the assumed actual sum was mentioned in the *Dublin Review*, which amazed me not a little, as no sum whatever at the time was stipulated or even mentioned. But the hardest blow at me was attempted by the Pope himself; for Cardinal Weld, hearing my picture so well and so much complimented by foreigners, had thought of the plan of making it a public work, by presenting it the Pope to be placed in the Cathedral of 'St. Paul beyond the walls' then rebuilding, and on the part of His Holiness it was most graciously accepted (though without having been seen). The death of Cardinal Weld was doubly painful and terrible to me, for in addition to the losing of so dear a friend I soon had cause to suspect that a conspiracy existed against me to prevent me from ever placing my picture in the church. How to defeat or counteract this taxed my imagination more than the invention of the picture. I had long suspected, and soon foresaw, that a host of enemies were up in arms against me, with Cardinal —— at their head; yet I could not conceive that they aimed at the exclusion of my altar-piece from the church the destination the late Cardinal had found for it, and one approved by His Holiness the Pope. Yet every kind of symptom presented itself, and I must indeed have been blind to all the priestly human nature not to have been at once aware of it. In quiet, or assumed quiet, uncertainty, and patience I went on enquiring from the various persons concerned in the Cardinal's will, how and when and where I should be allowed to place my work in the church. Cardinal Acton took me on one occasion to select a place, and he may have been sincere and deceived by the many made-up appearances that so well deceived me. He was a very religious man in his own creed, and had the name of a great bigot, but I had received from him so much kind attention during my scandalous trial against my servant's fellow perjurers that I could not then, and do not now, think he was insincere. Yet our visit resulted in nothing final, and, if it was not all pretence, it was like it in its results.

"Of course so important an object as my picture becoming a public work, the only one in Italy by an Englishman, was not to be upset or laid aside even for awhile on my part without my utmost effort. But my opponents were such wolves in sheep's clothing that I had no course but a creeping one, pretending only to receive impressions, and relying on the assumed generosity flaring up about me.

"The saddest and archest of my persecutors was Baron Cammucini, a famous Roman painter, who pretended to admire my altar-piece and to be my most useful friend. When the time arrived for my leaving Rome to educate my children in England, it was expedient that some real steps should be decided on. I visited the Baron for this purpose, and he volunteered his services to go the Pope on my behalf for the permission to place my work in San Paolo F. M. He came to me after the interview with His Holiness to assure me that he had satisfied the Pope that my picture was in every way a work proper and suitable to a Catholic Cathedral, and that His Holiness had expressed much kind feeling about it, and left the matter to the Baron to carry out. This, as he had so much admired and praised the work, and often assured me that he had said the same to the Pope, ought to have contented me, but it did not; for when the time came, he gave me for answer that the architects were out of Rome, and that I must leave my picture in his friendly hands, and that he would regard it more and have tenderer care of it than his own works.

"This was not business-like, and I am sorry to say that I even did not think it quite true.

"At this time the German artists, who were great admirers of my works, and most sincere and obliging friends, gave me a public dinner, at which was Signor Reinhardt, an aged artist in historical landscape, and one who was of interest to me as having been the friend of Schiller. At the finish of the dinner he asked, with some formality, what was happening with my picture, and where it was? I explained that nothing had really been done, nor had I been able to decide on anything. Then said he, 'I make you a little old man's advice, based on fifty years' knowledge of Rome. Write to the Cardinal Tosti, President of the Cathedral of St. Paul, and say in a few words as you can put it, '*that unless he can at once allow you to place your picture in the church according to the wishes and the gift of Cardinal Weld, you must at once take it with you to England as you are responsible for its safety.*'

"This I saw at a glance was deep advice, and as soon as I returned home, wrote the letter in Italian and sent it without a moment's delay. In a short time I received a visit from the Marquis Campana, who had been sent by Cardinal Tosti to conciliate me. Being a most valued friend, he was well selected. He told me that the thing was all so well arranged, but that my rude epistle had spoilt everything, and that I must at once write an apology to the Cardinal Tosti.

"I assured the Marquis that there was nothing of which I could be ashamed in my letter; on the contrary it was the real truth, and expressed what I should really do, viz.—'*take my picture away.*' He was grieved, and begged me to write again, which, as I was unable to do right away, I begged him to show me in what form and how I should write. He complied and wrote an answer, in most elegant Italian, *but saying nothing conclusive.* So I assured him as an Englishman I could not send such a letter, indeed that I could not depart from what I had written at first. Realising this, and that I was determined, he kindly undertook to go back to the Cardinal and try and adjust the thing.

"He returned and brought me an invitation to visit the Cardinal that evening at once, although it was ten o'clock. I was received with great politeness by His Eminence. He first enquired ' What could induce me to return to England after twenty years' residence at Rome where I had so much distinguished myself.' I told 'him it was the education of my four children. He was surprised, and offered me the run of all the Roman Universities and his own powerful help; but I assured him that that was not my object; that I wished them to grow up English in mind and body, and have the advantages I had had. He then adverted to the picture, and begged me to leave it with Baron Cammucini, and that they would all have the greatest regard for it, and place it, and do all the fine things for it that I could possibly desire.' Now all this kind of thing I had heard over and over again ever since St. Paolo's had been consecrated anew, while my picture was still left out, *or remembered only to be forgotten,* and I too well knew that the time was come to have a real business-like answer, and such an answer I was determined to have. Perhaps I saw some little misgivings in the Cardinal's handsome countenance that encouraged me in the idea that he was not altogether performing the awkward affair quite to his own liking. So I at once told him that I could not conscientiously consent to such an arrangement; that I must see the late Cardinal Weld's wishes truly and faithfully carried out, *or take the picture at once to England;* and that what made the thing imperative on my part was the expected arrival of Lord Clifford in Rome, who, as the Cardinal's son-in-law and executor, would be sadly disturbed at finding the late Cardinal's gift thrown on one side and treated with marked disrespect.

"'Indeed,' I added, 'that I could not believe His Holiness the Pope would allow such a thing, as he so greatly esteemed the memory of Cardinal Weld, and had so graciously accepted the gift of my picture, and that the Cardinal had often told me of his conversations with His Holiness, not only about the gift, but also about the subject of the picture.' Cardinal Tosti was moved at this my appeal, and he said, ' Well, well, you can place it for the present in the Sacristy, and as to its final destination in the Church, that can be determined after the restorations in the church are completed.'

"At this I was well content, and as my motto is 'to let well alone,' I thanked His Eminence and wished him good-night and returned home to sleep sound on my success.

"Early in the morning, before six o'clock, I received a visit from an architect of the church; he had come to receive my orders about placing my picture in the Sacristy according to Cardinal Tosti's directions. ' But a change had come o'er my dream.' I had waked up with a bold idea, and the architect's visit helped me. I said that I had determined *not* to to place my work in the Sacristy, as Cardinal Weld's order *was to place it in the church*, and to this purpose I at once pointed out to him a fine arch in the church that would suit my picture in shape and light. He saw nothing to prevent this place being thus occupied, and offered at once to go back to the Cardinal to get his consent. The architect soon returned, and surprised me with the longed-for permission, and the whole arrangement was made at once. Before ten in the morning I arrived with my picture and its ponderous carved frame, and plenty of workmen to strain it and frame it at twelve. I had the high gratification not only of seeing it raised up to its capital place, for which in secret I had longed for three years, but also that the monks and priests of the church were much struck with my work and complimented me upon it. Indeed, I well knew that if I could once succeed in placing it, the rest would follow. And now the rich colouring of my picture and its attempt to revive the fine old art, fascinated all the clergy present, and much as I knew they had opposed it before they saw it, as a work of heresy and even blasphemy, so now it seemed to accord with all their extreme theological theories wherein the earliest principle was triumphant. My happiness was complete—*my work was effective and in its place.*. I left crowds admiring it who had been attracted to the church by the astounding fact that the picture by a heretic had for the first time been placed in a Catholic church. I had soon perceived by their cunning looks and signs that I was gaining more credit by having placed it than even having painted it, for I afterwards learned that the conspiracy against my picture and myself was known to everybody, so that amongst the persons present (and there were many artists) not only had I sympathy at having overcome serious obstacles, but I had what was in the Italian eyes the greater glory of having defeated the priests, from Monsignor Wiseman downwards, and so, in some measure, having assisted the cause of Italy and the Italians. On my way home I met the Duchess of Cambridge on her way to be assured of the fact, besides numbers of my friends, Germans as well as English. They all congratulated me on the wonderful fact, which everyone said had appeared to them impossible to accomplish. When I got home an astounding instance of Baron Cammucini's perfidy awaited me. In accordance with my request of the day before, when he had assured me that he would do his utmost, even more than he could do for his own work, if it was necessary that I should leave it to his care, he had now sent the Baroness to inform me that the architects of the church *were all away from Rome*, that my picture could not possibly be put up, *or even taken there*, and that I must leave it to his *friendly* care. My wife explained *that I was at that moment with the chief Architect and his assistants placing it in the church, and that the said Architect had been twice with me that morning.* The poor Baroness, finding herself the bearer of such a vile falsehood, was much overcome, and nearly fainted, and I was on my arrival not a little glad not to see her, or ever to see

Baron Cammucini again, for I should have lost all my patience with a man of such mean cunning. He wrote me a most complimentary letter on the occasion, in which he fought shy of his own failure and depravity, and assumed a total unconsciousness of it. What a degradation of human nature, for he was in an elevated position, and had failed, signally failed, in a meanly jealous endeavour to exclude my altar-piece from the Cathedral of St. Paul *by hook or by crook*. When I arrived in London I heard all the details of this deep-laid conspiracy, which it was thought was certain to demolish me and my picture. Afterwards I heard from Rome that the Pope admired my work, and pronounced 'that the heretic Englishman had produced one of the finest Madonnas he had ever seen.' This high compliment I received through the Prince Santa Croce.

"As regards the future well-being of the picture I was aware that the arch whereon I had placed it was only temporally bricked up, and that in the course of time it would be opened to connect the transept with the nave, for the transept being finished these arches were closed to remain until the opening of the nave. This opening took place six years later, and then it was expedient to remove my picture to the sacristy, where it now remains, waiting, I believe, for a place in one of the chapels of the nave now in progress.

"When I chance to meet Cardinal —— I fancy I see in his glance a touch of shame (but a very slight one) for having failed (for it is in the *failure* the sin is and not at all in the crime) in such a deep-laid plot. He was in London at the moment I placed my picture, and I have always regretted that I was so unfortunate as not to have had the first telling of news to him and to have seen his mortification. I hear often of my picture from travellers, and that it is well preserved and greatly improved in tone and looks, and like a work of the fine old times in comparison to the other two in the church, the 'Assumption of the Madonna,' by Agricola, and the 'Conversion of Paul,' by Cammucini, both inferior works, and inferior even to the usual efforts of these two artists."

(Written during the period of Severn's residence in London.)

III.

APPENDIX TO CHAPTER XII.

A REMINISCENCE OF SEVERN.

The following brief note, written by Professor Eric Robertson, about the period of Severn's interment beside Keats, is worthy of preservation as the record of a stranger who saw the old artist in his last days. It is in too subdued a tone to be a truthful portrait, but it is an interesting impression.

"It is not two years since Joseph Severn, the friend of Keats, slipped away noiselessly from the world. English visitors in Rome, attending a concert at the Sala Dante, or buying prints at the Government Stamperia, or casting their luckpennies into the Fountain of Trevi, were few of them aware that within a stone's-throw could be found a man full of memories of a great English classic, the Jonathan of a sweet-singing David, who, alas, never came to his throne!

" Passing up the stairs of the Sala Dante, and traversing a dim carpet-less gallery, Severn's visitors sought a most unpretending door, bespeaking the intercession of a sweet, faint little bell that in its unworldly chime seemed to strike the keynote of the abode, as one might say. When the inmate's faithful attendant had responded to this appeal, it was necessary to wait a few minutes while she ascertained whether Mr. Severn could receive. It always appeared to cost her master some reflection before he could decide upon seeing anybody. As if by way of apology for this inevitable delay, the lobby was converted into a kind of ante-room, the walls of which were hung with a few fine engravings. Severn set great store upon one of these, a unique and exquisite rendering of the well-known picture we have been allowed until lately to call Guido's 'Beatrice Cenci.'

" The studio was sombre, and arranged with as little conventionality as the painter himself, ' everything about him betokening a careless desolation.' ' Desolation ' is scarcely too strong a word to convey the impression given by the chamber and its tenant. He dwelt entirely alone, apparently from choice, for he had attached relatives and a large circle of warm friends in England.

" The spectacle of this old and frail man, likely soon to drop into a foreigner's grave, would have been sufficiently full of melancholy interest; but when one remembered him to be a relic of a time long gone by, and heard him speak of nothing but a generation of dead men, one had a sense of 'death in life' that quickened the whole effect into one of real desolation. He knew little of the world as it existed around him: he lived in the past. He could have shared the feeling of Lamb when he cried, ' Hang posterity! I write for antiquity.' Severn in the last year of his life was still painting portraits of Keats, the beautiful boyish Keats of his memory. He never tired of talking about his friend. He would lay before you a volume of Shakespeare's poems, in the fly-leaf of which Keats had scribbled his ' Last Sonnet.' Then you would learn that as Keats and Severn were one day lying under becalmed sails in the Channel, the poet grew quiet for a space, and by and by drew this volume from his pocket and wrote some verses in it, and handed the book over to his companion. It is in this sonnet that these fine lines occur:—

> ' And watching, with eternal lids apart,
> Like Nature's patient sleepless Eremite,
> The moving waters at their priestlike task
> Of pure ablution round earth's human shores.'

"David Vedder has a curiously similar thought :—

> 'The ocean heaves resistlessly,
> And pours his glistening treasures forth ;
> His waves—the priesthood of the sea—
> Kneel on the shell-gemmed earth,
> And there emit a hollow sound
> As if they murmured praise and prayer.'

"From Keats's works the discussion might pass to Keats's person, and the painter would tell you he considered Lord Houghton entirely in error in writing of Keats's 'blue eyes.' If any man could talk with certainty of their colour he himself could, and he could affirm that they had no tinge of blue, but were a warm grey, almost brown. Thus occurred a sort of Glaukopis-Athene dispute that Lord Houghton and Severn carried on in private letters, Lord Houghton to the last maintaining his description unmodified. The painter had not a very exalted opinion of Fanny Brawne, of whom he said the only true likeness was to be found in one of the two figures in Titian's 'Sacred and Profane Love.' The pictures in the studio, other than these portraits of Keats, had no great interest for the amateur.

"One, of the 'Cana Marriage,' evinced a touch of genius in representing the transformed water poured from one pitcher at first transparent as crystal, but changing colour in its arc, like a rainbow, and descending red into the other pitcher. Severn was proud of this idea. But it was characteristic of the man that when he had painted in the miracle, with a few sketchy figures in the background, he abandoned the design for a new memory portrait of Keats at the age of eighteen. It would seem, indeed, as if his connection with the famous, unfortunate poet had cast a shadow over his life and caused his artistic vigour to droop. The world to him was but a world that had lost Keats. Rome itself, with its innumerable associations, was to him but the grave of Keats.

*　　　*　　　*　　　*　　　*　　　*

"To the wall of the house in which Keats breathed his last at Rome there was recently attached a commemorative tablet. Severn was too frail to assist at the simple ceremonial of unveiling it. Who knows, but that a greater veil now drawn aside, the faithful friend may see of the man he loved something more than the empty name—may catch again his well-remembered tones?"

[E. S. R.]

From the *Dublin University Review*, vol. xcvi.

INDEX.

x

LONDON: PRINTED BY WILLIAM CLOWES AND SONS, LIMITED, STAMFORD STREET AND CHARING CROSS.